THIEF *of* LIES

a Library Jumpers novel

ALSO BY BRENDA DRAKE

Touching Fate
Cursing Fate

ALSO IN THIS SERIES

Guardian of Secrets

THIEF *of* LIES

a Library Jumpers novel

·BRENDA DRAKE·

ENTANGLED PUBLISHING, LLC

Entangled Publishing, LLC
2614 South Timberline Road
Suite 109
Fort Collins, CO 80525

Entangled Teen is an imprint of Entangled Publishing, LLC.

Visit our website at www.entangledpublishing.com.

Edited by Liz Pelletier
Cover design by Alexandra Shostak and Kelley York
Interior design by Heather Howland
Photos by Shutterstock/31moonlight31
Shutterstock/kaisorn
Shutterstock/Manuel Alvarez
Shutterstock/Ron Dale
Shutterstock/Gabriel Georgescu

ISBN 978-1-63375-602-1
HC ISBN 978-1-63375-221-4
Ebook ISBN 978-1-63375-222-1

Manufactured in the United States of America

First Edition January 2017

10 9 8 7 6 5 4 3 2 1

For those not afraid to jump no matter the dangers.
And to Kayla, my first fan, who is fearless.

Chapter One

Only God and the vendors at Haymarket wake early on Saturday mornings. The bloated clouds spattered rain against my faded red umbrella. I strangled the wobbly handle and dodged shoppers along the tiny makeshift aisle of Boston's famous outdoor produce market. The site, just off the North End, was totally packed and stinky. The fruits and vegetables for sale were rejects from nearby supermarkets—basically, they were cheap and somewhat edible. The briny decay of flesh wafted in the air around the fishmongers.

Gah! I cupped my hand over my nose, rushing past their stands.

My sandals slapped puddles on the sidewalk. Rain slobbered on my legs, making them slick and cold, sending shivers across my skin. I skittered around a group of slow-moving tourists, cursing Afton for insisting I get up early and wear a skirt today.

Finally breaking through the crowd, I charged up the street to the Haymarket entrance to the T.

Under a black umbrella across the street, a beautiful girl

with cocoa skin and dark curls huddled next to a guy with equally dark hair and an olive complexion—my two best friends. Nick held the handle while Afton leaned against him to avoid getting wet. Nick's full-face smile told me he enjoyed sharing an umbrella with her.

"Hey, Gia!" Afton yelled over the swooshing of tires across the wet pavement and the insistent honking of aggravated motorists.

I waited for the traffic to clear, missing several opportunities to cross the street. I swallowed hard and took a step down. *You can do this, Gia. No one is going to run you over. Intentionally.* A car turned onto the street, and I quickly hopped back onto the curb. I'd never gotten over my old fears. When the street cleared enough for an elderly person to cross in a walker, I wiped my clammy palms on my skirt and sprinted to the center of the street.

"You have to get over your phobia," Nick called to me. "You live in Boston! Traffic is everywhere!"

"It's okay!" Afton elbowed Nick. "Take your time!"

I took a deep breath and raced across to them.

"Nice. I'm impressed. You actually wore a skirt instead of jeans," Nick said, inspecting my bare legs.

My face warmed. "Wait. Did you just give me a compliment?"

"Well, except…" He hesitated. "You walk like a boy."

"Never mind him. With legs like that, it doesn't matter how you walk. Come on." Afton hooked her arm around mine. "I can't wait for you to see the Athenæum. It's so amazing. You're going to love it."

I groaned and let her drag me down the steps after Nick. "I'd probably love it just as much later in the day."

As we approached the platform, the train squealed to a stop. We squeezed into its belly with the other passengers and then grasped the nearest bars as the car jolted down the rails. Several minutes later, the train coasted into the Park Street Station. We followed the flow of people up the stairs and to the Boston Common, stopping in Afton's favorite café for lattes and scones. Lost in gossip and our plans for the summer, nearly two hours went by before we headed for the library.

When we reached Beacon Street, excitement—or maybe the two cups of coffee I had downed before leaving the café—hit me. We weren't going to just any library. We were going to the Boston Athenæum, an exclusive library with a pricey annual fee. Afton's father got her a membership at the start of summer. It's a good thing her membership allows tagalongs, since my pop would never splurge like that, not when the public library is free. Which I didn't get, because it wasn't that expensive and would totally be worth it.

"We're here," Afton said. "Ten and a half Beacon Street. Isn't it beautiful? The facade is Neoclassical."

I glanced up at the building. The library walls, which were more than two hundred years old, held tons of history. Nathaniel Hawthorne swore he saw a ghost here once, which I think he probably made up, since he was such a skilled storyteller. "Yeah, it is. Didn't you sketch this building?"

"I did." She bumped me with her shoulder. "I didn't think you actually paid attention to my drawings."

"Well, I do."

Nick pushed open the crimson door to the private realm of the Athenæum, and I chased Afton and Nick up the white marble steps and into the vestibule. Afton showed her membership card at the reception desk. I removed my notebook and pencil from my messenger bag before we dropped it, Afton's purse, and our umbrellas off at the coat check.

Pliable brown linoleum floors muffled our footsteps into the exhibit room. A tiny elevator from another era carried us to an upper level of the library, where bookcases brimming with leather-bound books stood against every wall.

Overhead, more bookcases nested in balconies behind lattice railings. The place dripped with cornices and embellishments. Sweeping ceilings and large windows gave the library an open feel. Every wall held artwork, and antique treasures rested in each corner. It was a library lover's dream, rich with history. My dream.

A memory grabbed my heart. I was about eight and missing my mother, and Nana Kearns took me to a library. She'd said, "Gia, you can never be lonely in the company of books." I wished Nana were here to experience this with me.

"Did you know they have George Washington's personal library here?" Afton's voice pulled me from my thoughts.

"No. I wonder where they keep it," I said.

Nick gaped at a naked sculpture of Venus. "Locked up somewhere, I guess."

The clapping of my sandals against my heels echoed in the quiet, and I winced at each smack. Nick snorted while trying to stifle a laugh. I glared at him. "Quit it."

"Shhh," Afton hissed.

We shuffled into a reading room with forest green walls. Several busts of famous men balancing on white pedestals surrounded the area. A snobby-looking girl with straight blond hair sat at one of the large walnut tables in the middle of the room, tapping a pencil against the surface as she read a book.

"Prada," Afton said.

I gave her a puzzled look. "What?"

"Her sandals. And the watch on her wrist... Coach."

I took her word on that because I wouldn't know designer stuff if it hit me on the head.

Nick's gaze flicked over the girl. "This is cool. I think I'll stay here."

"Whatever." Afton glared at Nick's back. "We're going exploring. When you're finished gawking, come find us."

"Okay," Nick said, clearly distracted, sneaking looks at the girl.

I slid my feet across the floor to the elevators, trying to avoid the dreaded clap of rubber. "Are you okay?"

"I'm fine." By the tone in Afton's voice, I suspected she didn't like Nick ditching us.

"At least we get some girl time," I said.

I must have sounded a little too peppy, because she rolled her eyes at me. She pushed the down button on the elevator. "Yeah, I can give you the tour before we get to work. The Children's Library has some cool stuff in it."

I didn't see the point of riding an elevator when you could get some exercise in. "We could take the stairs. You know, cardio?"

"How about *no*. My feet are killing me in these heels." The doors slid open, and we stepped inside. "Did you know there's a book here bound in human skin?"

"No. Really?" The elevator dropped and my stomach slumped.

Afton removed her sweater and then draped it over her arm. "Really. I saw it."

"No thanks."

"You can't tell it's actual skin," she said. "They treat it or dye it or something, silly."

"I bet they *die* it." The doors rattled apart. There was a slight bounce as we exited the elevator, and I clutched the doorframe. The corner of Afton's lip rose slightly, and I knew her mood was improving. I released my death grip on the frame then followed her into the hallway. "Besides, isn't it illegal or something?"

"Well, the book is from the nineteenth century." Afton shrugged a shoulder. "Who knows what was legal back then?"

"Why would they even do that?" This entire conversation was making *my* skin crawl.

"It's a confession from a thief. Before he died, he requested his own skin be used for the book's cover." The spaghetti strap on Afton's sundress fell down her arm, exposing part of her lacey bra, and she slipped it back in place.

A thirty-something guy passing us gaped, then averted his eyes and hurried his steps, probably realizing Afton's underage status. I rolled my eyes at him. *Jeesh.* Every single move Afton made was sexy. Nick was right. I walked like a guy. I leaned into her side. "Did you just see that perv check you out?"

"Oh, really?" She looked over her shoulder. "He's not all that bad for an older man."

Ugh. "You seriously need a therapist. He's almost Pop's age."

She laughed, grabbed my arm, and turned on her scary narrator voice. "They say this library is haunted."

"Stop it. Are you trying to freak me out?"

She snickered. "You're such a baby."

We stepped into the Children's Library and stopped in the center of the room. A massive light fixture designed to resemble the solar system dominated the ceiling. The hushed rumble of two male voices came from one of the reading nooks. I crossed the room, paused at the built-in aquarium, and inspected the fish. Afton halted beside me.

"This is great," I whispered, not wanting to disturb whoever was in there with us. "Fish and books. What's not to love?" Spotting a sign referencing classic books, I searched the shelves for my all-time favorite novel.

The male voices stopped and there was movement on the other side of the bookcase. I paused to listen, and when the voices started up again, I continued my hunt.

Warmth rushed over me when I found *The Secret Garden*. With its aged green cover, it was the same edition I remembered reading as a young girl. The illustrations inside were beautiful, and I just had to show them to Afton. Coming around the corner of the case, a little too fast for being in a library, I bumped into a guy dressed in leather biker gear. My book and notebook fell and slapped against the floor.

"Oh, I'm so sorry—" I lost all train of thought at the sight of him. He was gorgeous with tousled brown hair and dark eyes. Tall. He flashed me a crooked smile, a hint of dimples forming in his cheeks, before bending over and picking up my forgotten book.

He held the book out to me. "*Mistress Mary, quite contrary, how does your garden grow?*" He'd quoted a verse from *The Secret Garden* with a sexy accent that tickled my ears.

I stood there like an idiot, my heart pounding hard against my chest, unable to think of a response. The fact that he had read the book and could recite a line from it stunned me. And impressed me.

Say something. Anything.

"Good read there," he said when it was obvious I wasn't going to speak. He winked and nodded to a guy behind him before ambling off. When he reached the end of the row, he paused and glanced back at me, flashing me another killer smile, and then he disappeared around the bookcase.

Tingles rose in my stomach. *He looked back at me.*

The guy following his Royal Hotness gave me a final appraisal before departing. His stringy blond hair hung over his large forehead. It looked like he hadn't washed it in weeks, and there was probably an acne breeding ground under it. He grinned, and I broke eye contact with him, making for the nearest window.

Oh God, you're so lame, Gia. You could have finished the quote or anything less tragic than not speaking at all. The response I would have said played in my head. *With silver bells, and cockleshells, and marigolds all in a row.* Why? Why hadn't I said that?

The window overlooked the Granary Burying Grounds. I hugged my books to my chest and spoke to Afton's reflection in the windowpane, listening to the guys' boots retreating from the room, not daring to sneak a look. "I've been to that graveyard before. Mother Goose is buried there."

She strained her neck forward to view the tombstones below.

I shifted to face her. "Did you see that guy? He was—he was—" I was still at a loss for words.

"Probably European by the sound of his accent," she said, her eyes shifting over the tourists weaving around the gravestones below. "The taller one is delicious, though."

"I know, and I just stood there. He talked to me, and I just stood there."

"Well, maybe you'll see him again." Her outlook was always positive.

I sagged against the window frame. "I'd probably make a fool of myself again."

"I don't get the appeal," she said, squinting out the window then straightening. "It's just a bunch of old stones etched with names you can hardly read."

I feigned a shocked expression. "It's history. Sam Adams and Paul Revere are buried there."

"Don't you get enough history in school?"

"Never. I could walk in it all day."

We sat at one of the tables, flipping through picture books. It was Afton's favorite thing to do at libraries. The illustrations inspired her art.

Afton sighed. "I'm hungry. Let's get some lunch."

We grabbed our bags from the coat check and texted Nick. He told us to go without him. Afton and I gave each other puzzled looks. He never refused food. We downed lemonades and pretzels on the Common then returned to the Athenæum. I sent a message to Nick that we were back before checking in my bag.

After Afton dragged me on a tour from breathtaking rooms framed by towering bookcases and soaring windows to a balconied patio, we rode one of the small elevators to the fifth-floor reading room. Except for a few patrons, the area was vacant. We found the books we needed for Afton's and Nick's summer projects and then settled at one of the tables in the middle of the room. The sucky part about going to a private school was that each summer we had to write an essay over the break. Since I hated having to-do lists hanging over my head, I'd finished mine already.

"Mint?" Afton extended a tin while flipping through a small textbook on Crispus Attucks, an African American minuteman shot during the Boston Massacre.

"Sure. Thanks." I grabbed one then popped it into my mouth. After flipping my notebook open, I readied my pencil to make notes on Samuel Adams for Nick.

The guy I'd bumped into in the children's area strutted

to a table across the room from us, carrying a large book. He stood out in the conservative atmosphere of the library with his messy hair and tight leather outfit clinging to his toned body. In an easy movement, he sat down and started thumbing through the volume.

From our table, I snuck glances at him. He ran his hand through his tousled hair as he studied the pages, and I couldn't look away. It was like everyone in the room vanished; every sexy movement he made was choreographed just for me.

His gaze snapped up, catching mine.

Busted. I choked on my breath mint.

His intense stare held me for several seconds before the corner of his lips curved up, and his dimples made an appearance. I cleared my throat. The mint sliding down my esophagus was somewhat painful.

Okay, stop staring and do something. I gave him a bright smile, fumbling my pencil in my trembling fingers until it dropped. His eyes sparked with amusement, and he nodded at me.

"Shhhh," Afton said in response to the pencil clattering against the table.

I glanced at her. Focused on her book, a strand of her dark hair twisted around her finger, she hadn't even noticed him. A gust of air came from the guy's direction and rustled her hair. I looked back at him. The pages of his book fluttered, and then settled back in place.

He was gone.

CHAPTER TWO

"W hat the—"

"Shhh, Gia." Afton glared at me over her book. "*Hello?* We're in a library."

I stood to get a better view, scanning the room. The biography on Samuel Adams slipped from my hand and then clunked onto the table.

"What's wrong?" Afton asked.

Rain streamed down the glass panes of the tall arched windows. A hazy light cast shadows over the nooks and recesses of the room. He hadn't moved to any of the other tables.

"That guy just vanished."

"What guy?"

"The wicked hot guy from the children's area. He was sitting over there." I pointed at the empty chair. "I turned away for a nanosecond, and he disappeared."

Afton leaned forward, a frown on her perfectly painted face. "You see, it's moments like this," she said, barely audible, "when you might run into Romeo, that you should wear makeup and ditch the ponytail. You're sixteen, not twelve, you know."

"I have lip gloss on."

"Root beer flavored Lip Smacker doesn't count."

"Get serious. I swear that guy just vanished."

"You probably imagined him."

"Whatever, he was there." I pushed my chair away from me. Was he? Or did I imagine it? I was determined to find out.

"Where are you going?" Afton's frown deepened.

"To find that guy," I said, already walking away.

"He probably went out the back or something," she whispered after me.

"I would have seen him walk away," I said over my shoulder, a little too loudly, judging by how the man sitting at the settee across the room jumped.

The dark clouds outside made the reading room bleak and somewhat sinister. With the old graveyard right outside the windows, I envisioned all sorts of Revolutionary ghosts soaring around the burnished metal-disk light fixtures hanging from the white wooden arches of the cathedral ceiling. It felt like an ice cube skittered down my back, and I inhaled deeply. The musty smell of books filled my nose. *Get over it, Gia. Seriously. How dangerous can a library be?* But that didn't stop me from jolting when a girl slid her notebook along a table.

Creepy plaster busts of famous men stared down from the niches above. A small table and two spindle chairs stood between the stairwells in the alcoves, surrounded by the balconied bookracks. The smacking of my sandals against my heels startled a woman sitting in one of the alcoves. The guy wasn't in any of them.

I slinked up the stairs to the gallery, ears pricked. He hadn't gone up there. What was wrong with me? He was just some random guy.

I headed back toward Afton, hesitating as I passed the

table he'd occupied. The book he'd been reading lay open to a full-page photograph of a room in a library in Oxford, England. *He might not be real, but the book he was reading definitely is.* I hesitated then reached out and closed it. The title, printed in gold letters, read *Libraries of the World.* The book was proof I'd seen him, otherwise, how had it gotten here? No one else had been in this part of the room.

The heavy reference volume sat awkwardly in my arms as I carried it over to the table where Afton sat with wide eyes. "See," I said under my breath. "He *was* there. This is his book."

"You took *his* book. That's just a whole lot of wrong."

"No, it isn't. He's obviously done with it."

"You don't know that. You didn't see him leave." Her eyes darted around the reading room. "Put it back before he returns."

"He probably went down the back stairs."

"Or just went to the bathroom."

I flipped the cover over. "I can't believe someone like him is into libraries or reads children's classics."

"Like him? What do you mean?"

"He looks like he'd read a muscle magazine, not this."

Afton came to my side and leaned over my shoulder. "What'd you say it was?"

"It's a listing of the world's libraries." I leafed through the pages, pausing at every photograph. Each library was uniquely beautiful. A shiver rode down my spine as I traced each picture with my fingertips. "Wouldn't it be awesome if we could go see each one up close and personal?"

"Yeah, that would be awesome, if I were a book nerd like you."

"Well, the buildings are amazing. Does that appeal to your inner architect?"

She slammed her hand on the page. "Stop flipping so

fast. Look at that fresco. I wish I could paint like that."

A voice came from behind us. "What's up?"

Afton gasped, and I started. *"Nick!"*

The man sitting on the antique settee in the middle of the room angrily rustled his newspaper and glared at us. The woman from the reading nook passed us on her way out, giving us a disapproving look.

Afton placed a finger to her lips. "Shh."

Nick dropped a hand on each of our shoulders and glanced at the photograph. "Whatcha reading?"

"Wow, you finally decided to join us." I swiveled around in my seat to face him. "Wait. Let me guess. Did Miss Beacon Hill leave or something?"

"Are you pissed at me?"

"No," I said.

"Are you sensitive impaired?" Afton whispered, shrugging Nick's hand off her shoulder. "Of course she's mad. She's researching *your* summer essay on Samuel Adams while you goof off. You should be doing your own work. And about that, what lame-ass chooses a subject because it's a name of a beer, anyway? Oh. Wait. That would be you."

"I never asked you to research for me, Gia," Nick said.

"R*iii*ght. You don't have to ask, she just does it, and you always take advantage of her."

"Guys," I interrupted. "I really don't mind research. Actually, I love it. So can you both just chill, already?"

"Sure. Whatever," Afton said with a tight smile.

The man with the newspaper sighed, stood, and stomped off, leaving us alone in the reading room.

I tossed another page. "Check out this library in Paris. It's *so* awesome. *The Bibliothèque nationale de France.*"

They leaned over to get a better view. "Wow, those arches are massive," said Afton.

"I'll show you massive." Nick waggled his eyebrows at her.

Afton straightened and rested her fists on her hips. "Oh no, you didn't just say that."

"Hey, what's this?" Nick reached over me and grabbed a folded piece of yellowing paper. He unfolded it carefully. "Damn, it's old. I think it's written in Latin or something. What do you think?"

"It must have fallen out of the book." I took the paper from him and studied the fancy script. "It's definitely in Italian. Jeesh, Nick. You're more Italian than I am."

"And your point?"

"You should know this," I said. Nick and I took years of Italian lessons together, but he'd never gotten it. His lack of passion for his Italian heritage bugged me.

"Well, I do know it's talking about a door," he said. "*Porta* means door, right?"

"Yeah, it's door. Open the door."

"Well, that's just strange," Afton said. "It was probably someone's bookmark or something."

"It looks ancient," I said. "It's in formal Italian, and the script might be calligraphy, I think."

Nick leaned farther over my shoulder and tried to read it out loud. "*Apre–apra–*"

A vision of a young boy wearing Victorian clothes came to me. The paper slipped from my hand, and my breath hitched. The boy stared down at the book, which lay open on a table, and he struggled to say the same phrase just as Nick had. He reached into the pocket of a threadbare coat, pulled out a folded piece of paper, and read it.

"Gia?" Nick's voice brought my attention back to the paper.

"Yes?" I answered, distracted, still stunned by what I saw. The image felt real. As if I were there standing behind the boy, my hands twisting together while waiting for my turn. My turn at what, I didn't know.

"I asked how to pronounce it," he said.

I inhaled, deeply, because I needed air, and tried to focus on Nick's words. "Pronounce it?"

"The paper?"

"Oh, sorry." I picked the slip back up and studied it. "It's *aprire la porta.*"

The book quivered and its spine thumped against the table.

"It's an earthquake," Afton shrieked.

"In Boston? I don't think so—" The words jammed in my throat as a strong wind swirled around us, smashing me into Afton and Nick and squeezing us together until I couldn't breathe. The wind whirled faster and faster, drawing us into the page. My heartbeat sped up and when I tried to call out to them, nothing came out.

The squeezing pressure intensified and then it was gone. Wheezing and kicking my legs, I grabbed for something to hold onto, but there was nothing. We were in a pitch-black void. Afton and Nick panted nearby. And before I could call out to them, we fell, the cold air speeding past and wailing in my ears.

Shit, shit, shit!

Afton let out a piercing scream and Nick cursed. My sandals were sucked away from my toes.

"Oh my God! Oh my God!" Afton cried.

I recited the Hail Mary.

Nick repeated each verse.

Musty air punched my face.

My stomach clenched.

Legs thrashed.

Arms flailed.

We plunged farther.

And farther.

I jerked to a stop, suspended mid-air in inky darkness, my legs level with my body. Afton's and Nick's silhouettes were gray masses against the blackness, their whimpers hushed against the wind.

Then we plummeted again.

I held my breath.

Silence.

Cold.

Fear.

Smack!

A dim light tickled through my eyelashes. Sprawled across a carpet, I tried to move, prickly rug fibers scratching my cheek. One sandal hit my head and the other landed on my back. A thud sounded to the right of me and another thud to the left. Books tumbled down around me from the shelves of a nearby bookcase.

Terror pumping through me, I lay there for several minutes, evaluating the pain. My left shoulder and hip throbbed, but nothing was broken. "Afton?" I called out. "Nick?"

"Yes," he groaned.

"Are you okay?"

"I think so."

"Afton?" She didn't answer, so I got to my knees and crawled over the books to her. I shook her shoulder. "Afton?"

She didn't move, but she breathed. I pulled her head onto my lap and Nick scooted to my side, wrapping his arm around my back. The world was a Tilt-A-Whirl, and I wanted desperately to get off. I needed to stop freaking out and get help for Afton, but panic rocked my insides and rooted me firmly in place.

Nick muttered something, and I only caught the word "dead."

Tears wet my cheeks, and my nose started running. "What did you say?"

"Are we dead?"

I sniffed. "I don't think so."

Nick pulled a wad of tissues he always kept for his fierce allergies from his pocket and then passed them to me with a shaky hand. "Here, they're not used."

"Thanks," I said, taking the wad and then blowing my nose.

Afton stirred. "*Ouch,*" she moaned. "What happened?"

"We fell through a wormhole," Nick said.

Afton sat up slowly. "What's a wormhole?"

"It's a shortcut through space."

"This isn't *Star Wars* or one of your video games." I helped Afton to her feet. "It's some sort of...something." But nothing I'd ever experienced before.

"Okay. I'm freaking." Afton's lower lip quivered. "We fell. It was dark. This can't be happening, right?"

"Oh, it's happening." Nick struggled to his feet. "Where do you think we are?"

A dim light illuminated the stadium-sized room. Above us, circular windows resembling flowers rimmed the edge of a vast domed ceiling. Underneath the dome, massive concrete arches vaulted over cherry wood bookshelves. Library lamps with green glass shades lined the tops of several long tables stretched across the room.

We'd landed in a reading room I recognized.

Fear grabbed me, but I sucked it back, willing myself to stay calm. My arms and legs betrayed me, though, trembling uncontrollably. "I think we're in the library from the photo in that book. The one in Paris." My voice came out shaky. Though certain we were in that library, I hardly believed it myself. I had to stay calm and figure this out.

I turned to Afton and asked, "Are you hurt?"

"I'm fine. I think I just fainted." She wobbled a little before righting herself. "Do you think that guy had something to do with this?"

"Maybe," I said, searching under the scattered books for my sandals. I found them and struggled to put them on with trembling hands. "I don't know. What time was it back home?"

"Three or so," Nick said. "Why?"

"This library's closed. Isn't it like a seven or eight hour difference between Boston and Paris?"

"It's six hours," said Afton. "What's your point?"

"Then it's about nine at night here, and I'm guessing we're stuck in this library until morning."

"Th-this is a dream," Afton stuttered and clung to Nick. "We're going to wake up. We have to wake up."

"You'll be okay." Nick wrapped his arm around her.

"We should see if anyone is still here," I said.

Nick raked his fingers through his thick, dark hair. "How can you do that?"

"Do what?"

"Act like we took a trip on Delta or something, instead of being warped here by some insane magic."

"Look, I'm freaked out, too, but let's not panic."

"*Hello*, already panicking here," Afton said. "I just want to go home."

Pounding my feet and shrieking wasn't going to get us out of this mess. Funny how I normally was the one scared of everything—with reason—but here I was keeping everyone calm. I looked around. "Crap. I don't have my bag. Do you guys have your cell phones?"

"No." Afton swept a strand of hair away from her mascara-soaked cheeks. "It's in my purse." I handed her an unused tissue, and she wiped her inky tears away.

Nick dug his cell phone out of his front pants pocket and stared at it. "No service." He held it up and walked around, searching for a connection. "Nothing."

"It's because you don't have international roaming on your phone," Afton said.

I headed to the door. "Let's find something."

"Like what?" Nick snapped.

"I don't know...something...a *landline* maybe."

"Oh yeah, let's call our parents. I can hear it now." Nick imitated my voice by raising his to a higher pitch. "*Hello, Pop. My friends and I got warped to Paris. Can you pick us up?* They'd think we were on drugs or something."

"Oh, please." Afton's voice sounded strained. "Could you just stop with the sarcasm already?"

"What do you want to do, then?" I asked him.

Nick shrugged. "Go find a phone, I guess."

I glared at him before crossing the ginormous reading room to the nearest door. Nick and Afton trailed behind me. When I touched the doorknob, a loud wail came from the other side of the door, and I snapped my hand back.

"Is that an alarm?" Afton asked.

"I don't think so—"

Something like an animal's claws scratching across the floor screeched from behind the door. I gulped. That didn't sound like any guard dog I'd ever heard before.

"What the *hell* is that?" Nick said.

Afton grabbed Nick's arm tighter, her eyes wider than her makeup compact.

I stumbled back. "Wh-whatever it is—" *Thud!* Something heavy slammed against the door. *"Hide!"*

CHAPTER THREE

I grabbed a stapler and crouched behind the nearest cabinet. Nick and Afton ducked down beside me. I pulled the leg down on the stapler, held it up, and readied it to shoot.

"Yeah, that'll work," Nick said.

"What are we doing?" Afton squeaked out. "If it's security, they can help us."

"How are we going to explain us being here after closing?" I whispered. "We're trespassing. And we're in a foreign country, we could get arrested—"

The door slammed against the wall, followed by heavy panting.

"That sounds like one big puppy," Afton said.

"Be quiet." I motioned for them to follow me as I squat-walked down the length of the cabinet to the other end. The dog sniffed the air, making a sound like an overheated game console.

"Gross," Afton said in a small, choked voice. "Seriously, gross. What is that smell?"

"A security dog with road kill breath, I'd say," Nick whispered back.

I peered around the corner but couldn't see it. Its howl skittered down my spine, and a nearby table rocked as it brushed by, almost toppling the lamps and sending their pull cords chiming against their brass bases.

A shadow caught at the corner of my vision. I tensed and spun around. Nothing was there.

The dog's pants grew closer. The stink made me dizzy and I struggled to focus. We needed a safer place to hide. Across the room, bookcases lined the wall, and there was a balcony right above them. "Follow me," I whispered over my shoulder.

Nick scooted closer. "To where?"

"See that balcony?" I pointed to it. "We can hide."

"How are we getting up there?" Afton said.

"We have to climb the bookcases." I eyed Afton's sandals. "I think you should ditch the spikes or you won't make it."

"Crap. These are my faves." She unbuckled the straps and removed them. "Okay, ready."

I scooted around the corner and smacked straight into a guy resting on the heels of his boots and peering around the side of the cabinet. It was like running into a muscled barrier—he barely swayed. Intense dark eyes stared at me from the eyeholes of a knight-like helmet with gold wings. Threaded through the straps of a small shield, his arm bent across his chest for protection. The ornately textured handle of a sword stuck out of a metal scabbard at his side.

I fell back on my butt, gasping, and scrambled away from him.

He raised his finger to his lips to silence me, and, like a tracking panther, slipped around the corner and sneaked off in the direction of the animal's sounds.

In a flash, an Asian girl appeared and sank to her knees

beside me. She wore a black leather catsuit and a black-and-jade samurai helmet with a mask that covered half her face. A katana with a green corded handle balanced upright in her hands. She nodded at me and then slithered after the guy. Three other teenage boys, all wearing a cross between biker and knight-like gear, hurried past me.

"Where did they go? And why do they have swords?" Nick stretched up and peeked over the top of the cabinet. "I can't see them. Is anyone else concerned they have weapons?"

A crash sounded across the massive room, then scrambling feet, grunts, and an animal wail. Paws pounded against the floor and headed in our direction.

Afton clamped onto my arm. "Holy crap, it's coming toward us."

The security dog sniffed the floor on the other side of the cabinet. A staple dislodged as I strangled the stapler with nervous hands. The dog bumped against the cabinet, almost tipping it over on us.

"Come on. We have to get out of here." I jumped up—stapler in hand—and froze.

Not. A. Dog. I jumped back and hit the wall. The beast resembled a rhino, with a large tusk curving up from its snout. Blood oozed from cuts in its side. With each shake of its head, gooey saliva showered everything. Its sharp horns stabbed the cabinet and then tossed the crumpled wood to the side. What the— I must have hit my head. Hard. I was hallucinating.

Its crazed red eyes fixed on me. I hurled the stapler at its snout, then threw a front kick while it was distracted, the ball of my foot landing squarely on its jaw. The damn thing didn't even flinch. It snorted and readied itself to charge.

"Run!" I yelled to Nick and Afton.

My heart racing, I sprinted after them. A bookshelf exploded behind me and splinters pelted my calves; searing pain fired across my skin.

"*Shit*. That hurt."

Nick darted glances over his shoulder. "Hurry, Gia!"

We scrambled onto a table, thumped across the length of it, and pounced onto the next one, each spring propelling us farther down the row. The beast's hooves stomped behind me. *Thwack. Thwack. Thwack.* It crashed into the tables as it charged after us, leaving broken furniture in its wake.

Nick and Afton climbed one of the bookcases against the wall, clambered over a banister, and thudded onto the balcony. I scaled the shelves after them and latched onto two newels of the banister.

I held tight, clenching my teeth, straining not to let go. *I'm going to die!*

The beast rammed the bookcase, and I lost my footing on the shelf. Books tumbled out as the solid case collapsed onto the creature's back. It twisted upright, eyes set on me.

With my legs dangling just above its head, my sweaty hands began to slip down the rails. "Help!" I brought my knees up to prevent the loss of my feet.

Nick and Afton each grabbed one of my arms and pulled me up and over the banister. Hot tears of relief filled my eyes. My legs were weak as I staggered to stand.

I peered through the rails of the banister at the exact moment the guy and his friends rushed the beast, sinking their swords into its flesh. The beast collapsed to the floor, the impact resounding like thunder against the library walls.

The four guys towered over the only girl in the group as they examined the bleeding heap on the floor. The guy I'd collided with behind the cabinet removed his helmet, exposing tousled brown hair.

My breath punched out of me. It was the guy from the Boston Athenæum.

Blood splatter dotted his metal chest guard and dripped from the sword in his hand. The ease of his stance suggested confidence. His strong shoulders flexed under his shirt as he brought his helmet down then rested it on his side.

His gaze went up to the loft, brushing over Nick, me, Afton, and then darting back to me. I backed away from the banister. *This can't be happening. It's not real.* It was as if my mother's bedtime stories were coming to life.

The Athenæum guy returned his attention to the group beside him. I inched forward and clutched the railing, straining to hear them.

"I could hardly see anything," one of the other guys said. He removed his plumed helmet, releasing sandy tufts of hair. "We should have used our light globes or, better yet, our battle ones."

The Asian girl pulled her sword from the beast. "Yeah, maybe you'd get lucky again and hit another human."

"It was clearly an accident."

Light globe? I glanced at my palm, a memory warming the skin there.

The other two guys slipped their helmets off. One, who looked to be East Indian, had a bad case of helmet hair with dark waves smashed against his head. The other guy's short black dreadlocks were so sweaty they glistened.

"She's right," the dreadlock guy said. "There wasn't an open shot." He grabbed a box of tissues off a nearby table and passed it around. The group wiped their blades.

The Athenæum guy spoke next. "What took you so long to respond to my call?"

"There was a delay in the connection," said the girl. "Something interrupted it. The hound slipped through the gateway before the jump was detected."

Hound? Gateway? I should have been petrified, but I was too focused on the conversation below to think about the stinking carcass or that there were five people talking about us like we weren't there. It was like I almost knew what they were saying, but couldn't quite grasp it. The meaning was just beyond my reach.

"So what about the humans?" the East Indian guy asked. They all had accents.

"Same as always," said the Athenæum guy. "Get them home. Wipe their memories of the events. Cover their trails. Hopefully no hunters will find them."

The girl sighed. "You'd think Paris would come up with a better way to secure their libraries so humans aren't locked in after closing."

"They're not as cautious as us," said the sandy-haired guy.

"This wasn't a lock-in. The Monitors detected their jump through the gateway book," the Athenæum guy said.

The girl flashed him a startled look. "They couldn't have. Humans can't jump."

The sandy-haired one glanced our way. "That means they're—"

"We have an audience," the dreadlock guy said.

"We'll sort this out later," the Athenæum guy said. "We must secure the situation first. I met Edgar earlier, and he's heard of a wizard conducting illegal experiments. Go back to Asile and inform Merl. Tell him about the humans." He nodded toward the East Indian guy and dreadlock guy. "Don't use your phones or window rods to transmit any information about this incident. We wouldn't want to announce our findings for undesirables to hear."

The two went over to where we had first landed in the

library. The guy in dreadlocks wore a red leather vest. With his horned helmet cradled under one arm, he slipped his sword into the scabbard attached to his waist. He snatched up a book from the pile on the floor, placed it on a nearby table, and flipped through the pages.

The East Indian guy placed his Spartan-like helmet between his knees and held it there. Blood dotted his metal vest. He didn't have a sword. Instead, leather sheaths attached to fingerless gloves with steel knuckles were strapped to his forearm. A silver blade extended out from each sheath and over the top of his encased hand. He pushed something on the gloves' palms with his middle fingers, and the blades retracted. He tugged them off, tucked them into his belt, grabbed his helmet, and placed his hand on the other guy's shoulder, saying something I couldn't hear.

The pages of the books on the floor nearby fluttered. The East Indian guy's hair swooshed angrily around his face. The two guys' pants lashed at their legs, and the flaps of their vests slapped against thick leather belts. Their bodies spun together until they turned into a multi-colored tornado and vanished into the page.

I gasped and stumbled back, and Afton grabbed my hand tight. A quick breath cut through my lungs. Tremors ran up the length of my arm. I wasn't sure if it was my hand shaking or hers. Or both.

"Where did they go?" Nick said, crowding close to us.

"They…they disappeared," Afton squeaked.

"They went into the book." I dropped Afton's hand, leaning forward to get a better view of the scene below. And I knew what had happened. "Just like we did."

"Is anyone hurt?" The guy from the Athenæum called up to us, his voice smooth and deep.

"I-I don't think s-so," Nick answered, a quake in his

voice. He then looked to us. "You guys okay?"

I tightened my hands into fists and took several calming breaths, trying to stop my body from trembling. Other than the rug burns on my knees and the welts on the backs of my legs, I was alive. "Yeah, I'm fine." Physically, maybe.

"It's safe to come down," the Asian girl shouted. "The stairs are behind you."

We went down and then stepped out of the stairwell. The stench from the beast hit me, making me queasy. I swallowed the bile rising up in my throat.

Afton kept her grasp on Nick's arm. "What was that *thing*?"

Athenæum guy's stare was on me again. "Just a minute, you're that girl in Boston—the one in the reading room?"

Wait. He remembers me? My heart jerked and then jackhammered against my chest. "Y-yes," I stammered.

"We should make our introductions," the Asian girl said. "I'm Lei, and the rude one is Arik." She removed her helmet, releasing a long black braid that fell against her back.

"Did you say Eric?" Nick asked.

"No. It's *Ah-ric*," she said and holstered her katana in a sheath fastened to an emerald-encrusted belt around her waist. Nick and I had become obsessed with the swords after streaming all the *Kill Bill* videos on his laptop one Saturday. But seeing a real one was scary. It looked like it could cut someone's head off with a single swing. Unlike the other four, Lei didn't carry a shield.

"I guess that leaves me. I'm Demos," said the sandy-haired guy. He wore a metal chest plate molded to resemble a muscled torso. A helmet with a red plume dangled from his right hand. His liquid blue eyes lingered on Afton.

"What the hell is going on here?" Nick said. "Is this some sort of joke? Is this for real?"

"I don't understand your meaning," Arik said. "What's

your name?"

"Nick."

"Well, Nick, I assure you this is real."

"Yeah, welcome to your new reality," Demos said.

"I'm Gia, and this is Afton," I blurted, taking her hand again. Her fingers were ice-cold and she shivered uncontrollably.

"It's a pleasure to meet you, Gia," Lei said.

Arik attached his shield to his back with a belt strapped diagonally across his torso, and Demos did the same.

"Exactly what were you hoping to accomplish with the stapler?" Demos asked.

"I, uh, there wasn't anything else," I said.

"Well, I must say, you did look menacing with it."

"Which one of you spoke the key?" asked Arik.

Nick quirked a brow. "The what?"

"Right. If you want to play it like that," Lei said, "then tell us who sent you here."

"That book in the library—"

Arik looked at me with those dark eyes. Their thick lashes distracted me and I froze again, unable to form words.

Seriously. Say something. He must think I'm in need of a brain transplant.

"What book?" Arik urged.

"Yes, that book, you know…the one you were reading. It…well, one minute we're in Boston and the next we ended…we ended up here." I had to sound like a stuttering idiot trying to catch my breath between words. I needed to get a grip on myself, but each time I looked at Arik all thoughts escaped me.

"How did you know the key?"

"What key?"

"The key is a phrase spoken in Italian," Lei answered.

My stomach lurched at that. "Do you mean *aprire la porta*?"

"Yes, that's the one," Demos said. "Who spoke it?"

"I did."

Arik looked sharply at me. His gaze dropped to my chest, and with two quick strides, he was right in front of me. "How did you get the scar on your chest?"

I glanced down. My shirt had shifted south during the mad dash over the balcony. I yanked it up to hide the mark. The crescent-shaped scar was my barometer—I'd never let my shirts go below its highest point.

"*Well?* How did it happen?"

I covered the spot and took a step away from him. "It happened when I was a baby. My mother didn't say...she wouldn't tell Pop...she felt really bad about it. I couldn't ask her. She died when I was four." I realized how terrible that sounded and added, "Obviously, it was an accident. She was a good mother."

"Uh-huh." Arik raised an eyebrow at me then turned to Lei and Demos. "Do any of you know what a crescent brand does?"

"I think it's the shield charm," Lei said. "I've seen it in old charm chronicles, but no one knows how to create one. If that's what it is, are you aware of what it means?"

"She's a witch," Demos said around a wide grin.

I blinked. "I'm not a *witch*." I was sure of it.

"You have to be kidding," Nick said. "There's no way she's a witch. Wait, what am I saying? They don't even exist."

Lei came over and placed her hand on my arm. "Demos thinks that because only a witch can create a shielding brand. But he's mistaken, because witches can't travel the gateway books, and apparently you can."

"Bane Witches can travel," Demos countered.

Lei gave him an incredulous look. "Bane Witches are evil. It distorts their faces. Does she look that way to you?"

"You all are crazy," Afton snapped, spinning around, her eyes searching for an escape. "We have to get out of here."

Demos caught her arm. "Hold on there. Nobody's going anywhere."

"Get your hands off me." Afton yanked away from his grip. "You had blood all over them. And you can't keep us here. We're leaving. Gia? Nick?" She stormed off.

Arik's gaze dared us to make a move, his hand on the hilt of his sword, his broad shoulders and large biceps menacing under his fitted vest.

Nick and I just stood there, both of us too scared to follow her.

Demos chased her, saying over his shoulder, "I think now would be a good time to erase their memories."

"You know we cannot wipe them now," Arik said. "It would immobilize them for hours, and we must get them to safety."

Demos dragged Afton back to the group, chairs toppling over in the struggle. Nick wrenched her from Demos's grasp and wrapped his arms around her to keep her from running again. "What were you thinking?" he hissed near her ear. "They could kill us…you."

Lei crossed her arms, giving us a disapproving glare. "Maybe we could calm them. Besides, if she's a wizard, erasing her memory won't work."

"She can't be a wizard. She's female," Demos said, his breath heavy. "That is, unless she's hiding something." He glanced at my nether regions.

First he calls me a witch. Then he thinks I'm a guy? I glared at him. "*I'm* a girl."

"Don't be such a chauvinist, Demos." Lei shook her head

at him. "There have been female wizards. Well, not many, but there have been some. She could be suppressed. She isn't fey. I don't see a glamour rim around her. And she's definitely not a creature of any sort. She could be a Sentinel. Arik?"

His gaze traveled over me. I wrapped my arms around my chest, uncomfortable at the way he scrutinized me.

Nick scratched the back of his neck. "What's a Sentinel?"

Lei said, "We're like security guards for the libraries. There are many beings traveling through the gateways, searching…well, anyway, some can be dangerous, just like this hound here." Her foot landed on the beast's hindquarters. "We take care of them—"

"If she's a Sentinel, then she'll have special skills," Demos said. "Can you conjure magic or fight, Gia?"

The right corner of my mouth started twitching. It's a tic I get when I'm nervous or lying, or nervous because I'm lying, whichever. I *had* experienced magic before, but I wasn't going to tell them about it. Not that I could anyway. I froze each time I wanted to tell someone my secret. And what I'd done was nothing in comparison to all I'd heard and seen today.

Besides, I didn't even know who these people were. But I did know I wanted to stick around them in case one of those scary beasts showed up.

Nick gave me a sidelong glance. "Gia fences for our school's team, plus she's a badass kickboxer."

"*Nick!*" I dug my elbow into his rib.

Nick grabbed his side and glared at me. "Well, you *are* like another species."

"Stop it." I shoved him this time, hoping to shut him up. Sure, I had earned trophies in fencing and won matches in kickboxing, but so had others. How did that make me different?

"There's no need for violence." He shrugged away from me. "See? You're a fighter."

"I can't be one... I'm awkward."

Afton shot me a sympathetic smile. "You're only awkward at girl stuff."

I stared at my unpainted toenails. She was right. I never felt like I fit in anywhere.

"My bet is she's a witch." Demos still had that smug grin on his face.

"Stop teasing her." Lei turned to me. "Well, have you ever conjured magic?"

"*No*. Are you crazy?" I bit my lip to stop the twitch.

"Enough already," Arik said. "You're frightening her. It's not our place to straighten this out. We'll turn in our report to the council, and they can figure out this mess. Right now, our duty is to get these humans safely home and cover up any scent of them."

Lei retrieved her ringing cell phone from her hip pocket. "Yes? Uh-huh. Uh-huh. Certainly, we're on our way." She pressed the screen to end the call. "The Cleaners will be here in ten. We have to leave."

"What are Cleaners?" I said.

"They do exactly what the name implies," Lei said. "They'll use their magic to tidy up this mess, and they'll take care of this." She nudged the beast with her booted foot and then turned to Arik. "So, what's the plan?"

"We'll split up," he said. "Library hop to throw off the humans' scent."

"Why?" I blurted. "Why do you have to throw off our scent?"

"When a human enters the gateways, they leave a scent behind," Arik said. "Some of the less gentle Mystiks will kill any human who discovers the Mystik world. The lot of them—

hunters and hounds—will gather your scent before long."

"*What*?" Afton's eyes widened. "They can't kill us. It's illegal. We have to call the police."

"It's not illegal in our world," Lei clarified.

"Who are these Mystiks, anyway?" I asked.

"They're wizards, Sentinels, and other mystical beings," she said.

Afton grimaced. "Where exactly are these things?"

"We're not *things*," Lei spat. "Wizards and Sentinels are part human. We have a stake in protecting humans. There are some unusual creatures living among us in the Mystik world. And not all of them are bad. They're gentle and kind, most of the time."

"It's the other times I'm worried about," Nick said.

"Why haven't we ever seen any of these creatures?" I asked.

"Because when they're in your world, they mask their forms or conceal their abilities," Lei said.

"This is crazy." Nick shifted nervously. "I don't know what to believe anymore."

"No worries, ducky." Lei placed her hand on Nick's arm. "We keep the Mystiks from entering your world, and we take care of the naughty ones. Besides, your people have monsters of their own to handle. The wizard havens are against harming humans. You'll just have to trust us to protect you."

"Let's get a jump on it before the hounds descend on us." Demos quirked a smile at Afton. "Get it? Get a jump. We're going to *jump* into the gateway."

Afton pinched a look at him. "Hilarious."

I glanced at the creature on the floor. If there were more of them coming for us, I wanted to leave fast.

Arik issued orders. "Demos, you take Afton to Spain,

then—"

"He's not taking her," Nick broke in.

"You haven't a say in the matter. Lei, take Nick to Ireland, and I'll take Gia to Italy. Then we meet in Boston. Are we clear?"

"Yes," said Lei. She went over to the book, spoke something in Italian, and studied the page. The only word I caught was "window."

"What is she doing?" I asked Arik.

"She turned the photograph into a window," he said. "She can see inside the library and ascertain if it's safe to jump."

"I'm not sure if that's reassuring or terrifying," Afton said.

Nick slipped his arm over her shoulder. "We're going to be okay."

Demos cocked an eyebrow at Nick. "Is she your girlfriend?"

"Oh, please, I am *so* not his girlfriend," Afton said.

"Then why doesn't he want me to take you?"

"Demos, enough already. Get going," Arik said.

"Don't get your knickers in a twist. I'm going. Come on, sweet." Demos grabbed Afton's hand and led her to the book. "It's easier if you jump up the instant the book tugs at you. So when you feel the suction, just hop in with me. Got it?"

Afton tried to pull away from him. "No. Are you freaking crazy?"

"Ah, come on, you can trust me." He clutched her waist and gave Nick a smirk as he did. *"Aprire la porta."*

Afton shrieked as the book sucked them in. They vanished in a wake of flipping pages, just like the others who'd disappeared earlier. It creeped me out that I was beginning to understand what they were doing. I bet my mother had known about this, too.

Nick crossed his arms. "I'm not going through that again."

"It's your only way home." Arik clapped Nick's back. "That is, unless you'd prefer to purchase an airline ticket."

"It can be tough when you're a beginner, love," Lei said. "Just remember, we jump when we feel the pull. Concentrate on keeping your legs down and you'll land on your feet, not your face."

Arik snickered. "Or your arse."

Nick untangled his arms. "We're so screwed. We probably tripped an alarm or got caught on security cameras."

"The instant someone enters a library by way of the gateway books, magic immobilizes all alarms and cameras," Arik said.

"Okay, let's go before we're hound snacks," Lei said to Nick.

"Will you just stop saying stuff like that already?" Nick raked his fingers through his hair.

"Sorry, ducky," she said and stepped over to the book. "You ready?"

He stared at her for several seconds before joining her. "Let's do this."

Nick was so anxious to leave after Lei spoke the charm that he almost jumped into the book by himself. Lei snatched the back of his shirt and fell in with him.

Arik shot me a crooked smile. "Are you ready?"

I caught my breath. "I guess so."

He thumbed the pages until he found the right one, grabbed my hand, and recited the charm. When a pressure tugged at me, I jumped up with him. A powerful burst of wind lifted us above the book and then dropped us feet first. My foot kicked the book, turning the page before we entered the gateway.

Arik cursed.

CHAPTER FOUR

Arik clutched my hand as we plummeted through the inky void. Chilly air rushed across my body and my teeth clattered. He raised his hand and said a word I couldn't hear over the wind's howl. A ball of light sprouted from his palm and lit up my frosty breaths. There was nothing else to see within the gateway—no walls, ceilings, or floors—only his light searching the blackness.

I struggled to keep my skirt from flying up in the turbulence. I didn't want him to see my underwear. We slowed, and my legs went level with my body. I thrashed around, trying to get my feet underneath me. Arik made it look easy, like skiing on air. In contrast, I mimicked a novice on the bunny hill, frantically struggling to stay upright.

We shot out of a book cabinet, knocking open its doors and spilling books. I landed on my feet, barely, and stumbled into Arik's rock-hard arms.

"You all right?"

His amused gaze touched my face and my stomach belly-flopped. I swiftly pulled away from him to hide my flushing cheeks. "Yeah, I'm good, thanks."

Arik glanced around, a concerned look igniting on his face. "Bugger," he snapped under his breath.

A smell like antiquated, dusty books mixed with pine cleaner lingered in the air. It was warm and my fingers tingled as they thawed. We were in a large room. Every single wall, pillar, and arch had murals of saints and bible scenes painted on it. Gold trimmed everything. I'd seen this room before when I was younger. Father Mortimer had shown us pictures of it at Sunday school. *The Vatican?*

The tapping sound of booted feet came from a hallway on the right. A girl and five guys, all about my age and dressed in what I assumed was Sentinel gear, entered the room.

Arik brought his mouth close to my ear. His warm breath brushed my neck, sending chills across my skin. "Follow my lead. They can't know you're human."

"Okay." I was about to lie in the Vatican. And I was pretty sure committing even a minor sin in this place would put me on the damnation list.

"Well, well, Arik, we weren't aware you were to pay us a visit," a guy with a large nose and dark curly hair said. He broke from the others and crossed to us, his boots click-clacking against the black-and-white checkered floor.

Arik took my hand and gripped it tight. "Antonio?"

"Who did you expect? Jesus Christ? Maybe the Pope?" Antonio frowned. "The Vatican library is off limits without permission. Have you forgotten the protocol? Your Monitor is supposed to send ours a request to visit. What are you doing here?"

"I meant to jump into the Florence library," Arik answered.

"It isn't like you to make mistakes. Who's the girl?"

"She's a Sentinel."

"Why is she in human clothes?"

"We're performing some jump exercises. She's in costume."

"Really?" Antonio rubbed his chin. "This has nothing to do with the human scent permeating the gateways, does it?"

"I haven't encountered any humans, but we did run into another unattended hound. It was one of the Writhes'. And this isn't the first time this evening we've come across one."

"We've stumbled on a few, as well. That's why we're here tonight, protecting the Vatican. Though there aren't many traveling the gateways these days with—" He stopped as his dark clay-colored eyes settled on my face. "You're Italian—"

Arik stepped in front of me, blocking Antonio's view. "We have to get back."

"I wasn't aware we had a novice from Italy at the academy." He pursed his lips as he eyeballed me. "How old are you?"

"She's fourteen and was privately tutored until recently." Arik scooted back, causing me to move toward the book-case. "We're being timed."

I lowered my head so he couldn't tell I was older. The ponytail was my saving grace. Everyone said I looked younger with one.

"Certainly. I'd love to watch your trainee transport."

My stomach hit the floor. *Great. What if I can't do it this time?*

"I apologize for the breach," Arik said. "It won't happen again. We'll be on our way. Good evening."

Antonio inclined his head. "Good evening."

Arik rested his hand on my lower back. I was acutely aware of every twitch of his fingers as he guided me to the cabinet. He removed his hand to grab the gateway book, and a shiver ran up my back. After finding the photograph of the Boston Athenæum, he placed the book on the floor.

"You remember the key?"

I nodded.

He grabbed my trembling hand. "Don't tense like that. You'll mess up. Are you ready?"

"Yes." I drew in a deep breath.

Antonio studied us. "She's a fledgling. Don't push her."

Arik squeezed my hand. "You can do it."

"*Aprire*, um, *apri—*"

"No pauses."

I relaxed my breathing and focused on the page. *"Aprire la porta."*

We jumped into the gateway.

The others were waiting for us when we entered the Athenæum. "That first step's a real bugger, eh? At least you didn't land on your face like Alpha Male over there did." Demos nodded toward my friends.

Nick was beside Afton in the middle of the room, shifting his weight from foot to foot—something he always did whenever he had pent-up energy. Lei stood guard by the doors, scowling at Nick's anxious display.

"I put the book on the floor," Demos continued. "Landing can be tricky when the book is on a table or in a bookshelf."

"Thanks?" I wasn't sure how to answer him. I'd already landed through a bookcase. Twice. Since I'd made it home in one piece, there was no way I'd ever go through that possessed book again.

Lei crossed the room to Demos. "We should go already, before our trail is discovered."

Arik looked from Demos to Lei. "I must see our wards safely home. Incidentally, Gia and I jumped into the Vatican library by error."

Demos snickered. "Splendid. You'll get an infraction from the Wizard Council for that."

"You're one to judge," Lei said. "How many times have

you had to sit out a mission because of your bad marks?"

"Hey, at least I'm entertaining," Demos said. "No one wants to live up to your perfection, Miss *I-never-have-any-fun*."

"I know how to have fun," Lei muttered.

"We happened upon Antonio and his band," Arik interrupted. "They've also encountered hounds in the libraries. Be certain to inform Merl to increase security. Also, have him check the Monitors about the delayed response with the hound."

Nick's forehead puckered. "Who's Merl?"

"He's our haven's High Wizard." Arik undid the buckle of his belt and removed it from his waist, then wrapped it around the attached scabbard.

"That's an insane name for a wizard."

"His full name is Merlin," Lei said. "I should add he isn't the King Arthur one. His father thought it a riot to name his wizard son after a fictitious wizard. Merl hates when someone addresses him as Merlin."

"Yeah, Merl's father was a blast. Bless the old bloke," Demos said. "Merl is more serious than his father was."

Arik frowned at Demos. "It's time to leave."

"It was a pleasure meeting each of you." Lei bowed her head toward us. She spoke the key and jumped into the gateway book.

Arik took off his vest and tossed it to Demos. He extended his scabbard and blade. "Can you take care of these for me?"

Demos took them. "Certainly." He inclined his head to us while diving into the book.

"Let's be on our way, shall we?" Arik walked off toward the elevators.

"Oh, great," Nick whispered. "Here's where he kills us."

"You're such an epic moron. He could've killed us ages ago." Afton rushed after Arik.

"That's not nice, Afton," I said and gave Nick a sympathetic look. "You know how she is…"

"No joke. She's got bite." His gaze followed her. "I like her that way."

Nick and I stopped beside Afton and Arik to wait for the elevator. Arik gave me a sidelong look. "You handled yourself quite well back there, in the Vatican."

I smiled all the way to my toes at the compliment. "Thank you. I was a mess, though."

"Nah, you were a real peach." He smirked, a mischievous glint in his eyes.

My eyes widened. *How freaking embarrassing.* He did see my *peach*-colored panties. And they weren't sexy Afton-type panties; they bordered somewhere between little girl and granny glam. Ever so casually, I smoothed down my skirt, thankful it was in place.

The elevator dinged and the doors slid open. I avoided eye contact with Arik. This was going to be one long elevator ride.

"We have to get our things," Afton said as the doors closed.

"What time is it?" I asked.

Nick checked his cell phone's screen. "It's almost four."

"The front desk closes soon." I yanked the claim ticket out of my skirt pocket.

We retrieved our purses and umbrellas from the coat check and then stepped outside under leaden skies and drenching rain. I wrestled with my weather-beaten umbrella, rain pounding on my head until it opened, then I dashed down the steps after the others with the loose handle wiggling in my hand.

Traffic jerked and stopped on the street, horns blaring and brakes squealing. Arik's biker-knight apparel caused many questioning glances. The rain plastered his dark hair against his forehead and dripped a trail of water down the side of his strong jaw. His every move was easy and sure. I'd checked out hot guys before. Not one swaggered like Arik. I'd felt attraction before, too, but this was way different. Each time he looked at me, it was like a thousand wings took flight in my stomach.

"Do you want to get under?" I yelled over the downpour clapping against the fading petals of my rose-colored umbrella.

He flashed me his dimples. "No, thank you. The rain is refreshing."

Lightning shocked the dark clouds, making them look like purple smoke. Nick and Afton were several feet ahead of us, arguing about something. Nick's black umbrella bounced snappishly over their heads. I hurried to catch them.

"What's wrong with you two?" I flinched at a sudden smack of thunder.

"He's mad that I called him a moron," Afton said with irritation.

"I am not. I'm used to your crap."

"That's not nice," I said.

"I know," Nick agreed. "She has no filter."

"I do, too," Afton protested.

"Really?" I fumed. "I meant you both aren't being nice. And don't you think we have more to worry about than this?"

"You *do* have more to worry about," Arik said, catching up to us. "That hound in Paris was sent by a Writhe."

"You're insane," Nick said. "I feel like we're in some

weird video game."

"This isn't a game," Arik said. "I don't think you fully understand. Our Monitors detected your presence in the gateway and so did the Writhes. They'll kill you if they find you. I can't be certain if any other hunters sensed you. If they did, they'll track you. This very moment you're leaving a trail, and there's nothing I can do about it."

My voice quivered. "But we did that library hop thing, so they'll lose our scent. Right?"

"It won't erase it, just slow them down." Arik stopped and spun around, his eyes fixed down the street. "We have to get somewhere fast."

"Why?" I turned to see what had distracted him. "What's wrong—?"

A mountain with legs charged up the street. The man, bald and scarred, didn't have to dodge pedestrians, because they hurried out of his way. Terror shrieked through my body. *The bad people.* The thing I'd feared my whole life was barreling down on me.

"Who's that?" Nick asked.

"A hunter," Arik said.

"Hurry! The T is just around the corner!" Afton hustled up the street. Nick chased her, and Arik and I ran after them, flying around the corner into the Park Street station.

The creep was gaining on us. Arik grabbed a trash can and slammed it into the hunter. The man swayed on his feet, and Arik snatched my hand and pulled me down the steps, pushing between people along the way.

This isn't happening. This is not *happening.*

My foot slipped on the last step and I nose-dived. Ripped from Arik's grasp, I hit the floor. Screams pulled from my chest as I slid and crashed into a line of bicycles. A kickstand cut into my leg. The taste of salt and copper exploded on my tongue. I touched a crack in my lip, blood staining my fingertips.

Arik dropped to the floor beside me. Inside the train, Afton and Nick waved at us to hurry before the doors shut.

The hunter reached the platform. There wasn't an iris or a pupil in either of his white marble eyes. A scowl crossed his mangled face as he sniffed the air. He passed us and headed toward Afton and Nick.

"He smells them and not me," I whispered to Arik between breaths. "Why?" When I tried to move, the pain in my leg brought me back down to the floor.

"Stop moving," Arik hissed. "Your brand shields you. He can't sense you."

Just like a bloodhound latching onto a scent, the hunter hurdled over fallen people and bolted for the train. Afton yanked the opened umbrella from Nick's hand and threw it at the hunter's feet. He tripped over it and landed on all fours.

The doors slid shut. The hunter jumped to his feet and slammed his bulk against the train, and the car rocked on the tracks. The passengers inside screamed and moved to the other side of the car as the train sped off. People on the platform ran from the hunter, screaming and crying. The ones that weren't fast enough he punched or tossed out of the way.

The hunter sniffed the air again. His head shifted from side to side as he paced.

As he neared Arik and me by the bike pile, I struggled to get up again. I had to get away before he found me.

"I said don't move. Hunters are nearly blind, which heightens their other senses," Arik whispered in my ear, holding me tight against him, perfectly still. "It's a sort of sonar. They can only detect movements and scents."

I held my breath as the hunter passed. He growled and
bounded up the steps, knocking people down. He crashed
through the station doors. Glass clinked against the concrete
and shrieks came from the streets above.

Arik eased away, and I tugged my skirt down to cover
my thighs. The cut in my calf was deep and pulsing blood,
but I hardly noticed. All I could think about was the way
that beast had rammed the train. How could you stop
something like that?

Arik ripped a section from the hem of my skirt and used
it to bandage my leg, and I tried to keep my mind off the
pain by surveying the destruction the hunter left behind.
Several people lay around the platform, moaning and crying,
with bashed heads and broken limbs. The scene was horrific,
like one of those disaster movies in real life. What kind of
world had we stumbled on? And if there were more like
him…? What if he got hold of my friends? We couldn't hide
forever.

I grabbed Arik's arm. "You've got to help Afton and Nick."

"I won't leave you."

"He wasn't after me. He's after them." I opened my
messenger bag—twisted around my chest—and retrieved
my cell phone. "I'll text them to meet you." I slid my finger
across the screen to turn it on, racing my fingers over the lit-
up keys and typing out a quick text to Nick's phone. "Um…
not at the station. But where?" I paused. "Quincy Market.
It has tons of tourists." I finished the text and hit send. "It'll
take that hunter a while to sniff them out. Do you know
your way around Boston?"

"No."

I glanced around for something to scribble directions
on. A map stand lay on its side by the steps, the contents
littering the floor. "Grab a map."

Arik snatched one and brought it to me. I took a pen out of my bag, unfolded the paper, and flattened it on the floor. "We're here." I stabbed our location on the map with the pen. "Go down Washington and then jog over to Congress." I dragged the pen across the route. "They'll meet you in front of Faneuil Hall, right here."

He sat on his heels, his beautiful, dark eyes glossing. "You're hurt. I can't—"

Sirens sounded somewhere outside. "I'll be fine." I shoved the map at him.

"So brave," he murmured.

What a joke. I wasn't brave. But Afton and Nick needed his help more than I did. "Just go already."

Arik nodded and brushed my cheek with the back of his hand and my breath caught. As he scaled the stairs, tears gathered on my eyelashes. I blinked and the tears made their escape, running down my cheeks. Before he disappeared through the doors, he looked down at me with worried eyes.

Then he was gone.

CHAPTER FIVE

I adjusted on my bed, wanting desperately to scratch the cut in my leg. It'd been thirty-five hours and the stitches stung. Thirty-five hours without sleep. Thirty-five hours since my life had been normal, and all I'd had to worry about were fencing tryouts. Thirty-five hours, and now I was on the Mystik world's Most Wanted list. I was terrified and excited. Terrified a hunter would find Nick, Afton, or me. Excited to find out more about this other world. A world that seemed familiar to me.

Arik had gotten to Nick and Afton before the hunter could find them. He'd escorted them safely to their homes. Even though he said we were safe, saying some crazy stuff about erasing our trail, I still worried. He mentioned we had guardians watching us, but I never saw anyone who looked like they could be one. Nothing seemed certain, and I felt on unstable ground.

No matter how many times I told myself it wasn't real, the gash in my leg reminded me it was. We were so screwed, and there was no going back to not knowing the truth.

I wiped the tears away with the edge of my sheet and

then lifted my heavy eyelids, blinking at my Hello Kitty alarm clock. Kitty seemed as stunned about the time as I was. "Three," I moaned, rolling onto my back. Cleo, my calico cat, protested as she dodged my feet.

I scooted up against the headboard and grabbed the concoction Nana Kearns had made for me from the nightstand. I unscrewed the lid off the jar and inhaled. It smelled woodsy when I slathered it onto my leg. The ointment the doctor had prescribed didn't work as well as Nana's gunk. Relief was instant and the itch was gone.

The memory of the ball of light on Arik's palm while we were in the gateway came to me again. I kept replaying his actions in my mind with the hopes of discovering the secret to creating the light. I'd seen the same light in my hand before, when I was younger. It had freaked me out at first, but then I struggled to find it again.

I replaced the jar, held up my palm, and tried to remember what I'd done to make it appear. The first time was when I was four. Even though I was so young then, the memory was still vivid.

The globe had appeared out of nowhere. I'd been alone in my room, playing with a ball of light, when my mother came to tuck me into bed. She dropped her dishtowel, rushed over, and slapped the ball from my hand. Sparks flickered around me. She begged me to never do it again, warning me that if the bad people saw it, they'd hurt me.

The bad people scared me. I'd buried my face in my teddy and shuddered. She'd picked me up, sat on the bed, placing me on her lap, and chanted something.

"*I bind you to our secret.*" That was what she'd said. Oh hell, she'd spelled me. That's why I couldn't tell anyone about the magic.

I strangled my covers, trying to stop my hands from

shaking. Why had she hidden this from Pop? He could have helped me. Prepared me. By not telling him, she left me vulnerable.

An image of her kissing the top of my head and smoothing my hair away from my face came to me. I begged her to tell me the bedtime story. My favorite one.

Oh my God. The story. She had tried to prepare me.

She'd always started it the same way. I glanced at Cleo and muttered, "In a faraway land, a mighty knight…" Cleo yawned and began bathing herself. I was losing my audience.

"It was a girl knight, Cleo." Old dreams ran through my head. They were a little girl's dreams full of vivid colors and a magnificent castle. "She fought horrible creatures to protect humans…" I swallowed hard. *Protect humans.* Reality colliding with make-believe.

The story never changed. The young woman fled to protect her baby from an evil that could destroy the entire world. But because the baby was hidden, the world stayed safe. The memory warmed me, yet it ached at the same time. I longed for what could've been. A life with my mother in it.

Would she have told me, as I got older? I'd never know. She died shortly after that memory. There was a connection between her tales and what the Sentinels had said in Paris, though; I was sure of it. I just had to figure it out, starting with the ball of light.

I sighed and turned on the bedside lamp. Arik had spoken one word to create the light. The second time the light had appeared on my palm, I was ten and practicing my Italian, so it made sense the word was in Italian.

My eyes burned as I stared at the brightness coming from my lamp, just as I'd stared at Nana's lamp when I was ten. "Light. *Illuminare.*" I rattled off the words I had been practicing that day. "*Lampada. Lume. Luce—*"

The flesh on my palm warmed. Little flickers of light zapped across it and then disappeared just as quickly as they'd appeared. I bounced a little on my bed with excitement, and I tried again. "*Luce.*"

Nothing happened.

I tried several more times.

Still nothing.

Frustrated, I turned off the lamp and flung myself back against the pillows. The hot, humid night thickened the room, making my skin clammy. I kicked the covers off and rolled to my side.

Curling up under my covers, I was vaguely aware of every noise around me: the tick tock of my alarm, the rustle of leaves on the tree outside, the clanky sway of the fire escape. Through my slotted eyelids, the black pitch of Saturday night turned into the gray light of Sunday morning. A shadow moved across the grayness and I bolted up from my pillows.

A firm hand landed on my mouth, quieting my scream. "Hush," Arik said.

Relieved it was him and not some crazed killer, I exhaled. My breath punching through his fingers sounded like a deflating balloon. "Okay, you can let go now." The words came out muffled against his palm .

He removed his hand and plopped down beside me. I scooted up against the headboard, pulling down the hem of my black cami to cover my stomach. Surprised to see him in street clothes, I took a second glance at the jeans and black T-shirt hugging his body nicely.

"How's the leg?" He gave me a crooked smile, his gaze dropping to my chest.

"Did you just check out my boobs?" I whispered. *Please say yes.*

"No." He smirked. "Okay, yes. I am a guy."

That you are. I yanked the covers up to my chin and suppressed a smile.

Cleo hissed at Arik and dropped from the bed. "Way to serve and protect," I said with a laugh. "You could at least scratch his eyes out or something." She let out a protesting mew and hopped onto my desk chair, staring at Arik suspiciously.

His dimples deepened. "Cats have their own agendas, and they don't include their slaves."

"I'm not her…oh, never mind. What are you doing here, anyway? Pop will kill you if he catches you in my room. Wait. *How did you get in?*"

"I used the ladder."

"You mean the fire escape?"

"You say it's an escape. I think entry." The way he spoke with that accent and showed that dimply smile, sent goose bumps across my skin. "How are you faring?"

"How do you think I'm *faring*? I'm terrified. I can't sleep or eat."

"You were sleeping when I got here."

Was I? Maybe. Barely?

We sat there staring at each other, neither of us saying a word. I lowered my gaze; his eyes on me were so unnerving. I didn't do silence well, so I searched for something to say. Our meeting in the Athenæum came to me. He'd quoted my favorite book. "So you've read *The Secret Garden*?"

"Yes," he said. "Several times."

I glanced up. "Really?"

"You sound surprised." He rubbed the back of his neck.

"Because I am."

"What's your favorite part in the book?" he asked.

My favorite part? Were we really discussing a book? I'd

never had a conversation like this with a guy before. "Um, I'd have to say the one where Mary finds a hidden room in her uncle's house and meets Colin and finds out that he's her cousin. After that, she no longer feels alone. What's yours?"

"When she discovers the garden and it changes her."

"That's a good one." *Did he say that because I'm a girl who just found her secret garden? Will it change me?* "Most guys I know would never read it. Why do you like it?"

"Sentinels are sort of like Mary, aren't we?" His voice was quiet. "We're alone in the world, taken from our true parents. I like to think of the libraries as our secret garden. Our escape."

The emotions in his voice made my heart ache for him. I was lucky. I knew what it was like to have a real family. I had Pop and Nana, and the memory of my mom.

Not able to look him in the eyes, I decided we needed a less emotional subject. "So where are you from?"

"I was born in a small market town, Framlingham in Suffolk, England." Something like a bittersweet smile crossed his face as he mentioned the town. "I haven't any memories of the place. I was a baby when I was taken."

"You'll have to go and visit one day. I was born here. In Boston, I mean. Not like right here in my room. A hospital." My cheeks heated at how ridiculous that sounded.

He laughed.

Gah. Really, Gia? I glanced around my messy room to avoid his stare, wondering if he got into anything while I was sleeping.

From the corner of my eye, I spotted him shift to see where I was looking. Our eyes met again and the corners of his mouth lifted. "Don't worry. I only glanced at your journal on your desk."

I stifled a gasp. "You didn't."

He chuckled. "No. I wouldn't invade your privacy. Besides, it's too dark in here to read."

"Funny." I tossed my pillow at him. "So what are you doing here? You didn't come for small talk."

"I came to get you. Get dressed. Pack a change of clothes and anything else you may need." He skulked to the window, turned, and winked at me. "Meet me in the café down the street."

"Why?"

"I'll tell you in the café."

My hand flew to my chest. "Am I in danger? *Is Pop*?"

"Not if you do as I ask."

"Why doesn't that surprise me?" I said sourly.

He straddled the windowsill. "Just hurry."

"You know, that window was locked."

"Yes, it *was*." He grinned and ducked through the open window, barely making a sound as he went down the fire escape. Cleo darted after him.

A change of clothes? I flung the covers aside, stumbled out of bed, and rushed to the window to ask why I needed to pack an overnight bag, but Arik was already on the street below.

If I called out, Pop would hear. "Great," I seethed.

I packed a bag and tiptoed to the bathroom, listening to hear if my uninvited guest woke Pop. The apartment was still, so I took a quick shower, wrapped a towel around myself, and darted for my room.

"What's going on?" Pop asked as I was shutting the door. He held his favorite mug his aunt had sent him from Ireland with some saint on it. Fresh ground coffee beans scented the apartment and steam rose from the coffee, which told me he hadn't been up long, so he probably hadn't heard Arik in my room.

"Nothing," I answered through the crack. "I'm just late, as usual."

"Where are you heading off to this early in the morning?"

"I'm going to the library with Afton. We're finishing our summer essays." I hated lying to Pop after the whopper I'd told him about how my leg got hurt. I couldn't forget the worry in his eyes when he'd arrived at the hospital as the paramedics unloaded me from the ambulance. I never wanted to do that to him again.

I tightened my lips to stop my tic. Guilt sickened my stomach. Pop didn't deserve my dishonesty. It hadn't been easy raising a bratty me in those early years. I won the stepfather lottery when my mother married him. Some of my school friends' fathers weren't as concerned about their kids as Pop was about me. And I was a shit for lying to him.

"The library, again? Don't you think you should rest your leg?"

"It feels fine. I've been using Nana's ointment on it." I stuck my injured leg through the door.

Pop bent and examined it. He was a paramedic, so every time I got hurt it was a big deal. "Well, all right, it's healing nicely. Just don't overdo it." He scratched the back of his neck. "You spend a lot of time in libraries. Don't you ever get bored?"

"Most parents would be happy about that."

Pop just didn't get my love for libraries. I likened it to his passion for Fenway Park and the Boston Red Sox, which helped him to understand, a little, but he still had his doubts. Libraries weren't a necessity for him, because he only read sports magazines and the *Boston Globe*. I wondered if my draw to libraries had something to do with the magic hidden in them.

"Well," he said. "I'll make eggs."

"But we're stopping at the café first." At least that wasn't a lie.

He turned something over in his head. "Do you need money?"

"No. I still have some of my babysitting money."

"Well, be home by six for dinner, okay?"

"Sure." I shut the door.

I listened until he thumped away then I shimmied into my jeans. After layering a couple of tank tops on me, I wormed my feet into my black Converse, threw my wet hair into a ponytail, and did a quick check in the mirror. "Ugh, you're a mess." I gave my reflection the stink eye.

Cleo hopped up on the windowsill, startling me. "Crap! You scared me, squeaker." I rushed over, shut the window, and locked it. As I ran my fingers across her fur, she arched her back. "You have to stay inside, okay? If you're lucky, Pop will give you some of his eggs."

I slung my backpack over my shoulder and grabbed money from my dresser. The floorboards tried to rat me out as I sneaked into the bathroom and shoved my toothbrush, paste, and deodorant into the pack.

With my back to the wall, I scooted down the hall and hid my overstuffed backpack from Pop's view. "Later!" I lifted my umbrella from the stand by the door.

"Stay in a group," he said from his old worn-out recliner, the morning paper blocking his face.

I wanted to be nice, make up for my lies, but he'd get something was up. It sickened me to be so deceiving. Standing in the hall, I tried to think up the best Gia response for the situation.

"*Hello?* I'm not five," I finally said, and then shut the door before he could call me over for a lecture. I glanced back at the door, wanting to go back in and give him a hug. Instead, I zipped up my hoodie and struggled down the steps. The dissolvable stitches pulled angrily at my leg wound with each movement.

Rain drenched the street. I forced the umbrella open and hobbled down Baldwin Place.

The attack on the Park station platform was all over the news. They reported the man was high on drugs. The police were searching for him. But I knew they'd never find him, which made me uneasy to leave the apartment.

The thought of the hound we encountered in the Paris library and the bald freak in the subway haunted me. I'd been jumpy ever since. I swore there were unknown voyeurs hiding behind the darkened windows of the tall buildings crowding the narrow street, and I imagined some sort of evil looming within each hidden courtyard or flower-bedecked fire escape. Now that I could put a name to the horrors my mother hinted at when I was young, I was more anxious than ever.

I sprinted—the best I could with a gimpy leg—to the end of the road, fearful someone or some*thing* might jump at me from the shadows. I turned the corner and went straight into the café.

After closing my umbrella at the door, I searched for Arik. He was kicking back in a seat at a table in the middle of the café, and my heart squeezed at the sight of him. I moved toward him, but he shook his head and lifted a cell phone to his ear.

He pretended to talk into the phone as I approached. "Don't acknowledge me. Act as though we aren't acquaintances. Take one of the tables against the wall."

I brushed past him, slid into a chair at the nearest table, and kept my eyes on the window, acutely aware of Arik at the table diagonally to my left. My cell phone vibrated in my front pants pocket. I leaned back, tugged it out, and slid it open. "Hello?"

"It's Arik. Now listen carefully—"

"How did you get my number?"

"Nick gave it to me when I rang him earlier. He's on his way here. Act as if you were waiting for him, understand?"

"Yes," I said. "What's going on?"

"Do you see those two men across the street?"

People rushed by, peering into the windows as they passed. On the corner of Baldwin and Salem, two men—one stocky, the other lanky—crowded a street lamp.

"Who are they?"

"I'm not certain. I spotted them just now when I sat down. They're most likely tracking me."

I swallowed hard. "Why would they track you?"

"Probably because my recent jump history happens to match the human scent's path."

My stomach dropped. "Jeesh. It's been days already. Will our scent ever go away?"

"The scent is imprinted in the gateway. Hounds will eventually lose the body scent, but the Monitors will always have record of the jump. You needn't worry, you're shielded."

"We have to stop Nick from coming here. They'll smell him." I scanned the street, mentally willing him not to show up.

"I attempted to reach him, but there wasn't an answer." Arik paused. "But not to worry, I have taken measures to distract them from Nick's scent."

My hand tightened around my cell phone. "What does that mean? Is that supposed to make me feel better? And where were you the past few days? You said you'd come back. Remember?"

"It might be easier if you asked one question at a time."

Ugh. He was irritating me. "Okay, where were you?"

"I had to arrange some things. We've had guards keeping watch on you three." Arik fell silent when Erin, a girl from my math class and a server at the café, came up to my table.

"Hi, Gia, will it be the usual?" she asked.

I forced a smile. "Yes, please."

Erin, a red cloud of hair haloing her face, placed both palms on the table and leaned over. "Did you see the eye candy over there?" She nodded at Arik. "A total rebel type *and* a smoldering accent. I'd love to get to know him better." She winked and sauntered back to the counter.

Arik chuckled.

"Whatever," I muttered into the phone. "Can't we just explain to those men that it was an accident? We didn't mean to jump into that book."

"There's no reasoning with them. They've got Nick's and Afton's scent." Arik exhaled, sending a burst of static through the phone. "Because of the evils humans inflicted on Mystiks long ago—tortures and killings—many fear humans learning of our world. The treaty between the Wizard Council and the Mystik League only protects humans unaware of its existence."

Would that mean they'd be hunted forever? I choked out, "But...but would they really kill us? Just because we went through that damn book?"

"I'm afraid so," he said. "The havens were created as a safe place for the Mystiks and wizards to avoid persecution from humans. The last time a human traveled the gateways was close to a hundred years ago. After a wizard married a human, he brought her through a book to his haven . A group of Mystiks tracked her down and burned her at the stake, making the wizard watch her agonizing death. It's not a pretty story. It was a clear message to the Mystik world to prevent such tragedies in the future." He paused. "Those bleeders outside won't stop until the humans are dead. As I see it, we've two options…flee or fight."

"You want to fight *them*? You're crazy." The image of Lei's katana blazed in my mind. We could never battle Mystiks who had weapons and skills like that. And even if I figured out how to conjure that ball of light, what good would that do? Still, there was no way I'd live the rest of my life on the run.

Nick rushed in, dripping rain onto the floor. He spotted me and pushed past a group of kids leaving the café. He was dressed all in leather with biker boots, which suspiciously resembled what the Sentinels wore, and flung himself onto the chair directly across from me. "Hey," he said, panting.

I mouthed a *hello* to him.

"I'd rather fight," Arik said. "But since I must get you three to safety, we're fleeing." He paused. "We've discovered something about you, Gia. You're not fully human. You're a Sentinel. We're meeting someone who will explain everything to you."

Not fully human? A Sentinel?

"I'm not—" I stopped, remembering the men across the street. They were real. That hunter and hound in the library were, too. And there was something to Arik's claim. I rubbed the scar on my chest. My mother had started preparing me before she died. The stories. The Italian lessons. All to equip me for this day. I needed to find out the truth, and so I agreed to take another plunge into the rabbit hole. "Okay."

"Have coffee with Nick," he said. "Take your time. When you're finished, meet me at the Athenæum. I'm going to lead those men on a wild chase, and I'll meet you there as soon as I'm rid of them."

"What about Afton?" I asked.

"She's being retrieved and will be at the library." He rose and dropped a couple of dollars on the table.

I wanted to tell him not to go, not to leave me. That I was scared. But he had to, for Nick and Afton's sake. "Just be careful, okay?"

There was a long pause before he spoke. "Don't do anything rash. I wouldn't want you to lose that lovely head of yours."

Our cell phone connection ended.

Despite my worry, I smiled. *Did he just say I was lovely?*

He ambled out the door as if there weren't two scary men watching him. The men who came out of the shadows and followed him were definitely the type you'd cross the street to avoid. The lanky one zipped up his gray hoodie as he stepped off the curb. The stocky man, wearing a leather jacket, tossed a cigarette butt in the gutter and followed. Both had dark stringy hair and scruffy five o'clock shadows. They headed in the same direction as Arik. When they disappeared around a corner, I turned to Nick.

"Tell me everything… I mean *everything*. And why are you wearing those?"

"They're Arik's. We traded clothes to throw off my scent… to throw off any *thing* searching for me, so they'd follow him, not me."

"How's that supposed to work?"

"Apparently, his clothes will temporarily mask my smell. Confuse them. I don't know. It all went down so fast. He rushed out and told me to meet him here—"

Erin put down a paper coffee cup with my skinny caramel latte on the table. "Hi, Nick." Erin assessed him. "Wow, you're a biker wannabe now. Vitaminwater, right?" She walked off before Nick had a chance to reply.

"She hates me."

"What did you expect? You did break up with her after only one date."

"Funny. It was *three* dates. Hurry up and drink that." He stood. "I've got to get out of here."

"What about your Vitaminwater?"

"I didn't order it. She just assumed I wanted one." Nick stalked outside.

After placing six dollars on the table, I grabbed the coffee cup and the rest of my things and then shuffled around tables to the door.

Nick paced the sidewalk. "Can you be any slower?"

"I paid good money for this coffee. Besides, Arik said to wait before we left."

"I'm not hanging around for any of those...whatever they are to find me."

I swung my backpack onto my right shoulder and slipped my hand through the strap of my umbrella as I scanned the area. We skirted around other pedestrians, hurrying along at a sort of trot-walk pace toward the Haymarket station, hoping something didn't jump out from the shadows between the buildings. "Where's your bag?"

"What?"

"Arik had me bring a change of clothes. Didn't he ask you to pack one, too?"

"No."

I pulled on the shoulder strap of my pack, hoisting it farther up my back.

"I wonder why he told me to and not you?"

"They know everything about us. He must know your pop works graveyard tonight. Maybe that's why he called Afton. He probably wants you to stay with her so you won't be alone."

"Oh. Right. That makes sense." I remembered Pop's request that I be home to have dinner with him before he went to work, and I felt bad about ditching him. Because of his work schedule and my activities, dinners and Sunday night TV were our only alone time.

We shot down the steps to the subway platform and spotted Arik attempting to blend in at the edge of a group of kids. His eyes widened when he spotted us. He quickly turned his head to watch for the train.

I grabbed Nick's elbow. "Crap. *Nick.* I knew we should've waited."

"Shit. Just act normal."

The two thugs were on the ledge waiting for the train. The taller one caught me watching them, and a sinister grin twitched his lips.

We were so screwed.

CHAPTER SIX

I glanced up the tracks for any sign of the train. The tunnel was dark. The taller man watched me so intently I was sure he had caught me looking at Arik. Sweat trickled down my back, behind the pack, even though the platform was chilly.

I turned and started jabbering nonsense to Nick.

"What's wrong with you?" he snapped. "Are you on a caffeine high or what?"

"One of those creepy men caught me staring at Arik," I said through clenched teeth. "I was pretending to talk to you to throw him off."

"Man," he whispered. "Ever since Freaky Friday, it just keeps getting weirder, doesn't it?"

"Seriously, tell me about it. Arik keeps implying I'm not human."

"You're human, Gia. Haven't you been to doctors? If you weren't, you'd be cut open in some lab on a gurney, with men in white jackets examining your insides."

"Not funny. I'm scared." Not just because of the men watching Arik, but also from having no idea what I was or how my life might change. Would they expect me to become like them? Maybe I spoke some Italian and jumped us through some gateway, and a few times I conjured that ball of light, but I had none of the abilities of the teens fighting that *hound* in Paris.

The train squealed to a gradual stop beside the platform, and the doors swished open. Everyone crowded together, squeezing through the compartment doors and into the belly of the car. Arik went to one side, Nick and I shuffled to the other, and the two men stayed in the middle.

"Just stay calm," Nick said.

For the next fifteen minutes, we swayed back and forth until the train slowed into the Park Street station. Outside the window, people rushed along the platform. The crowd squeezed toward the doors, waiting for them to open.

A self-assured girl with long black hair darted along the platform. *Lei?* And behind her came Demos and the other two Sentinels, dressed in regular street clothes.

"Come on." Nick clutched my arm, and I let him lead me off the train. We moved up the steps with the crowd, and the moment we came out the doors, I pulled back on Nick's lead. "What are we doing? We have to help them."

"No. Arik said not to stop…to keep going until we reach the library."

"But—"

I turned toward the station's doors, and Nick yanked me back. "But nothing, Gia, you have to listen to me. They're tracking me, and I doubt your kickboxing skills are a match for them."

"They can't sense you with Arik's clothes on."

"You always half listen. Arik said if I wore his clothes, it would confuse them. It won't eliminate my scent."

I glanced at the doors and then back at Nick and sighed.

He was right. There wasn't much I could do to aid them, and I might be more hindrance than help. "Yeah, okay. Let's go."

Afton stood outside the doors of the Athenæum, nibbling at her cuticle. Her wrinkled pink dress shirt and loose black pants looked as if she'd slept in them, and she wore ballet flats instead of high heels. The outfit was completely unlike her.

"She's a mess," I whispered to Nick.

"Yeah… She looks terrified."

When Nick reached her, Afton flung her arms around his neck. "I was so worried," she said into his shoulder.

Nick patted her back. "You don't have to worry. We're okay."

She pulled away from him. "If anything happened to you guys… What are you wearing?"

"I was going to ask you the same thing," Nick said. "I'm wearing Arik's clothes. It's to cover up my smell."

"I'm wearing my mom's dirty clothes for the same reason."

"Why were you worried about us?" I asked. "You're the one who's alone."

"I'm not alone." She inclined her head in the direction of the library. "I have my own personal warrior for protection."

A man somewhere near forty stood up from his seat on the steps. His eyes struck me first, soft green and soulful. Waves of tea-colored hair brushed his forehead. For his age, he was extremely fit and muscular. He wore a black leather trench coat, and when he bolted down the steps, it flapped open, exposing the ornate handle of a sword strapped to his waist.

The man stopped in front of us. "Blimey, you resemble your ma," he said in a thick Irish accent.

"What?" My voice cracked. "Who are you?"

"I'm your da."

I barely remembered how I got to the café or when I sat down and ordered the generous breakfast the waiter placed in front of me. My head swam. It reminded me of the time Nick took us to Jessie's party, and I'd guzzled too much spiked punch (no matter what Nick said, I didn't know it was spiked at the time).

I lifted the glass of orange juice in front of me and took a long sip. Ever since Friday, I'd felt like I was falling. Like the ground was no longer beneath my feet. Who was I? Or rather, *what* was I? And who was this man sitting across from me? Was he really my father?

I clunked the glass down. "So what's your name?"

"Carrig. Carrig McCabe."

"How do you know I'm your daughter?"

"Your mother was Marietta, well, Marty, right? She be pregnant with you when she left."

I stared at the eggs on my plate, processing his words. "Yeah. She was my mother. Why did she leave?" My gaze went to him. His brows were scrunched, a worried expression on his face.

"I loved her with all me heart. She left to protect you."

"I don't know anything about my birth father. For all I know, you could be a phony."

"As certain as the nose on me face, I be your father."

"Then why didn't you come for me before this?"

"I've searched far and wide for Marietta and me baby," he said. "Her trail led to New York and then we lost her scent. There weren't any signs of her after that, and I relinquished all hope of ever finding her."

The walls felt like they were closing in on me. My stomach twisted, and I shot to my feet. "Excuse me, I need the restroom." Afton made to follow me, scooting her chair back. I shook my head, stopping her, and hurried to the bathroom with my heart pounding in my ears.

My legs were numb and my weight unsteady on them. I leaned against the door, trying to calm my rushing breaths. Panic was a crazy thing. It hit without warning. I'd had several attacks after losing my mother but hadn't had any since I started playing sports. It taught me how to silence my head, to ease my breaths and control the beast.

Tacky pictures of flowers hung on the wall in the small bathroom. Only one stall, a sink, and a big rubber plant made up the room. I locked the door and hunched over the sink.

I wanted Pop.

Tears burned my lids. I caught them with my fingertips before they fell and then studied my reflection in the mirror. My green eyes had red streaks and my face was paler than normal. My head throbbed, and I loosened my tight ponytail. I gave my image a sharp glance. *Get your head in the game, Gia.*

I was losing control.

"Why didn't anyone tell me about him?" I said, as if my reflection could hear me. I shook my head and reached for the faucet.

I did tell you, baby. I flinched at my mom's voice. It sounded so real. Alive. I glanced around the empty bathroom. My mother was haunting my head. I was definitely on the crazy train now.

Once during story time, I had asked my mother what my

father looked like. She'd tapped my nose and said he had soft green eyes, just like mine. I examined my face in the mirror. The color of my irises, my nose with a slight upturn at the end, and my full lips—all matched his.

Okay, so he could be my father. Now what? I had to find out all I could about Carrig and his world. I had to know the truth.

When I returned to my seat, Nick, Afton, and Carrig stared at me as if I was a mental patient just let out of the psych ward.

"What? I'm fine," I said.

"I have something to show you," Carrig said. He retrieved his wallet from the inside pocket of his trench coat, pulled out a worn photograph, and slid it across the table to me. The edges were tattered and the colors faded. A younger Carrig beamed in the snapshot, his arm wrapped around my mother's shoulders. Her belly was huge and round, her smile wide and bright.

I had never seen my mom this happy in a photograph before. We didn't have many photographs of her back home. There were tons of me with Pop. All taken by my mom. She avoided cameras, and now I knew the reason for it…to stay hidden. But why?

All these years I had based my mom's contentment on the one video we had of her. It was my fourth Halloween, and we were dressed like angels, dancing and giggling around the kitchen. The picture was jerky because Pop was laughing along with us while he was recording. I had always believed Mom was happily in love with my stepfather, but now I wasn't so sure.

The next item Carrig slid over shocked me. I caught my breath as I scanned the letter written in my mother's curly script. My head fogged, the edges of my perceived reality of my parents' happy marriage vaporizing with each word I read.

My dearest Carrig,

I will never love another as I love you. I must flee to protect our little one. I fear we are the prophecy. I know of a Pure Witch who will place a protection on the baby and me. Please don't follow us. It will mean death for all three of us. I pray that one day our family can be together. If this ends badly, know you have made me happier than anything else in my life. I risk all for our love, and I will die protecting our baby.

Always yours, M ☆

I dropped the letter on the table. *It isn't real. It's a fake.* She loved Pop. She married him.

But there was no mistaking my mother's characteristic curly M with a star at the end of the line for flair. Every birthday, Christmas, and Easter card to Pop from her—stacked in our memory box back home—had the same exact signature.

Nick and Afton watched me with those concerned gazes again, so I stared out the window, trying to regain my composure. People rushed by on the sidewalk, and vehicles braked, jolted forward, and sped off on the boulevard. A black cat slinked across the street, reminding me of Nana's cat, Baron.

"I'm not expecting you to believe me right off," Carrig

said, bringing my attention back to the table. "But think of the events of the last few days, and ask yourself if it might be true."

"Why didn't someone tell me?" I rubbed my eyes with the heels of my palms. "I'm sorry. This is a lot to take in." I took the paper napkin off my lap and wiped my nose with it. "My mother's letter mentioned a witch?"

"I'm not too sure I should be telling you this part," Carrig said. "You haven't taken the rest so well, yeah?"

"I'm fine. What could be worse than all the other stuff that's happened? At least you're not a deadbeat dad, like I'd thought. My. Entire. Life." I lifted my glass and took a swig of juice, trying to seem unaffected, even though I wasn't. What I really wanted to do was go work out, kick some bags, and gather my thoughts.

"All right, then." He took another sip of his coffee and cleared his throat. "There be only one Pure Witch in these parts skilled enough to master a shielding charm. Her name be Katy Kearns."

Juice spurted from my mouth, spraying Nick and the table.

Nick flinched. "*Gross*, Gia!"

I set the glass back on the table. "You said *Katy* Kearns?"

"Yes."

"*Nana?*"

The bell on the door jingled. I'd stopped checking to see who came into the café, but Nick's shocked expression caused me to turn. "Nana?" I croaked out.

Nana regarded Carrig. "You might have told me where to meet. If it weren't for Baron, I wouldn't have found you."

"Me apologies," Carrig said. "The area be unfamiliar to me, so I was not entirely certain where we'd end up."

Nana dropped her designer tote bag on the floor by

the table and smoothed a stray strand of hair back toward her chignon. Pop and Nana had the same striking red hair, but hers was streaked with gray. Nana was short and petite, while Pop was big and tall. He took after his dad instead of Nana. Wearing white slacks, a navy blue blouse, and a printed scarf tied elegantly around her neck, she was dressed as if she just stepped off the cover of an over-fifty magazine. At sixty-three, Nana looked younger and was in great shape for her age.

"Nick, be a good boy and get me a chair," Nana instructed. She waved her hand in the air as if she was shooing an insect, but I didn't see anything.

Nick raised a brow, giving her a curious look, then stood and offered his seat.

"Thank you. Now that's a good boy." Nana patted Nick's arm. "Would you mind getting me a cup of hot tea? Earl Grey, if they have it, dear." She scooted the chair closer to me, eased gracefully onto the seat, and cupped my chin with her hand. "I never wanted to hurt you." Her soft gray-blue eyes stilled me. The same tender eyes that had eased my fears a bazillion times before. "What I'm about to say may sting, but you're to remember it was done out of love."

I sniffed and nodded.

"Good." Nana released my chin and gave me a reassuring smile. "There are two kinds of witches in the world. Bane Witches, who wield poisonous hexes, and Pure Witches, who invoke spells and charms for good causes. I am the latter."

Afton dropped her fork on the table. "You *are* a witch?"

"Is *Pop* one?"

"No," Nana said. "His father was human. He didn't get any of my magic."

Memories of my visits to Nana's quaint duplex in Mission Hill came rushing in—her black cat that watched me with dissecting eyes, her collection of leather-bound books written in Latin with sketches of plants and animal parts in them, and the eccentric older women who made up her literary tea group. Even the concoction that healed my wound better than the doctor's ointment. All strange in their own right, but put together, they told a different story. Nana wasn't just odd— she was a witch. An honest-to-goodness witch. Who'd kept the truth from me, kept me hidden from my father.

My whole life had been a collection of half-truths and lies. Maybe to protect me, but it was hard to accept. I wasn't sure whether to be angry or scared. What people could be so horrible that Mom had given up someone she'd supposedly loved to hide me? Wizards… Mystiks… Hunters… who knew what else. My mind swam. What did they think I could do? I had so many questions I didn't know what to ask first.

Nick returned, balancing a small steaming teapot in one hand and a cup and saucer in the other. He placed them both in front of Nana.

"That was fast," Afton said.

"It's just hot water and tea bags." Nick pulled over another chair and leaned back in it, balancing on two legs. "What'd I miss?"

"Nana's a witch," Afton whispered.

"So nothing new, then," he said, slamming the chair back on all fours.

Nana cleared her throat, giving Nick a stern look. "May I continue?"

"Um, sure, have at it." Nick picked up his fork and drummed it on the table. When Nick was nervous, he tended to get fidgety. During tests at school, the teachers were always on him to settle down.

"Without distraction."

Nick paused mid-tap. "Oh, sorry."

"Thank you," Nana said. "Sentinels are born with a certain gene that enables them to create light and weapon globes for battles. The Monitors can detect the gene, which allows them to track a Sentinel while jumping through the gateways. After your mother fled the havens, Gia, she sought my help. She told me people with ill intentions were searching for her and her baby. I used a branding charm to shield the two of you from discovery. It's how you got the scar."

My hand flew to my chest. "You *branded* a baby?"

"I'd never harm a child. I applied a numbing potion to the area beforehand." She dabbed the corner of her mouth with her napkin, avoiding eye contact with me, then cleared her throat again. "As I was saying, your mother and father were both Sentinels. The wizard laws forbid Sentinels from having children together because a seer prophesied that a child from such a union would herald the coming end for both the human and Mystik worlds. Marty fled to keep you safe."

Nana removed the top of the teapot, grabbed the tags tethered to the two bags inside, and dunked them up and down. Her lips pressed into a tight line. She did that whenever she couldn't get up the nerve to deliver bad news.

"Just say it, Nana," I urged.

"It is believed that you are that child."

CHAPTER SEVEN

"I'm...*what*?" I knocked my glass over.

Nick watched the river of juice course across the table. "I think she said you're the Doomsday Child."

Nana and Afton grabbed napkins from the silver dispenser on the table and caught the flow before the orange stream cascaded over the table's edge.

"*Nick*." Afton shook her head and dabbed at the table. "Can you be any more insensitive?"

He scowled. "What the hell? She's not the only one dealing with all the shit going down, lately."

"Watch your language, young man," Nana warned.

"I'm sorry," I said, still stunned. "I've made a mess."

"Nonsense, it was an accident, is all." Nana added her napkins to Afton's pile.

I rubbed my temples to soothe a blossoming headache. "Let's say I believe you. Why didn't Arik and the others know about me? And now that they know, aren't I in more danger from them than anyone else? And...and...if you were hiding me, how did Carrig find you?"

"So many questions." Nana pursed her lips. "Firstly,

only Arik and Asile's high wizard, Merl, know the truth, and they will protect you. Your birth may have put the end in motion, but they believe you're the key to stopping it, as well. The others are unaware of your parentage. You must never tell anyone who your birth father is. The wizards and the Mystiks believe the presage hasn't been born yet, and we shall keep it that way for as long as possible. To answer your other question, Cleo is my spy, you might say. She informed me about your phone conversations with Nick and Afton—the ones where you rehashed the accidental jump to Paris and the narrow escape with a hunter on the subway. I figured you were in danger and your best protection was Carrig. I contacted him through an address your mother once gave me for emergencies. Thankfully, he received my note."

"Cleo?" I said. "My cat?" My head started to pound. More lies. Branding spells. And furry spies. Can I trust anyone?

"I can talk to animals, especially cats. Most witches can. You've heard of familiars, right? Baron is mine. Cleo belongs to your aunt. We sent her to watch over you"—she rolled a teaspoon handle between her fingers—"to be my eyes, so to speak."

"Gia, it's a great honor to be a Sentinel," Carrig said and puffed out his chest.

"I know something of Sentinels from video games," Nick said. "They're badass guards that protect things."

"'Tis sort of the idea—" Carrig seemed irritated by Nick's interruption. "They were created from knights, and have very little magic compared to wizards but are great fighters."

"Wicked," Nick muttered. "So it's an actual word?"

"*Duh*, it's in the dictionary." Afton rolled her eyes. "It actually means guard. I mean, seriously, how *do* you get good grades?"

"For Jaysus sakes," Carrig growled. "Will you stop your blathering and let a man think?"

We all nodded.

Nana took my hands. "Are you doing okay, dear?"

"How can I be fine? My whole world just... I don't know." I lowered my head, trying to garner the strength to be brave. "Can you tell me something? Did my mother ever love Pop?"

She squeezed my shaking hands. "Of course she did, sweetie. Your pop fell in love with her the moment I introduced them, and shortly after, he asked her to marry him. He was so delighted to be a father to her newborn daughter. You're his entire world, Gia."

"You said *he* loved her, but did *she* love him?"

Nana released my hands, lifted her cup to her lips, and put it down without taking a sip. "I believe she cared deeply for him, but it couldn't replace the love she had for Carrig. It was that love that caused her death."

Carrig choked on a mouthful of toast. "What?"

"We were out shopping, Marty, Gia, and I," Nana said. "Little Gia had darted into the busy street. Marty caught her and handed her to me. Before Marty stepped up onto the curb, something across the street distracted her. Her face brightened, and she tried to cross traffic." Her voice cracked. "That's when a van struck her. The last thing she spoke was your name, Carrig. I believe she saw you."

"It wasn't me. I've never been here before today." Tears tumbled from Carrig's eyes. He lowered his head and wiped them away with his fists.

Not one of us moved or said a word. When it seemed he wouldn't recover from the news, I placed my hand over his balled fist, and he looked at me with surprise. I knew how he felt.

I removed my hand and turned my attention to Nana. "I guess Pop doesn't know about any of this, huh?"

"Marty never told him, figuring the fewer people who

knew your true identity, the less likely you'd be found." Nana lifted the teacup again, and again she placed it down without taking a sip. "She feared if the havens found you, they would train you to be the force the seer foretold."

"'Tis not clear what be your abilities," Carrig interrupted, fully recovered except for the red rimming his eyes. "No one has had two Sentinel parents before."

"So I'm a freak, right?"

"Now then, don't be flattering yourself. You're merely special, is all." A hint of a smile crept over Carrig's lips. "Our professor of wizardry will determine just how special that be when he meets you."

Nana removed a black travel case from her tote and then retrieved some sort of hand-held tool from it.

A shocked expression crossed Afton's face. "Is that a tattoo gun?" She'd know the tools. The year before, she had been obsessed about getting a butterfly on her foot, but her parents wouldn't let her.

"It is." Nana pulled out a power cord and handed it to Nick. "Will you plug this into the wall, dear?"

"Nana, people are watching." I imagined someone using a cell phone to record her and post it on YouTube.

"Don't worry. I've placed an illusion spell around our table. People only see us eating breakfast and talking."

Nick gave the plug a curious eye, shrugged, and stretched it across to the wall.

"What are you doing?" I asked Nana.

"I'm setting up." She reached into her tote and retrieved a set of rubber gloves, a handful of wrapped needles, and several bottles with colored ink. Next, she pulled out a jar with a small amount of clear liquid inside, a spray bottle, and various other items I'd never seen before.

"Wow, Nana Kearns is a tattoo artist," Nick joked.

"Well, I find branding people archaic," Nana said, as she worked at putting her tools together. "Plus, with the activists in the Mystik world preaching to witches to stop cruelty to humans, I switched to tattooing charms into the skin instead of branding them."

I glanced at the other tables. No one paid attention to Nana and her makeshift tattoo parlor. A girl coming from the bathroom walked by and stumbled over the cord stretched across the floor. She looked back, shrugged, and continued to her table.

"Who are you inking a charm on?" I asked.

Nana held up the bottle containing the clear liquid. "There's barely enough potion left for two. I got the shielding spell from an ancient spell book I found in Romania. Ruth Ann from my tea club borrowed it, thinking it was a simple spell book. Your aunt Eileen got it back for me. When she returned with the book, someone had torn out the page with the recipe and Ruth Ann had vanished. There are some dangerous spells in that book. To be safe, I placed a charm on it. It won't leave the house again, you can be certain of that."

"Two tattoos will be enough," Carrig said, stopping Nana's rambling.

"*Naaana.* Who are you putting tattoos on?"

"Afton and Nick, of course."

"Oh, no you're not," Nick said.

Afton's eyes fixed on the needle Nana was attaching to the gun. "My dad will bust my butt if I get one!"

"Nonsense. You have no choice if you want to live," Nana said, as if Afton had just refused sugar for her tea.

Carrig turned in his chair to face Afton and Nick. "You wouldn't want any beasts like the one you encountered in Paris finding you, wouldja?"

"It only stings a bit," Nana added. "That's what the girl said, anyway. I normally do evil-eye protections, luck charms, and things of that matter." Nana twisted the black ink bottle into the gun. "I'm getting good at tats."

Needles freaked me out, and this one looked extra sharp. "Uh–um– What girl?"

"I'll tell her as you get about working on Nick," Carrig said. "It's nearing twelve, and Afton's da will be here shortly. And Nick should go with her."

"I can't go home," Nick said. "Those guys know where I live."

"They only know the neighborhood you live in. Hunters be like puppets with no brains. If they can't sense you anymore, they can't find you."

Nick looked doubtfully at Carrig. "I hope you're right."

"I am," Carrig said. I believed the conviction in his voice.

"Okay." Nick swallowed hard as he unbuttoned his shirt. "Stick it to me." He puffed his chest out.

Nana flipped the switch on the tattoo gun and it buzzed angrily to life. She started inking a black line into Nick's skin. Again, I looked around, but no one seemed aware of the crude tattoo parlor in the middle of the café.

"Right, then, where shall I begin," said Carrig, rubbing the stubble on his chin. "Every eight years a new generation of Sentinels be born to certain humans with mixed blood who be unaware of their Sentinel ancestry. On the rare occasion, one comes from a wizard with less magic in their bloodline. When a Sentinel is conceived, their changelings begin to grow in the Garden of Life within the fey nation. The changeling be an exact twin of the Sentinel. All Sentinels be having one."

"Fey nation?" The confusion on Afton's face mirrored how I felt. "Where is that?"

"It's in the Twilight realm. A place just beyond this world."

I gave him a confused look. Or maybe it was disbelief. Because this stuff was crazy. It couldn't be real. I was about to say just that when he put his hand up to stop me.

"Don't be saying a word," he said. "Just listen. About ten days after a Sentinel's birth, the appointed parent faery switches the baby with his or her changeling. The changeling lives the life of the Sentinel, and the parent faery raises the Sentinel until he or she be old enough to attend one of the academies for training. A human's changeling never knows what he or she truly be—they simply live the Sentinel's intended life as their own."

"That's cruel," I said, unable to stay quiet any longer. "How can you take babies away from their mothers?"

"It may seem cold-hearted," Carrig said, "but the Sentinels protect the libraries and keep both worlds safe. The fey created them long ago by crossing the blood of wizards with knights to protect the human world from the Mystiks. It be a small sacrifice, so it is. Most of the families be unaware of the exchange, anyhow."

"I bet their mothers know," I said.

"Truthfully, they don't. Every hair, freckle, and birthmark be the same on the babies."

"Okay, then what?" I said. "You know, what happens when a Sentinel finishes her education?"

"When they turn sixteen, they become guards of the libraries, maintaining the safety for all who enter them. They keep the entries into the wizard and Mytik havens secret from the human realm. After eight years of service, they retire, marry their assigned betrothed, and have children."

"Assigned betrothed?" I repeated.

"To prevent the prophecy, the Wizard Council makes marriage matches for the Sentinels."

Afton snorted. "That's pretty archaic, isn't it?"

"That it be," he agreed.

Nick wrinkled his nose. "It would suck if you had to marry a dog."

"Or a dumbass," Afton added, looking directly at Nick.

Nick was about to fire off some stupid remark, but I interrupted him. "Sixteen is kind of young to risk your life, isn't it?"

"It's an ancient system," Carrig said. "Back then, sixteen was considered adulthood."

"Then you're kind of old to be one," I said.

"I'm a Master Sentinel," he said. "I remain in service to educate and lead the many groups in my district."

My mind went back to the changelings. If I was a Sentinel, then I had one. There can't be someone exactly like me in the world. I'd know it. Feel it. *Wouldn't I?*

I swallowed hard and asked the question I wasn't sure I wanted the answer to. "Do you mean there's another me walking around somewhere?" It seemed like his response would never come. When he finally nodded, I blinked in disbelief. "So where's my changeling now?"

Carrig had a way with dramatics. He had me at the edge of my seat waiting for his answer again. "Your changeling was brought to your home this morning," he said. "To live your life, while you be trained as a Sentinel. Katy has already tattooed her."

I bolted out of my seat, the chair falling back and hitting the floor with a clang. "What the *hell* are you talking about? No one's taking over *my* life."

•••

Nana had barely finished inking the black crescent moon charms on Afton's and Nick's chests when Mr. Wilson pulled up in front of the café to pick up Afton. Nick hitched a ride home with her, and I was depressed to see them leave. I wasn't sure when I'd ever see my two best friends again.

I kept playing what Nana told me in my head. That this changeling was only borrowing my life. It was mine, and I would be able to have it back. But could she really be like me? And all she had to do was touch my things to get my memories? To know what I know? My secrets. I felt horribly violated.

My life had been stolen from me in the blink of an eye, and Nana had allowed it to happen. It was as if a dark cloud rolled over my head, suffocating me. I gasped for air. Each breath felt heavy in my lungs. And Pop wouldn't know a stranger had moved into our home. He'd have Sunday dinners with someone who didn't know him. Didn't love him. How cruel was that? I couldn't let that happen.

Nana's hand covered mine. "Calm breaths. I'm right here with you."

I nodded and wiped away a few tears that had slipped from my eyes. Though he was across from me, Carrig's words sounded far away as he told Nana the plan.

We were to jump from the Athenæum to England. One problem: we needed a membership card to get into the library. Nana went to get one, leaving me alone with this stranger against my wishes. I begged. I even used my best tactics to change her mind—sad eyes, a little whine in the voice, and persistence. She didn't cave.

I stared across the table at Carrig.

He stared back.

So awkward. Why didn't Nana tell me about all this? How could she let them take me away? I trusted her. *How*

could she lie to me? Why? I always knew I was different.
Not many guys could beat me in fencing and kickboxing
matches. There was an energy inside me, burning just under
the surface of my skin. I was just like the man sitting across
from me; I was a Sentinel.

"When did my changeling go to my house?" I said, breaking the silence.

"Early this morning. I first brought her to your
grandmother to shield her, and then she went."

"Where has she been all this time?"

"There be nowhere for your changeling to go when
you went missing." He leaned back against the chair. "Merl
brought her to me. I took her in and raised her as me own.
She's a good girl, and she doesn't want to be in your life any
more than you want her in it."

"I hadn't thought of that. She must be scared, too."

He tugged a hanky from a pocket in his trench then
wiped the sweat from his brow. Wearing a trench coat
in August was epically ridiculous, even if you needed to
hide a weapon. No wonder he was sweating. He should've
just concealed a knife in his boot or something more
inconspicuous. "She knows the risks. That you must fulfill
what you be born to do. Protect the libraries." He leaned
over the table and patted my hand. "The only t'ing I care
about be the safety of me two girls."

I barely felt his touch. My entire body was numb. Like
my mind went off and left it behind or something.

I cleared my throat. "Well, apparently she'll be safe with
Pop, and I'll be in mortal danger."

He studied my face with sad eyes. "Gia, you are me flesh
and blood. I never wanted me child to face the dangers I
had to. Your mother never wanted that, either. That be why
she ran. She was a brave woman to run. I love her more for

it, though it broke me heart."

I couldn't count how many times I imagined my birth father—who, by the way, never looked like Carrig—telling me things like this.

He continued. "When Merl handed me the changeling and bid me to raise her, I could not refuse. He knew you were me child and the dangers of anyone discovering you be the presage. So I transferred to Tearmann and hid your changeling in a cottage outside a remote village in Ireland. Each moment, each hour, and each day I thought about you while I watched the changeling grow." Sadness hinted in his eyes. "I should be calling her by her name—Deidre."

"You raised her alone?" I asked.

"At first. I wanted to join you and Marietta with Deidre and me. To be a real family. I searched many years for you both. Every lead was futile." He turned to see the clock on the wall behind the counter. "'Tis getting late."

"No one asked me if I wanted to go to…whatever that place is called. You can't make me." The café suddenly felt hot. I tugged at my collar. *This insanity has to end. It just has to.*

"It's Asile," Carrig said. "And you don't have a choice in the matter."

That's what you think, I wanted to say, but the scowl on his face made me think better of it. Instead, I said, "You mentioned an arrangement you made with Merl earlier, what is it?"

"I almost forgot…" Carrig's face went vacant, as if someone had unplugged him. I watched him carefully, scrutinizing every tic and twitch. He looked pretty scary with those large shoulders, strong hands, and intense eyes. Then, like a rebooted computer, his eyes focused on me. "Jaysus, I'm knackered. What was I saying?"

What just happened? Whatever it was, it sort of freaked me out. I glanced around the café and was relieved to find it was still crowded.

"Right, that be it," he said.

I blinked with surprise.

He wiped his brow again. "We're not heartless, you know. We won't take your family and friends away from you entirely. You'll be training with me for the remainder of the summer while Deidre stays at your home posing as you. During the school year, you'll attend our academy. You may return home on weekends and holidays."

"Great." My shoulders sank. "Only weekends and holidays, huh?"

"Sorry. It's me best offer."

The stern look on his face told me he meant it.

"I can live with that," I lied. Besides, I probably didn't have much of a choice. "At least I can still see Pop and my friends, I guess."

He grinned. "Good. Now then, do you have any questions?"

"If my brain wasn't in overdrive, I'm sure I'd have plenty," I said. "The only one I can think of is…well…What if I suck?"

"Do you mean at fighting or magic?"

"Did you say magic? I can't do *magic*." I fisted my hands, my nails digging into my palms. I debated whether I should mention the magical episodes—or rather, disasters—I'd caused before.

Carrig looked amused. "Of course you can. You're a Sentinel. Your magic just needs summoning, is all.

"Okay. No pressure, right? It's not like I'm *the one* and the fate of the universe rests in the palms of my hands or something lame like that."

No pressure? Seriously. Pull it together, Gia. Breathe. Breathe.

"Well, 'tis sort of like that, you know. You might be *the one*," he said all serious.

My stomach flipped as I studied his face. "Are you messing with me?"

A smile reached his eyes. "Indeed, I'm messing with you. I believe we will be needing many to face what be before us, not just one. The coming be more terrifying than any nightmare you've ever imagined. And it won't stop with the Mystik realm. It will destroy the human one, as well. Everyone you love will be in danger."

So I had no choice. "One more thing. Brian Kearns is my father, so I'd prefer you treat me like a student and not a daughter." I could've sworn hurt flashed in his eyes, but the smile stayed on his face.

"Deal. However, you might regret those boundaries. I'm a harsher teacher than I am a father."

The bell jingled and Nana rushed to the table. "Got them."

Carrig stood. "Shall we be on our way, then?"

I faced Nana. "You're going, too?"

"I would never let you go alone, dear." Her eyes did that warming thing when she smiled. "I'm sorry, Gia, I hated lying to you. I believed I was protecting you."

I swallowed back the emotions clogging my throat. She had always been there for me. Always there to give me a hug when needed. Always at every match. Always.

I wasn't sure I was ready yet to forgive her, but I understood what she'd done.

"I know you were," I said, my voice quivery. "I love you, Nana."

"I love you, Bug," she said.

She hadn't called me that since I was little. It meant more right now than it had at any time before. I held it in my heart as we headed to the Athenæum. A dark gloom hung over me like a reaper waiting for a corpse, the anticipation of the unknown scratching at my nerves.

CHAPTER EIGHT

The clouds stuck to the tall brick buildings like gray cotton candy. Rain chased down the gutters and clapped the ground, drenching the red cobblestone sidewalks, making them look glassy. It felt good to stretch my legs after sitting at the café table so long, even though it was hard to keep up with Carrig's long stride. "So where is Asile?"

"We go through England to get there," Carrig said.

"How?"

"Through a hidden tunnel behind a bookcase in an Oxford library. The Wizard Council had the tunnel systems constructed to connect all havens to a nearby library."

"The havens. Are they in this world?" I asked.

"No. A different realm connected to this one. Created by wizards, but it broke into pieces by unstable magic and made the havens sort of like islands—isolated from each other."

Okay. Mind blown. I decided that maybe asking questions wasn't such a good idea. Each answer was unbelieveable. And made me question my sanity.

"You'll love Asile," Nana said as she kept pace with me. "I've been to other havens and it's just like visiting European villages. It'll be like you're studying abroad."

I smiled. She had a way of always looking on the brighter side of things. Even in the middle of an apocalypse.

"You know," I said. "Haven means safe place. And these places you're talking about don't sound very safe to me."

"It be an old name," Carrig said. "When created, they be places for the Mystiks and wizards who sought shelter from human persecution. Just like all good t'ings, a few rotten apples spoiled it."

The Sentinels waited on the steps of the library. Dressed in street clothes instead of the leather warrior costumes of last Friday, they resembled normal teenagers. Loose black waves tumbled over Lei's shoulders, and Demos's sandy hair stuck out in a purposeful way. The other two Sentinels, who had helped kill the hound in the library the first day we transported through the gateway, introduced themselves.

"I'm Kale," one said. His messy dark hair framed his face.

"Jaran," the other added. His short black dreadlocks looked freshly washed compared to the other day in the library.

Arik, still in Nick's clothes, looked like he'd been in a fight. There was a cut on his cheek and his eye was puffy. His shoulders seemed to be holding the weight of both worlds.

What happened to him? I took a step toward Arik, but Lei shook her head, halting me.

I was sure it was my fault, and it felt wrong. I didn't want anyone getting hurt because of me. I tightened my fingers around the handle of my umbrella, thinking I could use it as a weapon if we ran into any of those hounds in the library.

Nana pushed through the red leather doors of the Athenæum, taking Demos, Kale, and Arik in first with her membership card, and after fifteen minutes, I took Carrig, Jaran, and Lei in with mine. We met Nana and the others in the fifth-floor reading room where I had initially spotted Arik.

We broke up into groups and sat in different parts of the room. Nana and Lei sat with me at one of the large tables. The others took seats around the room while Carrig and Arik settled into one of the alcoves between the bookcases, their heads close together, seemingly in deep conversation.

After the room emptied of other visitors, we hid under the larger tables.

I bumped my head against the overhang of the table. "How come we just don't jump now while the coast is clear?" I asked, rubbing my head.

"Too dangerous," said Carrig. "Transporting so many at a time would leave an energy trail."

Nana placed an invisibility spell around us, and we waited until the library had closed and all the employees had gone home for the day. Only dimmers lit the floor, and the library became even more silent.

"Let's be on our way." Carrig edged out from our hiding place. "Jaran, get the gateway book. Kale, retrieve our items from the coat check."

I crawled out from under the table. "Oh no, our stuff. They know we're still here."

Nana straightened her shirt. "Dear, you underestimate my abilities. Our items magically disappeared after they were checked." She winked at me.

Jaran hurried over to a bookcase at the far end of the room, grabbed the familiar leather-bound book, and rushed back. He dropped it onto the table and flipped the pages.

Arik went to the book and spoke the key. The colors of his body bled together, and he went in with a swirl of rainbow-colored smoke, the book quivering in his wake. After a few seconds, the book stilled.

I looked to Lei. "What's wrong with Arik?"

"A compelled cornered him," she said leaning close. "They torture their victims with visions of past regrets before they go for the kill."

I gasped.

"It's a ghastly business," Lei added. "The life span of the wizard controlling the compelled diminishes during the compulsion. The wizard has to be really desperate or insane to use it."

"How awful. Is there some way we can help?"

Lei patted my back. "Don't worry about it, ducky. He'll be back to normal soon enough. We're taught to overcome their mind games. Some visions take longer than others do. This one had to be bad."

"Gia," Carrig said. "Demos will escort you through the gateway."

Kale strode across the reading room, carrying my back-pack and Nana's tote bag. He'd forgotten my weapon—the red umbrella. It was one of the few things I owned that belonged to my mother. With Arik gone and everyone anxious to leave, I didn't have time to retrieve it. I'd have to get it later. Kale handed my pack to me. I thanked him, slipping my arms through the straps.

Carrig studied my face for a moment. "I'll be going through the gateway with Ms. Kearns. Are you okay to jump?"

"Yeah, I'll be fine." Who was I kidding? I was terrified to jump. I wasn't sure who to trust, and my danger radar was blaring out of control. How bad could it be, anyway? *I could break my neck, or wind up back in the Vatican, that's how.*

"All right, then," Carrig said. "After the book be silent, follow us."

Demos nodded. "Will do."

The other Sentinels jumped first, in case danger waited on the other side of the gateway. Carrig grabbed Nana's arm, and they vanished into the pages. I stared at the photo-graph of the Bodleian library in Oxford, England. Trying to get up the nerve.

"It'll be all right," Demos said. "I'll be right behind you."

Before I could psych myself out of going, I rattled off, "*Aprire la porta.*"

This was my third time through the gateway, and already I was getting used to the falling sensation. It was easier to keep myself upright, though it required a lot of limb flailing. I landed on the hard floor with a loud thump and staggered forward before stopping.

Demos flew out of the book right after me.

"Bravo, Gia." Kale applauded. "You were born to jump."

I smiled at him, taking deep breaths of musty air. "I guess so." I dashed to Nana and gave her a tight hug. "How was your jump?"

She patted her chest. "I hadn't jumped in years. It knocked the wind out of me."

"I know, it's a real rush, right?"

"That it is. Excuse me, I must ask Carrig something." She headed over to where he was talking to Jaran and Demos.

Arik shuffled off from the group as well, shoulders slumped.

I sidled up to Lei on my right. "I don't think he's getting over it. What happened to him?"

"We got separated from him. The two men following us were only decoys. They led Arik to an alley where a compelled man waited." She glanced at him. "He must've had Arik longer than we suspected. Tortured him. Arik's the leader of our group, so he doesn't want any of us to see him weak."

Arik stood in the moonlight streaming through a tall gothic-style window. Dust danced in the beams of light around him, making him look like he was in an old silent movie. His silhouette was small in comparison to the height of the dark bookcases bordering the room.

The tilt of his head made me aware he was staring directly at me. My stomach jolted, and I reeled away.

Carrig ordered everyone to follow him, leading us down a corridor of bookcases. A row of desks sat between each set of shelves we passed. Dark wood arched overhead. The coffered ceiling had many squared tiles with depictions of open books on their surfaces. Carrig stopped at the third bookcase on the left.

"This is the passageway to Asile." He pulled down two wooden knobs flanking each side of a house-shaped box fastened to the bookcase.

"*Ammettere il pura,*" he said.

Admit the pure. I was certain now that the reason my mother wanted me to take Italian lessons was because, so far, all the keys were in Italian.

The floor quivered, and the bookcase wheezed and creaked as it slid open, exposing a staircase plunging into the darkness.

All the Sentinels, except Carrig and Arik, held up their palms and in unison said, "*Luce.*" Light. A glowing sphere the size of a softball formed in each of their palms. One by one, they went down the dark stairwell, the light from the globes bouncing on the rock walls. Carrig aided Nana down.

Arik produced a globe and stepped over to me. The blood around the cut on his left cheek had coagulated, and there was a knot by his right eye.

I reached to touch it but pulled my hand away when he frowned. "Does it hurt?"

"I'm mint. Get going."

I scowled at him and adjusted my pack. "Why are you mad at me?"

He watched the others disappear down the steps. "I'm

not angry with you."

"Then what's your problem?

"I haven't a problem."

"Well, you were nice to me earlier and now you're glaring at me."

"This morning?" He raked his fingers through his dark, tangled hair. The light globe in his other hand lit up his beautiful face. The globe reflecting in his eyes looked like a star in a pitch-black sky. "I fancied you. Your bravery. How quickly you responded in the Paris library, the way you wielded that stapler. Even your willingness to attempt the jump from the Vatican without my help. But you are a Sentinel. There are laws—"

"You fancied me?" I interrupted.

"It wouldn't matter if I am...*was*. Sentinels can*not* be together. The punishment is severe."

"Doesn't matter anyway. I'm the Doomsday Child. You should keep far away from me." I spun on my heel and headed for the stairs.

Arik seized my arm before I took the first step. "Who told you that?"

I whirled around to face him, yanking my arm from his grasp. My foot caught on a raised part of the floor. I fell forward, and he caught me with one strong arm.

"Easy there," he said, keeping the light balanced on his palm.

I stared into his dark eyes, shrugging out of his hold. "Carrig. My nana. They both told me."

His face fell serious. "Shite." He paced in mad circles, glancing at me a few times before he stopped. "Oh, Gia," he said, grabbing my hand. "I won't let anything happen to you."

I pulled back. His fingers gripped mine tighter, and my hand sparked under his touch. I bit my lip to stop its tremble. "That compelled man showed you something about me," I said. "Didn't he?"

"No. It was all about me… Some tragedy of my own. The compelled can only see their captive's past and fears. No need to worry. You're safe here. Trust me."

"What did he show you?"

"I…I can't…"

"You ask me to trust you, but you won't trust me."

He lowered his head and studied our linked hands. "I was fourteen and in training. A hound had attacked my group in the library. My parent faery, Oren, was with me. The hound sunk its teeth into Oren's leg, and the beast pulled him through the gateway book. I froze. By the time the older Sentinels reached Oren, he was dead. That's what the compelled showed me. He also revealed that I would face the same choice again in the future. And I will fail again—" His voice cracked. "I miss Oren very much. He was a loving father. It's like the hound tore a piece of my heart away when he took him."

I squeezed his hand. "You were just a boy. It wasn't your fault."

"Many have said the same, but I'm still haunted by it." His voice was gravelly with emotion. "In the throes of sleepless nights, I still see the horror in Oren's eyes as the beast dragged him away."

My thoughts caught up with me. *I'm going to a place where these creatures live. If they find out who I am, they'll kill me. I'm going to die.*

My mouth went dry. "I'm scared," I croaked, swallowing back the gumball-sized lump in my throat.

Time stalled as he stared at me, his dark eyes so intense and full of compassion. "Gia," he said finally, voice soft. His face was mere inches from my own. He smelled like sweaty leather and soap. His jaw was tight, causing only hollows in his cheeks where his dimples came out when he smiled.

I focused on his lips, staring at the cleft just below the bottom one. My heart raced as his arm came around me and I leaned into his embrace, feeling the warmth of his body. My heart felt like it would fly out of my chest. He rested his cheek against my head, and his warm breaths whispered against my hair.

Something scurried over my Converse, startling me. I yanked away from him, teetering on the edge of the stairwell. He caught me before I fell backwards, losing the light globe he held in his palm. It burst, and little flashes zapped the air.

He laughed. "You're dangerous."

"*Oww*," I snapped, grabbing onto my injured leg.

"Are you all right?"

"It's just the cut in my leg," I said. "My stitches pulled. Something ran over my feet. It was way too big to be a rat."

"The rats down here are rather huge. They've lived here for centuries. They won't harm you."

"Says you." I glanced around my feet, my skin crawling.

He chuckled. "We should catch the others." He seized my hand in his and turned my palm up. "There's a charm that releases one's light globe."

"Yeah, I heard you say it. *Luce*, right?"

"That's correct. Clear your mind and think only of light."

"Wait. What? I can't—"

He placed a finger on my lips to stop me. His crooked grin made tiny flutters rise in my stomach. "We won't know until you try," he said.

Thinking of anything other than Arik at that point was tough. But Nana's lamp with the three stained-glass parrots perched on a base of bronzed twigs came to mind. It was the lamp I had stared at during one of my many attempts to ignite the light and had managed to create a flicker of gold on my palm. That lamp fascinated me because when lit, the parrots became a prism, casting a rainbow on a nearby wall.

"*Luce,*" I said.

Nothing.

I added a little more force.

Nada.

Arik supported my hand with his. My pulse jumped.

"Try again."

"*Luce.*" Light flickered above my palm and a softball-sized bubble of light popped to life. I had light! *In the palm of my hand.*

"Shall we?" He motioned to the stairs with a nod.

Our footsteps echoed off the cut-stone walls as we charged down the steps. There was barely room for one person to go along the tunnel at a time, so I led the way with the ball of light hovering over my palm.

Too busy admiring the light, I stepped on a rock and it rolled under my foot. The action caused my stitches to pull again, and I stumbled and hobbled a bit before regaining my balance.

"Careful there, you'll sprain your ankle," Arik said.

I wrinkled my nose at the rank stench of the cave. Water trickled down the sides and dripped from the ceiling. Rocks underfoot turned and rolled to the side or tumbled down the steep passageway. It was a claustrophobic's nightmare.

Arik's heavy boots sounded behind me. I glanced back, catching his gaze, and quickly turned back, watching my steps and tugging the bottom of my hoodie down with my free hand.

"Anyone else know you can create a globe?" Arik asked.

"No."

"How many times have you conjured one?"

"I want to tell you, but my mom used some sort of spell to keep me from speaking about it."

"Hold up," he said.

I stopped and faced him. He cupped my face in his hands and I sucked in a startled breath, almost dropping the glowing ball. I tried to back away but he kept hold of me. "What are you doing?"

"Removing it." Up close his eyes were captivating, if not a bit tortured. "*Annullare tutte le magie*," he said and released me.

"Did it work?"

"Not certain. How many times have you conjured one?" He gestured for me to continue walking.

"A few," I said, heading down the cave. "The first time was a total accident when I was like four. The next one was when I was about ten." I peered over my shoulder at him. "I guess it worked."

"I believe so. And how did you know the charm?"

"I didn't. I was practicing my Italian when the light flickered on my palm. It was a complete accident. I can't remember how I did it when I was four. Maybe I overheard my mother say it."

"Let's keep it our secret for now, all right?"

"Why?"

Behind me, Arik panted, a low rhythmic beat that matched the thumping of my heart. "It would be wise," he said between breaths, "with all that's going on lately, that we keep your lineage to ourselves."

The cave grew colder and I shivered. "Why do you only protect the libraries? Those hounds could get out and hurt people."

"There are wards around them, preventing Mystiks from

exiting. To enter the human world requires a clearance. It's very difficult to obtain one and once received, a device is inserted under the skin, allowing passage through the wards. Our job is to keep the peace between the different races traveling the gateways and assure the safety of all humans."

"I see," I said. "So have you ever jumped into a famous person's library? That would be so cool."

"Unfortunately, no," he said. "We only guard libraries that have gateway books. And I'm not aware of any private collections with one."

"Right."

When the cave widened, we trotted next to each other, trying to catch up to the rest. I slowed down when the pain in my leg was too much to keep up. Arik's pace eased.

"Do you need a rest?"

"No. I can walk. It's jogging that's killing me."

"We'll take it easy, then."

A fat drop of water landed on my arm, and I wiped it away, hoping it was water and not drool, or something else gross.

We followed the cave for twenty minutes or so before the tunnel began to tighten again. Arik motioned for me to go first. He had an insanely hot grin playing on his lips, which made me nervous.

"Why are you smiling?"

"I'm impressed," he said. "For a novice, you've retained your globe for quite some time."

"I totally forgot it was in my hand," I lied. My arm ached from holding it out so long, but I was determined to keep my globe lit, especially since he'd just said that.

We were getting nearer to the four globes blazing down the corridor ahead of us. "Here's a bit of fact for you," he said. "The havens' tunnel systems accelerate our actual speed. A day's walk in the human world takes only about an hour in a tunnel. Notice we don't feel like we're going any faster than a stroll."

"Really?"

Arik grasped my shoulder and pulled me to a stop. "Your shoulder is tensing."

I shrugged his hand off. Every time he touched me, my stomach reacted, and it was starting to freak me out. *Get a grip, already. He's just a guy.*

"Let me take over the light for a bit," he said.

"Okay." I wasn't going to argue with him. My shoulder was tired and sore. I lowered it, and the globe popped. Sparks shot across my hand. My arm felt like a rock at my side after keeping it raised so long.

"Why would anyone want to go to these havens?" I asked. "They have hounds and hunters and compelling creeps."

"The havens were once peaceful." The globe he carried lit up the side of his amazing face. His silhouette bounced across the cave wall. "There's been unrest lately," he said. "Caused by a vengeful wizard named Conemar. Don't trust anyone. Just Merl and myself. We aren't sure where loyalties lie."

"What does this Conemar guy want?"

Something crunched under his boot, something that had a hard shell. I cringed and fought the urge to scratch my skin off.

"What do most lunatics want?" he said. "Power. He wants to rule over both the human and Mystik worlds. He needs the keys to release an extremely powerful being. One that can cause natural disasters and bring people to their knees."

"That makes me feel *so* much better."

He gave me a sideways glance. "I'm sorry. I don't mean to scare you. We'll keep you safe. That compelled man found me fast in the subway." He kept his voice low as we continued toward the others, who were scaling a set of steps in front of us. "It makes me think the wizard compelling him was tipped off by someone from our Haven. So we must be careful."

I stopped. "Then why are we going there?"

His foot paused on the bottom step and he turned to face me. "Because it's the only place to protect and prepare you for whatever may come. You'll be safe as long as we keep who your biological father is a secret. Shall we continue?"

I nodded.

"All right, then." He sprang up the stairs.

I carefully went up after him, my leg wound screaming at me with each step. The idea of a wizard casting a compulsion spell gave me the creepy-crawlies. So did the enormous rats in the tunnel. There was no way I was going to be left alone down there for even a second.

Halfway up, I looked back over my shoulder. Without the light globes, it was eerily dark. Somewhere in the depths, there was a sound like nails scratching on rock. *It's only rats*, I reassured myself. Arik went through the door. My heart sputtered as I scrambled up the last steps, ignoring the pain. I froze there on the landing, stuck between two worlds, desperately clinging to one while called to embrace the other. If I went through the door, my mother's stories would come true, and I could never go back.

Arik reached his hand out to me. "It'll be all right. I won't leave you."

Stop fooling yourself, Gia. There's no going back.

I took his hand and crossed over the threshold, unsure of what I would find on the other side.

CHAPTER NINE

We came through a trap door into a stark room about the size of my bedroom. A bluish light peeked in from a door left ajar across the room. We headed for it, the floorboards squealing under our weight and disturbed dust clouding the air. I coughed.

We exited a small outbuilding, and I took a deep breath of fresh air—an earthen smell of mud and grass. Thin streamers of silvery light hung from a crescent moon that tilted in a black sky stippled with stars. A shadowy silhouette of a castle protruded from a dark hill like a shrine. Smaller buildings surrounding the castle reminded me of grave markers in an eerie cemetery.

"The castle ahead is our tribe's haven," Arik said. "Do you see the light on the horizon? Just beyond the hill is the city of Asile."

We crossed a long pasture. The silhouettes of the others disappeared over a rise in the path ahead of us.

"Where *exactly* is Asile?"

"On the border of England," he said. "The Mystik world has seven main wizard havens. The others are in Ireland,

Spain, France, Italy, Russia, and South Africa. All are near hidden cities."

"*Okaaay*," I drawled. "I get we're in England, but what part…you know, can you give me a familiar landmark to go by? Like, say, Stonehenge or something?"

"Well," he said. "Asile's true location is kept secret. It's in another realm and cloaked by magic. The only entrance and exit is the outbuilding we just came from, and the walls surrounding Asile have wards that prevent anyone from venturing past her boundaries. All the havens are the same. There are many labyrinths in the Mystik world and many entries that can lead to traps. It's a world intertwined with mysteries and dangers. You'd best stay within the walls."

I stumbled over the beginning of a rocked pathway with tangled bushes and thick grasses choking its borders. I braced myself—hands hitting hard against the ground—and barely avoided smashing my face against the stone. I sprung to my feet, waving Arik's offered hand away.

I scolded myself as I swiped my stinging palms across my jeans, brushing away the tiny pebbles sticking to my skin. *How freaking embarrassing, Gia. He definitely thinks you're a moron now.*

Arik shook his head and snickered. "We should have one of our curers see to your leg."

"I'm fine. It just needs to heal." I hobble-trotted ahead, keeping my eyes on the path as I went. His snickers followed me. I glanced over my shoulder at him. There was a playful spark in his eyes.

"What?"

"You're stubborn, aren't you?"

"I like to think I'm determined." I turned back and continued up the path.

Ahead of us, the others stopped at a wooden door in a

brick wall surrounding the medieval-looking castle. In the night shadows, the vines snaking up the length of the wall looked like dark invading creatures. Smoke puffing from the chimneys of the small homes at the base of the castle incensed the night air.

Carrig pushed the thick splintering gate open. He waited for us to pass, and then he leaned his weight against the stubborn door to shut it.

We walked into a manicured courtyard. It had several intricate stone walkways cut into its grasses that branched off to the many entries into the castle. Salt-white benches and planters surrounded a circular patio in the middle of the courtyard.

As we approached the main entrance, two stately doors crawled open. Twenty or more men in black uniforms with metal breastplates lined the entryway. A few creatures were in their ranks—some with fangs, some with horns, and some with unnaturally colored skin. I smiled nervously at them as I passed. Not one returned the gesture.

After the black veil of night, it took a moment to adjust to the light of the foyer. A chandelier loomed above our heads, one of its flame-shaped lightbulbs flickering final bursts of life, casting ominous shadows on the walls. A door on the right led to a darkened room.

This isn't at all *intimidating.* I wiped my clammy hands on my jeans and wondered, again, what I'd gotten myself into.

Lei stopped beside me. "No need to worry, ducky. It looks scarier than it is."

"I-I'm not scared," I protested.

"The look on your face and the quiver in your voice says differently."

I straightened my shoulders and stuck my chin out,

trying to seem less terrified. A massive tapestry of a gray-bearded man holding a smoky globe in his outstretched hand hung high above the stairs. "So who's the man on the rug?"

"Rug?" Her eyes went to where mine were focused. "Oh, you mean the tapestry. That is the Seventh Wizard, Taurin. He's the founder of our haven. He's sort of creepy, isn't he?"

"That's an understatement," I muttered. My ears started to thrum. The tapestry fluttered and turned fluid, ripples rushing down the fabric like wakes across a lake. An electric current forked across the globe cradled in Taurin's hand, sending out a series of crackles and thunders. His eyes sparked to life and stared directly at me. Goose bumps erupted across my arms. Overhead, the chandelier flickered before dimming. All the voices around me dissolved, and the present faded.

I stood just behind Taurin and right beside a blazing sconce. He balanced an electric ball on the tips of his fingers.

"Stand back," he yelled at a cloaked figure across the corridor.

"I shall not," the other man hissed. "Give me the Chiavi, Taurin."

Chiavi? That's Italian. It's the plural form of Chiave— key. He wants keys? For what?

"Thou art an infectious, dog-hearted lout," Taurin said, taking a step toward the man. "The havens fester in thy greed. I will not surrender the trinkets. The Tetrad shall stay entombed forever."

Taurin raised the ball, but before he could lob it at the cloaked man, a knife pierced his back. The electric ball fell and then exploded on the ground, blowing a hole into the floor and charring the wall nearby. Taurin's body crumpled to the floor.

My hand was wet, so I inspected it, but I found myself looking at long, thick fingers and a massive palm. It wasn't my own; it was a man's hand. Blood dripped down the blade of the knife in the man's hand. A hand that was just used to kill a man. I would have screamed, but the body wasn't mine, either, and I couldn't make the mouth work.

"Fool, now he is unable to tell us where he hid the Chiavi!" the cloaked man yelled down the corridor at me.

A vision of seven thin, smooth rods about the length of a hairbrush went through my mind. The body I now mentally shared tagged the rods as the Chiavi. When combined they made one magical key. A key to what, though? The cloaked man turned fuzzy and my ears started thrumming again.

"He would never give them up," came out in a deep voice. "By torturing his sons, we shall find the charms..." I tried to dig deeper into the mind, learn more about the key, but the words vanished as I slipped into darkness.

"Gia, you all right?" Lei's voice pulled me back to the present and into the light.

"Um..." I inspected my fingers. The bloody knife had vanished, and my hand was my own again. Great, now I'm seeing things—a vision from inside the body of a murderer. It felt like I'd stabbed Taurin myself, which creeped me out.

I had to work to avoid shuddering. There was some sort of significance to what I'd *seen*, but I knew I couldn't tell anyone. *Don't trust anyone*, both Nana and Arik had said. I gave Lei a slight smile. "Yeah, I'm fine."

A man somewhere in his forties, wearing a tweed jacket, hints of silver in his dark hair, cleared his throat as he stepped into the foyer. I moved to Nana's side.

Carrig headed over to the man. "Good evening, Merl."

"I trust your journey was safe?" Merl said.

Carrig shot his hand out. "For the most part, we've made it unscathed."

Merl hesitated, giving him a curious look before shaking his offered hand.

What's up with that?

Carrig looked at Nana and me. "This be Gia and her grandmother, Ms. Kearns."

"You may call me Katy," Nana said.

Merl's face brightened. He stretched his hand out to Nana, and she took it. "I'm delighted to meet you." His deep, warm voice sounded as if it dripped with syrup.

"It's a pleasure to make your acquaintance," Nana said, their hands lingering in a hold.

Ew. It was time to interrupt Nana's obvious flirting. "I'm Gia."

Merl released Nana's hand. "Yes, I'd know you anywhere. You have your mother's beauty. Our people are quite excited to have a most talented Sentinel's daughter return to Asile."

My cheeks warmed. "Thank you. Um, but how did they know I was coming?"

"The story about how you were found and that you are the daughter of Marietta Bianchi and Brian Kearns was placed in Asile's weekly Scroll. I have found if you give the public information, fewer questions are asked."

That's clever. And it would've made me feel a little less nervous if everyone's eyes weren't on me.

"You both must be tired," he said. "Faith will show you to your rooms."

"We want to room together," I blurted. There was no way I was going to sleep alone in this enormous spooky place, especially after the freaky vision of Taurin. I was sure the castle was a haven, all right—for ghosts, and not the normal ghoulish type. Any poltergeists living here would be deceased wizards, warriors, or worse. I couldn't imagine what would be worse, and that's what scared me most—the unknown.

"That's a good idea. Adjoining rooms will do," Nana was saying as I drifted back to the living. "Don't you agree, Gia?"

"Oh. Sure. Adjoining rooms," I said, uncertain.

"I'm Faith," said an extremely pale girl, startling me.

Where had she come from?

"Follow me, please." She sounded American.

As Nana and I shadowed the apparition, or rather Faith, Arik gave Merl the details of his face-off with the compelled man. "When I left the subway station, he cornered me in an alley—"

A door slammed shut on their conversation. I assumed Merl, Carrig, and the Sentinels had gone into the room off the entry for privacy. I made a mental note to find out more about compulsion.

Faith's drab blond hair swayed limply against her back. She glanced back several times to make sure Nana and I were following. Her pale skin glowed in the dim light of the foyer, and her willowy body looked starved for food.

We climbed the curved staircase to a landing with a thick mahogany banister. On each side of the landing, two tall archways led to long corridors. Our footsteps echoed against the stone walls. A strange herby smell hung in the air, reminding me of when Afton would burn incense in her room.

I leaned over to Nana as we went to the right. "You were flirting with Merl. He's too young for you."

"Nonsense." She waved me off. "He's one hundred and two, which in wizard years is about forty-eight. That's what the Mystik tabloids say, anyway."

I stopped. *Mystik tabloids?* Realizing I'd fallen behind, I rushed up to them. "So if he was human, that would make you fifteen years older than him. And that would make you a cougar."

She laughed. "I never go for men my age. They're too… old."

Okay. I'm done with this convo. Seriously. Old people and flirting. So not right.

I decided to inspect the artwork, hoping to forget the subject of Nana's love life. In stark contrast to the heavy paintings and metal weaponry hanging on the walls, delicate crystal sconces lit the halls. There were more corridors and staircases at every turn. We snaked through several adjoining passages until we stopped at a door halfway down a smaller hallway.

"This is your room," Faith said, looking at me. She unlocked the door and then pushed it open. Her head snapped in Nana's direction. "Yours is next door, but you may go through this room with us." She smiled, her large canine teeth coming out to greet us. I swear I heard theme music from a horror movie go off somewhere.

She held the key out to me. I hesitated before taking it from her bony fingers. "Um, thank you. I'm sure we can find what we need."

"They didn't tell you about me, did they?"

"Is th-there…um…something to tell?" I stammered.

"There's always something to tell," she said. "Ms. Kearns, please step inside."

I shook my head at Nana and mouthed *No!*

Nana just smiled and walked straight into the lion's lair, and I was stupid enough to follow her. As I passed by Faith, I almost gagged. She smelled ripe.

The room was just like a hotel suite, except the furnishings were medieval couture.

I dropped my backpack on the floor. "What, no TV?"

"There's a media and game room in the basement, along with a snack bar," Faith said. "It's always open, if you feel like going—"

"No. No, I'm good." There was no way I'd go off on my own in this place.

I inched cautiously across the room and peeked into the bathroom. There was a door leading to another room.

Faith swung the bedroom door shut behind her. Then she glided to the bed and sat on the billowy comforter. "I take it you haven't seen my kind before." She crossed her abnormally long legs, resting her frail hands on bony knees. Her chest was unusually wide and lacking in the boob department. She reminded me of a greyhound. "You needn't be frightened of me."

"Why would we be frightened?" I asked uneasily.

"Not only do I work on Merl's security team, but I'm also a Laniar," she said. "Actually, your kind mistakes my kind for your fabled vampires. Because of these"—she opened her mouth and tapped her tongue against one of her long canines—"some of the legends about vampires began with Laniars, from when we lived openly with humans. Others believed us to be werewolves."

"Yeah. I get it. You're like a cross between the two." Her

teeth looked like they could puncture a tire. "Does your kind suck blood or what?" Fearing she might want a snack, I tried to pull a turtle, lowering my neck into my shoulders.

Nana narrowed her eyes at Faith. "If we're all about announcing ourselves, then I should warn you. I'm a Pure Witch skilled in the magic of Incantora. Are you aware of her legacy?"

"She had the power to make a person's insides erupt in flames, burning the poor soul from the inside out, right?"

"That's correct. This is my granddaughter, and I will incinerate you if you touch her."

"Or suck my blood," I interjected.

Faith snorted. "Contrary to popular belief, humans don't taste at all good. They're bitter and salty. Lucky for you, I'm on your security detail. I promise not to eat you while on duty."

"Yeah, lucky."

"You could have Herman, instead. He's an Aqualian." I detected a hint of teasing in her voice. "But he's kind of slimy."

I liked her, but she needed a spritz of perfume. "So, if you're staying the night, you could take a bath here. We won't mind."

Faith lifted a smile. "That would be fun. I don't remember the last time I had one."

"You don't remember?"

"No one ever told me how often I should take a bath. I was raised by the pack after my parents were killed." Faith sniffed her underarm. "Oh, that's bad."

"You mean you were *born* a Laniar?"

"Did you think I was made?" She laughed. "I'll say it again; we are *not* vampires or werewolves, or hounds, for that matter."

"I'm sorry," I said.

"No need to be sorry. I barely remember my family. I enjoyed living with the pack. I met Ricardo there."

"Oh, is he your boyfriend?"

"He was until he broke things off. I fell hard for his charms, so I was devastated and I left the pack. That's when Merl took me in."

"I had me a Ricardo in my younger days. It was a lovely, fleeting moment." Nana walked over and put her arm around Faith.

Oh God. Not this again. No one should ever have to hear their grandmother swoon about past, present, or future lovers.

"Come on, dear, we'll get you in the bath. A lady takes a bath or a shower each day." Nana was always taking in strays, even if they had sharp canines.

"Or, if you're like me and you work out a lot, you might want to take two a day," I added, following them. I grabbed a small knife from a cheese and fruit tray on the coffee table as I passed and then tucked it into my back pocket. Who knew what might be lurking in the corridors…or the walls…

Coaxing Faith out of the bathtub later was like trying to drag Afton out of a mall. The sun was rising, and apparently, Laniars fried in the sun because their skin was paper-thin and their blood combusted under extreme heat. I was beginning to suspect Laniars *were* vampires, but they just didn't like the stigma that came along with the name. I got it. I hated when people called me a tomboy.

After the bath, and against my protests, Nana insisted Faith stay on the couch in the sitting area instead of out in the hall. Not that she didn't seem okay, but I didn't want her to suddenly develop a hunger for salty food. Faith sank into the backrest cushions and flipped through one of Nana's many tabloid magazines.

I traced my finger around the gold curlicue design on

the comforter and stared at the curtain enclosing the bed, waiting for sleep to overtake me. I couldn't fight it any longer. My eyes burned. Anyway, if Faith wanted to eat us, she'd had enough time to have her two-course meal, flee somewhere, and be happily digesting us by now. Plus, I was more at ease about things after Merl had stopped by to check on us and assured me Faith wouldn't eat my face off.

"Gia, are you still awake?"

"Yes."

"We're not vampires."

What the heck? Can she read minds?

"I wanted to clarify, you know, just in case you were still wondering. Vampires are dead. We are living. I'm warm. Come touch me, if you don't believe me."

I figured if I didn't touch her, this could go on forever. I slipped out of bed, padded over to her, and placed my hand on her arm.

"You *are* warm. Toasty, in fact." Okay, so maybe she was telling the truth. I dashed back into bed, shut the curtains, and pulled the covers up to my chin. "Good night...um... morning. Whatever."

"Sleep tight," she said. "Oh, and thank you for being honest with me, for the bath, and for letting me stay on the couch while I guard you. This is much better than standing in the hallway."

"No problem." I slid a hand under my pillow to make sure the cheese knife was still there.

"One thing about Laniars, we make excellent protectors. Our hearing is better than a dog's."

"Good to know," I said around a yawn and shut my eyes, yielding to sleep.

•••

Images flicked across my closed eyes. I bolted down a long hallway lined with burning torches. Fear twisted my stomach as broken thoughts rushed through my mind.

I can't fail at this. Thousands of people will die if I do. Epic storms. Death. So many. So many already gone. I'm almost there. The trap. Where is it?

My heels clanked over something metal covered with straw. *The trap.* A sigh escaped my lips. I reached the end of the hall and turned the doorknob of the only door.

Locked? It should not be locked.

A slow, rumbling thunder echoed down the hall. I spun to face whatever was coming. A reflection flashed across the night-darkened window beside me. I expected to see myself, but instead, it was a beautiful young woman with long blond hair. She reminded me of a fairytale princess in her red-and-gold renaissance dress that touched the floor, except for the sword in her trembling hands.

A mountainous shadow moved down the hall, getting nearer. I gasped, or rather, Sleeping Beauty did. The sword shook as she readied it. The floor cracked from the force of the mammoth footfalls.

The creature stomped into the light. Its facial features were leonine—fierce eyes, flattened nose, cleft upper lip, and fanged teeth—all framed by a dirty-yellow mane that brushed the candelabras hanging from the ceiling. There was something different about this creature, though, something almost human. Claw-like nails twitched at his sides. Scars branched across his face and massive arms. He looked as if someone had cut him up and haphazardly sewn him back together, like an experiment gone epically wrong. And he had friends. Three other creatures followed him.

One had a boar's head with sharp tusks that protruded out from his lower jaw. Bristly black hair covered most of his body. Another one was a man with two large ram horns coming out of his forehead that pulled and distorted his face. His torso and upper arms were human, but his forearms and legs were that of a beast—deformed and hooved.

I thought the others were bad, but when the last monster came into the light, a scream jammed in my throat. His forked tongue darted in and out over rows of razor-sharp teeth. Scales covered arms and legs that bent like a lizard's limbs. The only human parts to him were his pumped-up chest, neck, and abdomen.

They all moved as one—every arm, foot, and head movement a perfectly synchronized performance. It was as if something invisible tethered them together in a diamond formation as they slithered down the hallway.

Lion Man reached her first. "Do not fear, Athela," he said. "It is I, Barnum."

"It *cannot* be," Athela said, pointing the sword at him. "Thou perished in the great battle. I prepared thy lifeless body for burial."

"Mykyl brought me back to life…as this *being*."

"My father did this?" I knew Athela's horror as she eyed the thing in front of her.

"Yes, Mykyl did this," he roared, the windowpanes shaking from the force. "He could not leave me in my glory, a warrior slain. Instead, I am a beast, and my soul is connected to the other warriors he resurrected."

"Why did he do this to *you*?" she asked, taking a step back.

"He only needed a body, and I was already dead."

Fear fisted Athela's stomach and I felt it, too. I was her, or inside her, but she wasn't aware of me. I wanted to let her know I was there, that she wasn't alone, but I didn't know how. The terror inside her intensified, but she didn't scream.

She stood her ground bravely.

"What others?"

"Chetwin, Felton, and Harlan." He said their names as he pointed to each—Boar Man, Lizard Man, and Horned Man.

"Massssster, wilt thou sssshare her with ussss?" Felton's black tongue licked the air with each word.

"No!" Barnum turned and snarled at him. "She is my bride."

"We watch, then." Chetwin snorted. "There is no ridding thyself of us. Tell her."

"Tell her how only thy soul survived the change"— Harlan pounded his hoof against the floor—"and how her father stretched thy soul into our bodies. How we are one soul with four minds." His eyes focused on Athela. "Give thyself to us. It shall be as if thou art with Barnum."

Athela choked on a sob.

"Silence!" Barnum slammed his fist into Harlan's jaw. He stumbled back and the others went with him, pulling Barnum along.

"What will be my fate?" Athela asked.

"Be with me," Barnum said.

"Thou wilt have me shared with them?" Bile rose in her throat.

"No! I would never...I shall not let them..." Barnum shook his head as he trailed off. "I feel my humanity slipping from me, my love. I do not know what I will eventually become. In time, I may be fully evil."

"I am with child."

Barnum's head jerked up, and the others copied. He bent, reaching out and barely touching her cheek with his clawed hand. The others mimicked him, touching the air.

"No harm shall come to thee. Go now." Barnum

punched the nearest windowpane. Shards of glass rained down and clinked onto the floor, leaving a jagged gap just Athela's size in the panel.

Athela hiked up her skirts and stepped over the frame. She turned back to face him, tears drenching her cheeks. This was not her husband anymore. He was part of an evil, an evil that could end the worlds. The trap was set, and the beasts would rot for eternity in their tungsten tomb buried within a mountain known only by the high wizards. Her heart sank as she tried to imagine what hell her love faced. Not alive, and not dead. Forever frozen. She wanted him to know his memory would live on. A seed of hope until the madness took over and he was no longer Barnum.

Her sadness choked me and I wished I could hug her, console her. How horrible for all of them.

"Go with my love, Barnum," she said. "Your child will know what a great warrior his father was."

A loud squeal came from the ceiling and a heavy metal cage crashed over Barnum and his beasts. Dust punched Athela's face, and she covered her nose and mouth with her hand, coughing. Seven older men with graying beards rushed the cage, brandishing rods. Blue light shot out from the tips of the rods, and electric sparks ran across the metal bars of the cage.

Athela stared at one of the men. His ink-black beard and heavy brows were at odds with his strikingly pale skin. *Father. You betrayed me. Why could you not leave Barnum in his eternal rest? The others, as well? What evil consumes thee?*

The thoughts of revenge playing in her mind were dark and scary. She backed up, stepping on the hem of her dress and tripping herself. She landed on muddy grass. Cold wetness soaked through her dress. *Why wasn't the door unlocked? Did Father hope the creatures would kill me? Why—?*

I thought, *Probably because you saw something you weren't supposed to see. That's what happens in all the movies. You're minding your own business, stumble onto something you shouldn't, and in the next scene, they kill you.*

She stabbed the sword into the ground and then used it for support as she staggered to her feet. Her foot twisted on a clump of grass and we both winced.

Ouch. That hurt.

"Who is there?" Panic rattled Athela's voice.

Whoops. She can *hear my thoughts.* My mind raced, wondering what I could do to help her. Why isn't she running away? I'd have been out of there like yesterday.

She glanced around the field. "Show yourself."

I got an idea. *I'm your subconscious. This is where you RUN!*

Athela yanked the sword out of the mud, hiked up her skirts, and darted across the field into the darkness.

CHAPTER TEN

Either I was dreaming of jackhammers or someone was rapping on the bedroom door. The room was dark under the cloak of the heavy drapes.

The idiot banged louder.

"Okay, I'm coming!" It sounded like Faith sprang up from the couch.

"Who's bugging us?" I rolled onto my other side and slid the drapes over.

"I'm not sure," she said.

Our intruder pounded louder. I pushed myself up from the mattress. "Someone isn't patient," I said.

Faith's claws were ready as she eased the door open and peeked through the crack.

"Do you know what time it is?" asked a man.

"No." She opened the door wider.

A man with floppy brown hair, standing extremely straight and poised, frowned down at her. He pulled a watch from the vest pocket of his gray three-piece suit and then held it up by its chain, not bothering to look at it. "It is precisely three thirty, and Gianna was to be in my chambers by three. Carrig may have delayed his training for tomorrow, but my lessons are still on schedule." He looked past Faith and directly at me. "You have a lot to learn and little time in which to do it."

"What—" I cleared my throat. "Um…what lessons?"

"Your magic lessons, of course. Has no one explained this to you?"

I rubbed my eyes and shook my head. *There's that word again. Magic.* My stomach soured. *And, no. No one tells me anything.* But I thought it was best not to tell him that. Not with that stern look pulling on his face.

"Get dressed. I'll wait here for you."

Faith eased the door shut. "Shoot, I forgot to tell you. The man is Philip Attwood. Actually, you should call him Professor Attwood. He's very strict about ceremony." She fell back onto the throw pillows. "You'd better hurry. He hates tardiness."

"You think? He's very uptight." I dashed across the tiled floor, flinching at the coldness under my feet.

"No need to be nasty."

"Me? You could've told me I had a lesson."

"I *said* I forgot."

"Okay. Whatever. That man is full-on scary, just saying."

I ran to my backpack then dragged out jeans, a T-shirt, and a sweatshirt. After dressing, I yanked the door open. "See you later," I called back into the room.

"Chivvy along, now." He walked off, and I shadowed him down the hall. "I have too many duties to have an inconsiderate girl waste my time. I only agreed to work late because your training must start straightaway."

"I didn't know I was supposed to meet you. No one told me. If they had, I'd have been there *on* time." He didn't need to know I was a perpetual tardy violator. I made a quick mental note never to be late for lessons with him. Hopefully I'd learn enough helpful magic to make it worth putting up with his attitude.

He swung around to face me. "I fear, Gianna, we have gotten off to a bad start. I'm Professor Philip Attwood and you're to call me Professor Attwood. Not Mr. Attwood or Philip, you understand?"

"Yes." The man was definitely intimidating, so I didn't correct him on my preferred nickname.

"I am your mother's half brother."

"You're like my uncle?"

"I am, but don't assume I'll be easy on you because of it." He spun back around and continued down the hall. "Follow me."

Obviously. I rolled my eyes.

"Don't roll your eyes behind my back."

"How did—"

"I'm intuitive."

I slumped.

"Posture, Gianna."

I straightened my back, searching the walls and the ceiling for mirrors, but there weren't any. We rounded the corner and scaled a narrow stairwell. Professor Attwood stopped at a door with his name etched into a wooden plaque attached to it. He unlocked the door with a fancy long key and then pushed it open.

Several lamps placed around his office emitted a harmonious glow over the furniture. Pink and yellow notes had been pinned or taped onto the wooden faces of the bookcases occupying every wall. Stacks of books covered the dark wood floors, and mounds of papers and books landscaped the top of a large desk. For a man bent on promptness, he sure was messy.

In the far left corner of the room an enormous glass globe sat securely in the hawk-like claws of a pedestal. Bolts of bluish light zapped within the transparent sphere.

A white cockatoo rested on a thick wooden roost beside the globe. A round, clear stone dangled from a leather cord hanging from its neck. Smoke puffed up from what looked to be incense in a metal bowl on a table between two reading chairs, emitting a cedar scent into the room.

The bird's eyes were vacant and gray. "Is that bird blind?"

"Well, at least you're observant," he said in clipped tones. "He may be blind, but he can see more than anyone with eyes—"

"Who is it?" the bird squawked. "*Arrrk!*"

"Pip, this is Gianna," Professor Attwood said gently. "You aren't able to sense her because she's shielded with a charm."

"It's Gia," I asserted, then, at Professor Attwood's disapproving glance, instantly added, "Um, I mean, I prefer you call me Gia, please."

"*Arrrk!* Good day, Gia." Pip's head turned from side to side. "She be wizard?"

"No. She's Asile's missing Sentinel."

Pip fluttered his wings and paced his perch. "More. *Arrrk!* Something more."

The professor gave him a biscuit. "Calm down, mate."

Pip gobbled the biscuit. Then he stretched out his lovely white wings, rested them on his back, and lowered his head.

"Is he okay?"

"He's sensing the globe. Pip is a Monitor. The globe is how he sees. He can only view what comes over its sphere, what comes across the surveillance eyes, or what goes through the gateways."

"Surveillance eyes? That sounds like spying."

Professor Attwood let out a frustrated sigh. "The eyes only go in public areas. Should Pip sense a threat in what the eyes see, he sends out an alarm. Pip couldn't care less about any private matters."

"How does that work?" I touched the glass and then snatched back my hand. Its ice-cold surface had bitten my skin.

"It's made out of magical glass blown from sand found on the shores of Alato, the lands of the bird people. The magic makes it frigid."

Now he tells me. My fingers prickled.

Professor Attwood sank into a leather chair behind the desk and motioned for me to take the one across from him. He placed his elbows on his armrests, formed a steeple with his hands, and studied me with intense blue eyes.

Uncomfortable, I crossed my legs and stared out the window behind him, watching the clouds mingle over the countryside.

"Hmm…" He tapped his fingertips together. "How shall we begin? Sentinels usually commence their training at a much younger age than you are now, allowing more time to develop their magic."

"Can I ask you something?"

He nodded.

"Someone said Asile doesn't know where her loyalties lie. What did he mean by that?"

He parted his hands and leaned back into the chair. "There was an attack on a Mystik city a few days ago, and we're not certain which tribe was responsible for the assault. Many think an exiled French wizard was behind it."

"Do you mean Conemar?"

"That is the one. If it were him, then his adopted Haven, Estril, is backing him."

"Where is that place?" I asked.

"It's within Russia," he said. "Until the threat is eliminated, travel through the gateways has been restricted. Asile is one of the havens open to the entire Mystik world. Many come to visit our city, work in our Haven, or attend our academy. Anyone with ill intentions may have a plant here." He rocked forward. "I do agree with this *someone*; you should be careful. But you will have to trust me, so I can help you come into your power."

"Did you say a plant, like in a spy? What are they searching for?"

"There's a rumor mushrooming in the Mystik cities that a chart documenting the whereabouts of some powerful relics is hidden somewhere here in Asile." He swiveled the chair back and forth. "But that is not our concern at the moment. Our lessons are. Shall we begin? Have you ever created any magic, by purpose or by accident?"

I hesitated. "Well, yesterday I created a light globe."

"Only yesterday?" He stilled his chair. "Have you ever created a globe before?"

"By accident, when I was younger. Yesterday, I did it on purpose."

My leg started to shake. I was as nervous as that time I'd been called to the principal's office after reaching my tardy quota. Okay, maybe triple that time.

"You just performed one with no problems or false starts?" he asked.

"I had a few false starts. Arik helped me get it."

"I see. And your mother, did she ever talk about our world?"

"Sort of. I was four when she died, so, you know…" The right corner of my mouth started doing the nervous twitch thing, joining my spasmy leg.

"No. I don't *know*."

"Well, she didn't *tell* me, but told me by way of a story... sort of."

"I see. You resemble her, slightly. Marietta Bianchi." I swear tears were pooling in his eyes. "Your mother used to have the same tremble at the turn of her mouth. It was the only way under her strong Sentinel pretense that I knew when she was nervous."

"And how are you related, again?"

"We share the same mother. I was three when my father died, and shortly after, our mother married Marietta's father. A year afterward, Marietta was born and then taken away by her faery parent to train."

"How did you know about her? I was told no one was aware of the exchanges."

"Very few Sentinels are born to families in the havens," he said. "They're created in the human world, from parents who are distant descendants of the original knights. The ones the fey used to create the Sentinels. Marietta's birth was a rarity. The last such incident happened nearly sixty years ago. The Department of Magic Sciences determined it had to do with an anomaly in the Sentinel gene."

"That had to be strange having the two of them around."

"Changelings aren't allowed to stay in the havens. The truth of what they are and the existence of the Mystik world are kept from them. My parents were forced to relocate into the human world with her. I'd visit occasionally, but not often. They may look the same but a changeling has their own personality. Much like a clone would. The changeling was a horrid sister. Marietta, on the other hand, was a complete angel."

"I would've been born in the havens if my mom stayed here," I said.

"Yes." He stared at something across the room, a

somber expression on his face. "She would have been forced to leave, just as our parents had."

I glanced to where he was looking and it was a photo of him as a teenager wearing a cloak and holding a rolled document. *Graduation?* Was he thinking of how his parents were absent in the photograph as they were in his life?

A smile might have hinted on his lips just then, but I couldn't be sure, not with the weak lighting coming from the lamps. "Marietta and I discovered each other by accident. I knew instantly that she was my sister. Her resemblance to the changeling was precise, down to the mole on her cheek. I can hardly believe Marietta is gone." He spun the chair to face the window.

"But my mother's last name was Costa, not Bianchi. Marty Costa."

"Costa, eh?" He swiveled his chair back to face me. "It's the surname of a childhood friend of hers. She couldn't use her real name. She didn't want to be found."

Of course, she'd changed her name. "That makes sense."

He studied me. "Well, we needn't speak of sad things right off. Shall we get to work, then?"

I swallowed hard. "Sure."

Professor Attwood stood. "Well, then, each Sentinel can perform two globes. One is a light globe, which you can do, and the other is a battle globe." He walked around the desk to me. "Stand up and give me your hand."

I pushed up from my seat and then placed my hand in his.

"We'll start with fire. Flatten your palm." He unfurled my fingers. "Just focus on everything you know about fire. Imagine a flame burning, consuming your mind. Feel the heat. Smell the smoke. Hear the crackle. All magic starts from deep inside you, within the core of your being."

I stood there, thinking about fire. I even roasted a

marshmallow.

"Now, command it by saying *fuoco,* which means—"

"Fire. I know. I took Italian."

"Good. Go ahead and try it."

"*Fuoco!*" I said.

Nothing happened.

"Try it again."

I attempted it several times. Nothing.

"Okay, so we can eliminate fire. Let's try water."

I tried to create water, but it just made me thirsty. Next, I strained to conjure wind. We continued working through his list of possible globes.

A Sentinel's wizard ancestry determined their abilities. Whatever magic was their ancestors' specialty showed up in their globes. And there were many of them. Along with fire and water ones, we tried others—stunning, lightning, smoke screen, wind, and one that was like a sonic wave.

An hour passed without any results. No matter how hard I imagined, or thought, or focused, nothing happened, and I stomped my foot. Maybe I couldn't invoke globes after all. I'd had enough trouble keeping my light from winking out.

As frustrated as I was, he dropped my hand. "There's only one globe left. I hoped it wouldn't be the one."

"Why, is it bad?"

"It can be. It requires the person's blood and getting it from someone can be dangerous. If it's the one, you must promise to do as I say."

Yeah, that didn't just raise a red flag. If I believed in superstitions, I would've crossed my fingers behind my back when I answered, "I promise."

He reached behind me, grabbed a pushpin from a holder on his desk, and pricked his finger with the point. Panic fluttered in my stomach. I hated the sight of blood, and there was no way I was going to make a blood oath with a stranger. There's no telling what kind of diseases might transfer.

"I'm not going to prick you. I want to see if you can create a truth globe. I'm not certain you can. It's a difficult globe to conjure, but an ancestor of yours was able to master it."

I gave him my trembling hand. He turned it over, exposing my palm, and pressed his pricked finger above it. A drop of blood beaded and fell on my skin.

"As I said, you need a blood sample from the person you're verifying to perform this globe." His blood raced along the creases of my skin. "Now, in Italian you'll recite *show me the truth,* which is—"

"*Mostrami la verità.*" Lights flickered above my palm and then vanished.

"Well, we found your globe," he said, his face somber. "Now, try it again."

I tried several times to form the globe. A thin membrane would bud, grow, and shape into a bubble, but before it could fully expand, it popped. Professor Attwood's hand resembled an empty pincushion with all the tiny needle pricks glaring red against his pale skin.

"*Ugh,*" I moaned. "I can't do it."

"Yes, you can. Focus." He let another drop of his blood fall into the cup of my hand.

Tired, hungry, and frustrated, I glared at the pool of blood. Why wouldn't the damn thing form, already? Anger heated my face. There was a tug in my stomach and a vibration ran up my spine. My hand buzzed as if it had fallen asleep, and electric sparks zapped at my fingertips.

"*Mostrami la verità,*" I said.

Like a sprouting seed, a silver globe grew in the palm of my hand.

CHAPTER ELEVEN

I practically jumped with excitement, the globe jiggling in response.

Professor Attwood dropped the pushpin. "There, you have it!" he said. "Now, ask if I'm true. You can say it in any language, and it will answer you in that language. Remember, only keys and charms must be spoken in formal Italian."

"Why are they in Italian?"

"The keys and charms were once in Latin," he said. "A wizard adapted them into Italian. The change made for a better implementation of magic, so it caught on, and soon everyone used his system." He nodded to the globe. "Go ahead and ask."

"Is Professor Attwood true?"

His smoky image appeared in the globe and said in a tinny voice, "I am truthful."

"Now, simply pull your hand into a fist to close the globe."

I closed my hand over the globe, and it popped like a bubble, leaving behind little silver sparks. I sank into my chair and leaned forward, shaking uncontrollably. I wanted to vomit.

"I suspected you might have a reaction to the power," he said. "In a few weeks, your body will get accustomed to the power and the side effects will cease. You can avoid the reaction, by eating a healthy diet. Don't skip meals."

"Yeah, I haven't had breakfast. Or lunch"

Professor Attwood retrieved a juice pouch from a small refrigerator behind his desk and then handed it to me.

I gave the pouch a curious look.

"What's the matter? You don't like punch flavor?"

"No, it's not that. I just thought you'd give me a goblet of something, not this." I fumbled with the wrapping on the straw.

He took the straw, unwrapped it, and stabbed the pouch for me. "I'm addicted to these. The kids bring them back from your world for me." Professor Attwood returned to his seat while I sucked down the sugary goodness. "Truth globe wielders in ancient times were considered thieves. For they stole lies by revealing what was true. Anytime you aren't sure of someone, I want you to use your globe. However, you must be careful. It's best if you can find a way to get their blood secretly."

"Why?"

"If they are untrue, they may kill you just for asking."

"Oh." My shoulders sank. My ability didn't sound very useful. Or safe.

"The globe isn't suitable for battle, but it does come in handy for interrogations." He picked up a pen to take notes. "You won't be a forward Sentinel. Also, you'll feel weak afterward, so make sure to keep something sugary with you."

"What were my parents' globes?"

He looked at me sharply. "Parents?"

Crap. Crap. Crap. Think of something, fast. I tried faking calm, but the stern look on his face made me nervous. "Um, did I say parents? I meant *parent*." *Yeah. Good one.* Can I be any more tragic? I'm obviously not cut out for keeping secrets.

He raised a brow. "I clearly heard *parents*. If you meant your mother, you would have said *mother*. What aren't you telling me?"

I gulped, wavering between telling him about my parents or not. The truth globe had said to trust him. I hoped the hocus-pocus blood trick was legit and decided to go for it. "Carrig is my father. Marietta is my mother. Put the two together and here I am." I forced a grin at the end.

He dropped his pen. "I don't believe it. Why would Marietta defy the warnings? He's a Sentinel, for Christ's sake—a reckless one at that."

Reckless. I filed that away to think about later and bit my lip. Maybe Professor Attwood would tell me Carrig and Arik were wrong, and the prophecy didn't spell disaster. "It's a mistake, right? I can't be the Doomsday Child."

"If you are the presage, I believe you are our salvation, Gia, not our doom." His smile comforted me and I breathed a sigh of relief. "There is a way of knowing the truth. A drop of your blood should do it."

"You want me to perform a globe on *myself*?"

"Or we could just forget about it and never know the truth about your parentage." He didn't do sarcasm well.

Sighing, I snatched a pin from the holder, then sucked in a deep breath and pricked my finger, wincing at the sting. I squeezed the tip, letting a drop of blood fall onto my palm. I thought only of the globe and willed it to life. The familiar pull and tingle rushed through my body. The silver globe sprouted, and I recited the key.

Professor Attwood came around the desk and stood

beside me. "Ask it to reveal your true parents."

"Show me my real parents," I ordered the globe.

A blurry movie played across the surface of it. The actors were Marietta and Carrig. I wanted to reach into the globe and touch my mother. She was so alive, soft brown hair tumbling around her shoulders and full lips pressed together as she stroked Carrig's cheek.

Carrig pulled her into an embrace. "I love you."

"I love you, as well." A bruise shadowed the side of my mother's face. "It's against the laws for us to be together."

Okay, it was more like a *Lifetime* movie, except her bruise bothered me.

"When you were on the verge of death," Carrig continued, "I wanted to die me self. I cannot live without you."

"You are all I think about, my love," she said, tears drenching her cheeks. "I can hardly breathe when you're not around. We'll meet secretly, but we must be careful."

"We will," Carrig said, cupping her face and wiping the tears away with his thumbs.

I glanced at Professor Attwood. "Does that mean they're my parents?"

"The globe shows the truth. It cannot lie." He rubbed his temples. "I remember when Marietta was injured. She came out of the gateway book battered and bloodied. A hound had attacked her, and she was barely alive. Carrig did seem overly concerned about Marietta, and now I know the reason for it."

"Guess they weren't very careful." I popped the globe with my fingertips.

"They were foolish. The cost would've been banishment to—"

"Where? Where would they send them?"

"To Somnium. There are many isolated habitats within

the Somnium. It's a place of limbo. As if being in a dream state of nothingness forever."

"Well, that doesn't sound so bad," I said.

"Can you imagine nothingness? A desolate land that never changes, and where you are alone forever?"

I gulped. "That *does* sound bad. Where is it?"

"The entries into the habitats are in the libraries," he said. "We know the locations of some and use them as prisons. The ones we haven't found are like trap doors. You could come across one without knowing and it'll pull you in."

The traps Arik mentioned. I shuddered. "That's creepy. I'm never going in a library again."

"There is a way of sensing the energy around the entries of Somnium. I'll teach you."

"Well, that's good. I think. But what about humans? What happens if they get sucked into the Som...the Som-thingy?"

"Somnium," he corrected. "Humans are immune to the traps."

That sounded legit. "So what are we going to do about me being...you know?"

He gave me a questioning look.

"The Doomsday Child...the Coming or whatever you guys call it."

"I'm not certain, but we'll sort it out. I need to train you posthaste so you can protect yourself. The attack on the Haven yesterday is only the beginning. I fear other tribes will fall to whatever evil is about." He scribbled something on a notepad. "Is there anyone else who knows who your parents are?"

"Well, Carrig, of course, my Nana, Merl...and Arik."

He placed his pen down. "I wonder why Merl didn't tell me about you."

I shrugged.

"You must perform a truth globe on Arik immediately. I'm going to give you a book on charms and one about the Mystiks. Study ferociously, for you will need to prepare yourself in case of an attack. Learn each Mystik species' weaknesses." He went over to the bookcases and searched for the books. In small ways, his movements reminded me of my mom.

I thought about Pop with Mom. If she'd really cared for him. Then I imagined Pop with my changeling and knew she couldn't love him the way I do, although she probably would over time. Did he notice a difference between us? That she wasn't me? I resented that she'd slipped into my safe life while my whole world spun upside down. But mostly I was sad that she had kind, loving Pop and, except for Nana, I was pretty much alone. I wanted to tell Pop I loved him, but it would be months before I saw him again.

Professor Attwood grabbed several books from the shelf. "Time to go," he said, handing me the books.

"Where are we going?"

With his hand firm on my back, he ushered me swiftly to the door. "I have an appointment coming. You must seek out Arik and find out if he's trustworthy before dinner. I know you already trust him, but we should verify it anyway." He pushed a pamphlet into my hand. "This is a map of the castle. You will find the Sentinels' chambers listed on it. Your room is in the visitor corridor. It's all on the map."

"That's crazy. How do I get his blood?"

"You'll figure a way. Are you afraid of him?"

A picture of Arik flashed through my mind. Tall, broad, with a confident swagger, there was no doubt he could kill if he had to. But I trusted him. He'd saved my life more than once. "No."

"Good. If he wanted, you would already be dead."

"Thanks for that. I feel much better."

He raised an eyebrow at me. "Are you being sarcastic?"

I rolled my eyes. "Duh."

He smiled, which made him look less intimidating. "Just go. We haven't much time."

I had no idea why he was in such a rush. "Why—"

He popped open the door. Standing on the other side was a cloaked man, his hood pulled over to hide his face.

"Excuse me," I said, squeezing by him. The hood slipped back and I recognized the guy. "Hey, I know you."

"I'm sorry, we've never met," he said, moving into the office.

"Well, no, we didn't meet. But you were in the Athenæum with Arik. He said your name. Edgar, right?"

Professor Attwood scooted past him and took my arm. "I must ask you to keep Edgar's visit with me a secret. It's a matter of life or death. His."

I glanced through the crack in the door. Edgar attached a small metal device to Pip's globe. "What's he doing?"

Professor Attwood yanked the door closed. "It's his mission recorder," he whispered. "He's transferring the information to Pip."

"Who is he?"

"I asked you to keep his visit a secret." Professor Attwood gave me a warm smile. "Will you do that for me, and stop asking questions?"

I didn't like not knowing, but his pleading eyes said he wouldn't tell me even if I begged. "Okay," I huffed. Again, someone else wasn't giving me all the information I knew I needed.

"Good, then, I'll see you at dinner." He went back into his office, leaving me staring blankly at the door.

Because I'm the world's worst navigator, following the map Professor Attwood gave me proved a bad idea. After a series of missed turns and hurried backtracks, I ended up in the long corridor containing the Sentinels' rooms. I stopped at the door the professor had marked on the map and pounded on the thick wood. I yanked my hair tie free, letting long brown strands fall past my shoulders. He didn't answer. I knocked louder.

"You are seeking for Arik. No?" a girl barely older than me asked in a French lilt. She embraced a stack of towels as she came down the hall. Her blond hair swept her shoulders with the rhythm of her hips. Plain English words couldn't describe her beauty as well as sexy French ones could.

"Yes," I answered, studying her almond-shaped eyes, their color almost too blue.

"Well, 'e's not zere," she said, eyebrows arched to sharp points. "All Sentinels 'ave been sent on a…how do you say?" She puckered her puffy pink lips as she tried to find the correct word. "A mission, zat's it, no?"

"A mission? Do you know when they'll be back?"

"Perhaps a few days, perhaps weeks, zat's all I know. I'm merely the c'ambermaid."

"Thanks." I hugged the books to my chest so she wouldn't see the titles and headed back the way I'd come.

Before I went around the corner, I gave her a quick once-over. She stood with one hand on her hip and the other balancing the towels as she gave me an icy stare. With biceps like that, there was no way she was a c'ambermaid. She looked like a spy to me. I would have to tell Professor Attwood about her later. Right now, I wanted to get to my room and check in with Nana.

I had an eerie feeling someone was following me as I raced down the hall. I darted glances over my shoulder. Nothing. I skidded around a corner into another empty corridor.

Rubber shoes squeaked across the floor in the hall I'd just left.

I spun around and waited. "*Wh*-who's there?" I called.

No one answered. I hurried around the next corner, my heavy breaths pounding in my ears. Scratching noises sounded above my head. My gaze flew up to the ceiling. Nothing. A thud sounded down the hall, but it was empty.

I made it to my room. The air in the hall turned syrupy. My breaths grew shallow—lungs crushing from the pressure around me. "*Help…*" came out, weak and powerless. My fingers fumbled to get my room key into the lock.

An ominous energy surrounded me. It was like invisible creatures slithered across my skin. Concentrating hard on keeping my hand steady, I slid the key in and then quickly turned it. My head spun and my knees shook. I leaned against the door to steady myself. I wheezed. Spots flickered across my vision.

Panicking, I threw my weight against the door, stumbled into the room, and slammed it shut behind me.

The heavy curtains covering the windows made the room as dark as a cave. A gust of wind came from the window on the right side of the bed, causing the curtains to billow into the room. Just then, the bathroom door flew open, and I screamed. "*Shit*. Holy fu—" I covered my mouth at Nana's stern glare.

Faith sprang out from behind the curtains and then landed in a crouching position between Nana and me.

Nana was wearing a fancy floor-length dress the color of her soft gray eyes. For her age, she had a rocking body. "Gia, what's wrong with you? Slamming doors and swearing like a construction worker."

"Sorry, Nana. But you scared the crap out of me."

I slumped onto the bed. My hands and legs still shook. Something had pursued me from the Sentinel's rooms and tried to suffocate me outside this door. Or had it? I really needed to get a grip. This whole other world thing and spooky castle was getting to me.

"We're late for dinner," Nana said. "It's a formal affair and you'll need to wear a dress."

"I didn't bring a dress."

"There are some in the wardrobe." Nana fastened an earring.

"Faith, it's still daylight," I said. "What were you doing in the curtains?"

Faith straightened. "I felt something was wrong, so I was checking it out."

"But I thought you couldn't be in sunlight?"

"I only burn in *direct* sunlight. I was perfectly safe. Our side is darkened by the castle's shadow at this time of day."

"Well, I'm fine now, so you can go back to bed."

Faith pounced into bed and flung the covers over her head.

"Why are you so jumpy?" Nana asked.

"I can't tell you…"

"We've never had secrets before."

"Really? I would say all this was a *huge* secret on your part." I raised my palms for emphasis. "Wouldn't you?"

"Besides this." She frowned. "We've always been truthful."

"You mean *I've* always been truthful."

Her nose twitched. It's what happens when she's trying not to cry. I felt horrible for being snotty. "Forget about it," I said. "I can't tell you…um…not until I perform a truth globe on you. It's like the light globes, but it shows if someone can be trusted."

"You don't say?" Nana puckered her lips. "That's a

curious globe. We best do whatever it is in my room." Her
gaze flicked to the Faith pile on the bed. "We don't want to
disturb her."

Hunger pains hit me, so I grabbed a handful of straw-
berries, tiptoed after Nana to her room, and shut the door. I
performed the globe on Nana, and she checked out.

Nana smiled. "Never doubt my love for you, dear."

"I'm sorry." I studied my hands. "You know I love you.
It's just that everything"—I glanced up—"all this. It's just so
much to take in. I don't know who to trust anymore."

Nana gave me a tight hug, which helped calm my nerves
and kept me from hyperventilating. "Now, now." She patted
my back. "I know it's scary, but you're a strong girl. You can
handle this, and I'm here to help."

I pulled back and nodded. "Okay." I put on a brave face
for her even though I was terrified.

"Now, go get changed."

I washed my face in the bathroom before returning
to my room, and then searched for a dress to wear. Each
hanger I dragged across the wardrobe bar held one gaudy
dress after another. Whoever had stocked it didn't know
teen girls at all. I stopped at a brandy-colored dress with cap
sleeves, a corseted bodice, and a slight bell skirt. The dress
was more modern than the others. I wiggled it on.

Using Nana's cosmetics, I tried to replicate Afton's
smoky eyes and then pinned my hair up before examining
myself in the bathroom mirror. *Not bad.* I reached for
Nana's lipstick and decided against it, grabbing my root beer
flavored Lip Smacker instead. I imagined Afton's protest
as I swiped my lips with the waxy stick. The thought of my
friend painfully squeezed my heart, and I hoped she and
Nick were safe. She would enjoy dressing up for a formal
occasion like this. I sucked back the emotions threatening to

ruin my makeup and flicked off the light, then joined Nana in the corridor.

"I feel silly, and I can't breathe in this thing," I whispered to her as we approached the dining hall. I adjusted the bodice and scratched under the itchy material.

"Stop fretting. You're stunning."

Nana glided into the dining room. I huddled closer to her. The hundred or so people—and a few creatures—sitting around the many tables glanced up at once. There was a man so hairy he reminded me of Big Foot. Many Laniars were in attendance. A man with slimy looking skin and gills on the side of his head wore a curious suit with clear tubes snaking around it, circulating some sort of liquid. He had to be the Aqualian Faith had mentioned before. Not wanting to stare at the unusual beings, I kept my gaze forward.

Was it a special occasion tonight or was this how they always dressed for dinner? The men wore nice suits with tartans of all colors draped over their shoulders, as cummerbunds around their waists, or as neckties hanging down their starched shirts. Two men actually wore tartan skirts. Unfortunately, their knees were entirely wrong for the look. The women wore Renaissance-style dresses. It was like being in a time warp or at a medieval-themed dinner show. At least my tacky outfit blended in.

I almost tripped when I spotted Arik sitting beside the French girl from the hallway earlier.

C'ambermaid my ass.

CHAPTER TWELVE

The French girl's dress had easy written all over it. With one good cough, the rounds of her cleavage would pop right out the top. There was nothing medieval to the dress. The black sequins belonged on stage with the Pussycat Dolls.

Merl met us. "Wonderful, I see you found your way."

"Is Professor Attwood here?"

"He is. I'm glad you could join our celebration this evening. It's been six hundred years to date since the wizard havens formed their alliance." He offered Nana his arm and led us toward the tables. "Philip has informed me about your globe. I'm very pleased, indeed. No one has possessed a truth globe for centuries. There are so many things we can learn from it, but matters like this should be discussed in private, don't you agree?"

I opened my mouth to answer but shut it, realizing he didn't require a response. He was simply giving me an order.

Professor Attwood and the other men at the table stood as we approached. He pulled out the chair beside him and motioned for me to sit. Merl and Nana continued on to a nearby table.

"This is my niece, Gianna," the professor said.

The women around the table smiled at me from their seats.

"Gia," I blurted, and then added, "It's nice to meet you all." I returned nods as Professor Attwood introduced each person.

"I hear you're Marietta's child," an older woman, whose name I had already forgotten, said.

I shifted in my seat and smiled.

"Auntie Mae, I just told you she's Marietta's daughter," Professor Attwood answered for me.

"Oh yes, that's right. At my age, I can hardly remember my own name." Auntie Mae and I had the whole forgetting names thing in common.

A plate was already waiting at my setting. There were some sardines and green mush stuff artfully arranged on it. I wrinkled my nose. I hated fish—well, just dead ones. I grabbed a few crackers from a plate in the middle of the table and stuffed one in my mouth. When the waiter came by, I handed my untouched plate to him, smiling nervously when he raised an eyebrow.

After searching the dining room, I leaned over to Professor Attwood. "Where's Carrig? I don't see him anywhere."

"He went to Tearmann, the Irish haven. He'll return later tonight." He slanted closer to me. "You will have your first lesson with him at eight in the morning. Try not to be late. Carrig isn't as understanding as I am."

"Yeah, right, he must be a monster, then," I said.

He winked. "I wasn't so awful, was I?"

"Oh. No. Not at all," I said with a sarcastic laugh.

As I listened to the overly English conversation at my table, my attention kept homing in on Arik and the French girl. He caught me staring and smiled. I sucked in a sharp breath and adjusted in my chair, bumping into the soup bowl a waiter was placing in front of me. The soup slopped over the sides and landed on the saucer underneath it. "I'm so sorry," I said.

"It's not your fault," the waiter said. "I apologize for startling you. I'll get you another."

"Oh, no, please, leave it. It's fine."

He bowed his head slightly and backed away.

I tasted a spoonful. It was delicious, so I slurped it down. Before long, another plate landed in front of me. I studied the stuffed pastry. "Okay, what's this?"

"It's Beef Wellington. Eat it. You'll like it." Professor Attwood dissected his with a fork and knife.

I took a bite and was pleased. But the yummy food hadn't removed the bad taste in my mouth. My run-in with that French girl earlier kept annoying me. With everyone around our table distracted in conversation, I took the opportunity to talk to Professor Attwood.

I whispered, "Arik wasn't there when I went to his room earlier. In the hallway, I ran into that French girl who's sitting beside him now. She said he was gone on a mission, and he wouldn't be back for weeks, but he's here at dinner. Isn't that suspicious?"

"He was on a mission this morning. There's nothing to be suspicious about, no one knows how long a Sentinel will be gone." He cut a piece of beef and stuffed it into his mouth.

"She said she was the chambermaid."

He swallowed. "Her name is Veronique Lefevre. She's a Sentinel. She probably wondered why you were snooping around the Sentinel chambers. Anyway, she's here from the French haven."

"Who invited her here?"

"No invitation is needed. We move freely among our allies, and last I checked, France is our ally."

Auntie Mae's dinner knife slipped and clanked against

the plate as she tried to cut her beef. I glanced up and spotted Arik heading in our direction, wearing a black suit with a purple and black tartan cummerbund. He flashed me his dimples, and my breath caught. My knife slipped from my fingers and clunked onto the table.

Auntie Mae gave me an amused look. Another thing we had in common—klutzy hands.

Arik addressed the table, his gaze landing on me. "Good evening. May I have a word with Miss Kearns in private, Professor Attwood?"

The sound of my name off his lips melted me.

Professor Attwood wiped his mouth. "Certainly. It's entirely up to Gia, of course."

"Sure." I bolted out of my seat and instantly regretted it, hoping I didn't look too eager. I took a calming breath before saying, "Excuse me," to the table. Arik led me to the patio.

He gave me a sidelong glance. "You look lovely this evening."

His comment startled me. "No, I don't."

He smirked, his cheeks dimpling again. "I assume you're the type who doesn't know how to respond to a compliment. All you have to do is say 'thank you' and blush a little. Try it."

My cheeks were burning, so I definitely had the blushing part down. "Thanks. You look pretty hot yourself."

Something whizzed by my head. I spun around, searching for what I hoped wasn't some big, disgusting flying bug. Hovering in midair, right in front of my face, was an oval black stone the size of my fist. It slowly rotated until a yellow eye stared at me.

"It's only a surveillance eye," Arik said, placing a hand on my lower back and guiding me to the stone wall that encircled the patio. "There are several of them throughout the castle. The eyes connect to the Monitor."

The warmth of his hand on my waist sent a jolt of excitement through my body. I stepped away from him and placed both my hands on the cool stone banister to steady myself. "You mean Pip?" I glanced back at the floating eye.

"Yes. He reports any suspicious activities to Professor Attwood."

"What did you want to talk to me about?" I asked.

"How are you coping?" A strand of dark hair fell across his brow, and I wanted to smooth it back.

The night was chilly, so I wrapped my arms around myself to keep warm. "It's definitely been strange, but I'm adjusting."

"You're cold." He took off his jacket.

"No. Don't do that. I'm—"

He ignored my protests and draped his jacket over my shoulders, his fingers brushing my arms. Were the goose bumps dancing across my skin from him or the chilly air?

"Thank you," I said, inhaling his aroma on the jacket. There was a hint of some sort of cologne and the outdoors scenting the fabric.

"Veronique said she came across you at my door today. What did you need?"

"She told me she was the chambermaid."

"You startled her when she came from the linen cupboard. She'd never seen you before. For all she knew, you were a spy or a compelled."

"Do I really look like I'm compelled to you? And besides, I don't even know what one looks like."

"You could be one. They are normal people possessed by a wizard and compelled to do whatever the wizard wishes. When the wizard is working his magic through a compelled, the air around the individual is thick with power and it's difficult for anyone nearby to breathe—"

"Wait." I said and gripped his arm. "Are you kidding me? I felt that way earlier when I went back to my room."

"Are you certain? Veronique also felt it in the corridor. She said the feeling left with you."

"Yes, I'm sure. It freaked me out." I peeked over my shoulder and spotted Veronique sitting by Arik's empty chair. She focused on me as if she wanted me gone or dead. My bet was on the latter. "I didn't feel it in your hallway, though."

"When you haven't encountered it before, you might not notice it right off." He turned so his back was against the wall and he faced the dining hall. "Then whoever was in the corridor was following you, not her." His eyes searched the room as he spoke. "I think our secret about you is out."

"About that. Remember you told me to trust no one? I have to be certain you are true…" I trailed off, trying to think of how to ask him to give me a blood sample.

"I've had plenty of opportunities to kill you. If I wanted to, I'd have done it in your bedroom." He gave me a wicked smile, which made me wonder if he was thinking back to my skimpy cami. My cheeks felt even hotter. "You can trust me."

He was right. He'd had plenty of opportunities to shank me. I gathered my nerve. "Well, I need some of your—"

Gross. Blood freaked me out. In First Aid class, they'd taught us to use gloves to avoid catching diseases. Now, I'd become the official blood handler of the havens—no gloves required.

"Just spill it. What do you need?"

Well, how ironic. I actually wanted him to *spill it.* "I need a drop of your blood."

"I assume the good ol' professor found your globe. I'm impressed. Truth globes were believed to be extinct." He turned his back to the dining room. "Come closer to me."

Don't mind if I do. I scooted to his side.

He tugged a knife from an inside pocket of his dinner jacket. We stood shoulder to shoulder, facing the dark pastures, to shield the diners' view. He poked his index finger with the tip of his knife and grabbed my hand.

My stomach turned at the sight of the crimson streak he smudged onto my pale palm. Holding my breath, I performed the truth ritual. When the Arik in the globe said he was truthful, I expelled the air I held in my lungs.

I grabbed the wall, bracing myself. Lights floated across my vision. My arms and legs trembled. Every muscle felt like it had been through an intense workout.

"Are you all right, Gia?"

"Yeah, I'll be fine," I said. "Excuse me. I should go wash my hands."

Arik escorted me to the restroom. I handed his jacket to him before I went in. Staring at Arik's blood drying on my palm, it comforted me to know he was on my side, but I desperately wanted to learn more about him and Veronique. After checking the stalls of the bathroom to assure I was alone, I went to the sink.

"*Mostrami la verità*," I said. "Show me the truth about Arik and Veronique."

I almost dropped the globe when it showed the two kissing in what must be his room. A feverish kiss like that led to other things. *Please stop*, I pleaded in my head. As if someone had heard me, a loud knock came from the bedroom door in the globe.

"Arik?" A male's faint voice came from the door. "What are you two doing in there?"

Arik pulled away from Veronique. His voice came through the globe in a high electric pitch. "Bugger, it's Demos. We can't…the rules."

She placed her lips on his again and muttered against them. "I don't care about ze rules."

The knock sounded louder.

"Come on, Merl's in the corridor," a girl's voice I recognized called out. *Lei?*

The globe slipped from my hand and popped against the edge of the sink. *Gah. How stupid are you, Gia? Guys like Arik don't like girls like you.*

I was crazy to think he would. I was nowhere near as sexy as Veronique. There was no competition. Game over.

I scrubbed my palm clean under the scorching tap water. As I dried my hands, Veronique walked into the restroom. Her hips snapped back and forth as she clunked in on spiky high heels.

"Well, fancy meeting you here, no?"

"No. I mean, sure, whatever." I tried to get by her. "Excuse me."

She fixed a look on me. "How are you adjusting to ze havens?"

"I guess okay," I said, feeling uncomfortable at the concern on her face. Or guilty for not liking her after seeing her with Arik in that globe.

"Vell, if you need, I'm 'appy to help out." She smiled and swiped a lipgloss wand across her lips, staining them red.

Arik was leaning against the wall when I walked out of the bathroom. The smile on his face slipped, and he hurried over to me. "What's the matter? Did something happen?"

I dropped my gaze. "I don't get it. Why would you say you liked me when you're already with someone else?"

"Pardon?" he said.

My stare found his. "Veronique?"

He didn't say anything for several rushing beats of my heart. Not until his confused look changed to something like understanding. He smiled then. "There's nothing there, but I gather you've already formed an opinion of me. Maybe it's best to leave it at that. I'll show you to your seat."

"Sure. Fine. But I can find my own seat." I headed for the dining room, acutely aware of Arik's steps behind me.

He followed me the entire way back, and I avoided eye contact as he pulled the seat out for me. "Thank you," I said, sitting.

"Good evening," he said and nodded to the others at the table.

I snatched up my napkin and placed it on my lap. Everyone was too busy eating their desserts to notice how shaky my hands were. I stared at the dessert in front of me.

"It's a sticky toffee pudding," Professor Attwood said. "Eat it—"

"I know. I'll like it, right?"

The corners of his mouth turned up slightly. "I fear I'm becoming predictable."

Veronique smiled at me as she meandered past to her table, hips doing that snapping thing. I frowned as she placed her hand on Arik's forearm and, as Nana would say, *kittenishly* giggled at whatever he was saying.

Nothing there, my ass.

I dug my spoon into the sticky toffee and took a big bite.

N ot long after dinner, I sat at the desk in my room, leafing through the books Professor Attwood had given me. It felt good to be free from that corseted contraption. *How the hell did women eat back in those days?*

Reading about charms, spells, and all the stuff wizards could do was fascinating and scary at the same time. Some wizards had the ability to weave their minds to another person's or even two minds together that weren't their own. They used it for spying, and in some cases, stealing identities.

I yawned. "Great. Now we need firewalls for our brains."

I closed the book on charms, set it aside, and decided to read more about the Mystiks in *The Invisible Places* by Gian Bianchi, Professor of Wizardry. Someone had written a poem on the page before the first chapter. Black ink drops and a fingerprint smudged it. The title was in Italian, but the verse was in English, which struck me as strange.

Libero IL Tesoro

A religious man's charm hangs from his vest;
A school of putti, one of which sees further
than the rest;
Strong women flank the ceiling, the one in
Sentinel dress holds an enchanted point small
in size;
Behind Leopold she stands, one hand resting
on a crown and the other
holding a rolled prize;
With numbers in her mind and knowledge in
her hands, on her brow a crown does rest;
In front of the world, he wears his honor on
his chest;
Beneath destruction and rapine, he scribes the
word, while time falls;
All these things are within the library walls.

Poetry was all rhyme and no reason sometimes. Afton loved this stuff, and I wished she were here to help me make sense of it. I flipped the pages to the first chapter. Reading always helped me fall asleep, and this book looked boring enough to put me out fast.

The chapter was about how mystical beings once lived openly with humans, without concern for who witnessed their powers or their unusual exteriors. The number of humans grew rapidly until they surpassed the Mystik races. Some of the Mystiks turned evil, killing humans for food or for rituals. Out of fear, humans hunted and killed Mystiks— even the innocent ones—wiping out entire covens.

The Mystiks feared the differences between their races and refused to band together against the humans, so many of the weaker Mystiks sought help from the wizards. That's when the wizards cloaked their havens and built cities nearby for the gentler Mystiks to live protected. The gateway books were created by the fey to make travel between the havens faster. To keep rogue Mystiks from traveling through the gateway books and killing humans, the wizards commissioned the fey to create a force of magical knights—the Sentinels. With the help of their new force, the Wizard Council took control of the gateways and libraries. And because of the Sentinels, only eight percent of the nearly hundred attacks on humans each year by Mystiks ended up in loss of life.

I stretched my hands over my head and yawned. "Still, that's like eight deaths a year."

The next chapter was about Laniars. Mostly, it was the same stuff Faith had told me the night before. *Wait.* Where was Faith? I glanced around the room. She should have been there protecting me already. By the bed, her bag lay on its side, books, magazines, and a variety of small things strewn across the area carpet. Amber liquid dripped from an open can of an energy drink tipped over on the nightstand.

I could have kicked myself for not realizing earlier she wasn't in my room. If I didn't learn to be more aware of my surroundings—and quickly—we could be in serious danger.

CHAPTER THIRTEEN

I barreled into Nana's room. "Have you seen Faith? She told me she had to guard me at night."

Nana—mummified in the covers of the bed with her hands barely poking out to hold the book she was reading— peeked over her reading glasses at me. "Perhaps Merl summoned her?" Nana reached over and picked up the beige handset to a landline on the bedside table.

"You have a *phone*?" I had tried my cell phone several times and couldn't get reception.

"You can't make calls outside of Asile with it. One moment, it's ringing. Yes," Nana answered whoever was on the other line. "Merl, please." She placed her hand over the mouthpiece of the phone. "When did you see her last?"

"We saw her just before dinner, remember?"

Someone on the other line answered. "Why hello, Merl, dear. I'm so sorry to bother at such a late hour, but Gia is concerned for Faith—" He must have said something to cut her off. "No, she isn't here, and we haven't seen her since before dinner." She paused. "All right, we'll see you in a few."

After Nana hung up the phone, she slipped on her

robe and rushed into the bathroom. I followed. She started brushing her hair.

"How can you worry about your hair at a time like this?"

"Well, Merl and I did go for a romantic walk after dinner, and I think he was pretty darned close to kissing me."

Ew. Find a happy place. "Did you use a love spell on him?"

She twisted the bottom of a lipstick until a well-used red nub extended from the case, then swiped her finger across the red stick and patted the cream lightly onto her lips. "No, I didn't use a *love spell on him.* I don't use charms for my own benefit. I love the mess of life. I hate when things come too easy."

"Hand me the brush. You have a rat's nest on the back of your head." I took the brush and smoothed out the knot in her hair. Afterward, I paced until someone knocked on the door.

Nana opened the door. Merl wasn't alone. The Sentinels flanked him, wearing their battle gear.

"Has she returned?" Merl asked.

"No, but do come in," Nana urged.

Merl shook his head. "I haven't much time. Searchers and surveillance eyes are hunting the grounds for Faith as we speak. I gave her strict orders to stay with Gia and she'd never go against them." Worry weighed on his face, deepening the hint of wrinkles at his eyes.

Arik leaned against the doorframe, his heavy-lidded brown eyes studying me through the eyeholes of his helmet, arms folded, head cocked.

"Kale will stay here with you," Merl said. "Keep your doors locked and do not open them until I return."

I'd go nuts waiting to hear whether Faith was okay or not. I might not trust her totally yet, but I'd feel horrible if something happened to her because of me. "I want to help search for her."

"I'd prefer you stay here where it's safe," Merl said.

"She can tag along with me," Arik said. "I'll make certain she doesn't get into trouble."

"I'll get changed," I said, without waiting for a reply from Merl. Though I didn't want to be alone with Arik and have my feelings go all berserk over him again, he was my only way out of this room.

Our footsteps echoed across the wide corridors and high, arched ceilings as Arik and I searched the classroom and dorm halls without saying a word, which was completely uncomfortable.

Arik finally broke the silence. "You okay?"

"I'm good."

"I like your hair curly like that."

I brushed my fingers through my hair. The curl was from the bun I had in it earlier. "Thanks." The flutter in my stomach returned. I told myself he didn't mean anything by it, not with him having the hottest girl on the planet as a girlfriend.

"Are you feeling better? You were homesick…"

"Oh that, yes, thanks." We rounded a corner. "But now I'm worried about Faith."

"I'm sure she's fine," he said.

"Then why all the fuss? You know, why the search party and all?"

"You got me there. I was trying to ease your concerns." He searched the corridor. "Merl *is* worried. Faith would never leave her duty. With the current uprising in the Mystik world and a compelled at large in Asile, we're on heightened alert. Anything abnormal must be investigated."

I glanced at him sharply. "You guys haven't found the compelled, yet?"

"No. There wasn't any data recorded by the surveillance

eyes during yours and Veronique's encounter with the unfortunate soul. Not in the Sentinel hall or in the hall to your room. Whoever it was knows how to avoid our security."

I couldn't speak, fear muting my voice, the dim corridors suddenly feeling more sinister. Could someone have done something bad to Faith? Why? Was it because she was protecting me? My thoughts went to that feeling I had in the hallway. Maybe I led whoever it was straight to Faith.

When we came into the Sentinels' section of the castle, Veronique stepped out of her room wearing tight yoga pants and an even tighter t-shirt. She spotted Arik and me together and gave me the death stare again.

Fantastic. My shoulders straightened. The girl really was hot.

"What's 'appening?" she asked, her French accent lacing her words. "Zere's been much agitation in zee hall."

"We're searching for Faith. Have you seen her?"

"No. Shall I 'elp?"

"If you care to," Arik said.

I forced a smile. "It's probably nothing. Faith might just be out doing whatever Faith does." I wished she wouldn't come with us.

"No, no, I want to 'elp. Just a moment," she said and went back into her room. I hoped she was putting on a bra. When she came back out, she had a breastplate on and her sword strapped to her side.

A horn sounded somewhere outside the castle and we took off down the hall. We flew around several corners until we reached a door and barged through it.

The sky was purple with the threat of dawn. I dashed across the slippery, wet grass after the shadows of Arik's compact body and Veronique's svelte frame. The other Sentinels and some people I didn't recognize had gathered on the pasture down the hill from the castle. A pale figure was shackled to one of the thick maple trees.

I stopped beside Arik and Veronique. My stomach dropped. It couldn't be.

Arik turned and grabbed my shoulders. "Let's go back to your room."

"No."

I pulled away from Arik and ran toward the tree. Jaran tried to head me off, but I darted around him. And froze. It was her. "Faith!"

She was kneeling in the mud, her stone-white arms shackled across the tree. Head limp. Chin against her chest.

Arik trapped me in his strong arms. "You don't want to see this," he said.

"No. No. *No!*" I clung tight to him. Salty rivers ran down my cheeks. "It's all my fault," I whispered against his chest.

"It's no one's fault," Arik said, holding me up. His tenderness surprised me.

"It is too. It's because of me she's—" I stopped when I spotted Merl crossing the field.

"Everyone except for the Sentinels, go back to your rooms." Merl shooed the crowd and rushed to the tree. "Go on. Do as I say." He dropped to his knees in front of Faith and lifted her chin. "She's still alive," he called out. "Someone, fetch me the cutters."

I struggled to get loose from Arik's arms, but he tightened his grip. "Stay here. There's nothing you can do. You'll only be in the way."

Jaran returned with the chain cutters. While Merl held up a section of links, Jaran chopped at them. Sparks flew out from the impact.

"It won't budge." Jaran dropped the tool to the ground. "It's charmed."

Faith moaned and shook her head. "Leave me!" she howled like an injured animal.

Veronique pulled her sword from its scabbard and swung it at the chain. The blade connected with the links, chiming as loud as a church bell, but still it held tight. She stumbled against the force. "What 'as you?"

Merl glanced at the horizon. The purple sky had turned a dark pink, announcing the arrival of the sun. "Who did this to you?" he asked.

"I did this to me."

"Why?"

"Leave me. He's compelling me. I'm to kill you and Gia. I can't. I refuse to hurt you, Merl. And it's my duty to protect Gia. *Let me die.*"

"Someone wants to kill Merl and Gia?" Veronique asked. "Why?"

I pulled from Arik's grasp and ran to Merl's side. "Who's compelling you?" I choked out.

"I didn't see…he was cloaked." Faith lifted her gaze to me. "I'm so sorry about scaring you in the corridor."

"That was you?" The memory of Faith hiding in the drapes in my room flashed in my mind.

"These are my charmed shackles." Merl turned to the Sentinels. "Demos, go and retrieve the keys from my office."

"He won't find them," Faith said weakly as Demos bolted back to the castle. "They're hidden." A fierce look passed over her face, and she bared her teeth.

I stumbled back. "What's happening to her?"

"She's lost her will against the compulsion," Arik said.

"Someone take Gia to her room," Merl said. "Veronique, give me your sword."

"I'll take 'er." Veronique gave him her sword and grabbed me.

"No. Wait." She yanked my arm, but I didn't budge. "What are you going to do?"

"It's an act of mercy." Merl's voice cracked, and he cleared his throat before continuing. "I cannot reverse the charm on the shackles without the key. We can't chop the tree down. It's too thick. If we use magic…fire or lightning… we'd certainly kill her." Merl glanced at me. "Faith is like a daughter to me. I don't want her to suffer. Dying by sunlight is very painful."

"You have to wait for Demos," I begged. "He's getting the keys."

"You heard Faith, she hid them." Merl's eyes were glossy, his jaw tight.

I ran to Faith. "No! I won't let you kill her."

She pushed against the chains, gnashing her teeth and swiping the air as she tried to reach me. Arik jumped between us, pushing me back. "You want to get bit?" he said.

"There has to be something we can do," I said, dropping to the ground on my knees, just out of Faith's grasp. I covered my mouth with my hand to stop my sobs. But nothing could stop them. I shut my eyes tight. *This can't be happening. She can't die.*

The tears tumbling from my cheeks and nose landed on my hand. My palms pulsed and tiny tingles pricked my skin. I opened my hands and stared at my palms. They burned, but they weren't on fire. A pink glow swathed my eyes. For a long moment, I believed it was the pink light of sunrise and expected Faith to crumble before my eyes, but she didn't. Instead, the charmed shackles fell to the ground, releasing her. I stumbled to my feet.

Veronique stood gaping at us. "What just 'appened?"

"Get back." Arik pointed his sword at Faith. Veronique snatched hers from the ground where Merl must have dropped it and aimed it toward Faith as well.

"Get Gia away," Merl ordered, a ball of electricity swirling between his hands. "It's not safe."

"Don't hurt her!" I rushed toward the tree. Arik grabbed me around my waist, lifting my feet off the ground.

"Let me go!" I kicked his shin. He flinched, but kept his hold on me.

Merl threw the ball at Faith. The charge sparked across her skin, and she collapsed to the ground, bound by electric cords of light. He kneeled beside her, placed his fingertips around her face, and closed his eyes.

Faith's eyes rolled back, exposing the whites of her eyes. Her body shook violently.

I twisted in Arik's arms. "He's killing her!"

"Hush," he said. "He's only searching to see if she's still being compelled."

Merl removed his hand and the pulsing cords binding Faith disappeared. "Do you desire to kill me?" asked Merl.

"No."

"And Gia. Do you wish to kill her?"

"No." Faith shot me a smile. "Am I free?"

"Yes, but I want you to come with me. I must run a few tests to make sure you're completely released." Merl stretched his hand to her and helped her up. "Hurry. The sun is almost up."

Veronique turned to the others. "Did you see zat bubble?"

Merl released Faith's hand. "I think it was a rather large globe."

"Did it remove ze charm?" Veronique pressed.

"I'm not certain. I will have to look into it further." Merl headed up the hill. "We must hurry and get Faith to safety." Lei threw a black cloak around Faith's head and hurried along with them.

"You can let me go now," I snapped at Arik.

He released me. "Can you wait here with me? I want to talk to you alone."

"Why? What do you want?" I wasn't in the mood for a tongue-lashing, and only stayed because I was curious to hear what he had to say. The crowd broke up, and most moseyed up the path back to their rooms.

Veronique hovered behind. "Shall I wait for you?"

Arik removed his helmet. "No, there's no need."

She pouted and stormed after the last of the gawkers, leaving Arik and me alone.

I kept my gaze on the sun rising over the hills. I didn't want to play nice, I had a throbbing headache and my body was weak. "What do you want?"

"You were inside a bubble. It expanded beyond you and engulfed Faith. Then the shackles unlocked."

His revelation scattered my anger and I teetered off balance. I looked around, like some of the pink light might still be swirling about, and shook my head. How I'd done... whatever...was a mystery. "So, what was it?"

"I don't know. Are you all right?"

My legs were rubbery, and I was dizzy. And a little shocked. No, really shocked. A few days ago I couldn't conjure a spark of light without help and now I was flinging pink globes. "Um...maybe...I think so."

He dropped his helmet and cupped my shoulders, rotating me to face him. "This all has to be frightening for you."

His tenderness blew away the last of my irritation and my head drooped. "I'm—"

"And don't say you're fine. You don't have to be strong around me." He leaned closer with a serious look on his face.

I held my breath. He was too close. I took a shaky step

back from him, but stopped when he stared at me with a frustrated look.

He dragged his fingers through his messy helmet hair. "I apologize... I didn't mean..."

I stared off at the empty field. "No worries. I get it. We're just friends."

"*Just* friends, huh?" He sighed. "Friends don't think of each other the way I think of you. The danger you face. I feel driven to protect you. Maybe it's because I admire you so much. Facing a world you know nothing about and not cowering in a corner. You fought me—hard—to save someone you'd just met who wanted to kill you. And pushed me away when you were wounded so I could guard your friends. But that makes me worry about you more, because you're not being careful."

My chest tightened. I wondered what his game was. What he wanted from me, when he already had someone else, someone hot and sexy. "What do you want me to say to that?"

"I don't know. Something. Anything. Nothing."

"Okay, how about Veronique. The rules. Remember them?" Despite my resentment that he'd sort of led me on, I didn't want Arik banished to a prison in Somnium. No one deserved being tormented by an eternity of nothingness.

He heaved a deep sigh. "We've been here before. I told you there's nothing there."

I snorted. "Well, the body language between you two the other night suggests differently." I exhaled a slow breath. No need getting upset about it—there was nothing between us. I threw my hands up. "I'm sorry. I get it. You guys have to keep it a secret. But how can you risk being with her? That's a real dumbass thing to do."

He looked like I'd just slapped him.

"Listen," I said. "I just want to be your friend. I could definitely use one. I feel so lost here."

"Then there's nothing left to say." He stalked off toward the castle. "Are you coming? I must see you safely to your room."

"*You* have to see me safely to my room?" I called after him, rushing up the path. "What part of me screams damsel in distress to everyone around here?"

He stopped short and spun around. "Don't be daft. You're not safe. And play fighting won't cut it here. You've never fought a Mystik creature. It's not a game."

Daft? After that, I *really* wanted to punch him.

"I leave for a mission in the morning," he said over his shoulder as he led me to a side door. "Carrig will be here to watch over you."

"I don't need *watching over.*"

A frustrated breath punched out his nose. He shoved on the bar to open the door and leaned against it, holding it for me. His muscles rose and fell in all the right places on his body, and his nearness as I passed caused a shiver to run across my skin.

Silence clouded us all the way to my room.

"Hey," he said when we reached my door. "I apologize. Regardless of you being the…"

"Doomsday Child," I finished for him.

"I didn't say that."

"You didn't have to."

"I *meant*, even though the Coming has already happened—" He punched out a breath. "Regardless of how I feel, the laws are still the laws. I'm the leader of our band of Sentinels, and I must follow them."

Just like you followed them with Veronique? I knew a lame excuse when I heard one.

When I didn't respond, he added, "Try to stay out of trouble while I'm gone."

"You're not my pop." My hands shook at my sides as I thought about what he said. *Friends don't think of each other the way I think of you.* How can he say something like that when he's with another girl? I didn't buy any of his reasons. That he admired me? I'm nothing but a fraud, like I'm playing Nick's video games and pretending this is all make believe.

He grunted and his boots clacked down the hall.

I was not going to stamp or yell. I would not show him any weakness. "Goodbye, Arik...and be careful." I turned the knob and pushed the door open.

"Good evening," he grumbled.

I watched him until he vanished around the corner. Not once did he look back.

"Are you coming or going?" Lei flipped through one of my books, her crossed legs resting on top of the desk. Her hair hung like a shiny black curtain over the back of the chair. Her sword and scabbard were still strapped to her thin waist.

I shut the door and bolted the lock. "Why are you here?"

"I'm on duty until your bodyguard returns." She continued scanning the book. "Wow, did you know there were this many battle globes?"

I peered over her shoulder. "Actually, I did. Uncle... Professor Attwood showed me all of them earlier. What's your globe?"

"It's a lightning globe."

"What are the other Sentinels' globes?"

"Jaran performs a water globe," she said. "Once he flooded the National Library of Austria. Demos can do a wind globe. Stay away when he has one going...he's careless. Kale's is a stun globe. He stunned himself once in Madame Tussaud's in London. None of us could undo it, so we propped him up next to some Bollywood stars while we waited for a wizard to release him. People believed he was one of the wax figures and were taking pictures with him. It was rather hilarious."

"Why were you in Madame Tussaud's?"

"We chased a rabid feral there."

"A what?"

"They're shifters who only change into cats. Anyway, Arik can do a fire globe. He's the best. He can manipulate the fire into a thin whip, and he never hits walls or books. I can't wait to see which globe is yours." She turned a page and yanked her hand back. "Love a duck! Paper cut."

Lei dropped her feet to the floor and examined the cut. "It's a ghastly one. Those pages are thick." A couple drops of her blood fell onto the desk. She slipped her finger into her mouth and hustled to the bathroom.

Two tiny puddles of her blood beaded on the lacquer finish. I stared at the crimson pools before glancing at the bathroom door, which was slightly ajar. The faucet ran, and Lei hunted through the cabinets.

I swiped her blood off the desk with my finger and smudged it on my palm. Professor Attwood's warning caused me to hesitate. If she were untrue, she just might off me with that extremely sharp katana sword of hers. Before completely psyching myself out of doing it, I ignited a globe. "Can I trust Lei?"

"What's that?" Lei asked, coming back into the room.

I gasped as she crossed the distance between us, her hand on the handle of her sword. *Why the hell is her hand always near her sword?*

CHAPTER FOURTEEN

"Yes, I am trustworthy," Lei's image said within the globe. Lei's lips parted into a wide grin. "Brilliant. Yours is a truth globe."

"Huh?" I totally wasn't expecting that response. My body shook as the energy faded from it.

"Well, that's good." Nana said from the doorframe of the bathroom. "It would have been awkward if you weren't true, Lei." Nana went to the wardrobe, pulled out a nightgown and robe, and snatched my toiletry bag from the shelf. "Kale told me you found Faith. Is she okay?"

"Yes, she's fine," I said, with a hitch in my voice as I recalled Faith's limp body shackled to the tree. "But it was so *horrible*." She shut the wardrobe door. "What are you doing with my things?" I asked.

"You should take a hot bath and relax," Nana said. "It's been a long night."

"Go and take a soak, Gia, and I'll give Ms. Kearns the details," Lei said.

I snapped up a banana from the silver tray and peeled it. By the time I reached the bathroom, I had scarfed it down, my cheeks full like a squirrel storing nuts. After skinning out of my clothes, I sank to chin level in the hot water. For a few moments, I pretended I was home in my own tub. I missed Pop like crazy. I stayed motionless, letting the warmth caress me. When I felt better, I pulled myself out, dried off, and slipped on my nightgown and robe. I wiped the steam off the mirror and ran a comb through my wet hair, pausing mid-tangle at a knock on the door.

"Come in."

Lei eased in and stood behind me. I eyed her image in the mirror. We were almost the same height, but I was about an inch taller. "You're upset?"

"I'm fine." *Why am I always saying that? Am I fine? Or just trying to convince myself I am?* It wasn't like everyone in Asile was mean to me. *Well, except Veronique.* "Hey, what do you know about Veronique?"

"She's a nutter bunny." Lei studied herself in the mirror and rubbed at a black smudge under her left eye. "She's always throwing herself at Arik. I think he fancied her once, but it fizzled out after she showed her true spots. Be careful around her. The girl is dodgy."

So they're not together. Maybe I had a chance after all.

I smiled and dragged the comb through my hair again. "You have to admit she's beautiful."

"Yeah, a beautiful snake."

I laughed. "Why do you say that?"

"She spent a year at academy training with us," she said. "She had been privately trained before then. Sentinels work together in battles. She wasn't a team player. She only wanted to be the top Sentinel in all the games."

"Did she come out on top?"

"No. She could never beat Arik."

I smiled at that.

She gave me a curious look. "Do you like Arik?"

I paused, and then shrugged. "Of course, I do. I like you, too."

"I meant *like* like him."

"Does it show?"

"Like a nasty gash in your arm."

"Gross. Only a warrior uses analogies like that one."

She pursed her lips. "Was it too much?"

I picked up Nana's jar of face cream, scooped some out with my fingertips, and rubbed it onto my face. "Who am I kidding? I can't compete with Veronique. Heck, I don't even know if I want to try."

She gave me a sympathetic smile. "You haven't got the correct picture of yourself. Perfect heart-shaped face. Huge green eyes. Pouty lips. Your features are amazing. Men like to shake it up with a vixen like Veronique. But when it comes to love, they go for something deeper. Like you."

I gave her reflection an appreciative smile. "Thanks."

"It's useless, anyhow. You're a Sentinel, and it's illegal to be with another one."

I wiped the cream from my face with a wet washcloth. I decided not to tell her I was the Doomsday Child and it didn't matter if Arik and I were both Sentinels.

"Besides, we're supposed to stay pure for our betrothals."

Betrothal for *Sentinels*. But I was something different. No matter what Carrig said, I wouldn't be forced to marry a stranger.

She picked up Nana's perfume bottle, removed the cap, and sniffed it. "But don't worry," she said, wrinkling her nose at the smell. "It's eight years until wedded bliss, so a little flirtation is fine. Just don't get caught snogging, and whatever you do, don't bonk."

"Listen, I'm tired. I'm going to bed." I padded to the bed.

"Right-o," she said. "If you need me, I'll be on the couch."

"Okay." I yawned and slipped under the covers, tugging the curtains around the bed closed. As I drifted off, I thought about Pop and hoped Deidre was taking good care of him.

The dream came when I closed my eyes, on the edge of sleep. The wizard from the tapestry, Taurin, sat at an enormous wooden desk, writing something with a quill under the glow from a candelabrum. He didn't look so much a wizard as he did a king.

"Pardon my intrusion, Taurin."

Taurin looked up. "Ah, Athela, do enter."

Clutching a burlap sack to her chest, she hesitated before gliding to him, her elaborate dress trailing behind her. Her delicate face wore concern. "I wish to speak of thy son."

"Barnum?" He sounded surprised. "He's been dead for months, what have thee left to say?"

"My father has done a terrible deed that involves Barnum."

Taurin straightened. "Go on."

Athela seemed to look directly at me. "May we have privacy, please?"

"Of course, milady," the voice belonging to the body I was in said.

The man marched out the door and stopped just around the corner, where he hid in the shadows to view Taurin and Athela through the open door.

"I wish to speak of the four creatures my father calls the Tetrad. The havoc they have created with the elements was inhumane. The earthquake, storms…fires…so many dead… so many…women and children… infants." Each word was drenched with tears and her voice got softer until the last word was barely a whisper. "It is my father's doing. He should be held accountable for such atrocities."

Taurin stood, came around the desk, and handed her a silk hanky. "Thou art not to worry about the Tetrad. We have entombed it within a mountain."

She took the cloth and wiped her eyes. "My father used me to lure the beast. How could he risk…he knew the man-lion creature would be distracted by me. I recognized him straight off. It was Barnum."

"Thou art mistaken."

"No!" Athela shook her head. "He recognized me, as well, and he told me it was him. The other beings were his fellow warriors who died in the same battle. My father resurrected them and turned them into *those* creatures."

"It cannot be," Taurin muttered.

"Scry me if thou must. See for thyself." She lifted Taurin's hand and placed his open palm on her cheek. "*Please,*" she said, putting so much force behind the word that my heart broke for her.

Taurin spread his fingers across her face and lowered his head. Athela's body trembled and her eyes rolled back. Taurin's face twitched and twisted with a mix of sorrow and pain. It went on for several minutes before he let Athela go.

"It is the truth—Barnum—my son." His eyes settled on Athela's face. "Thou art with his child."

"I am."

"I must call on the Wizard Council."

"Thou must not. My father has poisoned the Council."

She dropped the bag on the table, whatever was inside clanking together. One by one, she withdrew several metal rods the length of her hand and placed them on the table. "I found these in my father's chambers."

"The Chiavi," Taurin said.

"Yes, all but the seventh. My father took the Chiavi from the other wizards. He will come for yours, then control the Tetrad. He wants to rule all the kingdoms. Thou must hide them from him."

"My sons and I will suffer this. Mykyl will not care that thou art his daughter. He will seek revenge for betraying him."

"A trusted servant waits with a carriage for me and I will leave this moment to—"

"Do not tell me where you will go. Tell no one else. Just go now, and do not ever return, for thy sake and my grand-child's sake."

Athela kissed his cheek and turned to leave.

As the man I occupied ran down the hall to get away before Athela came out of Taurin's chamber, I knew he was heading to Mykyl to inform him that Taurin had all the Chiavi. I was also aware I'd hitched a ride in the body of the man who would later stab Taurin in the back.

The dream haunted me the entire night, and I barely slept. I dragged my tired butt to the bathroom. After tying my hair back, I washed my face and brushed my teeth.

When I glanced in the mirror, I looked the same, but I didn't recognize myself. Dark circles strangled my eyes. My hair was knotted and wild. *I'm not the same. Who am I?* I choked on the lump forming in my throat. There was no going back to not knowing about this place. The nightmares would always find me, and I had to learn to deal with it. *Who am I?* Continued to play in my head. *Who am I?*

"Come in," Faith told someone, interrupting my pity party. "Put it over there."

Faith?

I grabbed a towel off the hook attached to the wall. It was still dark outside the bathroom window. Wondering who would visit us this early, I tightened my robe and charged into the bedroom.

Two men wheeled in a wardrobe.

"What's this?" I asked.

"I'm not sure." Faith's predator stare intimidated the two nervous men. When they had settled the new wardrobe beside the one already against the wall, they rushed off, slamming the door behind them without saying a word.

"When did you get back?"

"While you were in the shower." Faith pulled open the doors to the wardrobe, acting like nothing happened the night before. "It's your battle gear."

Leather pants, metal breastplates with a slight girly curve to them, and light blue blouses hung neatly on hangers across the rod. On the top shelf sat three silver helmets, each shaped like a cat's head. Five scabbards bedazzled with blue stones hung on one door, while two shields with tiger heads on them dangled on the other. The hilts of the swords were silver tiger heads with sapphire eyes. My heart hammering, I pulled the door wide, metal clanking against metal. Three pairs of calf-high leather boots were in the bottom of the wardrobe. All of this was real—I could no longer deny I was training to become a warrior.

I grabbed a pair of pants and wiggled into them. I

squatted to see if they'd bind or bust apart.

"They're tight but flexible, and the pockets—Love. Them." I tossed the blouse Faith handed me onto the bed and grabbed my black, long-sleeved T-shirt instead. "I'm not wearing that. It's not my style."

"But it's a uniform," Faith protested.

"Don't worry. It still is, just my version." I slipped the breastplate over my head, and Faith helped me fasten the straps on the sides. Then I finished putting on the rest of the biker-knight gear. "Fits perfect. How'd they know my size?"

"Someone must've scanned your body with a measuring charm." Faith examined me. "You look lethal."

"Thanks, I think."

"And—" Faith looked away then back at me "—thank you for saving my life, especially because you are still scared of me." She shook her head. "That was very powerful magic, breaking a charm spell no one else could. I'd heard you need lots of training. And you don't know how to conjure, but—"

"They're right." I looked at my new gear then out the window. "I have no idea what I'm doing. I'm not sure I could do that again." From the corner of my eye, I could see her still studying my face, and I focused on her. "But I'm glad whatever I did worked." I offered a small smile, and she returned it. The silence continued on for several moments, but it no longer felt awkward between us.

"You better go to breakfast, or you won't get to eat before practice," Faith finally said and headed for the bathroom. "Don't kill anyone with that sword—yet."

•••

The practice field was empty. Carrig was late, so I stretched and did some jumping jacks to warm up. When he finally bounded onto the grass, his face was all twisted and sinister. He spotted me staring at him and shook away the bull-that-just-saw-red look.

A feeling of doom rushed over me. Crap. He was pissed off about something, which was not good when sparring, especially for me.

"Good to see you warming up." He dropped a long, narrow duffle bag, and his gaze traveled over me. "Jaysus, you're a regular warrior in that gear." He kneeled beside the bag, pulled out two wooden swords and two small balls, and placed them on the ground. He reached his empty hand out to me. "Give me your sword."

I handed him my scabbard and sword, and he slid them carefully into the bag. "We'll be using practice swords and globes," he said. "We wouldn't want to be killing each other on the first day now, would we?"

"I'd prefer *not* to die."

He ignored my joke and got to his feet, handing me one of the practice swords. This was going to be a *long* practice. "We'll start at the beginning, then," he said.

"I'm on the advanced fencing team back home. I have all the basics down."

"Is that so? What be the basics?"

I did a quick leap forward with the dummy sword extended. "That's a *balestra* and this—" I said at the same time I hopped and lunged forward "—is a *balestra* with a lunge."

"Good. Show me more."

He lunged, and I took a step back, twisting my body a quarter turn to avoid his attack.

"That is an *in quartata*," I said.

"You do have good balance, I'll give you that. We'll

skip the basics. I'd rather teach you the reality of swordplay. It's not all *balestra* and *in quartata*. It won't be polite like fencing. There be no protections from a sharp blade but your wit and your instincts. And wielding your sword gets a little bit trickier when you have a shield and a battle globe to cope with."

"Okay. I'm ready. Teach me how to fight *dirty*."

There was no response to my humor. He was killing me. Figuratively, and possibly literally. Something wasn't right. He'd been nice at the coffee shop, and smiled, but not now. I'd told him to treat me like a student and not a daughter, but it seemed like there was more going on. It made me miss Pops even more.

"First off, has Professor Attwood found your battle globe?"

The odd scowl on his face surprised me. I debated asking for his blood and showing him my truth globe, but his weird reactions made me think it was better to lie—for now. "No. Why?"

"Once you have your globe, we'll practice with it." He got into an attack stance. "Your turn. Come at me."

Chapter Fifteen

At my lessons later with Professor Attwood, I told him about my uneasiness with Carrig, that I had lied to him about finding my globes, and that he was too aggressive during practices. He phoned Merl to discuss my apprehensions.

"Tell him I have bruises to prove it."

He placed his hand on the mouthpiece of the phone. "He says you shouldn't worry. Carrig is one of our best Sentinels. He's very trustworthy. And he'll speak to him about taking it easier on you during practices. " He returned his attention back to whatever Merl was saying.

I slumped in the chair. "I'm sure that will help."

He ignored my comment and continued talking to Merl. "Right then, I'll be by tomorrow." He hung up the phone.

"I know, I know," I said, seeing the frown on his face. "I should've stayed quiet, right?"

"Gia," he said with a straight face. "We don't interrupt a person when they're on the phone with the High Wizard."

"Sorry."

"As far as Carrig is concerned, don't provoke him during

training." Professor Attwood studied the cuckoo clock on
the wall.

"Me provoke him? Yeah, right." I crossed my arms. "You
know, Faith said he's never been this brutal to others he's
trained. Why is he so tough on me? I just don't trust him."

"We have a duty to protect those who dwell here," he
said. "It's best to handle matters like this cautiously. We are
dealing with magic, after all. Carrig is a powerful Sentinel. If
he is behind the recent uprisings, which I highly doubt, and
we approach him with this it could end badly. He could kill
you and possibly many others before he's stopped."

"Well, okay, but I don't want to be left alone with him."

"I'll post a Sentinel in the dining room on the off chance
your concerns are warranted. The dark windows are perfect
for viewing the training field without being seen from the
outside." He smiled. "Will that suffice?"

"I guess."

"Splendid. In addition to your truth globe, you created
a second one this morning that released a charm. I want
you to work on mastering that globe today after our magic
lessons. I have someone coming by to instruct you." He
jotted something down in his notebook. "You impress me. In
no time at all, you'll be chanting charms like a wizard."

I rubbed the armrest on my chair. "Can I tell you
something?"

He didn't look up, his pen scratching across the notebook page. "Yes. What is it?"

"Ever since I've been here, I've been having strange dreams."

He placed his pen on the desk and scrutinized me. After I
told him the details, he nodded, went to the window and stared
out. "Your dreams are true, accurately historic, even. Mykyl
did create the Tetrad. Each part of the Tetrad can control one
of the elements—earth, air, water, and fire. It destroyed entire

villages with earthquakes, hurricanes, tornadoes, and fire until the original seven wizards came together and trapped it. The spirit of a Seer must be giving you these visions—a way to prepare you for what might be ahead. You needn't fear them."

The past didn't bother me, but some spirit preparing me for a future that involved this Tetrad made my stomach churn. I needed to learn everything I could. "Mykyl was after some key. The Chiavi, he said. What are they?"

"They're seven magical keys that, combined, can unlock the Tetrad from its tungsten tomb. When Taurin discovered Mykyl wanted to use the Tetrad for his own goals, he hid them. Mykyl had Taurin killed, like you've seen. Taurin's sons avenged their father's death by ambushing Mykyl and crucifying him.

"War broke out, and the havens chose sides. France, Italy, and Ireland sided with Taurin's sons in England, and the rest sided with Mykyl's heirs in Russia. The two sides fought until they were at a stalemate. Taurin's sons were killed and the whereabouts of the keys lost with them. That was until eighteen-ninety, when a professor uncovered an old chest buried in a secret corridor within the hidden gallows beneath the Vatican. He was haunted by visions of destruction caused by the Tetrad and changed the Chiavi into various items and hid them within the world libraries."

"So," I interrupted, "just anyone can find these keys and release that thing? How come he didn't destroy the keys?"

"The keys were spelled and could not be destroyed," he said, glancing over his shoulder at me then returning his gaze to the window. "But to prevent the control of the Tetrad from falling into evil hands, the wizard havens signed a peace treaty and formed an alliance. For centuries now, all the Mystik races have searched for the Chiavi. The Sentinels have fought to prevent those with evil intentions from recovering them. Because of our efforts, the Tetrad remains entombed." He turned from the window. "Through your grandfather's mother you are a descendent of the Seventh Wizard, Taurin. From Barnum and Athela's child."

I bolted upright in my chair. "Wait. *What*? Exactly, what does that mean?"

"I'm not certain, but—"

"We'll sort it out, right?" I slumped again.

He chuckled. "I've said that before, yeah?"

"Yep."

"Back to charms, then," he said. "I want to quiz you on what we learned yesterday. What's the phrase to place a lock on the door?

"*Bloccare la porta.*"

"To unlock it?"

That was easy. It was the one that got me in this mess with the gateway book. "*Aprire la porta.*"

"Very good."

A knock came from the door.

Professor Attwood checked the antique clock on his desk. "He's early. Enter," he called to whoever it was.

It was as if whoever opened the door did it slowly for a dramatic effect. Arik poked his head in. My heart jumped into my throat and I straightened, uncrossing my legs, my foot connecting to the back of Professor Attwood's desk with a loud *thump*. He gave me a curious look.

"Am I early?" Arik asked.

"Perfect timing, actually," Professor Attwood said. "Gia is ready."

Uneasiness creeping down my spine, I glanced from Arik to the professor. "For what?"

Professor Attwood stood, shaking his legs to smooth his pants. "The remainder of your lesson today will be with

Arik. He's going to help you explore that new globe. I have a meeting at the Vatican. Hopefully, I can convince them to drop the charges on the unlawful jump last week." He leveled a gaze at Arik, then me.

Arik cocked an eyebrow. "Shall we?"

Friends don't think of each other the way I think of you, his words from the other night played in my head. This was going to be all kinds of awkward. "Um—" I cleared my throat. "Sure." I grabbed my hoodie from the chair and followed him out.

His gaze kept shifting my way as we walked next to each other down the corridor to a set of stairs. No guy had a right to look that gorgeous. It was distracting. A leather jacket flung over his shoulder, he wore jeans and a tight blue t-shirt that hugged him as if made to fit his compact body perfectly.

"Why aren't we in uniform?" I asked. "Aren't you giving me a lesson?"

"We don't need our gear. We'll just be working on that new globe of yours."

Each time we passed under a burning sconce on the wall, his chocolaty eyes changed to the color of the sap that dripped down Nana's large oak on a sunlit day. I shuddered under his scrutinizing stare as a leaf barely hanging onto that oak in the last days of fall, my stomach full of fireflies.

We ended up in the basement. It wasn't your normal basement. It was large with a high ceiling, decked out with overstuffed chairs, gaming tables, and pinball machines. Across one wall was a snack stand with an espresso bar. The girl attending it had long earlobes, small horns sticking out of her wide forehead, and cinnamon colored skin. She looked bored drumming her claw-like nails on the counter.

Spotting us, the girl straightened and flashed a sharp-tooth smile. "Hi there, Arik, you want a fireball as usual?"

"No thank you, Titania. Perhaps later."

"Okay," she said, slumping over the counter again and watching me with suspicious eyes.

"What's a fireball?" I asked.

"Coffee with chocolate and hot spices," he said. "You must try it. We'll get one on our way back. It'll burn the hair in your nostrils."

Gross. "I think I'll pass."

Arik laughed. "Suit yourself, but it is amazingly delicious once you get past the first sip." He stopped to open a wide wooden door leading into a tunnel with smooth rocked walls. The rubber soles of my Converse squeaked against the polished cement. "Where are we going?"

"I cannot say. We are not in private."

"What do you mean?" I glanced over my shoulder, and then strained my eyes to see farther up the tunnel. "There's no one in here but us."

He lowered his voice. "The walls listen."

"You mean *have ears*," I corrected. He darted a puzzled look at me, so I figured it needed clarifying. "The saying. It's the *walls* have *ears*."

"Does it really matter?" He returned his eyes to the dimly lit path in front of us. "Since you felt compelled to correct me, I assume my meaning was understood."

That shut me up. Pop was always on me about chastising others. I only did it because I would want to know if I was saying something wrong. I was about to apologize, but his body language made me speechless. Shoulders squared, jaw jutted out, he bounded for the door with a scowl on his face.

I stopped.

When he realized I wasn't beside him any longer, he spun around and took two long-legged steps to me. "What's the matter?"

"You're mad," I snapped, crossing my arms.

"We don't have time for childish antics, Gia."

"I don't want to spend the afternoon doing whatever it is I'm doing with you while you're angry at me."

He took another step forward, and I backed up against the wall. His body was so close to mine, I was aware of every rise and fall of his muscles as he breathed. "We hardly know each other, yet you seem to be an expert on who I am. I couldn't care less about petty things. When we walk through that door, we will be in the village. I must keep my focus. To guard you from any threats." Was he referring to how I'd corrected him just now, or to yesterday, when I'd accused him of having a relationship with Veronique? Maybe both.

"I—um…"

"Splendid, you're finally at a loss for words," he said, and his gaze softened. "Besides, didn't we agree to be friends the other night?"

Friends. Everything inside me collapsed like a house of cards. Either way, I'd obviously insulted him—whether he deserved it or not. But he'd also said he admired me and that he felt driven to protect me. The memory of his admission melted my frustration. When he looked at me, my stomach took off in a flight of wings. *It's because you like him, you dumbass. And you ruined it by opening your stupid mouth. Yet. Again.*

"We did. We're friends. Definitely friends." *Stop rambling, Gia.* "So, *friend*, we should get to that top secret place of yours, don't you think?" *Ugh. I'm such a loser.*

"Yes, we should." He spoke so slowly, I was sure he thought I was an idiot. Mercifully, he moved out of my space, and my brain started working properly again.

At the end of the tunnel was another huge wooden door. Arik opened it by swiping a metal security-looking card into the lock. Sunshine blinded me as we stepped onto a cobblestone sidewalk.

Without a word, he led me down the roads winding through the small village. People crowded the street, carrying packages and dashing in and out of shops. It reminded me of Nana's tiny Christmas village set, but minus the snow. Arik ducked into a bakery and approached the counter. The smells were so incredible my stomach rumbled.

He ordered biscuits, chocolate pastries, and two bottles of water. After he paid, we went through the kitchen, out the back door, and down a small alleyway. An awful sour smell came from the many overflowing trashcans. We came out of the alley and into a thick forest.

After trailing him through the dense trees for several minutes, I asked, "How much farther is it?"

"We're here." He stopped at a vine-covered wall about eight feet tall and climbed the vines to the top. "Come on. It's no trouble at all."

I scaled the wall, losing my footing halfway down on the other side. I landed hard on my ass, pain stabbing my tailbone. "*Shit.*" I sat there, stunned, until the pain subsided.

"You all right?" The concern on Arik's face was cute. Who was I kidding? Every expression of his was hot.

"Yeah." I stood and brushed off the dead grass, glancing around the area. It was a crumbling arena, overgrown with foliage. An earthen smell swirled in the wind. "What is this place?"

"It's an amphitheater," he said. "It was used for plays and other performances back in ancient times before it was destroyed."

"This could be your secret garden instead of the libraries," I said.

He stepped lightly across the overgrowth. "This isn't

my secret garden. Weeds and horrible memories haunt this place. After Asile's first high wizard died, it became a site for executions. It's the only place with enough room and privacy for us to practice in."

A recent rainfall had kissed the leaves. Mud slurped at my feet as I went over to him.

After placing the bag on the ground, he faced me. "Hold up your palm."

I raised it to him, and he placed his palm on top of mine. It took all my willpower not to shake under his touch. The warmth built between our hands.

"Do you feel the heat?" he asked.

Is he kidding? That's all I feel when I'm next to him.

I nodded, my eyes not leaving his gaze. "It's getting hotter."

The wind brushed his hair across his forehead and flushed his cheeks. "It's my battle globe. If I let it grow any more, it will burn you. When I was six, Oren taught me how to ignite my battle globe at will. Most Sentinels have to speak a charm. I practiced relentlessly until it became second nature to me. Just as walking or talking happens naturally. I believe you can learn this, too." He removed his hand.

"I doubt it." The wind cooled the heat of his touch from my palm.

He sighed, pulling out a small booklet from the inside pocket of his jacket. "Have some faith. You can create a light globe and your battle one. We're not sure what this third one is or what it can do. You should be able to conjure it the same way." He flipped to a dog-eared page. "A wizard found information in this log book about your mysterious globe. He discovered it while researching your family tree. Only one other possessed your globe. A boy who lived many centuries ago. It's a universal globe. Unfortunately, he died before his thirteenth birthday from the plague, so there isn't much information to glean from his experiences with it or what powers it possesses."

"Apparently, it doesn't protect against human diseases," I said.

"I suppose it doesn't." Worry scrunched his face and it took him several seconds before he continued. "I can imagine this is scary for you, so at any time you want to stop, we will."

"I can do this," I said, not very convincingly.

His finger dragged across the page as he read the entry. "It says here that you must think of things that make you feel protected to ignite the globe."

"Great. Just whatever makes me feel safe, huh?"

"Aye, give it a whirl."

The globe proved elusive. A light one sprouted first, then the truth sphere appeared. I wasn't sure how to separate them. Numerous things that gave me a sense of security came to mind. From alarm systems to people—Pop, Nana, and even Arik. But nothing worked.

Dark clouds rolled over our heads. A crack of lightning disturbed my train of thought. Rain sprinkled on us, dotting my palm with water, which made me wish I had my mother's red umbrella. Pain tugged at my stomach, my insides were on fire. A groan slipped from my lips and Arik grabbed my elbow just as my knees began to buckle.

"Embrace the memory," he urged. "Only think of it."

The umbrella? I used to sleep with it after my mom passed away. Carried it everywhere. It was a way to keep her with me. Electric sparks sped up my chest and across my arms. A pink sphere grew to the size of a peach pit on my palm before it busted.

"You have it!" His boyish excitement surprised me. "It startled you. That's why you lost control. Try again."

I concentrated on the umbrella for several minutes, willing the globe to form. When it materialized, it puffed up like blowing a bubble with pink gum. "What do you think it does?"

"All I know is that it released the charmed shackles from Faith. The entry in the book is unclear." He rubbed the back of his neck. "Try throwing it."

I cocked my arm back, the sphere wobbling like Jell-O, and tossed it. The globe flopped to the ground near us and burst.

"That's a horrible throw. Have you ever thrown a ball before?"

I glared at him. "Yes. It's just that this thing is awkward and jiggly."

He glanced up at the sky. "A storm is coming. We might have time to try once more."

My entire body went weak. "I don't feel so good."

"Shall we take a break, then?" He snatched up the bag and pulled out a chocolate covered pastry.

I shoved it in my mouth as though starved. Which I was. I hadn't eaten since lunch.

Amusement danced in his eyes as he watched me gobble it down like a troll. He took one out for himself, ripping off a piece and popping it in his mouth.

"Holy crap, this is delicious," I said with a full mouth. The sprinkling of rain turned into fat drops.

"I've not found any better." He removed bottled water from the sack, unscrewed it, and handed it to me. Something on the side of my face caught his attention. "You have a bit of something right there." He pointed it out.

"Oh." I rubbed at my cheek.

"You missed it." He rubbed the corner of my mouth with his thumb.

Surprised at his touch, I dropped the bottle and slipped back on my heels, grabbing his hand and pulling him down with me. I landed on my back in the mud. He fell on top of me, bracing himself with his arms so as not to smash me with his body. Cold mud crawled under my shirt and up my back. I shivered. Rain dumped on us.

Our faces were mere inches apart, his chocolate-laced breath brushing my lips—every bit of my body sharply aware of his nearness. The rain slapped the bag beside us and clapped the ground.

A serious expression pulled on his face as his head lowered closer to mine. He swiped my lower lip with his finger this time, causing an eruption of tingles to spread across my skin. "Those pastries are messy. I should have grabbed some napkins."

"No, I'm just a slob." I licked my lips, and his breath hitched.

What just happened? And why is he looking at me like that? I thought he was still mad at me.

He straightened his arms, his face moving away from mine. "Are you injured?"

"I don't think so." *Only heart palpitations.*

He scrambled to his feet and grabbed both my hands, yanking me up. "We best find cover before we drown."

We made a mad dash for the wall, rain drenching us. My feet kept slipping as I climbed up the vines beside him. The village roads were practically vacant of people. Our feet smacked the puddles as we sprinted to the door into the castle.

Dripping water and mud on the tunnel's floor, we tried to catch our breaths. I was freezing, but too lost in the moment to care. Arik's laughter had me completely entranced. His eyes danced and dimples deepened with each chuckle.

"You need to get dry," he said, a hint of amusement lingering in his voice. "Moreover, your entire backside is caked in mud."

As we walked through the corridors, we did a sort of hide and seek thing with our glances. He'd peek at me, and I would hide my eyes by looking at something on the wall. I'd look at him, and he would glance down at his feet. Both trying to conceal our smiles.

I was disappointed when we reached my room. "Well, thanks for seeing me to my door."

"It was my pleasure."

His pleasure? Did he mean that or was it just a thing to say?

"And thanks for the lesson," I added.

He pushed his wet hair away from his forehead. "You did well. Practice forming the globe until our next lesson."

Was that it? I didn't want him to go.

The door flung open, and Faith frowned at the sight of me. "Were you mud wrestling?"

"Certainly looks that way." Arik snickered then looked over at me. "I leave for another mission tonight. When I return, we'll commence our lessons."

"You should hurry and get cleaned up for dinner," Faith said, eyeing us.

"I suppose that's my cue." He hung there for several awkward seconds, eyes searching my face. "Good evening," he finally said.

"See you later," I said, trying to sound like his roaming eyes hadn't affected me.

When he nodded and ambled down the corridor, disappointment sunk in my stomach. Was he feeling the same way as me? All the signs pointed to yes. I shook my head.

What's the matter with me? Maybe there's nothing going on between him and Veronique, but he has a betrothed somewhere, so there's no point getting involved. Why set myself up? Arik's a one-way ticket to heartbreak.

I closed the door and headed to the bathroom but couldn't stop thinking about him. The weight of his body pressing against me and his warm breath on my lips teased my thoughts. He was the silver lining to the *suckage* that was my new life.

CHAPTER SIXTEEN

For weeks, I sparred with Carrig, learning to balance a ball and hold my sword with an arm laced in the tight straps of my heavy shield. He won every match, but I put up a good fight. Spending time with him was like being with a coach, not a father. The man didn't know how to work with teenagers. I actually felt bad for Deidre growing up with this guy. He busted my lip twice, cracked a rib, and cornered me until I fell down a rocky hill.

Nana was so angry she complained to Merl. He told her to stop fussing and that Carrig knew what he was doing, which only made Nana hotter.

It was coming up on three weeks and still Arik and the other Sentinels hadn't returned from their mission. Back home, school would be starting soon. I didn't know if I'd be back by then, which upset me. I didn't want Deidre to attend classes for me. I valued my GPA.

The day was thick with fog when I finished my training session with Carrig. After seeing my battered arms and blood-caked forehead, Professor Attwood canceled our lessons and sent me to my suite, where Faith gave me one look and guided me to the bed. I tucked myself in a fetal position, buried my face into the pillow and screamed. How could I take any more? It was too hard. I just wanted to go home. I hated this life, and I needed Pop.

Faith brushed tangled strands of hair away from my face. "Hold on. I'll get you something for the pain." She grabbed a bottle from the nightstand and poured a small amount of Nana's elixir into a shot glass, then held it in front of my face. "Here, drink this."

I tossed back the shot, draining the liquid in one big gulp.

"You stay here. I'll be right back." She hurried off to Nana's room.

I poured more elixir to the rim of the glass and slugged it down.

Faith returned with Nana on her heels, dousing a cotton ball with some sort of ointment.

"My goodness," Nana said. "You look awful. I swear that man is going to get a few choice words from me when I see him." She sat beside me on the bed and dabbed my cuts with the drenched cotton ball.

The pain subsided and my body seemed as though it was floating above the bed. All my fears dissipated like dandelions blown on the wind.

I giggled. "Nana, you should sell this stuff. It zaps the pain. Zippo. Gone-o."

"Faith, did you give her the elixir again?"

"You said to give it when she's hurt bad."

"How much did you give her?"

"Only a half shot glass, as you instructed."

I giggled again. "I snuck another. Well, a full shot, that is."

Nana frowned at me. "Young lady, you're insufferable at times."

"What's that mean?" asked Faith.

I hiccupped. "It means I'm difficult…I think."

"It's time to get dressed for dinner," Nana said. "You need to eat something to take off the edge."

"Okey dokey."

I was in a euphoric daze as Nana dressed me. She ignored my protests as she pulled a pink dress over my head. It was chiffon and had a black satin bow at the waist. So not my style. At least it was from this century. It took both Faith and Nana to squeeze my toes into the heels they'd picked for me. I was certain I'd add a broken leg to all my other injuries as we went down to the dining hall.

"Good evening," Veronique said, passing us on her way out the door.

"Good evening," Nana returned.

I swayed and Veronique grabbed my arm, helping Nana to steady me. Something musky tickled my nose. I coughed.

"Thanks," I said around a hiccup and yanked my arm from her.

"My pleasure." Veronique smiled and walked off.

I turned my head toward Nana. "Did you feel that?"

"Feel what, dear?"

"A wet, misty, stinky thing."

"No. Now pull yourself together. Everyone's watching." She smiled to the tables as we passed.

Food did help take the edge off the elixir, but it also brought back the pain. Auntie Mae's chattering scraped against my eardrums, annoying me more than usual. The massive headache didn't help. I made my excuses to the table and headed back to my room.

The corridors seemed tighter at night with the shadows draping them. Tiny winged creatures circled me, and I slapped at them. One hovered in front of me, her body thin and green like a praying mantis and a scowl on her beautiful face. She shook her head and waggled her finger at me, then flew off, the others chasing her.

Great. Now I'm seeing things. Nana should sell this stuff. Wait. "Maybe she does." My voice sounded slurred.

I stopped in the middle of the corridor, my head reeling and stomach nauseous. There was no way one extra shot of elixir would make me this tipsy. I'd snuck an extra shot before and never got this woozy. Really, I should be worried, but I couldn't focus enough to care. I squinted as I tried to see my way down to the end of the hall.

As I fell backwards, a pair of arms caught me and eased me to the floor. A spindly woman in her thirties with choppy red hair, pointy ears, and slanted gray eyes stared down at me.

"Are you real?"

"Yes," she said. "Are you hurt?"

"I don't think so," I said. "Who are you?"

"Sinead. I'm fey."

"Okay, are you Sinead or Fay?"

"No. My name is *Sinead*. I'm from the *fey* nation." She pulled me up by my arms. "Come on, help me out. We've got to get you to your feet."

Once upright, I checked out her back. "You don't have wings."

"I'm one of the Silent People. We don't have wings. Can you walk?"

"My legs feel like Twizzlers."

She wrapped my arm around her shoulders, held my waist, and led me down the hall.

"We've got to get to your room. You'll be safe there."

With each step, I willed my legs to move, and before long, Sinead was knocking on the door to our suite.

Faith jerked the door open. "What's happened to you?"

She looked from me to Sinead. "Who are you?"

"She helped me," I said. "Move and let us in, already."

"You're *drunk*. How many shots did you have? You're going to be in big trouble when Nana sees you."

"Zip it, Faith. The world is spinning."

Sinead dragged me to the bed and dropped me onto the pillows. "I think she was drugged," she said.

Nana burst through the door. "Young lady, you should be ashamed—" She stopped when she spotted Sinead. "What's going on here?"

"I'm Carrig's wife, Sinead." She collapsed beside me on the bed.

I rose to my elbows. "You're *whose* wife?"

"I've been trying to get into Asile ever since—" Her eyes teared. "I was with him when we went to exchange Gia and Deidre. I waited outside your house while he went in with Deidre to get the shield charm. After she came out, I took her to Gia's apartment, and Carrig waited with you."

Nana shut the door. "He did mention someone was waiting for Deidre. You were her escort?" Nana's eyes widened when she realized my condition. "What have you done to my granddaughter?"

"Nothing," Sinead said. "Someone else did something."

"Move over and let me take a look at her." Nana leaned over, grabbed my chin, and twisted my head side to side. "Your irises are slanted. Have you seen anything unusual?"

"Yes," I said before letting out a yawn.

"Delusion potion," Nana said and went into her room. The sounds of rustling bags, clanking bottles, and running water came from the bathroom. She returned with a glass of cloudy water. "All right, drink this."

I lifted my head and drank it down. It tasted like watery frosting. I sank back into the pillows and shut my eyes. After a while, I sat up. The three of them stared at me as if I had turned blue or something.

Finally, Sinead spoke. "How do you feel?"

"Much better. Good thing you found me."

"I was seeking you. Do you remember what I told you earlier? About waiting outside Ms. Kearns's house?" She pulled a slender dagger from a holster buckled around her hips, grabbed Nana, and held the blade to her neck.

"Stop!" I yelled, jumping off the bed. Without thinking about the consequences, I whirled and kicked at Sinead's arm. The blade flew from her hand and clattered to the floor. "What are you *doing*?"

Faith readied herself to pounce. Lip curled back, fangs bared, she growled at Sinead.

The fey gave each of us a sharp glare as she scrambled for the dagger, but I was quicker and knocked it under the bed and out of her reach. "The man who came out of the house was not my Carrig. I stood right in front of him with my usual glamour on, and he didn't recognize me." She growled at Nana. "Tell me what you did to him!"

"I didn't do anything. Wait. Let me think." Nana paused as she tried to remember. "I finished tattooing Deidre and she left. I was out of black ink. The supply store is only around the corner. Carrig stayed with my stepdaughter, Eileen, while I went to get more ink."

"You're lying," Sinead said. "Move away, Gia. This is not your grandmother."

"Yes she is." I held my ground in front of Nana. "I performed a truth globe on her. And besides, for all I know, you're lying to us."

"Good gracious." At my nod, Sinead reached under the bed and then holstered her dagger. "Of all globes, yours is a truth globe? I wouldn't wish that globe on my enemies."

"What's wrong with my globe?"

"It's not useful for battles. Did you perform the globe on everyone?" Sinead asked.

"Well, I've done Professor Attwood, Nana, Arik, Lei, and Merl."

Sinead inclined her head in Faith's direction as Faith eased out of her attack position. "What about her?"

"It won't work on Laniars. Merl scried her—she checked out."

"Right," Sinead said. "How much blood does it require?"

"It just takes a drop."

"Okay, perform one on me if it will help you to believe me. Then we'll come up with a plan." Sinead retrieved her dagger again. She seemed preoccupied as she pricked her finger and let her blood fall onto my hand.

Sinead's face resembled an insect's with the globe contorting her face. Her nose looked flatter and her ears larger, the points at the top more exaggerated. "I am truthful," the image said.

After I busted the globe, my eyes went to our new ally.

"I've had a bad feeling about Carrig all along. He's been ruthless on the practice field. He seems more concerned about training me to be a great fighter than learning anything about me. And he's never mentioned you to me." I turned to Nana. "Something must have happened when you went to get more ink. Can you think of anything?"

"No. Nothing. We took separate routes to the library. He said it wouldn't be good for me to be seen with him."

"Gia, have you ever seen more than the person saying they're true in the globes?" Sinead asked.

"Well…," I paused, fearing they'd think I was crazy. "After I did Arik's globe–um–well, before I washed his blood off my hand, I performed another globe."

"Go on," Sinead urged.

"I asked it about Arik's relationship with Veronique. The globe showed me—" I trailed off feeling wicked uncomfortable.

"It showed you more than what it usually does," Sinead finished for me.

"Uh-huh." The thought of Arik and Veronique together nauseated me.

Sinead put her hand on my cheek. Warmth surged through my body and my anxiety subsided. "With matters of the heart, we all fall weak. It's natural to be curious about your attraction."

"I'm *not* attracted to Arik."

"You can't hide your emotions from fey. I can feel every mood in this room. Now, try and extract the memory of that morning from Ms. Kearns." She gave me a warm smile. "Can you do that?"

"I'll try."

Nana went into the bathroom. When she returned, she pricked her finger with a safety pin and dragged her bleeding finger across my palm. I chanted the charm and a globe shimmered in my hand.

"Show me the morning of August the ninth in Nana's sitting room."

Waves rippled across the surface of the silvery globe. Color flickered across the sphere and Nana came into focus. She sat on a chair in her parlor, tattooing a girl who was propped on the ottoman in front of her and looked just like me.

"All finished," Nana said.

"Good." Carrig got up from Nana's antique loveseat. "Deidre must be getting to your son's house. An escort waits outside to take her. I won't be a moment."

Nana showed Carrig and Deidre to the door. She returned her tattoo supplies and began loading them into her tote. She held up one of the ink bottles and shook it. "Drat, not nearly enough."

A knock came from the door. Nana crossed the room and let Carrig in.

He settled back onto the loveseat. "You've a worry on your face."

"I don't have enough black ink. The supply shop is just around the corner. We can leave for the library from there."

Carrig struggled to get comfortable against the small pillows of the seat. "I think it's best you're not seen with me. I'll meet you outside the library. If it isn't any trouble, I'll wait here a bit until my partner returns."

"It's no trouble at all." Nana tied a floral scarf around her neck. "Would you like some tea while you wait?"

"A bit of tea would be nice, but not if it's any trouble to you."

"Oh, no, it's no trouble at all. Eileen!" she called in the direction of the kitchen.

Aunt Eileen, Nana's stepdaughter, blew in wearing her usual attire of head-to-toe black and a ratty floral shawl. She didn't have a real job. Nana paid her to help around the house.

"Yes?" She tilted her head, her red, over-teased bouffant shifting slightly.

"Could you fix mister—I'm sorry. I don't believe Marietta ever told me your full name."

"It's McCabe."

"Could you fix Mr. McCabe some tea? I have to run to the shop and get some more ink."

"Certainly." Aunt Eileen's heavy black-lined eyes landed on Carrig. "How do you take it?"

"Cream and sugar, if you have," Carrig said.

Nana grabbed her tote from the table and walked toward the kitchen with Baron slinking after her. "Make yourself comfortable. Oh, and Eileen, there's freshly baked lemon bars resting on the stove. Be a dear and bring Mr. McCabe one with his tea."

Before Nana departed the room in the globe, Sinead grabbed my hand. "Don't close your palm just yet. I've read about truth globes. The magic lingers for a bit after the donor departs the target area. We may get a glimpse of what happened while Ms. Kearns was gone."

Carrig fidgeted on the pillows, waiting for his tea. When Aunt Eileen came back into the room carrying a silver tea tray, he stood.

"Sit. Sit. I've got it." She placed the tray on the small coffee table in front of him. Carrig repositioned himself on the loveseat. Aunt Eileen poured tea into a dainty porcelain cup, and balancing it on a saucer, she handed it to him. She took a seat in a poofy chair across from him. "You may help yourself to a lemon bar."

"Thank you." Carrig took a sip from his cup. "Are you a witch, as well?"

"Yes."

Aunt Eileen was painfully shy. She never knew how to carry on a conversation. People misunderstood her oddness. She was never that way with me, though. She used to play with me for hours when I was younger and she had no other kids around.

"What's your specialty?"

"Potions." She studied her teacup.

"Right," Carrig said, reaching for a lemon bar. He took a big bite as he watched the minutes tick by on Nana's cuckoo clock.

They sat sipping tea in silence. Carrig drained his cup and placed it on top of the saucer on the table. He rubbed his temples, rocking a little, then he collapsed against the pillows.

Aunt Eileen smiled and walked toward the front door, disappearing from the globe's view. The front door squeaked as it opened, and several heavy feet stamped across the entry tiles before the globe popped.

It sounded like we all gasped at the same time.

CHAPTER SEVENTEEN

Carrig unloaded the practice equipment as I fidgeted with a practice globe, which was a small spongy ball designed to help me learn to fight while handling my battle one. The sun had barely risen above the horizon. We decided not to call, since someone might be listening, so Sinead and Faith were on their way to discuss our findings with Merl and Professor Attwood.

What played out in the globe looked like Aunt Eileen drugged Carrig, and whoever came into the room afterward did something to him. It wasn't a compulsion spell, because he would still have recognized Sinead in her glamour. Hopefully Professor Attwood could determine which one was used.

The sense of something big going down freaked me out, and I wished the Sentinels were back from their mission. I really needed someone to talk to.

"Uh, do you think we could try real swords today?" I asked, wishing I had my Converse and jeans on instead of battle gear. My boots weren't broken in yet and they felt stiff.

Amusement lit Carrig's face. "You think you're ready

for *real* swords, yeah?"

No. But I needed his blood to find out the truth. "I'm ready. I'd like to see how it feels. You know. Feel the weight of the sword. See what it's like when steel hits steel, and all."

"You don't say? You wish to be *one with the sword*?"

I frowned, slipping my arm into my shield. "Are you trying to be funny?"

"That's an American saying, isn't it?"

There he went again, flashing his Irish charm. The man ran hot and cold so frequently, I couldn't keep up with his moods.

"All right, then." He pulled his sword from his scabbard.

I slid my blade out of mine.

"One has to be careful with real swords. No lunging with it." He readied his stance. "Make sure to keep the blade at a distance. We wouldn't want an accident now, would we?"

"I know. I know," I said. "Just like the wooden ones, no body contact." Except he hit me all the time with the fricking wooden ones.

"Okay then, give me your best."

I took a deep, calming breath, ignoring the little voice in my brain that screamed using real weapons was a very bad mistake.

I brought my feet shoulder-width apart and raised my sword, my shield clanking against my belt. We waltzed around each other. I was definitely in better shape than Carrig, but he had more strength and experience. I steadied my breathing and glided my feet across the grass, never raising them more than an inch off the ground. In fencing, breathing and balance made all the difference in control, and I needed the advantage that our age difference gave me.

Carrig swung his sword. I parried. He flew by and turned quickly, sending another blow at me. I pivoted away, and his blade missed me by an inch.

I tossed my practice globe at him and he dodged it effortlessly. It thumped to the ground and rolled down the hill.

He threw a slow shot at me, as if I would fall for the fake. I beat his sword in the middle of its blade with mine. His shoulder hinted at a counter, so I swung low to block the strike. I was totally on the defense, which didn't leave me open to cut him. I shuffled around to make myself a harder target.

When Carrig started panting, I knew I had him. It always surprised me during our sessions that he'd wear out first. For a trainer and a leader, he was out of shape.

"What's the matter? Tired?" I mocked him as I spun away.

"Late night, is all." He advanced toward me.

I was mentally in the fight, flexible and ready for an opening. Carrig brought his feet too close together and stumbled a little. I jumped at the opportunity and flicked my sword, slicing his cheek.

"Shites!" He groaned. "You drew blood."

"You fell into my blade," I protested.

He wiped the blood from his cheek with an irritated growl. "Stay here. I'll be right back." He darted across the pasture and disappeared through the double doors leading to the dining room.

When he was safely inside, I turned so my back faced the door. I swiped Carrig's blood from the tip of my sword, smudged it into my hand, and recited the charm. The globe sprouted in my hand.

"Is Carrig McCabe true?"

His image blinked across the sphere. "It is unclear."

I gasped, dropping my sword. My hands shook and I couldn't catch my breath. *Unclear? What does that mean? It's not clear if he's true or not? What is he up to? So many* questions pinged my brain, causing white flashes of light in the corners of eyes. I swayed on my feet, dizzy, pain stabbing my temples.

"Why is it not clear?" I asked the globe.

Carrig's face faded, and an image of a black flag with a red flame blazing in the middle flickered within the globe.

"What is that suppose to mean?" Hot frustration burned through me.

I heard his footsteps returning, so I dropped the globe, its lights sparked in front of me.

Carrig held a napkin to his face as he approached. "It's just a scratch. There be no harm."

"I feel sick," I said with my back to him, the corner of my lip twitching out of control. "I think I need to lie down." Using the globe still sucked energy from me.

His hand dropped on my shoulder, and his fingers dug into my skin as he spun me around. "What's this? Sparks? I thought you hadn't come into your magic. What have you been up to?"

I backed away from him, my legs weak. "Nothing."

"You lie." He grabbed my wrist, causing my sword to slip from my hand and thud against the ground. "Do you think me a fool?"

I tried to wrench free, but his grip tightened. My heart slammed against my breastbone.

No one had shown up yet to challenge Carrig…Sinead, Professor Attwood, Merl, even Nana had more power than I did, and they knew how dangerous it was for me to battle him by myself. A guard was supposed to watch our sessions from the dining room. But I was alone, taking on an experienced Sentinel.

You can't depend on anyone else. You can best him. You have to.

I steadied my breaths and concentrated on the pink globe, willing it to come to me. Warmth rushed through my body, and my skin prickled. The globe encased Carrig and me. It formed and breathed around us, cradling us in its sphere.

Fear. Thoughts that make me feel secure. Anguish when I believed Faith would die. My emotions ignite the globe.

Sparks shot through my stomach and into my chest. I held on to the magic with all my will. The bubble lasted a little longer this time before the magic slipped from my hold and the globe busted.

Carrig sank to his knees. "What happened?" He looked confused. "Who are you?"

I stumbled backward and plucked up my sword. "You don't remember me?"

"No. I've never seen you before in all me life."

"But I look just like Deidre. You remember her, right?"

"I don't know a Deidre." He glanced around, shock evident on his face. "Where am I?"

Great. Either he has amnesia or he's playing me.

I pointed my sword toward his chest, staring down the blade at him. "What *do* you remember?" The sword seemed heavier than normal and my body seemed weightless. I pushed through the side effects of using the globe, struggling to keep my grip on the handle.

"The last thing I remember…I got off work, stopped off at the pub, and downed a few pints. Just a minute, a French lass was at the pub. She bought me a strong one and now, you and this." His face went pale. "What's going about here?"

What the hell? Was he cheating on Sinead? He was lucky I didn't slice him again. Instead I asked, "Do you remember the *lass's* name?"

"Christ, it was something like Ver…Vera…" He rubbed his temples.

No. It couldn't be. Could it?

"Veronique?"

"That'd be it. She's about this high." He raised his hand to indicate about five-eight. "With bosoms to here." He cupped his hands out in front of his chest. He exaggerated.

"Yes, that's her." I rolled my eyes. "Wait. She's a Sentinel, Carrig. Why didn't you recognize her?"

"Me name's not Carrig."

"Really." That globe must've hit him hard. "What's your name, then?"

"Sean McGann."

Sean McGann? I bit my lip as I processed his words. "Oh, my goodness. Are you Carrig's changeling?" My globe must have released whomever, or whatever, was controlling him. Or was this a trick?

"Bullocks," he muttered.

I had asked the globe if Carrig was untrue. Not Sean. I needed to verify his identity. "You know your Irish tales about magic?"

"Aye, I do."

"Well, that's what this is. Magic. I have to do something, and it requires a drop of your blood." I bent, lifted the corner of the bandage on his face, and rubbed my finger across the cut. The truth globe verified Sean was indeed Carrig's changeling. I had read about wizards weaving people's minds together in one of the books Professor Attwood gave me. Could it be that their minds had been woven together and that's why the globe was unclear? If so, what wizard was controlling them? And where was Carrig?

Apparently, someone had switched Carrig with Sean, and worse of all, Aunt Eileen had something to do with it.

Glancing from Sean to the darkened windows of the castle, I wasn't sure what to do. I thought there was supposed to be a guard there, making sure I was safe. Why wasn't he or she helping me?

I snatched up my sword, slid it into the scabbard, and reached my hand out. Sean took it, and I guided him to his feet. "I'm going to take you to a nice man. He'll make sure you get home safely."

"He won't be locking me up, now, will he?"

"No, I promise."

"All right, then."

We made our way across the practice field. Professor Attwood had said it would take a few months before the side effects of using magic would subside. And my body was already recovering quicker than it had before. Just under the surface of my skin, the pink globe pulsated. I unfurled my fingers, and a sphere easily formed on my palm, jiggling with my steps. It was like an extension of my hand. I willed it to grow as big as a basketball and to shrink as small as a golf ball.

"Will you stop messing with that t'ing ? It's bloody strange."

"Oh. Sorry." I popped the globe.

Before we made it to the castle, Arik flew out the double doors and raced toward us. Sinead was close behind him.

"Hurry! She's behind us!"

"Who is?"

"Veronique! Just don't stand there. Run!" Arik grabbed my arm and dragged me in the direction of the outbuilding. Sinead ran up to my other side.

"Sean, come with us," I yelled over my shoulder.

"Who's Sean?" Arik glanced back.

"Carrig's changeling. Long story. I'll tell you later." I vaulted over a rock. "What happened to the guard that was supposed to be—*guarding* me?"

"I'm not sure. He wasn't there."

I looked back to make sure Sean was following us. He was, but so was Veronique and a menacing looking man dressed in a guard's uniform. I stopped, fear twisting my gut.

Arik skidded to a halt. "Don't stop!"

Veronique held up her palm, producing a red globe. She hurled the globe in our direction. It turned into a fireball as it whizzed toward me. It flew past Sean, and he dropped to his knees.

Arik tackled me. My chin hit the ground hard and my breath punched from my lungs. The globe hit just a few feet away from us and rolled, leaving a burnt trail in the grass.

More fiery globes hit around us. Veronique formed them fast, rapid firing them at us.

"Stand up," he ordered, then called to Sinead, "Get the changeling to the outbuilding!"

I scrambled to my feet.

Arik tossed a few of his own fireballs at Veronique and the guard. She ducked one, and the guard skirted around two.

While they were distracted, he grasped my face in his hands. "Breathe. Stay focused." I nodded, and he let me go. "They'll get to us before we can get to the outbuilding. Toss light globes at Veronique. It'll distract her, so I can get closer to that guard and bring him down."

I took a deep breath to gather courage. The first one I threw was a few feet off target. But it puzzled Veronique and allowed Arik to take off for the guard. I kept forming and throwing light globes at her. It was like huge camera flashes blasting around her. She covered her eyes with her arms.

The guard charged past Veronique. Arik ran for him and shifted his globe into a flaming whip, lashing it out. It wrapped around the man's neck, bringing him down to his knees. Arik strangled the guard until he fell, unmoving, on the ground.

Arik sprinted back to me as I continued to throw balls of light at Veronique.

"Run!" he yelled, approaching.

My boots pounded against the ground, my heart feeling like it would explode in my chest. A fire globe hit the side of my boot and ricocheted off it. I glanced down at my foot. Though it felt hot, the fire hadn't penetrated the leather.

"That was too close," I panted.

Arik turned and flung another sphere at her.

We dashed into the outbuilding. Sinead slammed the door shut before another fiery globe could reach us. Flames licked through the cracks of the door.

"Hurry! Do you know a charm?" Sinead asked.

Quick, think. Think! You have to lock her out.

Facing the door, weak and trembling, I shouted, "*Bloccare la porta. Aperto solo per* Merlin!" The flames flicking through the seams of the door vanished, leaving behind wisps of smoke. I leaned against the wall, unable to hold myself up. Pain struck my head, and I slid down the wall, resting on my heels.

"Gia, what's wrong?" Arik kneeled in front of me.

"She…she wanted to kill us."

Sinead knelt on the other side of me and closed her eyes, mumbling something that I suspected was faery talk. It almost sounded like a song. The pain vanished and my arms and legs stopped shaking. She examined my face. "Better?"

"Yes, so much better. Thank you." I stood with her. "You can do that, but you can't do charms?"

"Fey can't conjure wizard charms."

"Charms are my specialty."

"You added to it," Sinead said.

"How did you know?"

"I've heard it spoken before."

"Oh. Well, not only did I lock the door, but I also made it so only Merl can open it. Professor Attwood taught me how to change up spells."

"Good thinking." Arik smiled. "Who's this Sean?"

"Carrig's changeling. I think their minds were weaved together or something."

"That would explain how Sean knew things about Carrig," he said. "A wizard must have done it, then compelled Sean. The wizard could then see and hear everything Sean did. Carrig was trained to resist this process. That must be why whoever it was used his changeling."

"If their brains were weaved together, how come Sean didn't recognize you, Sinead, or your glamour in front of Nana's house?"

"Because glamour is a magic and a wizard can't weave someone else's memory of it to another brain."

"Well, that's scary," I said. "Anyone could be a spy and we wouldn't know it."

"Not all the memories from the compelled transfer to the one compelling." Arik's eyes went to Sean. "If you pay attention, you can spot a slip up."

"Let's move. We have to get help." Sinead headed toward the stairs.

I formed a globe and held it high, its light surrounding us.

"Thanks." Sinead went through the trap door and skipped down the steps.

"No problem." I peeked back at Sean. He gave me a nervous smile as he clambered down after us.

"What happened back there?" I asked Arik.

"Veronique ambushed us on our way to Merl. I'm not sure if she's acting alone, but if she isn't, it won't fare well for Asile. Thank goodness, she didn't see Faith escape down a hall. Our only hope is for Faith to alert Merl or Professor Attwood about Veronique's attack before she can do whatever evil deed she's planning."

My thoughts flew to Nana. I prayed she'd be safe.

"We have to find the other Sentinels." Arik said, then turned to Sean. "Where are you from?"

"Galway," answered Sean.

"We'll take you to the Trinity College Library in Dublin. It's the best I can do."

"Anywhere 'tis better than here," Sean said tightly.

We reached the end of the tunnel and climbed to the top of the stairwell. Thankfully, the library closed on Sundays, or we would've had to wait all day. Above us was the entry into Duke Humfrey's Library.

Arik pulled a lever, and a bookcase slid open. We stepped up into the library, and the case trembled back over the opening. "Sean, sit there." Arik pointed to a reading chair and turned to me. "We have to find the book."

Each gateway volume had the same Dewey Decimal number attached to it, so no matter what library a jumper was in it was easy to locate.

"*Sei zero sette periodo zero due DOR,*" I recited the numbered charm to find the book. A row shook on a shelf of a tall bookcase against the wall, and the gateway book slipped away from the rest and floated over to us.

Sinead caught it, placed it on the table, and opened to a random page. She brought her hand up to her mouth and blew an air kiss across her palm. Several shimmery silver butterflies took shape and batted their wings as they hovered in front of her face. She spoke to the incandescent creatures in a language that sounded ancient, and they fluttered into the book. Their bodies and graceful wings melted into the pages, leaving behind a shimmery glow that faded within seconds.

"Okay, I give. What do the butterflies do?"

"They're tracers." She pulled me away from the table. "They can summon whoever I want from within the libraries. I've told them to retrieve the other Sentinels. We should keep back or they might land on us when they come out."

My stomach knotted in anticipation. After several minutes had passed and they hadn't shown up, I tried to distract myself.

"Exactly what are the Silent People?"

"The Silent People is another name for the fey. We move *silently*, stealth-like. We have some magical powers, and we're the gardeners of the changelings."

"Changelings?" Sean stood. "Aren't they supposed to be deformed creatures switched for normal children, and such?"

Sinead glared at him. "Those were lies told by horrible parents disgusted by their less than perfect children. A human discovered our secret about changelings and spread tales about them. And besides, are you forgetting you are a changeling?"

"I am not."

"All right, you two," Arik said. "Stop it."

Sean dropped back onto the chair.

"Sinead, did you say gardeners?" I asked.

"I did," she said. "When a Sentinel is born, a cocoon grows in the Garden of Life. After ten days, the Sentinel's changeling hatches as a fully developed infant. Inside the changeling's cocoon is a colored bead that's connected to the Sentinel gene inside the matching baby. It enables the parent faery to track down the baby. After we switch the two infants, the Sentinel becomes our responsibility. We raise them like our children. Our love for them is insurmountable."

"So, who's your Sentinel?" I knew the answer before I even asked.

"You are." Sinead paced in front of the book on the table.

Anxiety turned in my stomach. Was she mad when my mother disappeared with me? If she knew about my precocious period, when all grownups were stupid and I knew everything, she'd be grateful for dodging that disaster. I didn't know what to say.

"When I couldn't find you," she continued, "I wasn't sure what to do. Carrig came to me when he heard about the unmatched changeling. He told me he was the father of the missing Sentinel and Marietta was the mother. I was terrified. We knew you were the one the seer presaged, so we decided to keep you a secret. We raised Deidre together. In time, Carrig and I fell in love, and Marietta became his past. As for you, he figured you were better off ignorant of this life."

"Then you're not mad at my mother for hiding me?"

"Oh, no." A smile hinted in her voice. "She only wanted to protect you. I'd have done the same."

"Oh. Crap. I almost forgot," I said. "When I asked the globe what happened to Carrig, it showed me a black flag with a red flame in the middle."

Sinead grabbed her throat.

"It's the Esteril flag," Arik said. "Conemar has him."

"Conemar? That wizard from France? The one you said was behind the attacks on the havens?"

"Yes, him," he said. "He was born with an evil soul. A wizard compelled his mother while she was pregnant with him. In the course of the act, the man died. When a wizard dies during a compulsion, his or her victim becomes insane. It is very costly for a wizard to compel someone. Their life spans diminish while casting the compulsion spell. Usually, it would've taken months for the wizard to run out of life at his young age, but it only took weeks. The baby drained the wizard's life span at a faster rate than normal."

I swallowed. Chills ran across my skin. I didn't like this story. "Where is Conemar now?"

"He was exiled under the suspicion of murder. Esteril, the Russian haven, eagerly took him in. They hadn't had a High Wizard since the sixteenth century due to a curse an enchantress, Athela, placed on the haven. It is believed she went crazy when her husband died."

Yeah, I'd go crazy too if my father turned my husband's corpse into a beast.

"Am I to rot here?" Sean adjusted in the chair. "All this talk be spooking me."

Him and me both.

"You sit there and don't say another word," Sinead snapped. "When our friends come, we'll get you back to Ireland. Until then, keep your mouth shut."

"Jeez, give the guy a break. It's not his fault he's here."

"I'm sorry." Sinead exhaled. "I'm just worried about Carrig, and Sean reminds me of him."

The book shuddered against the table and the tracer flew out, dissipating into a thousand glitters that floated to the ground. The pages of the book flipped, and when it stopped, Demos swirled out and landed on his feet on top of the table. He leaped effortlessly to the floor.

"You rang?" A crooked smile teased his lips and a naughty glint hinted in his eyes as he inspected my body. "Gia. I dare say, warrior gear suits you."

CHAPTER EIGHTEEN

My heart swelled as I watched Arik stride toward Demos. I'd promised myself to keep my distance, but I couldn't help it. I took an anxious step toward him and stopped, remembering we had an audience. We'd just made it through something horrible together, and I wanted to hug him. He was so strong, fearless. But I turned away instead.

The grave look on Sinead's face must've struck Demos, because his smile slipped when he saw her. "What's happened?" He glanced at Sean. "Carrig, is something the matter?"

"That's not Carrig," Arik interrupted. "He's his changeling. Conemar kidnapped Carrig and switched Sean with him. He weaved their minds together."

"How?" Demos's eyebrows pinched together as he studied Sean. "And how was he able to jump through the gateway book?"

"While their minds are weaved together, Sean receives Carrig's memories and abilities," Sinead said.

"Gia must perform a truth globe on you before we continue," Arik said.

Demos agreed and after he had passed, we told him how my pink globe released Sean.

"I think it runs on my emotions," I said. "It removes charms and spells."

"I think that's why Veronique attacked us," Sinead said.

Demos's eyes widened. "Veronique?"

She nodded. "Yes. I'm not certain, but she could be involved with the recent assaults on the Mystiks."

Disappointment clouded Arik's eyes. "I must contact Merl."

Arik fished a thin rod from his pocket, which was actually two rods fashioned together. He pulled the ends apart and a blue glow kindled between them, creating a screen the size of an iPad. "Merlin Sagehill," Arik spoke into it.

"What's that?" I asked.

"It's a window rod. It's like a webcam, but powered by magic. It's our only connection to Asile. The charms around Asile block cell phone reception."

Several minutes passed.

I frowned at the thing. "It's broken."

"Give it time. He has to find a safe place to answer it."

The light between the rods blinked, and Merl's face came across the screen as a ghostly blue form. "Brilliant, I see you have Gia. Has she informed you of the goings-on?"

"Yes. How's Asile?"

Merl's eyes landed on me, which came across somewhat creepy. "Adding to the charm to open the door on my command alone was quite clever, Gia. We cornered Veronique at the outbuilding as she tried to escape." He addressed Arik again. "We scried her. She's conspiring with Conemar, who's behind the recent attacks on the Mystiks. He has spies in every Haven. Veronique overhead you talking to me about finding Gia, thus had Conemar spell Carrig. Using his changeling to observe her—" Static ran across the screen.

Arik tilted the rods to get a better reception. "What do they want with her?"

I leaned closer to hear Merl. "Yeah, what he said."

"From what I gathered from Veronique, they hoped she'd lead them...the chart...to locate...Chiavi."

"Wait, you're breaking up." Arik moved closer to a window with me stuck to him like static cling. The rod's reception improved.

Merl squinted at the screen. "Can you hear me better?"

"Yes, go ahead."

"Veronique sent Gia, Nick, and Afton's addresses to the rogue Mystiks searching for them. She got the information from your mission recorder. We'll discuss how she got access to it later, but for now, there are more pressing matters. Brian Kearns and Deidre are in danger—"

I sucked in a sharp breath. "What?"

Arik held up his hand to quiet me.

Merl didn't stop for my interruption. "You must rescue them and the other two humans, Afton and Nick. Bring them back to Asile. The Wizard Council has approved their travel here and registered them with the Monitors. They'll go undetected through the gateways."

"We will," Arik said. "But we haven't completed our mission. Most of the cities are secured, but I returned to Asile to tell you the Writhes' coven has fallen. There are few who survived."

Merl's face was grim. "I will send guards to retrieve the survivors. Report back when you have the humans. Go safely."

"Wait. My nana and Faith. Are they okay?"

"They are. I'll keep them safe," he said. "You're not to worr—"

The blue light between the rods went dark. Arik eased

them together and buried it back into his pocket.

I heaved a sigh, relieved they were alive, then remembered what Merl had said. I dashed back to the book. "Pop's in danger! We have to get him," I said, flipping through the pages to find the Boston library.

Arik caught my arm, stopping me. "Calm down. We wait for the others. Once they pass your globe, we'll leave."

"We can't wait—"

"Bloody hell, Gia. Will you just listen to me? We need the other Sentinels. There's no other way. We can't just rush to the rescue without help."

"I'm not going to risk waiting!"

He scowled down at me.

I watched his hard, dark eyes. "I'm going without you, then."

He blew out a frustrated breath. "Will you stop being stubborn and listen?"

I crossed my arms, tears burning my eyes. "No. He's all I have besides Nana. We have to go now. The rest can follow."

"Oh, bugger me." He threw his hands up in the air.

I was pretty sure he'd just cussed at me.

"What's wrong with you, Arik?" Sinead said from across the room. "Stop being nasty. Her family is threatened, and you are not sympathetic."

He growled and said in a softer voice, "I apologize. I didn't mean—"

"I'm scared." The tears I'd been holding back flooded over my lashes.

"Oh, now, don't do that." Arik's eyebrows pulled together with concern. "I won't let anything happen to your father and the others. Will you trust me on this? We need help, or we've lost before we've even started." He towed me into a tight embrace. "You remember the hunter in the subway. We'll be much more help to everyone if all of us are working together. Look what we did as a team against Veronique."

Every second of delay was killing me, but he was right. We needed all the Sentinels.

I sagged against his firm chest. I believed he'd probably give his life to keep that promise, and it scared me. As much as I didn't want anything to happen to Pop or my friends, I couldn't accept anything happening to Arik, either. I inhaled his manly scent, my head spinning. I needed time to get to know him better. Tell him how brave he was, how much I admired him, too. I swallowed back the emotions cramming in my throat, unable to gather the courage.

"I trust you," I said.

"Today is Sunday." His posture was more relaxed. "Your father is at work, Deidre is at your practice, Nick's just finishing his shift at his parents' restaurant, and Afton babysits for her neighbor. We should have a good hour before any of them returns home."

I tilted my head to see him. "How do you know all that?"

"From the guards that watched you during the days following the gateway breach—"

His reassurances relaxed me a little.

After each Sentinel had come through the book, I performed truth globes on Kale and Jaran, while Lei sat on a chair, cleaning her nails with a small dagger. After they both passed, Arik informed them of the situation. Sinead motioned for Sean to follow her and Jaran.

"Good luck," Sean said, glancing at me with honest sincerity in his eyes. "I hope your da and friends make it."

"Thank you," I said. "Good luck to you, too."

He took Sinead's offered hand and grabbed Jaran's arm.

"Wait," I said. "The letter from my mother and the picture of my parents, do you still have them? They were in your wallet."

He pulled out his wallet, examined it, and held it out to me. "This isn't me billfold."

I took it from him and retrieved the note and photograph from inside, then handed the wallet to Sinead. However small, they were another connection to my mother, just like the faded umbrella. I slipped the photo and note into my vest pocket and gave the rest to Sinead.

After Jaran spoke the key, the book sucked them into the photograph of the Trinity College Library in Dublin, Ireland.

"Poor Sean." Demos chuckled. "When Sinead clouds his mind, he'll never quite grasp all this was actually true. I bet he won't ever drink whiskey again."

"Or be tricked by hot blondes," I said before walking off to the nearest bookcase. I scanned the titles on the shelf, trying to stay calm. My head pounded and my throat tightened. I just wanted to get to Pop. Arik came up beside me and rested his hand on my back, the warmth of his hand soothing me.

"It's going to be fine," he said.

"I hope so."

Jaran and Sinead's return interrupted him. "That Dublin library needs a good dusting," she said, brushing her hands on her pants. "He'll have to wait until it opens tomorrow to leave. After I clouded his mind, he fell asleep behind a bookcase. He won't budge until someone wakes him. They'll think he got locked in."

Arik addressed the Sentinels kicking back around a table. "Let's make a plan." They all stood and gathered around him. I rushed over to join the circle.

Demos settled his arm across my shoulders. "How are you faring?"

"Fine, I guess."

He handed me a tan trench coat. "Here, put this on."

"What for?"

"Do you want all of Boston to see you in fighting gear? We all wear them."

"You do realize it's summer, right? We'll look suspicious in these."

"Just put it on." Demos winked. "Cheer up. Perhaps we'll be lucky and it'll be raining."

"I just want to *go*, already."

"We'll have to split up," Arik said, glancing at Demos's arm over my shoulder.

Demos withdrew his arm.

"All right, then." Arik glanced at each Sentinel. "This is the moment we've only read about in our studies. A time we never thought would be during our guard." He paused, his lips a straight line. "The Coming is here, and it is our duty to protect against the evils that will follow. I am not sure what we face, but there is not another bunch I would want to go into battle with than this one."

"Nor is there a leader I would rather follow than you," Jaran said as he straightened. "I will fight until my last breath for all that is good."

"As will I," Lei said.

"And I," Kale followed.

Demos smirked. "Such mush."

Lei glared at him.

"All right, no need to get hostile." Demos held his hands up in surrender. "I was just trying to make light of the situation. I'd be the first to run into the fray."

My knees were wobbly and my palms sweaty. How would they feel if they knew *I* was the Coming? I didn't even know what it meant. I wasn't like the rest of them. I didn't want to fight to the death. All I wanted was to get Pop, Afton, and Nick to safety. And get my life back.

Arik cleared his throat and continued. "Take everything but your helmets. Kale will go with Gia to get Afton. Demos and Jaran will retrieve Nick, and I will go with Lei and Sinead to Gia's home."

I stepped forward. "I'm going to my own home."

"It isn't wise," Arik said. "I know you're worried about your father, but we can't have you and Deidre together. Your neighbors may see." He smiled then, a half smile—a crooked, endearing smile. "I will return with your father unscathed."

He had a point. What would everyone think if they saw two of me? Pop, especially, would be really upset until I had a chance to explain. We needed to get him out of there quickly and quietly without a commotion, which someone might notice.

It was hard for me to leave Pop's safety to someone else, but I followed Kale through the gateway book and into the Boston Athenæum. I rushed out of the library with Kale on my heels, not waiting for the others to come through. I stopped at the curb, surveyed the dark angry clouds, and buttoned up the trench coat. At least it was going to rain.

"Do you have money?" I asked as Kale caught up to me.

Kale stared at me quizzically. "What?"

"*Money*. Do you have any?"

"What type?"

Really? Where did he think he was?

"The American type," I said.

"Oh, right." Kale fished through his pockets. He pulled out a bundle of Euros, several twenty-dollar bills, and a few Benjamin Franklins.

My hand shot up in the air when a taxicab approached

and I screamed, "Taxi!"

The ride to Afton's house seemed like it took forever. The taxi had to stop for too many red lights and jaywalkers. I let out an exasperated breath when a bus stopped in front of us and we had to wait.

Kale patted my jittery hand, which rested beside him on the seat. "You needn't worry. It is out of our control."

"How can you stay so calm right now? What if they kidnap Pop and take him to Conemar? We have to get to them before his rogue Mystiks. We all could die."

"Where I was born, they believe the soul is eternal and we live many lifetimes. This body is just one I will occupy during my journey. It comforts me to know this."

"Where were you born?"

"In Manipur, in Northeast India." Kale turned his attention to the window. "I've been there twice. The first time, I saw my changeling living the life that should've been mine, and the second time was"—he paused—"when I learned of his death."

"I'm sorry," I said, feeling bad for him. I never knew what to say when someone lost someone they cared about.

"Thank you," he said. He sighed. "It was difficult for me to see the sorrow my birth mother had over the loss. I wanted to show myself to her, tell her who I was, and make her love me like she had loved him, but that would've been senseless."

How will I feel to actually see Deidre living my life? Would I resent her, or care for her like Kale obviously cared for his changeling?

"I'm scared."

"Never think about the coming fight."

"No," I said. "I'm not scared of fighting, I'm afraid of losing who I am."

"You only lose what you choose to lose."

Rain streamed down the windows as I considered what he said. My life had changed so much in the last month. I wasn't the same person anymore. My magic wouldn't harm anyone, but I'd turned my fencing *epee* in for a sharp sword I might be forced to use. Would I kill someone? I wanted to believe I wouldn't lose myself, but who knew what fear might cause me to do?

The taxi turned off Massachusetts Avenue and onto Lexington. "We're almost there." I scooted to the edge of my seat and watched out the windshield. "It's that big white house."

The tires squealed as the driver slammed on the brakes, and I smacked my forehead against the window partition separating the front and back seats. I eyed the driver as I paid him. "They let you get a license, but me they don't, because I drive *too* slowly. Jeesh. Really. You could've killed us."

"Step away from the cab, please," ordered the driver.

I backed up, and he sped off.

Kale and I stood on the sidewalk and surveyed Afton's house, rain pounding down on us. The front door gaped open, and my stomach plunged to my feet.

Afton, I wanted to scream, but slapped my hands over my mouth.

CHAPTER NINETEEN

K ale lifted his chin in the direction of the door.

My heart hammering, I took measured steps beside him up to the house, alert for danger.

I settled my foot on the first porch step. "This is strange. Their house is usually locked up like Fort Knox, even when they're home."

Oh my god. No! Afton!

Kale grabbed my arm as I started to bolt inside. "Hold on. We do them no good rushing in unprepared."

But I couldn't stand still, rocking impatiently on my feet as I watched him.

He reached into his trench coat and pulled out a pair of gloves. He slipped them on his hands and wrapped the straps around each of his forearms, then hid his arms in the flaps of his black trench coat.

Right. I had to prepare. Had to start thinking like a warrior instead of a scared little girl. But it was hard to stay calm when I imagined a million different scenarios involving Afton—all of them ending badly. I gulped down my fear, drew my sword from its scabbard, and kept it close to my side. The shield resting on my back under my trench probably made me resemble the Hunchback of Notre Dame.

I trailed him over the threshold with my sword extended. "It's too quiet," I whispered.

Kale raised his hands and pushed his middle fingers against his palms. One sharp blade shot out and extended over his knuckles. Then he flipped his left one over and said a charm, forming his purple globe.

"I thought we weren't supposed to use globes outside the libraries?"

"It's a stun globe and won't destroy anything like Arik's fire or Lei's lightning ones would. Get behind me," he muttered.

I let him lead and readied my sword.

"Relax, Gia."

We circled around the entire first floor. Empty. So not good. Where was everyone on a Sunday?

Then we headed upstairs. The first bedroom was vacant. The next room was Afton's bedroom. The usual incense smell hung in the air. Clothes hung over the footboard of the bed and shoes covered the floor. Her list of Taylor Swift songs played from the dock on her nightstand. On her vanity, lotions, perfume bottles, and makeup containers crowded the table. Not a thing was out of place.

A loud clang came from the bathroom.

"Afton?" I called out.

"Hey, you're early. I just got back from babysitting," she said as she came out of the bathroom. "What the hell?" She looked from me to Kale and then to my sword.

I sheathed it. "Afton, it's me, the *real* Gia." I yanked the collar of my shirt down to reveal my scar. "See? No tattoo."

Afton came closer to examine it. "Oh, I've missed you," she squealed, throwing her arms around me. I hugged her back hard.

"Why is your front door open?"

"My mom went next door for tea. The lock's broken. One good wind and it blows open. They're fixing it sometime today." She pulled back, worry striking her face. "Why *are* you here? The other Gia is on her way over."

"Afton?" A familiar voice came from the door. "What's going on here?" Pop asked. "The front door is wide—" He dropped his car keys, his gaze shooting from me to Deidre standing behind him.

"Pop! You're safe." I dashed over to him and threw my arms around his waist. I couldn't keep the tears from burning my eyelids, and I sobbed into his chest. And then I realized he wasn't hugging me. I leaned back and glanced up at him. He was gaping, his eyes darting back and forth between my changeling and me.

Oh God. There was no lying out of this one. I loosened my grip and stepped away.

My double leaned against the doorframe and glared at me. "He wouldn't be here if you had a driver's license."

Pop turned from Deidre to me. "Why do you look like each other?"

"Um. You see—" I tugged my trench coat closed to hide my sword. "It's because *I'm* your daughter. The girl next to you is Deidre."

Pop studied my face. The confusion in his eyes broke my heart. "Are you twins? Wait, you can't be... I was there when you were born. Are you related?" His forehead wrinkled. It did that whenever he was confused. "Who are you?"

"We're not twins or related," Deidre said. "She's your daughter, not me."

I knew I wasn't supposed to tell anyone about the Mystik world, but did it really matter anymore? Pop would find out soon enough, since we were there to whisk him off to Oz.

I'd tried to tell him about the magical light before and never could. Would my words even come out?

Kale shifted his gaze from Deidre to me. "We're not safe here. We must go."

I nodded. "Yeah, let's get out of here." I looked at Pop. "We'll explain on our way. Please trust us."

Pop rubbed his forehead and glanced at Deidre.

"We should go," she agreed.

He nodded and followed her out the door, and my heart twisted in my chest. She was taking over my life. Over Pop.

Afton slipped her hand in mine. "Come on."

Sitting in the backseat of Pop's Volvo felt odd. Not only was Deidre taking over my life, but she also claimed the front seat. Where I've always sat since forever. It hurt so badly I felt like my chest had been torn open. Pop gripped the steering wheel so tight his knuckles turned white. His jaw muscle twitched, and I knew he was clenching his teeth. I hated making Pop feel this way. Scared? Confused? Both ?

I scooted forward and placed my hands on the back of the front seats. "Remember that time when I was going into the first grade and I was so scared I wouldn't go into the classroom? Back when you used to call me Bumblebee? You had told me it may sting at first, but soon it would be all honey. I never got what you meant. It was cute, though, and it still makes me smile."

Pop nodded. "I never was good at analogies."

"Nope."

He glanced at my double then returned his focus to driving. "So, Gia, who's Deidre? And how does she look exactly like you?"

I gulped. Deidre started to open her mouth, but I frowned at her. "This is going to sound like I'm crazy."

"I'm sure it will."

I explained everything to him while everyone else pretended to look out the window. I figured I'd show him my light globe later, when he wasn't driving. I wasn't sure I wanted to show him Mom's letter, though. Maybe he didn't need to know how much she'd loved Carrig.

He looked at Deidre again. "That explains why you've been acting odd lately."

"So you see, you have to come with us. You're not safe here. In Boston."

"My mother's a witch, huh? That answers a lot of questions." He rubbed his neck.

"I love you, Pop."

"You too, kiddo," he said, reaching over the seat and squeezing my hand. "We better hurry, huh? It's like having twins," Pop directed to Deidre. "I was beginning to get suspicious. You and Gia are polar opposites. She can't cook and she's a slob, and you can cook and you're tidy. I worried someone had clobbered you on the head during kickboxing lessons. I was about to call a doctor friend of mine."

Deidre laughed. "It's been such a rush. I hadn't time to learn about Gia's quirks."

"There's the parking garage," I blurted, wanting to end their conversation about my hijacked life.

"I see it," Pop said.

He kept giving me weird looks on the walk to the Athenæum. His shoulders were slumped, and his face looked worn out. I wished we hadn't had to drag him into this otherworld stuff, but at the same time, I was relieved he was there, and I relaxed. I squeezed his hand to show how happy I was to be with him again.

Demos was waiting on the steps for us.

A thought struck me. "We should call Arik and let him know Deidre and Pop are here."

"Right. They're most likely waiting for them at your apartment." Kale pulled his cell phone out of his pants pocket and poked the numbers on the screen.

"Yes?" Arik's voice blasted through the phone. Kale must've accidentally hit the speaker button. Clanging and crashing sounds came over the phone.

"This is Kale. What's going on there?"

"Sword fight. I have—"

Clang!

"To—"

Clang!

"Go—"

Clang!

Fear ignited within me. I wanted to rush to Arik. Help him.

A man walking by gave Kale a startled look.

"It's a video game," I said to the guy.

The man shook his head and continued on his way.

A grunt came over the phone.

"Mr. Kearns and Deidre are with us." Something crashed in the background. "What was that?"

"A telly. Apologies to Mr. Kearns." A growl came across with a burst of static. "Don't worry about us—" Something like glass shattered over Arik's last word. "We'll meet you there."

"How many are adversaries?" Kale asked.

"Too many—" *Clang!*

Without thinking, I started for the exit, but Demos grabbed my arm. "Let's go," I said. "We can help—"

Kale frowned at me then said, "Do you need us to assist you?"

"No." *Crash!* "We have it under control. Keep the others safe. That's an order." An end of call chime sounded.

"Now that's talent," said Deidre. "Talking on a mobile while sword fighting."

I gaped at her. Arik was in danger and she admired his multitasking skill?

Kale pushed the off button on the screen. He grinned at Pop uncertainly. "Don't worry about the mess. We have Cleaners who will fix everything."

"I don't care about the stuff," Pop said. "I'm worried about that boy. Aren't you?"

I turned to Kale, desperation lacing my words. "We have to help. He only has Sinead and Lei."

Something flashed in Kale's eyes when I mentioned Lei's name. "Yeah, all right. We better check it out. Demos, you'll come with me," he said. "Where are Jaran and Nick? He can keep watch on the others."

"We had a run in with a hunter," Demos said. "We got separated. They should be here in a bit."

"Shite." Kale glanced down the street. "I can't leave Gia alone with them. You'll have to stay behind. I'll go on my own."

Like hell I'm staying. "You don't know your way around Boston," I said. "I'm going with you."

"I've been here—" Kale hesitated when I gave a pleading look behind Pop's back. "All right. I could use a guide."

After some arguing, Pop agreed to let me go. Kale and I grabbed a taxi and had the man drop us off down the street from my apartment.

I adjusted the shield on my back and tied the trench's belt tighter around my waist. Kale stopped under the apartment complex's canopy. The place was quiet.

"How'd you know which building was mine?" I asked.

"I shadowed you the two days before you came to Asile. I was your guardian, so to speak."

I swung a sidelong look at him. "You had to be bored. Watching me."

"On the contrary, you have interesting habits."

I opened my mouth to ask what habits, but the door swung open and a man in his seventies stepped out. Good thing, since I didn't have my key.

"Oh, hello, Mr. Navarro," I said as I dashed up the steps. He wore a dark suit with a white gardenia stuffed in the lapel.

"Gia." He nodded, hobbling down the steps. "I have a date. I can't talk. I'm late," he answered my puzzled look as we passed each other.

"Have a good time," I called after him and darted through the door Kale held open for me.

Kale strapped on his hidden blades as we ghosted up the long interior stairwell leading to the apartment. We reached the front door in a matter of seconds. A loud crash sounded upstairs. Kale and I grabbed for the doorknob at the same time. He let me open it as he readied for an attack.

It was as if something had blown up inside the apartment. Papers and couch stuffing, mingling with smoke, floated in the air. Several charred books lay beneath the cooked bookcase, and the overhead lamp hung from the ceiling by a single cord. The ornamental mirror in the entryway was in shattered pieces on the floor.

"Good thing Mr. Navarro's hard of hearing," I said.

When we reached the top of the stairs, it was eerily quiet.

Broken glass crunched underfoot as I eased into the apartment. "What happened here? This is horrible." *Oh please, let them be okay.*

"This is dire," said Kale, his face etched with concern.

"Where are they?" I took another step.

Kale moved in front of me. "Careful. We have to assess the situation."

A loud crack reverberated throughout the apartment. Both Kale and I spun around looking for its origin. It sounded again above our heads, and I glanced up, plaster showering my face. With a final groan, the ceiling crashed down on us.

I lay on top of the shield strapped to my back, clawing frantically at the ceiling debris burying me. Powder choked my throat and suffocated my nose. Panic seared my mind and I willed myself to stay calm. I reached out, trying to grab onto something.

Two hands clamped onto my wrists and dragged me out of the rubble grave. I coughed, spitting plaster chunks and blowing powder out of my nose.

Kale dusted me off. "Are you all right?"

"I'm fine," I managed to say, shaking debris from my hair. I winced as I pulled a tiny shard of glass out of my cheek. Blood trickled from the cut, and I smeared it away with my fingertips. My head throbbed.

"Arik—Lei—Sinead!" Kale yelled.

"We're in here!" Lei shouted from the kitchen. "Arik's been stunned!"

Kale and I hurried through the narrow kitchen entry. Arik's head lay on Sinead's lap.

I sucked in a scared breath. His face was pale; his chest rose and fell, laboring for air. My hand flew to my mouth. *Oh no!*

Kale kneeled across from Sinead. "Did you see the bleeder who stunned him?"

Lei shook her head. "I only saw the globe whiz by. I didn't see who sent it."

"If you saw a globe, it had to be a Sentinel, and mine

should counter the stun." Kale raised his hand, forming a purple sphere. With a turn of his wrist, the globe dropped onto Arik's chest, and his body glowed violet.

Arik blinked. His hand twitched. He gasped and coughed, gulping at the air. Kale guided him into a sitting position.

He's okay! I expelled a relieved breath.

"Don't try to fill your lungs all at once," instructed Kale. "Do you remember where you are?"

"Of course I remember where I am. What happened?"

"I released my globe," Lei said nervously.

"What were you thinking? The ceiling fell down on us." Kale aided Arik to his feet. "You can't set off lightning in this small a space."

"I panicked. And so what? I stopped those Writhes." Lei walked over to the kitchen window that overlooked the fire escape. She pushed the curtain aside and peered outside. "The street is quiet. We should go."

"Wait a minute," Kale said. "What are Sentinels doing with Writhes?"

"Before one of the fried Writhes died, I got him to talk." Lei kept her gaze on the window. "The Writhes have joined Conemar in Esteril."

Conemar? I gasped. "Oh, no. Merl said he was sending help to the Writhes."

Arik stared at me until he realized what I was getting at. "It's an ambush. We must contact Merl." He reached into his breast pocket, dragged out the window rod, and pulled the rods apart. Static ran across the blue glow, and it suddenly went black. "Bloody hell. It's damaged."

Lei turned from her patrol at the window. "I'll try mine." She retrieved hers from her pocket and opened it. The space between the rods kindled. She put her mouth close to the screen and spoke Merl's name. Her screen blinked out. "No blooming connection."

"All right, then," Arik said with resignation. "We have to get to the others. We'll come up with a plan once we're in the library." He thumped out of the kitchen. Gone was his smooth stride. He was obviously struggling to rebound from the attack.

Lei hurried past Kale, her small hand brushing his arm. When Kale glanced around to see if anyone noticed the exchange, I looked away in Sinead's direction.

"Deidre is fine," I told her.

Sinead smiled. "Thank you."

"Did any of you see my cat?" I gasped and glanced around. "Cleo!" I called.

"When the fight broke out, she darted out the window," Sinead said. "I'm sorry. You'll have to leave her."

"As long as she didn't get fried, she'll be fine." I sighed. "She'll stay with Mr. Navarro. He likes to feed her tuna." I crossed the kitchen, stopping to lift a chair and push it up against the table. It was silly, I knew. Everything was destroyed so why do that? I was doubtful the apartment could be returned to normal even with the Cleaners. I wasn't sure anything would feel normal to me again. After giving the destruction one last look, I huffed out a breath and trailed Arik down the stairwell and out the front door.

A bright light flashed across the gray sky, and thunder cracked a moment later. Rain plastered my ponytail to the back of my neck. I ducked under a canopy.

"I'm sorry about your flat."

"Thanks." Hopefully, our insurance had battle coverage.

Arik pressed up to my side to avoid the torrent as we waited for everyone else. The scent of smoke clung to his clothes. With him that close, my blood rushed so fast through my body blood swished in my ears. "I can hardly stand you being mixed up in all this," he whispered while tucking a stray ribbon of my hair behind my ear. He suddenly backed away from me. It was as if he was warring with himself. "If you were to get hurt because of me—"

"None of this is your fault."

"It is. Veronique came to Asile to make amends. To be friends—" A sarcastic laugh cut off his words. "I guess I wanted to believe she'd changed. I trusted her. She gathered yours and the others' information from my mission recorder. I left it unattended. Because of me, Asile is in danger."

Trust no one, Gia, he'd said. He was so right. I placed a shaky hand on his arm. "Oh, Arik, I'm sorry."

"No. It's I who should be sorry, not you. I'm lead Sentinel for our group. I shouldn't have taken such liberties and should have worked harder to keep your secrets." He swiped his fingers through his wet hair. "With the recent goings-on, it's best we keep our wits about us."

"Friends, right?" The words tasted like metal and regret in my mouth. I wanted to be his everything. But what I wanted more was to make things easier for him.

His sad eyes locked with mine. "Right, then."

The longing for him to hold me sliced my heart into pieces. The door to my apartment complex opened and Kale stumbled out with Lei and Sinead following. I turned to face the street, the pieces of my torn heart jumbled in my chest. For Arik's sake, I had to let go of the hope of us ever being anything other than friends.

Arik stepped away from me, dragging my mess of a heart with him. "What took you so long?"

"I had to bandage Lei's arm," Kale said. "She has a nasty cut."

"We'd best be on our way," Arik said and headed up the street.

I lagged behind the rest as we rushed to the Athenæum. Every few minutes Arik ran his fingers through his wet hair to get it out of his face. Sinead kept looking back at me, giving me a reassuring smile from under the bucket hat that covered her pointed ears, which I returned with a forced one.

The nearer we got to the library, the sadder I grew about Arik saying he was sorry for taking liberties with me—for getting closer. With his sexy Irish accent, he called out instructions to the other Sentinels, leading the way along Boston's busy streets with his swagger and panther prowess. My heart squeezed at the sight of him.

Am I falling for him? We turned on to Park Street. *If I were, I'd know it, right?* I was so confused. By the time we darted up the steps of the Athenæum, I decided to stay as far away from Arik as possible. It was the only way to protect my heart.

CHAPTER TWENTY

A rik and Sinead sprang up the steps to the Athenæum's door. The rest of us loitered on the sidewalk below. Sinead turned toward the street, fanning the air with her hand, as if she was waving to someone across the way.

Kale came to my side. "It's glamour."

"What?"

"Sinead is cloaking our illegal entry into the library," he clarified.

"Oh," I muttered.

The clouds parted over the State House and glinted over the building's golden dome. The Boston Common was just beyond the State House. Pop and I used to picnic there, watching the blue tower light on the old Hancock building. *Steady blue, clear view. Flashing blue, clouds due.* Pop would recite the rhyme that helped everyone remember what the lights stood for. If the light was red, we stayed home. On the Saturdays it was blue, we'd sit on the grass, filling each other in on how our week had gone, before life got too busy. He'd hid his disappointment well when each time he'd invite me, I'd make an excuse. I never realized I missed those lazy Saturdays until now. I guess pending doom pulls on a person's heartstrings.

Arik slid a gold rod between the cracks of the heavy, ornate doors that were only closed and locked after library hours. When he was done, he pulled them apart, revealing the red leather doors hidden behind them. He held one open as the others passed through. When I went by, he gave me his usual crooked grin. My stomach twisted.

Sinead raised her arms and twisted her hands. The lights flicked on across the room.

My heart sailed when I spotted Pop in the lobby. I ran over and flung my arms around him. He held me tight as we rocked in our silent embrace. An embrace that said what words couldn't, that though he wasn't my birth father, he was my pop, the one who mattered most.

"Did you have any problems getting here?" Arik asked Jaran.

"We ditched a hunter and then had to wait awhile for the street to clear, but other than that, no problems," Jaran answered. "The library is as quiet as a tomb."

Pop and I let go of each other. I noticed Nick stood off to the side by himself, and I sprung for him next. He wrapped his arms around me.

"Man, am I glad to see you," he said. "The other Gia is driving me crazy."

I giggled and released him. "Glad to see you, too. How are things going with Afton?"

"I'm over her."

"What do you mean, *you're over her*?"

Nick shrugged. "I like someone else—you know."

"No. I don't *know*. I've been gone. Who exactly do you like?"

"Deidre."

"But you just said she drives you crazy?"

His lips pulled into a mischievous grin. "Yeah, I guess it's a good kind of insanity. It was weird at first, since she's identical to you, but your personalities are *way* different."

Really weird. "Wow. Thanks, I guess."

"Excuse me, I have boyfriend duties." He moseyed over to Deidre and Sinead, who were still holding each other. Deidre released Sinead and introduced Nick when he reached them. Sinead smiled as Nick slid his arm over Deidre's shoulders. Pop shuffled over and introduced himself to Sinead.

Arik, grouped with Kale and Lei, tried to get a connection on a window rod.

Jaran came to my side. "It was quite brave of you to go with Kale to help Arik and the others."

"Thanks for taking care of my friend."

"It's my duty." Jaran's eyes found Nick. "You know the way he dresses—I mean—well, I thought he preferred boys."

I chuckled. "Most people think that about Nick at first because he's into fashion, but he's totally into the ladies."

A flash of disappointment crossed Jaran's face. "Well, should you need of anything, please feel free to ask," he said.

Interesting. Is he attracted to Nick?

"Thanks, I will," I said.

"Splendid. Excuse me," he said and headed over to Arik's huddle.

Afton cut across the room and gave me a tight hug. "Were you in a cat fight or what?" She snorted, pulling a piece of plaster from my hair. "You look like hell."

"Thanks, just give it to me as it is. I hate when people sugarcoat things."

Arik stood in the middle of the lobby. "All right,

everyone. We'll be leaving shortly. I haven't been able to reach Asile. Sentinels, you know what that means."

"Yep." Demos carried in a large duffel bag and started handing out our helmets.

I stepped forward. "I'm a Sentinel, and I haven't any idea what not hearing from Asile means."

"You aren't part of this, Gia," Arik said. "You haven't finished your training."

I moved closer to him and frowned. "I've had enough training."

"I'm in command," Arik said, "and I say you stay behind."

"My globe can help. It shields," I argued.

"May we speak alone?" he asked.

"Sure. Whatever." I stomped after him to the nearest room.

Pop barged into the room after us.

"I must talk to Gia alone," Arik said to him.

Pop folded his arms across his chest. "She's my daughter. Her welfare's my concern."

Arik yielded. "If you stay, I must ask you to keep this between us. I don't want to scare the others."

Pop came over to me and held my hand. "I won't say a word."

Arik studied our linked hands for a moment then he looked up at us. "I'm afraid Asile is lost. We can only pray for survivors."

I gasped, dropping my helmet. "Nana?"

Pop's face twisted with concern. "She's there?"

"I'm afraid so," Arik answered for me. "If Merl was able to get her out—if anyone escaped, they'll be at the shelter."

"Where's the shelter?" Pop moved into his hospital emergency mode, unwavering under pressure.

"It's a charmed chateau hidden in the countryside

somewhere in France," Arik said. "We have to summon escorts from the French Haven to take us there."

I snatched my helmet from the floor. "We should just go and not risk alerting anyone."

"Only Couve's High Wizard and his Sentinels know the whereabouts of the shelter."

"How do we know they're on our side?" I said. "Veronique's from there."

"Her actions do not make them all guilty." Arik's face held both concern and strength at the same time.

"He's right," Pop said.

"The French Haven is in as much danger as us. Their council exiled Conemar to Esteril." Arik paced around a small reading table. "Conemar must have something big planned to feel confident enough to start a war. It would end badly if he acquired all the Chiavi and gained control of the Tetrad. It's going to get hot and too dangerous for you to be in the heat of it."

"Why didn't you guys put him in prison when you had him?"

"Just as the human world struggles to convict criminals, so do the havens. It's called justice."

"Well, justice sucks." I banged my helmet against my leg, ignoring the pain. "And now our world is in as much danger as yours."

"Have you forgotten? Mystik is your world, as well."

Pop came up behind me and dropped his hands onto my shoulders. "Calm down. We have to keep our heads straight."

"Don't misunderstand me, Gia." Arik let out an exasperated breath. "The human world is part of our world. Wizards and Sentinels are partly human. We'll fight to the end to protect both worlds." He turned his back and mumbled, "We're not monsters."

"Son, no one thinks you're a monster." Pop squeezed my shoulders, egging me on to agree with him.

"No, Arik. I don't think you're one," I said, faintly. The last thing I wanted to do was to make him feel like a monster. "But I can't stand by and not be in the heat of it. My birth started all of this. I'm a Sentinel just like you."

Pop removed his hands from my shoulders. "Can you give me a weapon?"

Arik turned around, startled. "I can't have you risking your life."

"I'm guessing it's already in danger." Pop's red unkempt eyebrows knitted together. "Don't you think I should be able to defend myself?"

Arik bent over, pulled a long dagger from his boot, and handed it to Pop.

Pop took the dagger. "What, no guns?"

Arik shook his head. "We don't use guns. The laws established at the Mystik Summits forbid their use in the libraries. Only hand-to-hand combat and magic abilities are legal. There are enchantments over the libraries that disable the propellants of bullets."

"What are the Mystik Summits?" Pop asked.

"It's an annual gathering of the Wizard Council and the Mystik League," Arik said. "They discuss matters to keep the Mystik world hidden from humans—"

"Wait," I cut in. "I read about this in a book called *The Invisible Places*."

Arik smirked.

"I don't see what's so funny," I said.

"The book's author is Professor Gian Bianchi. He was to be the next High Wizard of Mantello, the Italian Haven, before he died."

I blinked at him.

"You don't see the similarity of your names? Your mother's name is Marietta *Bianchi*. They have the same last name." He paused to see if I caught on. "He was your great-grandfather. You're named after him."

"I see." My mind wrapped around the importance of this revelation. I felt a little stupid for not noticing the name similarity before. "So I have a wizard gene–that's good, right?"

"Not really. We all have wizards in our lineage. Having more Sentinel blood than any Sentinel alive is, though." He studied my face. "I just wish you were better trained. You could have all the talents in the world, but without training, they're worthless."

I stiffened. "I could beat you any day."

"All right, you needn't get upset. I just meant as far as your magical powers are concerned. I've heard you have good sword skills."

"You think you know everything, don't you?" I said.

He smirked again. "I'm not so pretentious to think I know everything."

"Arik, we have guests," Lei said from the doorway. "The Sentinels from France are here, and guess what?"

Arik frowned at her.

"I gather you're not in a guessing mood, eh?" She grinned at him. "Bastien's with them."

"Why did *he* come?" Arik growled and then stormed off for the doorway.

"Who's Bastien?" I asked Lei as we followed Arik.

"Bastien Renard is the son of the French High Wizard, Gareth." Lei laced her arm through mine. "He's simply gorgeous, and kind, and is like a rock star around the Mystik world."

Afton joined Lei and me as we walked into the room. "Hot

warrior boys are here," she purred. "And. They. Are. *French*."

In the other room, two girls and three guys dressed in Sentinel garb stood behind a gorgeous guy of about eighteen or nineteen. His blue eyes sparked under the lights. A sloped nose ran in a straight line down his face, ending at a confident smile on his beautiful lips. Sweeping dark strands of hair framed his face. He wore black pants and a tight gray T-shirt, which hugged each chest and arm muscle perfectly. I got the whole rock star status Lei mentioned. The guy was so hot, it felt like the room temperature rose with him in it.

Arik walked up to Bastien. "Why are you here?" he asked stonily. "You're not a Sentinel."

"My father thought it best for me to assist you," answered Bastien. "These are dangerous times, wouldn't you say? A wizard can come in handy."

"I see you're missing a Sentinel." Arik's jaw tightened. "Do you miss your sweetheart, you Judas?"

"What are you talking about?"

Arik snatched the collar of Bastien's shirt. "Veronique. She told me she was dating you. She attacked our haven. You had to have known what she was up to."

The five Sentinels behind Bastien moved toward Arik. Jaran, Kale, and Demos cut them off.

"Tell them to back off," Arik ordered through locked teeth.

"Do as he says," Bastien choked out as Arik tightened his hold. "Listen Arik, I'm not with Veronique."

"She said she was dating a Renard."

"It wasn't me." Bastien clutched Arik's hands and tried to tear them away. "It was probably my brother, Odil."

"Arik, let him go." Kale grabbed his shoulder. "This won't solve anything."

Arik released his grasp on Bastien's shirt. "Odil? I forgot

about him. Has he been acting strangely?"

"He always acts strange."

"All right, then," Arik said. "You need to prove it. Will you let one of mine perform a truth globe on you and your Sentinels?"

I warmed with pride when Arik called me one of his.

Bastien seemed puzzled. "No one has been able to perform a truth globe in over three hundred years. I didn't know your haven possessed one." His gaze touched each Asile Sentinel. "Are they twins?" His eyes drifted from Deidre to me, and I drew in a shaky breath. "Hold on, now, is one a changeling?"

"Yes." Arik gestured to me. "This is our missing Sentinel, Gianna"—his hand shifted toward Deidre—"and her change-ling, Deidre."

Bastien's smile faded, and he stepped over to me. "It can't be. They told me you died at birth."

"Well, I didn't." I placed a shaky hand on the hilt of my sword. His silvery blue eyes were unsettling. "Wait. Why would they tell you?"

He took a step forward. "Because you're my betrothed."

I took two steps back. "I'm your *what*?"

CHAPTER TWENTY-ONE

I had to get some space, so I marched over to a vacant corner of the room. Lei and Afton came after me.

"He can't be my betrothed. He's a wizard."

Lei adjusted her belt. "Sentinels are betrothed only to wizards. Your bloodline determines what wizard level your husband is chosen from."

Afton laced her arm through mine. "This is so antiquated. But, hey, the boy is smoldering. I say go for it."

Bastien stopped in front of us. "You don't have to fear me, Gianna."

"It's Gia," I snapped. "And I don't. Fear you, I mean." I spotted Arik heading toward us. He looked as stunned as I felt.

"You better back down, Renard," Arik said.

"Don't push me, Sentinel. I wouldn't harm my betrothed."

"She's just a girl," Pop said, coming up to us. "She's no one's betrothed."

"Who are you?" Bastien asked.

"I'm her father."

"Well, she was promised to me," Bastien said and squared his shoulders. The angles of his chiseled face made every tilt of his head amazing. "It was a promise made between the High Wizards of Asile and Couve."

The way he scrutinized me made me a little dizzy but I ignored it. This was beyond crazy. No way was I going to feel anything toward some guy they'd force me to marry. "I'm sorry," I said. "But I don't care about a promise between people I don't even know."

"Come with me." Arik took my hand, and, still flustered, I let him lead me to the nearest room. "Listen, Gia, we haven't time for this. We'll deal with this later."

I nodded.

"Bastien, bring your Sentinels," Arik called over his shoulder. "We'll do the truth globes in here." He dragged two chairs together and motioned me to take one.

After I'd finished with the French Sentinels and their alliance with Asile was verified, Bastien sat down to have me verify his. Everything about him suggested royalty. I kept my focus on the globe, trying to ignore the intense vibe coming from him. He passed, and I was eager to get some distance between us. But he just sat there, not moving, staring at me with those eyes that held so much depth it was like falling into the ocean.

"You should be proud being betrothed to me," he finally said. "One day I'll be the high wizard of Couve and you'd be like a queen."

I adjusted uneasily in my chair. "What if you hadn't found me? Isn't there a runner up or something? I'm happy to give her my spot."

Amusement played on his face. "If you're trying to dissuade me, you're doing a horrible job."

"I take it you're not used to rejection," I said.

He lifted a smile. "I'll admit it's a rare occurrence."

Arik took a step toward us. "All right, we're finished here."

Bastien stood and leaned over to my ear. "You not wanting nobility intrigues me. I'm curious to learn more about you, Gianna." His whisper tickled my neck and sent a shiver down my back. I held my breath, every inch of my body at attention. He straightened, gave me a wink, and swaggered to the door with Arik on his heels.

Holy crap. I felt like I'd just melted in my chair. The boy was definitely confident, maybe on the side of arrogant, but something about him made me want to know more, too.

Arik glanced back and caught me watching Bastien's retreat. I dropped my gaze and played with the fraying hole in my jeans. The look on his face was somewhere between disappointment and anger. But why? He'd made it clear there could never be anything romantic between us.

Alone with the familiar smells of the library, I shut my eyes and inhaled the musty scent of old books. Sitting in the middle of history with the scent of aged leather and floor polish teasing my nose, I began to relax.

"Well, did they pass?" Lei entered the room. "Arik won't say. For some reason he's all puffed up like a blowfish, brooding."

I lifted my heavy head. "Yeah, they did."

"Are you okay?"

"I'm just a little weak. We haven't eaten in a while. I'll be fine in a moment."

Lei crossed the room, pulling a power bar from a side pocket in her cargo pants. "Sorry it's a bit squishy, but it's food."

"Thanks."

Lei pulled out another flattened bar, and we ate in silence. When she was finished, she extended her hand to me. "Come on, let's join the others."

"Yeah, okay." I grasped her hand and let her pull me up.

"This whole business about betrothals is a bother,

isn't it?"

"It's pretty stupid, if you ask me." I curled my hand into a fist. "There's no way someone else is going to pick who I marry."

"I'm not certain the Wizard Council realizes what one will risk for love." A sadness hinted on her face before she forced a smile. "On the upside, you could do worse. Most girls would think they won the betrothal lottery with Bastien." She headed back to the door, flinging her wrapper in a nearby trashcan.

I stopped. "Who's Arik's betrothed?"

She turned around, raising a curious eyebrow at me. "You're still pining for him, huh? She's a mage in Esteril. A very wholesome girl."

Blood rushed to my face. "I'm not *pining* for him."

"All right, Ducky, and I'll pretend to believe you."

"What about you?" I challenged her. "Can you give up true love for your betrothed?"

She shrugged.

"I bet you like the silent, strong type," I teased her. "Say, with an East Indian flare."

"I gather you've figured out Kale and I fancy each other." A mischievous smile crossed over her lips. "And no, I can't imagine being with anyone else."

I dumped my wrapper in the trashcan and followed her out of the room. Everyone's attention was on us when we walked into the lobby.

"We have a few from the human world with us," Arik was saying to Bastien when we joined them. "I must get them to the shelter."

"I think we should go to Couve first," Bastien said. "If my brother is Veronique's lover, I fear for my Haven. With our Sentinels gone, my people are vulnerable. If your Sentinels come with me, I will send one of mine to take the humans to the shelter."

"That will do," Arik said.

Bastien spoke to his Sentinels in a hushed voice. I couldn't make out anything he said.

Arik came over to us. "Jaran, I want you to go with Mr. Kearns, Deidre, Afton, and Nick to the shelter. The rest of you will come with me to Couve."

"What's Couve?" Nick asked.

"The French Haven," Lei answered.

Pop rested his hand on my cheek. "Promise me you'll be careful."

I rested my hand on his. "I promise."

"I'm not ignorant, you know?" He smiled. "I knew there was something different about your mother. I felt there was something more to my mother. And I'm sure there is something magical about you. It's hard to let go. Let you be who you're meant to be…but I know I must." The tears in his eyes mirrored mine.

Deidre stepped forward. "I've been trained to fight. I should go, as well."

Sinead's head snapped in Deidre's direction. "No. You must go to the shelter and help Jaran protect the others."

It was so weird having Deidre around. It was as if I was watching and hearing myself.

Deidre scowled. "As you wish, Mother."

Jeez, I would have begged and protested longer before giving up. Watching Deidre give in to Sinead's magic without putting up a good argument made me feel guilty about all the times I pestered Pop until he'd given in to my requests. A headache was building behind my eyes and I rubbed my temples.

Bastien was at my side in a flash. "If you aren't well, I'll aid you through the gateway."

"No, that's okay," I protested. "I can jump by myself."

Arik leaned against a wall across the room, eyeing us with a scowl. He angrily unhitched himself from the wall. "Let's get this over with," he said then jumped into the open gateway book on a nearby table.

One by one, the Sentinels jumped into the photograph of France's Senate Library. Before I jumped in, Bastien wrapped his arms around my waist, tugging me into the page with him.

"Let go of me!" I yelled.

His grip tightened. "It'll throw us off balance."

"You're really something, you know that?"

"I'm pleased you finally realize that." His breath puffed against my neck and my stomach twisted. We fell in silence for several minutes, until we landed in the middle of a battle.

Colored globes flew by like paintballs in an arena, smashing against walls and shields, bursting into flames, shooting whips of light, and blowing gusts of wind. Lashing swords, explosions, grunts, and yells echoed around the room. A French Sentinel fought off a hairy eight-armed man near us.

Across the room, Arik battled a hound, just like the one that had attacked Nick, Afton, and me in the Paris Library. Arik darted and rolled away from the beast. The hound charged him. A fire globe burst to life on his palm and he manipulated it into a fiery whip, snapping it at the hound until it backed away. Once the hound was in range, Kale stabbed it with his sword.

To my right, Demos held tight to a rolling track ladder with his sword extended, speeding across a bookcase toward a Writhe who was climbing the shelves. The track ladder stopped violently, and he swung his sword at what I recognized from the books as a Writhe. The blow fell short, hitting a shelf.

The Writhe soared to the floor, swinging a spiked mace. Demos shrugged with a cocky snicker and slid down the ladder, his sword meeting the Writhe's mace at the chain. The chain broke and the spiked-ball fell to the floor. The Writhe and Demos stared at the decapitated mace.

Thick veins branched across the Writhe's pale bald head like raised roots of a tree. The frozen expression on his face reminded me of a theatre tragedy mask. When the spell of the murdered mace wore off, Demos and the Writhe resumed their battle dance. The Writhe contorted his body away from Demos's sword, twisting and bending in different directions to avoid each blow. Demos chased him down an aisle of bookcases.

A Laniar sprinted on all fours and attacked a hairless creature with an oversized head, a spindly body, and tons of teeth heading for Arik. The creature whipped its tail at the Laniar, who clawed the demon with its sharp nails, then latched onto the creature's throat with its canines. Dark blood sprayed down the Laniar's pale chin.

I choked on a gasp and spun away. *Oh my God.* A wave of nausea swooshed through my stomach. Everything was in fast motion around me, I couldn't move.

In the middle of the room, Lei and Kale stood back-to-back, throwing globes at their adversaries. Lei hit three Writhes at once with a lightning globe, while Kale stunned a charging man shrouded in a cape. There were several cloaked men, their faces hidden in the shadows of their hoods, battling the other French Sentinels. I spotted Sinead fighting one, the hood slipping off and exposing the woman underneath.

Veronique. How did she get out of Asile?

Just as Bastien shoved me to the floor, a purple globe whizzed by my head and hit him. My helmet flew from my hand and rolled across the floor. Bastien slumped to the ground, and I scrambled to him. Though his body was immobile, he breathed. The stun globe had hit him.

On the floor, Bastien struggled to breathe.

Kale. He can help.

I searched the room for him. A small man in a colorful suit—a typical Napoleon Bonaparte type—bounded in my direction. Lightning flashed between his hands, and by the fix of his eyes, he planned to send it my way.

Panic surged through me, and I threw up my hands as if I could block the man's attack. A pink globe sprouted and engulfed Bastien and me. The man slid to a stop in front of the globe.

He titled his head to the side and cracked his neck, bouncing the electric currents between his hands. A wicked smile played on his lips. "Well, well, Agnost's prophesized child. Impressive, Gianna. You may be of use, after all."

Put on a brave face. You can't let him know you're afraid.

"Conemar," I sneered.

"I see my reputation precedes me." His lips twisted into a smirk. "Your great-grandfather refused me. That is why I put my knife between his ribs. You would be smart to give up now."

He touched the pink membrane separating us and closed his eyes. A force pushed against the globe. I gritted my teeth, willing the globe to hold. After a while, he removed his hand.

"Good girl. This globe is strong. I've never seen one grow like this before," he said, running his hand across the outside as though he was searching for a weak spot. His gaze landed on Bastien. "Poor Bastien, shall I tell him I just killed his father, or do you want the honor if he wakes up?"

I glanced down at Bastien, still stunned on the floor. His gaze was frozen on the ceiling, and tears slid down his temples. My heart twisted, knowing Bastien had heard Conemar's confession.

There was a *plunk*. Conemar had punched his arm through the globe, and his meaty hand clamped my throat.

"Your globe is easily breached. You must learn to master it."

I gagged against his tight grip. Lights flickered across my vision and I turned faint. I focused on a pulsing sensation deep inside me. It had to be where the globe originated. I put all my will into pushing that feeling out, thinking only of strengthening the globe.

Conemar's grip loosened as the pink membrane strangled his wrist. "You can't win," he hissed. "Drop the globe. Join me and your friends won't die. Think of the power we'll have by controlling the Tetrad. Whatever you want will be yours. Where's the chart, Gianna?"

"Chart?" I croaked.

"The poem with clues to finding each Chiave." He placed his other hand on the globe and pushed harder. "It is said only the presaged can find the Chiavi. A charm on the chart would locate you the moment you entered Asile."

"What are you talking about?" The pink sphere rippled under his effort. "You're fricking crazy. I haven't seen any damn chart." But the image of the book *The Invisible Places* by Gian Bianchi flashed in my mind. The scribbling on the first page was a poem. Professor Attwood had given it to me the first day I was in Asile—it did find me, so to speak. It had to be the chart.

"You have seen it." Conemar crinkled his brows together. The right one shot up higher than the other as he studied my non-poker face. His face was familiar, but I knew I'd never met him before. Or had I?

I concentrated on keeping my palm lifted and the globe

up. "Are you cracked?" I choked out. But I was weakening and the globe was slipping. My insides churned and I struggled to ignore my growing panic and stay focused.

His hand tightened around my throat again. Long fingernails dug into my skin. He frowned. "I can't kill you. I need you. But it doesn't mean I won't cause you great pain."

As I started to pass out, Bastien sprung to his feet, knocking my arm and causing the membrane to bust. My globe must have countered the stun on Bastien. He tackled Conemar, plucking his grip from my throat. I fell to my knees, gasping. Tears stung my eyes and my neck burned where Conemar's nails dug into my skin.

My anger gave me the strength to push to my feet. I pulled my sword from its sheath, fuming. Bastien had Conemar pinned to the floor. Struggling to breathe and too weak to hold Conemar, Bastien lost his grip and rolled over gasping. I rushed over, placing the point of my sword to Conemar's throat before he could get up. I glared down at him. "How does it feel to be cornered?" I pressed the point against his neck. A drop of blood beaded from his skin. "It sucks, doesn't it?"

Conemar smirked. "Go ahead, kill me, and you'll never see your father again."

"Do you mean Carrig?" I spat. "I don't even know him."

Conemar paled. "Well then, kill me, if you have the nerve." He tilted his head and light refracted against his face, again illuminating familiar-looking features and causing me to take a step back. Who was I? This wasn't me. I couldn't kill someone. *I can't do this.* My hand shook and I almost lost the grip on my sword.

"I knew you hadn't the heart for it," Conemar said, scrambling to his feet.

Bastien had regained his breath and dived for Conemar.

A massive hound jumped up on the table beside us, and under its weight, the table crashed to the floor. I spun and lunged at it with my sword. I pushed hard to get the blade to pierce the creature's neck. It was like pushing a toothpick into leather. I yanked the sword out and stabbed the hound again. It howled and dropped to the floor. I slumped, bile burning my throat. *I could kill.* The fear shook me. I wanted out of this nightmare.

A black globe landed at my feet and dark smoke exploded from its sphere, blinding me as it rolled over my head and engulfed the room. The sulfur smell was overwhelming. Bastien and Conemar scuffled somewhere within the smoke screen. Bastien grunted.

"Bastien!" I called out.

"I'm fine," he answered back. "Keep alert. I lost Conemar."

"Retreat!" Conemar yelled from within the smoke.

An explosion knocked me to my knees, whipping my hair across my face. The blast dispersed the smoke. As I gasped for air, Demos threw another wind globe, which cleared the other side of the room. Through the thinned smoke, I spotted Conemar searching the gateway book.

He readied to jump. I willed my pink globe to life and threw it in Conemar's direction, hoping it would distract him. My anger made the globe soar. Just as the globe was about to hit Conemar, Kale stepped into its path as he charged after Conemar and it popped against his body.

Conemar rolled sizzling electric currents between his hands until an orb of energy formed. Kale raised his palm and spoke the charm to ignite his globe. Static zapped above his palm, but nothing formed. He looked at Conemar, and back to his palm, a quizzical expression twisting his face.

Lei drove her sword into a Writhe that blocked her way to Kale. She jerked her blade free, and the Writhe collapsed at her feet.

A sinister grin spread across the wizard's lips as he cocked his hand back to fire the charge at Kale.

"No!" I screamed.

Before Lei reached Kale, Conemar shot the electric bolt into him, and Kale slumped to the floor. Lei dropped beside him and dragged him into her arms. Arik turned his fire globe into a whip and lashed it out at Conemar.

Veronique slid in front of him and blocked the whip with her shield, sparks ricocheting off metal. Using the distraction, Conemar plunged into the gateway book, the disturbing smile still plastered on his face. Veronique sailed in after him. Several cloaked figures followed. The rest of his men lay dead or injured on the floor. A few of Bastien's guards were among the dead.

My breath froze in my chest and I stood there stunned. My heart pounded in my ears, drowning out all the noises around me. I'd never seen a dead body in real life before. The sight of so many made me sick. I bent over, holding my side and catching my breath.

Bastien sat dazed on the floor. I hurried over and knelt in front of him.

"Are you hurt?"

"Just got the wind knocked out of me," he said, struggling to his feet.

I grabbed his arm and helped him up. Once he was steady, I rushed over to Lei, who still cradled Kale in her arms.

"I'm sorry—" My voice cracked. "It was an accident."

"Get out of here. Leave us alone!" Tears dropped from her cheeks and landed on Kale's laboring chest.

I took a step toward her. "Lei, I'm—"

"Just *go away*," she said, almost inaudibly.

I couldn't move.

CHAPTER TWENTY-TWO

A rik hurried to Lei's side. "Is he breathing?"

Demos and Jaran joined them.

Lei just rocked Kale without answering.

"*Lei*," he said more forcefully, "is he breathing?"

Sinead approached from behind Arik and gently grasped Lei's shoulder. "Let me see him."

Lei nodded and stood. Arik wrapped his arms around her and guided her a few steps away from Kale.

Lei glared at me. "It's your fault. What did you do to him?"

"I–I'm sorry," I stammered. "I was aiming for—he stepped in the way."

"Give her time," Bastien whispered, taking my elbow and leading me across the room to a chair.

It's my fault. He's going to die, and it's my fault.

I plopped down on the chair, feeling weak and queasy but not as bad as when I first used my battle globes. The side effects were lessening. While Sinead worked on Kale, I held my breath, hoping I hadn't killed him. When his leg moved, I exhaled. He groaned, and I let out a sigh. Once Sinead eased him into a sitting position, I sobbed into my shaky hand.

Lei flew to Kale, snaring him in her arms. She didn't seem to care who witnessed her kiss him. "Is he going to be okay?"

Sinead nodded and then gave me a sympathetic smile.

The Sentinels surrounded Lei and Kale. I felt like an outsider. Actually, I felt like an epic idiot for throwing my globe without knowing what it would do. It disabled Kale's globe, leaving him vulnerable. He could've died, and it would've been my fault.

Bastien gently touched my arm. "Don't worry. It was an accident. Things like this are unavoidable during battles. It can't be helped."

I caught Arik staring at us, and he diverted his eyes, barking orders to his Sentinels.

"I must get to Couve," Bastien said. "To my father."

"I'm so sorry, Bastien."

He grabbed my hand. "Follow me."

With a sigh, I staggered alongside him into the hallway, too exhausted to think, to do anything besides follow along. The battered French Sentinels labored out behind us.

I rolled my neck to relieve the tension. Beautiful paintings stretched across the ceiling. Set in elaborate gold-trimmed frames, they depicted Roman women in everyday life. One was dressed like a warrior.

I dropped Bastien's hand. "The woman on the ceiling. I know this."

He ignored me, shuffling over to the Sentinels, a stunned expression still on his face.

"Know what?" Arik asked from behind me with Sinead trailing him.

I flinched. "Crap, you startled me." I glanced back up. "The mural. It's a clue to finding one of those keys—"

"Hold on," Sinead said. "We must keep this secret.

Bastien, can you put up a shield to hide our location and to keep this conversation private?"

Bastien nodded, then chanted something with his arms outstretched. A wave of light shot out from him and spread across the ceiling.

Sinead returned her gaze to me. "Now what's this about a clue?"

"In my great-grandfather's book, there's a poem written in it," I said. "I think Gian put it there for one of his heirs to find. By what Conemar said to me, I believe it's a chart with clues to finding the Chiavi. It describes that woman in it."

"A perfect place to hide the chart," said Arik, "since Gian's edition has been out of print for eighty years. I can't imagine why no one else came across it."

"It's charmed. Apparently only the Doomsday Child can see it."

I studied the fresco on the ceiling, trying to remember the poem. Commotion distracted me. Demos and Lei shuffled in, aiding Kale behind her. The jagged cuts on their faces and arms trickled blood, and their clothes were rumpled and torn. Demos helped Lei lower Kale to the floor.

Bastien crossed the hall to us—his face grim and his eyes red. "I must get to my Haven. If your band isn't able to continue with us, then stay."

"Let us recover a moment, and we'll accompany you to Couve," Arik offered.

Demos hopped up from his position on the floor beside Kale. "We have to go now. What if they need help?"

One of the French Sentinels closed his window rod. "I just spoke to the commander of the guards. The attack is over, and the situation is under control. What's your order?"

Bastien's eyes flicked around room, as if taking

inventory of everyone's condition. "All right, my Sentinels need to take a breath, as well. We'll leave on the half hour."

Arik inspected me. "Your neck is marked," he said. "Are you okay?"

"I'm fine." Seeing the concern on Arik's face gave me hope that he still cared, even though I knew nothing could happen between us. He had a *wholesome* girl waiting for him.

"You're unharmed," Arik flung spitefully at Bastien. "What did you do? Hide behind her skirts?"

"No, he didn't," I said, my voice shaky. "He was hit by a stun globe...and...and he stopped Conemar from killing me. It's all my fault."

"No," Arik said. "None of this is your fault. It's all mine. I should've made you stay behind."

My hands clenched, and I shook my head. "No. I forced you."

Arik cupped my shoulder. "I am the leader. All responsibility rests with me."

Bastien shoved Arik's hand from my shoulder and stepped in front of me. "Don't touch her."

I backed away from them, shaking my head. There was more going on here than two guys battling for control, and I didn't like it.

"Don't try me, Renard." Arik formed his hand into a fist.

Demos moved between them. "Hold on, now, no one likes a possessive male." He guided Arik back.

"Speak for yourself, ducky," Lei said, wiping sweat from Kale's forehead with a tissue. "I love me some possessive male action."

Kale gave her a pained smile.

"Don't worry. I won't blast a million watts into him," Bastien said. The sadness in his eyes broke my heart. *How can he be so strong? He just found out his father was murdered.* I'd fall apart if it was me.

Arik gave him a sharp look.

Is Arik jealous of Bastien? A mixture of happiness and guilt rushed through me. One guy I *couldn't* have, and the other I *wouldn't* have because I refused to be betrothed.

I stepped between Arik and Bastien this time. "Stop it, Arik. Conemar said he murdered Bastien's father."

Arik's face softened. "Are you certain?"

"No," Bastien said. "But I must get back home. My mother—" his voice broke and he turned away from the group.

"We must figure out what Conemar is up to," Demos said "And, what exactly does Veronique's presence here mean?"

"I wondered about that, as well," Kale said weakly.

Lei yanked out another tissue from a box in her hand. "Sinead, you were fighting her. Did you find out anything?"

"I searched Veronique's thoughts," Sinead said. "Bastien's brother Odil got into Asile by pretending to carry a message from his father and then freed Veronique from her cell. They narrowly escaped."

"This doesn't make sense," Bastien said, punching the wall beside him and wincing in pain. "How could he do this? How could he kill *our father*?"

Sinead placed her hand on Bastien's shoulder. "I know your brother. He is selfish and easily led. You must stay strong for your mother."

Bastien lowered his head and nodded, holding his injured hand to his chest.

Arik dabbed at a cut on his lip with his fingertip. "If Veronique and Odil barely made it out, then Asile still stands. Merlin must've put up stronger wards."

"Wards that block window rods," Lei added.

Watching Lei in her helmet woke words buried deep within my mind: *Look to the one in Sentinel dress.* One of the images painted on the ceiling was of a woman wearing a golden helmet and a chest guard. Sitting on a rock and studying a map stretched out before her, she held a sword in one hand and a spear in the other, with a shield leaning against her side.

"That's it!" I paced, my face lifted toward the ceiling. "It's something about a small pointy thing in her hand. Oh, her sword. It's small from down here. The Chiave has to be here somewhere." I twirled around, trying to see every piece of artwork in the place. There weren't many, mostly paintings and a white plaster statue of a curvy woman. The plaque said her name was Saint Agnes.

"Care to fill us in on what's going on?" Jaran asked.

"She found the chart in a first edition book of *The Invisible Places*," said Arik.

"Shhh. Let me think." I struggled to recall the poem. "Does anyone know anything about the first Chiave? The book I read said the Writhe's found it or have it."

"The textbooks have it wrong. Writhes didn't find the Chiave, nor do they have it," Sinead said. "It was found in the Vatican's Library by Gian Bianchi. It was a cross pendant. Ever since Gian's murder, it's been missing. It's believed the killer took it from him and hid it somewhere."

Hot flames seemed to consume me. My face burned. "Conemar said he killed Gian."

"That's interesting," Sinead said. "The Writhes had accused Toad, a Laniar, of the crime. Toad was found insane and sent to the gallows beneath the Vatican."

I swiped sweat from my forehead with my sleeve. "There were Writhes fighting with Conemar today."

"If the Writhes are indeed with Conemar," said Arik,

"then most likely an innocent Laniar was imprisoned for the crime. Which means Conemar and the Writhes have been conspiring together ever since Gian's death."

"When did Gian die?" I asked.

"It was 1938," Kale said.

"So that means they've been planning world domination for over seventy-five years at least," I said.

"Conemar was accused of murdering the seer, Agnost," Kale said. "If he was indeed Agnost's killer, then he's been plotting even longer. Agnost was murdered in 1898."

He was born with an evil soul.

"My God, how old is he?"

Demos fidgeted with his sword. "Our textbooks put Conemar in his thirties at the time of Agnost's death, so I'm assuming he's nearing the hundred and fifty mark—midlife for a wizard."

"Didn't Gian write something in his blood before he died?" said Arik.

"He wrote *Libero il Tesoro*," Sinead said.

"Free the treasure," I translated. "That's the title of the poem."

A loud crack reverberated above our heads.

Lightning shot across the ceiling as the fresco came to life. A bird squawked and a horse neighed. The boy holding the horse's reins blew on his horn. The breeze brushing my face carried the sweet smell of grass and the spicy aroma of flowers.

The warrior woman in the painting stood and leaped from the ceiling to the floor. Her skirt caught the air in a parachute of soft peach. She was like an Amazon—a tall warrior woman. The helmet and chest guard she wore were as golden as her skin.

The woman reached her sword out to Sinead, who took

it without hesitation. Then the woman hurled herself back up and into the painting. The wind receded, the lightning stilled, and the woman, horse, boy, and bird froze back into their places within the fresco.

No one moved or made a sound. Several addled minutes went by before anyone stirred.

"We have a Chiave." Sinead held the sword out to Arik. "It must be in the care of our leader."

Arik seized the sword.

The hallway erupted in celebration. All but Bastien, who whispered something to one of his Sentinels. The guy's face hardened.

Lei stopped in mid-celebration. "What's going on here? How did Gia know where to find a Chiave?"

My throat tightened. What could I say? The grim expression on Arik's face did nothing to make me feel better.

Arik cleared his throat. "Gia is the daughter of two Sentinels."

The collective gasp echoed against the walls.

"I knew she was dangerous," Lei spat.

"You're saying we're in the end times?" Kale's voice was scratchy.

Bastien's Sentinel sidled up next to me, sword drawn, as if to protect me.

"No one touch her," Bastien warned.

Arik took an angry step toward Bastien, his hand on the hilt of his sword. "Why would we hurt her?"

My chest tightened as I scanned the Sentinels—would one of them try to hurt me? *Trust no one, Gia* rang in my mind.

Sinead stepped into the middle of the group. "Her birth may have put the events in motion to cause the end of the worlds as we know them, but that doesn't mean she will cause the destruction. You've all taken an oath to protect innocents. No matter what. Gia is an innocent. She's one of you. You cannot turn your back on her. I can feel every emotion in this room, and I'm surprised by some." She looked pointedly at Lei. "What I feel from Gia is her desire to do what is right."

"I'm with you, Gia," Demos said.

I smiled at him, and my muscles relaxed a little.

"I will never let you lose who you are," Kale added.

"Thank you," I mouthed, remembering the cab ride when I told him I was afraid of losing myself. I swallowed the emotion building in my throat, trying to keep it at bay.

Lei huffed, not saying a word as she checked Kale's wounds. I wanted to be anywhere but in the same place as her. Her coldness toward me could have frozen an ocean.

Arik came to my side, leaned over, and lowered his voice. "Follow me. I have to talk to you, privately."

It sounded like an order, so I crossed my arms. "Don't boss me, like the others. Remember *I'm* not a Sentinel yet."

"Are you barmy?"

I loved how his strong brows pushed together over his dark eyes when he wasn't sure about something. "What is that supposed to mean? Speak English, already."

"I live in England. *I* am speaking English," he said. "Have you gone mad?"

I raised an eyebrow.

"Will you *please* follow me? Is that better?"

"Much better, thank you."

I plodded after him into a long corridor with interminable rows of coat racks lining the walls. It had to be where the senators left their coats and stuff when visiting the library.

"What is it?" I asked when we were out of view from the others.

"Remove your sword."

"Why?"

"I want to replace the Chiave with your sword. No one has seen yours or the Chiave up close. They won't even notice the difference. It's the only way to keep it safe."

"All right."

He took my sword and handed me the Chiave. I slid it into my scabbard and ran a finger over the golden hilt. An intense pain hit my breastbone. I gasped. My hand flew to my chest, and warm liquid drenched my fingers. I staggered into Arik's arms.

Arik removed my hand from my chest. "You're bleeding." He pulled back, examining my wound.

"I think someone shot me," I mumbled against his shoulder. I buried my chin into my neck, straining to see the wound. My scar was bleeding. I swiped the bloodied mark with my fingertips.

"There isn't a wound." Arik paused. "I think your blood is calling you."

"What the hell is that supposed to mean?" I panted, more than a little freaked.

"A calling is used to communicate with spirit seers. They're seers who have died." He rubbed his chin. "Usually, a seer cuts themselves and uses their blood with a crystal ball to get a vision from a spirit, but you're not a seer. So it has to be coming from the other side."

"Are you saying a ghost made me bleed?"

"Yes, I believe so. I've heard about spirit seers trying to communicate from the other side through nosebleeds and bloody tears and such. Perhaps you should try and perform a truth globe with it."

"That's just crazy."

He punched out a breath. "Will you please try?"

"Okay." I smeared the blood onto my palm. "What do I

ask it?"

"Perhaps, you should ask it what it wants."

I frowned at him. "You know this is creepy, right?"

He nodded. "But just do it."

My hand twitched as I created a truth globe. The silver sphere struggled to form in my hand. Pain shot across my brain, and I winced.

"What's the matter?"

"I guess it's just a side effect of using the globes." The pain subsided, and the globe balanced on my palm. "What would you like to show me?" I asked it.

I gasped as the sphere's shape changed. It became a silver hourglass, then the bottom half split into legs and the top half grew arms and a head. When the process was complete, a beautiful silver image of a naked woman perched on my palm. Her thigh-length hair draped over the front of her body.

"It is an honor to come before the one Agnost presaged," the woman said, sounding like she spoke through a tin can. "I am Agnes, the spirit of the Chiave found. Until all the Chiavi are recovered, this one will serve you well. This sword is a destroyer of all swords. May you fare well, heir of the Seventh Wizard."

Agnes's silver body thinned and stretched until it turned into a line of silver smoke and dissipated.

"Now, *that* I've never seen before," Arik said.

"Why am I not panicking?" I lowered my shaky hand. "This is crazy. It's a dream. It has to be." My breath quickened.

Arik took my face in his hands. "You *are* panicking. Take a deep breath."

I gulped in some air. "I have to get to Asile and get Gian's book."

"We must get to Couve."

"No," I protested. "You don't understand. The chart is

inside that book. It's on the desk in my room."

"Calm down," he said. "No one in Asile knows the chart is in your book. It will be safe until we return."

"How can you possibly know that? Conemar asked for the chart. It's right in the open. Anyone can find it."

"If they knew where it was, he wouldn't have asked you for it. We can't afford to lose an ally. It's imperative we aid Couve. Will you trust me?"

"Yes, okay," I said with a shaky voice.

"Good." He let go of my face. "Remember, keep mum about the sword exchange."

I nodded, placing my hand to my cheek where his had been.

When we joined the others, Bastien met my gaze. His eyes were almost the color of blue ink on white paper. I absentmindedly rubbed at my throbbing scar. "You're bleeding," he said. The tender concern on his face made me speechless. Why did this guy seem to care so much when he didn't even know me?

"It's not her blood," Arik lied for me, walking between us and blocking my view of Bastien. "Let's be on our way."

We entered Couve through a secret door behind an antique card catalogue. The tunnel was the same as Asile's—dark, damp, and musty. Golf carts, tethered to outlets in the wall, waited at the bottom of the stairwell.

I hopped into the front passenger seat of the last golf cart with Demos and Sinead. It was a tight fit. If I reached my arm out, I could touch the wall racing by.

"Hey, there's only room for one cart in here," I hollered

over the revving engine. "What happens if another one comes from the other side?"

"We die," Demos shouted from the driver's seat around a wide grin.

I rolled my eyes. "Seriously?"

"Did you see the red and green lights above the tunnel as we entered?" Sinead said from the back seat. "The lights let the driver know if he can go through or not."

"Oh." I hadn't seen them. I glanced up at the ceiling on our next turn. There were two square lights, and, thankfully, the green one was lit.

The carts buzzed around corners for nearly an hour before the tunnel came to a wide cavern. We stopped at another staircase and plugged the carts back in. The narrow steps were slimy underfoot, so I grabbed on to the railing going up. We stepped into an outbuilding identical to the one in Asile and went through the door.

The castle of Couve sat on the bank of a large lake. The salt-white walls gleamed in the setting sun, its reflection twinkling on the water. Moss crept over a retaining wall surrounding it. We pushed through the gate and walked the narrow cobbled streets snaking through the tiny village at its base.

Bastien's aristocratic demeanor was gone. His shoulders sagged with the sorrow of his father's death.

Small gatherings of people lined the interior walls of the castle. People crowded each room off the foyer, and many sat on the wide stairway that led to the upper floors. Bastien moved into the crowd. When the somber people noticed him, they gave him compassionate smiles or whispered their sympathy as he passed by, and his shoulders drooped even more. I wanted to ease his pain, but the closer he got to the entrance, the faster he moved, and I couldn't catch him.

Bastien returned each smile given him with a warm one. His hand gently patted each person he passed. Witnessing the love his people had for him, despite his anguish, made me admire his bravery. I would have been a slobbering mess, but he spared time for a nod or quiet word.

The crowd slowed him, enabling me to reach his side. He looked down at me, and a faint smile pressed at the corners of his mouth. We ascended the stairs together. Everyone else kept a respectful distance, but I saw him as someone in pain, and I wanted to be there for him. I knew how horrible it was to lose a parent.

We crossed a catwalk and headed toward a closed door. It unnerved me to catch Arik's tortured eyes on us through the railing of the banister. Was he jealous? The confusion in my heart flipped my stomach.

I tore my gaze away from Arik and focused on the door ahead. Bastien turned the knob and pushed the heavy door open. I stopped, and he turned to face me.

"I'll wait for you here," I said.

"You don't have to. You could go with the others."

"No, I want to. I'll stay." I gave him a warm smile.

He nodded. As he closed the door, I caught a glimpse of a woman with a regal posture kneeling beside a body stretched across a low table and draped with a sheer cover. Candles flickered dim light across her face. She brightened slightly after spotting Bastien.

"*Mon cher fils*," she said, grabbing the side of the table and pushing herself up to her feet. "*Une terrible—*"

The door closed. I sat down on the floor, leaned against the wall, and hugged my knees. The only noise in the quiet corridor was my own breathing. Images of the recent battle haunted me. Nana and Faith facing unknown dangers in Asile terrified me. And whether Pop, Nick, and Afton made it to the shelter safely or not worried me.

I wanted to go home. I wanted things back to the way they were.

I needed Nana and Pop.

Time crept by as I waited for Bastien, and I closed my eyes. But the nightmare of where I was and who I didn't know I was, strangled my breath. Gia Kearns didn't exist anymore. She'd been lost somewhere on that first day when the gateway book ripped her from her world, dumping her in a dark hole. A fog surrounded me.

I startled awake when the door suddenly opened.

"*Je t'aime, Mère*," Bastien said.

"*Je t'aime, mon fils*," his mother returned.

I slid up the wall to my feet. "What did you say to her?"

"I told her that I love her. Shall we meet the others in the dining hall?"

"If you want to stay with her, I can find the dining hall on my own."

His face was heavy with sadness. "She asked that I tend to our guests. As firstborn, I have certain duties to uphold."

"Such as?"

"Such as making sure you eat something."

"Seriously? I think that should be the least of your concerns."

We headed down the catwalk. "In all seriousness, I must, as my mother said, put on a brave face."

He certainly had the brave face down, all but the sad blue eyes part.

What do you say to someone after suffering a great loss? I decided to make small talk to lift the uncomfortable feeling I had. "How come you don't have an accent like your mother and Veronique?"

"I spent my youth in Asile training to be a wizard and

a few years in the States studying with a Native American witch, affording me the opportunity to practice my English. Veronique trained with a private coach in the French countryside, so her English is unpolished."

I watched my feet as we went down the staircase. We walked in silence through the lobby and down a long corridor. I couldn't imagine how he was feeling. The loss of my mother when I was four still stung even after all these years. If I were to lose Pop, I couldn't handle it.

"All this must be scary for you." There was sincerity in his voice. Despite the fact that he was beyond gorgeous and somewhat arrogant, there was an ease to him, a welcoming spirit. No wonder his people showed him so much love.

"It is. I just want to be home." He halted, and I stopped to face him.

He brushed a strand of hair away from my cheek. His touch was soft, caring. "It will never be the same for you, Gianna, but perhaps you will find new relationships here. Meaningful ones. You won't lose those relationships back home," he said. "They are your foundation. Your tether to that world."

It was as if he could see into my soul, and I felt naked. I turned from him and continued walking down the corridor.

What's going on with you, Gia? Get your emotions in check.

He strolled beside me. "I didn't mean to upset you."

"No, you didn't. It's just been a long day." Why did he make me so nervous? "It's weird that someone I just met understands me so well."

"That's encouraging." His lips raised slightly at the corners. "I'd like to get to know you better, if you would allow it."

I understood how he earned his rock-star status. He was the complete package—sexy and sincere, but I needed to stay away from him and his charm. I would fight this betrothal arrangement every way I could. Still, he was hurting, and I refused to be rude. "I'd like that."

"This is the Hall of Honor for our Sentinels," he said. Portraits of men and women from ages ago decorated the walls, and bronzed statues of knights stood between each door we passed. "When a Sentinel dies in service, they are immortalized here."

I read the dates on the plaques nailed to each statue's stand we went by. "Wow, they all died young."

"A Sentinel enters service at sixteen and leaves it at twenty-four. If they die after their service, it is usually from natural causes, and they're buried in their family's crypt." Bastien halted in front of a statue of a young woman.

The vision of the woman falling to the ground, a sword stuck in her chest, flashed through my mind. I gasped, my hand flying to my heart.

CHAPTER TWENTY-THREE

The woman was only twenty-two when she died. Though cast in bronze, I imagined her eyes burning with life, her soft brown hair flowing behind her as she ran, and her willowy body fooling her opponents into believing her weak just before she wielded her sword and each blow she threw was a strong, solid hit. She never gave up. She never lifted her guard.

The vision sped to the young woman sitting on an iron bench, seemingly lost in thought, surrounded by a brilliant array of flowers, with her sword leaning on the bench beside her. She read a letter, and her voice played in my head.

Dearest Cousin,

I know you asked that I don't risk sending you updates, but I know if it was me, I would want to receive them. I just hope you still check your postal box. Your baby is doing wonderfully, growing strong

*each day, trying to crawl and keep up with
Gia, even. I send you my love and hope you
are doing well.*

All my best, Marietta ☆

The woman lit a match, set the letter on fire, and
dropped it in the planter beside her. The flame gobbled up
the white paper until it was ash. A twig snapped behind
her, and she turned. Her eyes widened with surprise when
a shadowed figure skewered her with her own sword. My
breath hitched as her expression froze when death took her,
and she collapsed to the ground.

"Gia," Bastien said grasping my shoulders. "Are you all
right?"

"I'm fine. This woman"—I read the name from the
plaque—"Jacalyn Roux. She died sixteen years ago. Who is
she?"

"She was a Sentinel. She died when she was almost
twenty-three."

"How did she die?"

"In the gardens of Couve," Bastien said. "The guards
found her pierced through the heart with her own sword."

"Why would someone kill her?"

"It isn't certain. Some think she committed suicide
by falling onto her own sword, but those who knew her
believed she was murdered."

"Oh, she definitely was murdered."

He glanced over to me. "Why do you say that?"

"I've been having visions ever since I came to the
havens," I said. "I had one just now of her murder."

His hand on my arm startled me, and I drew my eyes

away from the statue.

"Come on," he said. "Let's not linger on such morbid events better left in the past." He ticked his head toward the hallway. "Shall we join the others?"

"Do you know what happened to her baby?"

He gave me a confused look. "She never had a baby."

"Are you sure?"

"I'm certain." He led me to a door at the end of the hallway, and we eased inside the room. Arik and the others were already sitting at a long table with silver trays piled with sandwiches, fruits, and cakes spread across its center. Their faces were somber as they ate in silence.

My mind spun as we crossed the long distance from the door to the table. Who was Jacalyn? What did my mother have to do with her? And what was up with that letter she read? What happened to the baby?

There must be a connection. I just couldn't piece it all together. A thought struck me: If Jacalyn had lived in Couve, maybe some of her belongings still existed.

Bastien escorted me to an empty seat beside Demos, and before he left, I leaned toward him. "Are there any personal items of that woman's around? Like old photographs or letters?

"She was my mother's dear friend," Bastien said. "Her room has been untouched all these years. My mother is sentimental like that."

"Do you think after we eat, you could bring me there? It's *really* important."

He gave a slight nod. "Certainly."

I slid into the chair, and he strolled down to the end of the table, settling in at the head.

Arik sat across from me. His usual mischievous grin was a straight line of disapproval. I redirected my attention to the food tray in front of me, mindlessly adding a sandwich, vegetables, and fruit to my plate.

"You seem lost in thought, Gia," Arik said from across the table.

"I—guess I am."

He still wore a scowl. "Not to worry. Since Couve is stable, we'll join the others at the shelter after our meal."

"There's something I have to do before we leave," I said.

"Do you care to tell me what?"

"Come with me. I don't want to talk about it here."

"All right," he said.

After dinner, he followed me to the French Sentinels' Hall of Honor. "What are we up to?" Arik asked as we waited in the hall for Bastien.

I walked over to Jacalyn Roux's statue. "Do you know this woman?"

Arik studied the statue.

I grew impatient. "Well, do you?"

"I don't believe so, why?"

"She died the year I was born, and before that, she was missing for a year." I paused to catch my breath.

Arik crossed his arms. "Why does it matter?"

"I had a vision of her. She read a letter from my mother telling Jacalyn her baby was doing well. Jacalyn's baby. The baby was with my mom. With *me*."

"I still am unclear of the importance," Arik said.

"Really?" Frustration boiled inside me. "Why would someone want to hide a baby? And with my mother who was in hiding herself? What happened to this baby? Who's the father? Bastien said she never had one, so why does my mother mention she had? And even more important, why am I having visions from people I don't even know?"

"All right. It does sound suspicious," Arik said. "But I'm

not certain we'll find any answers to your questions."

Bastien came up behind us. "What questions?"

"The mysterious baby questions," Arik answered.

"So, you told him." I detected annoyance in Bastien's tone. "Sorry I kept you waiting. I had to get the key to Jacalyn's room. The room was thoroughly searched when she died, so I doubt there will be any answers there, but I'll take you anyway."

Bastien brought us to a room deep within the castle. A gust of dusty air punched our faces when he pushed the door open. Arik and I moved into the middle of the room as Bastien switched on the blush-colored porcelain lamps draped in cobwebs.

The warm light illuminated the dust floating in the air. The room was a young woman's forgotten sanctuary. There was lots of white painted furniture, a light-pink comforter, pink drapes, and white-lace pillows, all seemingly antiqued under layers of dust.

Arik tugged open drawers of the nightstand. I crossed over to the vanity and picked up a hairbrush. Strands of dark brown hair were caught in the bristles. I placed the brush back, making sure to put it in the same exact spot. It wasn't hard to do, since there was a clean silhouette of the brush in the dust. I eased the top drawer on the left open and sorted through the miscellaneous items thrown haphazardly into the drawer. The middle drawer held hair ties, makeup brushes, emery boards and the like. I sighed. "Find anything?" I asked the others.

Bastien riffled through the bottom drawer of the bureau by the window. "Nothing here."

"Nor here," Arik added as he peeked under the bed. "It might help if we knew what you hoped to find."

"I don't even know–a diary or something?"

Bastien pressed his face against the floorboards as he peered under the bureau. "How about letters?"

"You found letters?" I dropped down beside Bastien. He smelled good, like expensive cologne. His arm brushed mine, causing my skin to go goosepimply. I jerked away from him. *What the hell was that?*

Shaking it off, I strained my neck to see under the bureau. Behind it, a wooden panel in the wall had slipped out of place. Several letters stood in a line within the gap. Bastien and I got up from the floor and pulled the bureau from the wall. I removed the panel and tugged each letter out of the opening, dropping them on the floor.

After plopping on to the area rug, I pulled my legs into a pretzel, picked up the nearest letter, and opened it. Bastien and Arik sat down on either side of me.

"Oh. My. God. This is a love letter from—" I read the sender on the envelope.

"Who's the letter from?" Arik asked, impatiently.

"It's from Professor Attwood."

Bastien picked up a letter and read it. "This one is from Marietta to Jacalyn. She mentions her excitement over Jacalyn's news and says she and Carrig are hiding out in Ireland. Marietta is twelve weeks along."

"Does it mention what news?" I asked.

"No, but Marietta finishes the letter—I can't believe this." Bastien looked at me. "*Friends in motherhood.*"

"See," I said. "I told you so."

Arik stretched his legs out in front of him. "So they both were pregnant at the same time."

"Listen to this," Bastien said. "*I cannot imagine how it must feel to give birth alone. I feel it is your beloved's right to know the father. He will understand your mistake. Dearest cousin, fear not for your baby, for it is my baby with the price upon its head. I shall send for you when I am settled. Always, Marietta.*"

I gasped. "Omigod. What does that mean? And how are they cousins?"

"They can't be cousins. It must be a term of endearment." Bastien folded the letter and slipped it into the envelope.

"How about this one," Arik said. "*We must never tell of our discovery. A grandfather like ours is one to be admired, and I fear the scandal would bring him shame.*"

"Who wrote that?" I asked.

"Marietta did," he answered. "She also says she was sorry to hear Sabine was distraught over the news. Who is Sabine?"

"My mother," Bastien said.

"We should ask her," I said.

"I always knew she hid letters 'ere someplace," Bastien's mother said from the opened door.

"*Maman*," Bastien said, scrambling to his feet.

She waved him away. "Please sit down, Bastien."

Bastien obeyed.

She stayed in the doorway as if it was too painful to enter Jacalyn's shrine. "Jacalyn and Marietta," Sabine said. "We all met at ze Sentinel's school in Asile. After Marietta returned to her own 'aven, we all exchanged letters. Zey became Sentinels and I became ze wife of a High Wizard.

"A few summers afterward, Marietta's mother died, and Jacalyn went to Asile to console 'er. Since Marietta's father was expired as well, it was up to Marietta and Philip to sort through zair mother's belongings. They discovered the unpublished memoir of Marietta's grandfather, Gian. He admitted to 'aving an affair with Jacalyn's grandmother, and conceiving a child from zat union—Jacalyn's mother."

She sighed. "I did not realize zat Jacalyn and Philip fell

in love. I wish I knew—"

"Wouldn't that make Jacalyn and Professor Attwood cousins?" Arik asked.

"No," Sabine said. "Marietta and Philip share ze same father and 'ad different mothers. Jacalyn is related to Marietta through her mother."

My legs were falling asleep, so I adjusted them. "Did you know about Jacalyn's baby?"

Tears pooled in Sabine's eyes, and she left them there, until she blinked, and they fell onto her cheek. "No. I do remember seeing 'er a few months before she disappeared. She hardly spoke. If she'd 'ad a baby, well, I did not know. My poor Jacalyn—"

Sabine pulled a lacy handkerchief from her bodice and dabbed at her eyes, then continued, "Jacalyn 'ad spent time training Sentinels in Esteril and met her betrothed, Conemar, there. 'E was obsessed with 'er. After realizing how evil 'e was, she brought her case to dissolve their betrothal promise to the Wizard Council. I believe 'e murdered 'er because of it. But it could not be proven." She covered her mouth with the hanky, muffling a sob.

Bastien jumped to his feet. "I should see my mother to her chambers." He turned to me. "You should come with us."

"No. I have to hide the letters."

"With the recent attack, I don't want you to be alone in the castle."

"I'll be fine," I said. "Arik's here."

Bastien looked from me to his mother, then to Arik. "All right. Will you guard her?"

"I kept her safe before you were in the picture," Arik said, sounding irritated.

Bastien ignored Arik's statement and steered Sabine out the door.

Arik hopped up. "So there's wedding bells in your near future."

"Really?" I shoved him lightly before picking up a handful of letters. "Don't be ridiculous. I'm not engaged to him."

As if. No one is going to make me marry anyone. Besides, I'm only sixteen, and there'd be time to figure that crap out.

I glanced at him gathering envelopes with one hand and dragging the other one through his hair. He caught me staring, and the corners of his lips lifted. He had the hottest smile I'd ever seen. But we were friends, and it was all we could ever be.

Sirens went off somewhere in the castle. "What's that for?"

"I'll see what it is," he said, dropping the letters in his hand and pulling out his sword. "You stay here and hide the letters. Lock yourself in." He stormed out the door.

I shut the door and bolted it behind him.

Back and forth I went, snatching up letters and slipping them into the opening in the wall. When all the letters were back, I secured the panel, moved the dresser into place, and waited for Arik to return.

The window flew open, and the drapes rose like pink airfoils in the wind. Between the flapping of the drapes, a dark shadow crouched on the windowsill.

"Wh-who's there?" I stammered.

"A Sentinel with your skills should not fear the shadows, Gianna." A young Latin man with extremely long legs, a broad chest, and a thin waist hopped down from the window and sauntered into the room's light. He wore a dark suit with a white T-shirt under the jacket and his dark hair slicked back from his forehead. "Do not fear me," he said as he neared.

"I'm not afraid of you," I said, gulping my fear back and

standing my ground, though I desperately wanted to back away.

A smooth smile spread over his lips. "You're a horrible liar."

"Who are you, and how do you know my name?"

"I am Ricardo."

"Faith's ex?"

"She spoke of me?"

I drew the Chiave from my scabbard and held the blade high for him to see. "Don't come any closer, or I'll decapitate you."

He stopped and held up his hands. "Now, you wouldn't want to do that; it will make such a mess." He chuckled under his breath.

I tightened my grip around the hilt of the Chiave. "Touch me and I'll kill you."

His laugh unnerved me. "Did Faith say I was on the bad guys' side? She may be a guard for Merlin, but I am his oldest friend. This castle is under attack as we speak. We haven't time to argue whether you will go with me or not." He pulled a cell phone out of his pocket and reached it out to me. "I won't hurt you." He crossed the distance between us. "Merlin has a message for you. Just play the video."

"You mean Merl," I said, trying to give him my best death stare.

He grinned. "I'm the only one allowed to call him Merlin."

I took the phone with my free hand. He had it already on the video. Before I pushed play, a knock came from the door. I stared at Ricardo, wanting to open it, but worried what he'd do if I tried.

"Gia!" Arik pounded harder on the door.

"Are you going to get that?" he asked.

Not sure he could be trusted, I wouldn't take my eyes off him.

The door splintered from its hinges and crashed to the floor. Arik rushed in, with Lei and Sinead on his heels. Several more Laniars flew into the room from the open window behind Ricardo and landed on either side of him. One of the female Laniars snarled at Lei, who stood unmoved.

"Ricardo?" The tension in Arik's shoulders relaxed.

"Arik, you're just in time to hear Merlin's message." Ricardo slowly exposed his long, sharp canines.

"How were you able to get a message from him?" Arik asked.

"I was in Asile when it was attacked. My pack pushed Conemar's men back so Merlin could reset the wards."

"Watch them," Arik directed Lei and Sinead, pointing at Ricardo and his gang of Laniars. Then he leaned over my shoulder to view the video. "Go ahead, push play."

My finger shook as I did. Merl flashed to life on the screen.

"I'm sorry for having to use this technology, but I didn't want to risk lowering the wards to use my window rod. Thanks to Ricardo and his friends, Asile is safe, for now. The wards surrounding Asile are holding, but we need help before Conemar breaks through them. Ricardo has gathered our allies from the Mystiks. I appoint Arik as lead. You must alert all the havens. Have them send as many Sentinels, wizards, and guards as they can afford. Gia is to go with Ricardo. He will see to her safety from here forward. Be careful and may Agnes guide you."

I pressed the screen, and it went dark. "How do we know he's not being forced to say this?"

"The password, *May Agnes guide you*," Lei replied. "She's the patron saint of Asile."

Agnes? That was the silver woman's name that formed

from my globe. Did the saints have something to do with the Chiavi?

I faced Ricardo. "How did you know I was here?"

"The werehounds tracked your scent from a shirt Katy…excuse me, your Nana…gave us."

"Can your pack help us save Couve?" Arik asked him.

"They will, but Gia must go with me." He noticed the protest forming on my lips. "Merlin said no exceptions. I'm to get you to the shelter."

From the corridor came yells, scuffles, and the continual wail of the warning siren.

"I can't go with you," I said. "I have to fight with them."

"She can't fight with us," Lei said, glancing at the door. "She almost killed Kale."

I turned to Sinead. "You know what I can do."

Sinead gave me a pity smile. "Yes, but you have no control over it. Let Ricardo take you to your father and friends."

I thought of Kale lying motionless, near death, and I hated that she was right. As much as I wanted to stay, I might be more hindrance than help. I caved. "Okay," I said, defeated.

Lei flew out of the room with the Laniars on her heels. Sinead hugged me, then rushed after them. Arik moved over to me and cupped my face gently in his hands. His eyes held the intensity that always drew me to him.

I swallowed my breath in anticipation. All the sounds around us went silent.

He bent and lightly brushed my lips with a kiss. His lips were soft and oh, so tender. Butterflies swooped and curled inside me, and it felt like the ground disappeared from beneath my feet. He pulled back a little and said, "Regardless of the fact that you're a royal pain in the arse, I fancy you. Listen to Ricardo and don't do anything rash." He gave me another kiss and rushed out the door. My heart twisted in my chest as he disappeared. I touched my mouth and exhaled. He liked me. It was against the laws, but he told me he fancied me. Maybe we had no future, but we had *now*.

"What a sweet display," Ricardo said, dragging me out of my haze. "I'm not one for rules or laws, but I'd be careful there. The punishment would be much worse for him than you."

"Why?" I stared at the door as if I'd see Arik there.

"He's a leader. He knows better." Ricardo headed to the window. "Are you ready to fly?"

"Did you say *fly*?"

CHAPTER TWENTY-FOUR

Ricardo gave me a wicked grin, complete with sharp canines. "Well, not exactly *fly* per se." His dress shoes clicked across the floor as he sauntered gracefully to the window. "Shall we be on our way?"

"You do realize we're five stories up, right?"

He beckoned me with his fingers. "Trust me. I won't drop you."

I took a deep breath and grabbed his hand.

"We're going down the side of the building," he said. "Remove your shield and sword."

My free hand rested on the hilt of the Chiave. "I can't leave the sword."

"You must."

"I won't go if I have to leave it."

He eyed me suspiciously. "Okay. Leave the shield. Put the sword on your back."

I removed my shield and dropped it on the floor. Then I unstrapped my scabbard and belted it across my chest.

"Ready," I said.

He gathered me to his side. "Extend your free arm for

balance as we go down. Do you understand?"

"Yes—"

Before I added anything else, Ricardo flew out the window with me and ran down the side of the building. We raced down so fast, his legs were a blur.

I dragged my feet against the sandstone wall and held my arm out for balance. It was like a scary drop on an amusement park ride. My heart quickened with the rush of adrenaline. The ground sped toward us. He arched his back and pushed away from the wall with his feet, pulling me with him, our feet aiming for the ground.

"Pull your knees up!" he yelled.

I drew them up right before his feet hit the ground with a loud *thwack*. "No time to reflect on how magnificent I am," Ricardo said and headed for the outbuilding.

I stumbled after him on wobbly legs. "That was wicked awesome."

We rushed along the cobbled streets, screams and cries echoing through the village.

"Stay in the shadows," he ordered when I stepped into the light of a nearby lamppost.

Dark figures hunched in front of the pale plaster of the outbuilding. When we neared them, the animals looked like seriously buffed Dobermans. I stopped. "What are they?"

"They're werehounds, but you needn't fear them. They know you are Gian Bianchi's great-granddaughter," Ricardo said, affection icing over Gian's name. "He is a hero with the Mystiks. He fought for our rights when others turned on us. It is an honor to protect you. Just walk by them. They won't harm you."

I smiled nervously at each werehound I passed. A couple of them sniffed me as I went by, their breaths beating against my boots. "How did Conemar's men get in?" I stepped over a fluffy tail.

He shooed a couple of werehounds out of our way. "With Couve's High Wizard dead, the protection wards broke. A less powerful wizard made a spotty attempt at bandaging the old wards. The true mystery is: Who let Conemar into Couve earlier today? My bet is on Odil."

Ricardo held the door to the outbuilding open for me, and I stepped inside. I removed my scabbard from my back, belted it to my waist, and created a light globe in my hand. He led the way down the narrow steps to the tunnel.

"Why do you suppose they attacked Couve twice?"

"Only a few men entered during the first attack." He unplugged a golf cart. "Probably to kill Gareth and remove the wards for the bigger attack."

"Gareth?"

"That is Bastien's father's name."

"How evil do you have to be to sacrifice your own father?"

"Odil has been a burr in his father's side since birth, but I highly doubt he'd let someone kill his father." Ricardo slipped into the driver's seat of the golf cart. "I bet he's not aware of the consequences from his actions. He's not the sharpest tooth in a Laniar's mouth."

I rolled my eyes and slid into the passenger seat.

He turned the key, and the cart whirred to life. I dropped my light globe when he turned on the headlights. He backed the cart up and guided it down the tunnel.

"In spite of their differences, Odil loved and respected his father. No, something else is at hand and comes from Conemar, I am certain. I must get you to the shelter before I sneak into Esteril and find out what's going on there."

"You're going to Esteril?"

"Yes. In order for Conemar to weave Sean's and Carrig's minds together, the two must be alive. I believe Carrig might be in Esteril." He flicked his eyes at me and returned them immediately to the tunnel. "Carrig is a powerful Sentinel, and we need his skills to defeat Conemar, so I'm willing to risk it."

"I *know* Carrig is in Esteril," I said. "I had a vision of it."

"You're favored by the spirit seers? Gian was as well. They show you what they think you need to see. Be wise and remember all you've witnessed."

"Why do the visions have to be so nightmarish?"

"Only by understanding the evil events of our past can we learn to prevent future disasters." The blaze of the headlights ricocheting off the tunnel's walls illuminated his perfectly aligned, sharp white teeth. I pulled up the collar of my leather vest, hiding my neck. He smirked. "I will deliver you unharmed to the shelter."

Everything about him was smooth and dark, like melting chocolate. No wonder Faith was heartbroken over him. "Why did you dump Faith?" I gripped the window frame as he swung the cart around a corner.

"Most Laniars have no control over the desire to love many." He kept his focus on the winding tunnel. "It's a survival thing. Unfortunately, Faith is different and has many human feelings. Monogamy, one of them."

"I see." My toes clenched in my boots as he veered around another corner.

"I saw Katy when we rescued Asile. She told me to tell you she's well."

Nana had mentioned she'd gotten together with a Ricardo when she was young. *Oh no. Eww.* "You're not *the* Ricardo. The one she had a romance with years ago, are you?"

"I am. She was a fiery little witch back then. A true beauty."

My stomach churned. "I don't want to hear any more."

He laughed.

"Anyway," I said. "I've decided to go with you."

"What do you mean, you've decided?"

"I'm going to help you save Carrig. You're right, we need him—I need him if I'm ever going to master my powers."

"You know, Merlin—not to mention Arik—will stake me." He slammed on the brakes as we came to the end of the tunnel.

"I'll say I followed you. You had nothing to do with it. So, how do we get into Esteril?"

"Well, they will let me in, but not you. We can't get you through the wards without a wizard. It's best I go alone."

"I can take care of the wards."

He got out of the cart. "It won't work. The moment you enter the library, they can track you."

I walked around to his side of the cart, stood in front of him, and pulled down the collar of my shirt.

He eyed my chest. "You're too young. Even I have standards."

"Gross. I mean this." I pointed to my scar. "This is a charm. It shields me from the Monitors and this"—I held up my palm and formed a pink globe—"disables wards and stuff." I popped the globe, tugged up the neckline of my shirt, and waited for the side effects of conjuring. They didn't come; I felt fine. "One more thing," I said. "If you're tricking me, *I* will stake you."

"Impressive, but you're not going with me. I'm taking you to the shelter first."

We scrambled up the stairs. Once in the library, he found the gateway book and opened it to a photograph of a library I didn't recognize.

"How do you know where the shelter is? I thought only—"

He raised his hand to stop me. "It was my home for many years. I testified against Conemar and was sent to the shelter for protection."

"They didn't blindfold you or something?"

"I'm too cunning for them. I withstood their attempts to wipe my memory. You don't live as long as I and not pick up tricks."

"I see."

"Blast it all," he snapped, leaning closer to the page. "One of Conemar's search parties is in the library leading to the shelter."

"How can you see that?"

"My ring." I glanced at it. It was large and gold with a lion's head on it. "Merl spelled it so I can see into the libraries through the photographs."

I practically fell over him trying to see the photograph. "Oh no, can they get in?"

"Personal space, please." He pushed me away with his back. "No, they'd have to know the key. No one knows the key but the Couve Sentinels and their High Wizard. And me, of course."

"Veronique does, and she's on Conemar's side."

"Merl wiped Veronique's memory of all keys and important information when she was captured." He slammed his fist on the page.

"He should have wiped her entire memory." My lip twitched. I hoped he hadn't notice the jealousy lacing my words.

"That would have killed her and is against the laws." He eyed me suspiciously before returning his attention to the book. "Damn it. You'll have to go with me. But you must stay out of sight."

"I can do that."

He looked up. "I have a feeling you won't."

...

The library in Saint Petersburg was spooky at night. I pulled a history book from a shelf and hid behind a display case under the white arches of the ceiling. When my eyes began to droop, I put the book down, got to my feet, and paced. I spun around to face a movement in my peripheral vision, sliding the Chiave out of my scabbard and readying it for an attack. Nothing was there.

"Get a grip, Gia," I muttered to myself, slipping the sword back in its case.

I checked the time on Ricardo's wristwatch, which he'd given me before he went through the bookcase. I was to leave in an hour if he didn't return by then. He gambled on the bulk of Conemar's men either being at the battle in Couve or stationed at the siege on Asile. He hoped he would be in and out with Carrig before being noticed. I wasn't sure what his plan was, but I had a terrible feeling about it.

"What are you doing here?"

Startled, I whirled around on my heel. "Sinead? How did—" Three tiny fairies with multi-colored wings and spindly green bodies flew around her. "Hey, I saw those fairies the night I was drugged. They're real?"

"They're not fairies; they're sprites. I had them follow you. They came for me when you didn't go to the shelter, and you came here instead." She frowned. "Are you trying to get yourself killed?"

"We couldn't get to the shelter. Conemar's men were there."

Sinead took a step closer to me. "Where's Ricardo?"

"He went to Esteril to rescue Carrig."

Her pointy ears pricked back, and she crouched to the floor behind the display cases. "Get down." The sprites darted off.

I squatted beside her. I whispered, "What is it?"

"I'm not sure. Stay here." She crawled to the end of the long display stand, peered around it for several seconds, then stood.

"Well?" I rose.

"A rat, is all."

"A rat? *Gross*." I tried to scratch the heebie-jeebies from my skin.

She ignored my freak out. "So what's Ricardo's plan?"

"I don't know." I checked the wristwatch again. "If he doesn't come back in another twenty minutes, I'm to leave and go back to Couve." I pointed to a large wooden eyesore with dusty books aligned on its shelves. "He went through there. I think our cover is blown. They can't read me in the libraries, but I bet they know you're here."

"I'm sure they do." She motioned with her pointer finger for me to get down. "Someone's coming for certain this time."

"Great," I seethed, returning to my hiding place behind the display.

"Whatever happens, stay down."

"What are you going to do?"

"They sensed me here. I have to go with them willingly, or they'll discover you. So don't do anything stupid. Once it's clear, go to Asile. The sprites will make sure your path is clear."

I tensed. "But—"

"Do as I say. I'll help Ricardo."

She worked her magic on me again. Its hypnotic control sent a chill slithering down my spine, but I tried to fight it.

Focus, Gia.

The bookcase shook and rattled as it slid open. A glass front bookcase nearby reflected the room. Several muscled guards stormed the room. Even the young women were menacing—tall and broad shouldered.

"Hold on boys," Sinead said to two young male guards. "I come in peace. I'm here to speak to Conemar."

The guards each seized one of her arms. "Oh, you will speak with him. When he returns," the taller, bulkier one said, his accent as thick as his arms.

"She's fey, and she's trying to compel us," one of the girls said. "Remember our training and block her magic from your minds."

The two guards dragged Sinead away.

I held my breath, waiting for them to leave. A woman's voice spoke a charm in what sounded like Russian. I had assumed all keys were in Italian, but obviously, they weren't. I kept repeating the phrase within my mind, trying to memorize it.

The bookcase rattled open, boots slapped down steps, then the bookcase slammed back into place. I peered over the display. The sprites flew around me, all talking at once. It was like an annoying buzzing in my ear. "One at a time. I can't make out what you're saying."

One with shocking red hair fluttered in front of my face. "You have to go after her." Her voice whistled like a quiet teakettle. "You can do it. You're the presaged."

"I think she compelled me or something. I want to go but can't."

"It will wear off. Go help her when it does. We will clear the path to Couve and the Shelter."

"How are you going to do that?"

"Not to worry. We have our tricks."

They flew off, leaving me alone in the library.

After several excruciating minutes warring against Sinead's magic, I blew out an exasperated breath.

My globe! It can undo spells. I held up my hand and willed it to life. The pink membrane engulfed me, releasing Sinead's magic. Thankfully, there weren't any aftereffects, other than a slight tingle in my stomach.

I hurried to the bookcase and spoke the key. It took several attempts to get the pronunciation of the Russian charm correct before the bookcase finally opened.

Too frightened to fire up a light globe, I felt for each step with my boot as I eased down the wet stairwell. Drops of water fell from the ceiling and landed on my head. At the bottom, I dragged my fingertips across the rough wall to guide myself down the pitch-black tunnel. I couldn't believe I was doing this, but I had to risk it for Sinead. Ricardo didn't know she was there, and I had to tell him, somehow.

I took a deep breath to calm my nerves and wrinkled my nose. It smelled as if something had died in the tunnel. The darkness freaked me out. The scurry of tiny critters' feet sounded below me. Something with many legs fell on my arm and skittered across my skin. I shrieked and quickly slapped it away.

Since I had probably woken the dead with that scream, I figured it wouldn't hurt to ignite a globe. After I had, I wished I hadn't. Tons of spiders and other nasty bugs crawled across the walls and ceilings, and on the ground, several rats rushed in and out of holes in the mortar. I centered myself within the tunnel and stepped carefully over the fast moving hairballs underfoot. I shuddered with every step I took.

Nearly twenty minutes later, I reached the bottom of another staircase. I inched up the stairs and paused at the door. After extinguishing my light globe, I created a pink one in its place and threw it at the door, hoping to eliminate any wards attached. This time the magic shocked me. I rested against the door and waited for the spins to stop.

Using magic sucks.

After jerking the door open, I crept inside. Figuring I was in an outbuilding just like the ones in Asile and Couve, I continued to the other side where I hoped the door to the outside would be. Fur coats hanging on the wall by the door brushed my skin as I passed.

I stepped outside onto a cold and barren field, shivered, and darted back inside. Unbuckling my scabbard, I slipped it off and placed it on the floor. Then I grabbed one of the furs from the wall, slipped it on, and belted my scabbard around it.

Icy snow bit my face. Crouching low to the ground, I hid in the shadows. A dark, menacing castle sat on top of a rocky hill. Attached to a pole on the highest tower, a black flag with a red flame blazing in the middle flapped in the biting wind.

My heart pounded louder in my ears the closer I got to the castle of doom. Instead of going through the front entrance, I went around the side. Soft drapes blew in and out of a couple of glass doors left ajar on an enclosed patio. I crawled over the wall and landed softly on the stone patio.

I tiptoed to the doors and peered around the drapes. Only a long dining table with a dozen or so chairs filled the room. The Chiave protested with a *shiiiiing* as I removed it from my scabbard, and I paused, listening for any movement inside. With cold, stiff hands, I held the blade out in front of me and then continued inside.

I crossed over to a door and eased it open a little. My heart knocked so hard against my chest as I peeked through the crack, I was sure someone could hear it. Opening the door wider with my boot, I tightened my hold on the Chiave and inched into a scary-movie vacant hallway. One direction led to a vast sitting room, so I hurried down the other direction instead and ended up in the foyer.

On either side of a wide staircase were two openings leading to the back of the castle. The corridor on the right brought me to the kitchen, and I doubled back. Across the corridor, a narrow stairway went down and disappeared in the darkness.

A dungeon? I hope. Dungeons are always underground.

The stairs were slick and dangerous as I plunged down them into the unknown. Small sconces, casting dim light throughout the narrow corridor, gave a sense of doom over the iron doors with small barred windows lining the walls. Like a victim, I pushed all reasoning aside and headed down it.

Score. I was right. Definitely, a dungeon.

A Russian man's voice came from behind me, saying something I didn't understand. I spun to face him. Two men filled the corridor in front of me, both heavily armed.

CHAPTER TWENTY-FIVE

The Russian man spit out more foreign words.

"What?" My breaths turning shallow, I backed away from them slowly. "Um, I was looking for a bathroom." *Lame.*

"You're American?" The other man spoke English, albeit with a very heavy Russian accent. "What are you doing down here?"

I recognized him. "You were with Arik at the Boston Athenæum and then at Professor Attwood's office," I said without really thinking.

The guy's eyes widened.

The other man looked puzzled and said something in Russian to him.

"Edgar, right?"

"Who are you?" Edgar focused on my face.

"Gia. I'm—"

"Gianna Bianchi. What are you doing here? You're exposing my cover."

From the other man's face, it looked like he was figuring something out. He pulled a dagger from his belt and pointed it at Edgar, saying more stuff in Russian. I made out Arik's name and a word that sounded like spoon.

"Spy?" Edgar acted stunned and readied his fists.

The man repeated the word and lunged at Edgar.

Edgar dodged the attack and caught the man in a wristlock. The dagger clanked to the floor. "Hand me the dagger," he said.

I snatched it up and gave it to him. "What are you going to do?"

"I have to kill him."

"What?" I stumbled backward, shocked. "You can't *kill* him."

"I have to. He knows who I am."

"Then you are a spoon, I mean, spy?"

Edgar grinned. "If you're on the right side. Are you a spy?"

"Um, yes?"

"Carrig is down the hall." The man struggled in Edgar's grip, and Edgar tightened his hold. "I'll get rid of Val here and distract the other guard. Get out of here fast, you hear me?"

"Where's Sinead?"

"Who?"

"She's a faery. Carrig's wife."

"I haven't seen her. Now hurry and get out of here."

I nodded and watched as he shuffled away with the man.

"Go!" he yelled over his shoulder.

I bolted down the corridor. "Carrig," I whispered through the small barred windows in each door I passed. If Carrig was still locked up, where was Ricardo?

Something thudded against the metal door at the end. I stopped short and flattened myself against the opposite wall. *Crap. What the hell is that?* I heard it again, then, "*Oomph,*" and then, "Shite! Who be there?"

Yep. It was Carrig. He sounded just like Sean McGann. I went to the door and pulled on the handle. Of course, I should have expected a locked door, but I was hoping for one of those doors that locked on the inside and not on the outside.

"Stop hitting the door," I said. "I'll find something to get you out."

"What the bloody hell are you doing here?" His voice was dry, like sandpaper dragged across each word.

A guard station was at the end of the hall. I hurried to it and riffled around the desk, hunting for a set of keys to unlock the cell door. Each drawer I searched came up empty. I blew out a frustrated breath and glanced around at the walls.

A rack in the corner held encased swords, but there were no shelves to hold anything else. The walls were bare. There wasn't even a nail to hold a ring of keys. Rust-colored stains spotted the wall directly across from me. The splatter surrounded a chair pushed against it. I was sure I didn't want to know what had happened there.

Hurry. Hurry. Despite the chill, sweat was running down the back of my neck. I was running out of time and options.

While dashing around the desk, my scabbard caught on an open drawer, and I tugged it free. The hilt of the Chiave glinted against the dim light. Agnes had said it was the destroyer of all swords. Could it cut through all metals? I hustled back to the dungeon door.

"Deidre, your sword won't budge this door," Carrig said through the bars of his cell as I lifted the Chiave above my head. "You'll just mangle the blade."

"It's not an ordinary sword." I swung the Chiave hard against the top hinge. The blade sang against the steel, breaking the first hinge, the vibration stinging my hands. I did the same to the middle and bottom ones.

"Move aside," Carrig ordered. He threw himself against the door, and it fell outward, smashing onto the tile floor with an echo that thundered down the corridor. If the bad guys didn't know we were here before, they did now. He stepped over the door and out of the cell. "Deadly brilliant, Deidre."

He thinks I'm her. I decided we didn't have time for a meet and greet. "We have to hurry," I said.

"I don't understand. Why did you come for me?"

"It's a long story. We must find Ricardo."

"He's with you?"

"Yes. He came in before me."

"Shite." His fist tightened, and it looked like he wanted to hit something. Hopefully, not me. "That thickheaded mongrel. This will be his death. How long has he been here?"

"An hour," I said. "Maybe a little more? There's one more problem, though. The guards have Sinead."

"Daft, daft woman—she'll kill me, I swear."

He didn't notice I called her by her name instead of Mom or Mother. I wasn't even sure what Diedre called Sinead.

He rushed to the guard station and grabbed a scabbard and sword from the rack against the wall. He strapped them on and ran down the corridor.

I chased him up the stairs and into the kitchen. He plucked a butcher's knife out of a wooden block and handed it to me. "Put it in your boot. There be a pocket on the side." He grabbed a boning knife and gave that to me, too. "And put this one in the other boot."

I bent over and found a pocket on the inside of both boots, slipping a knife into each one before straightening. Carrig was sliding a knife into his boot.

"Now, keep close behind me." Carrig stormed out of the kitchen.

My boots slipped across the tiles as I struggled to keep up, the handles of the knives pressing against my skin. He was definitely more in shape than his changeling was. Plus, his response to me was a lot friendlier. We searched each room on the first level and continued to the second floor.

A woman's voice hummed from somewhere down the hall. I stopped on the landing. "Do you hear that?"

He froze and held his hand up. "It's *Moon Glory*—one of the fey's songs."

"It's her," I whispered.

"Smart woman, that one." There was pride in his voice. "Leading us to her without alerting her captors of it."

We followed the song down the hall to the third door.

"I'm in here," Sinead called out.

"Step aside," he said at the door. He backed up and spoke a charm, a green globe forming on his palm. He hurled it at the door. Wind blasted the door off its hinges, pitching it across the room. Splinters and debris swirled around in the aftermath.

"How come you didn't do that to your cell door?" I asked.

"The cell was charmed to disable battle globes."

Sinead clambered over the rubble and threw herself into Carrig's arms, kissing him all over his face before stopping at his lips.

I averted my eyes. "Hate to break up your love-fest," I said over my shoulder, "but we're busted."

Two guards came charging down one direction, while a third came at us from the other way. Carrig stormed after the two guards. I yanked the boning knife from my boot and threw it at the lone guard, aiming low so I wouldn't kill him. The blade sunk into his leg. Blood sprayed from his wound, and he fell to the ground, groaning.

Sinead rushed by me, holding a small statue in her hand. She smashed the guard over the head, knocking the man out cold.

Carrig had knocked out one guard and was now fighting the second. The two foxtrotted around each other in a series of long, slow steps and short quicker ones. The clang of sword beating sword rang down the corridor. Panting. Grunting. When Carrig had an opening, he sliced the guard's arm and slammed the hilt of his sword against the man's head. The guard slumped to the floor. Carrig nudged him with his foot before rushing down the hall to us.

"Do you know where they took Ricardo?" He pulled a tapestry off the wall and wiped his blade clean with it.

Sinead looked up from bandaging the guard's leg, putting a final knot in the table runner she'd shredded with her dagger to use. "They took him outside."

"Leave him. We must hurry." Carrig flew down the corridor, a determined look on his face.

Sinead grabbed my hand and towed me after her. We raced down the steps, through the corridors, out a side door, and onto clumpy grass.

"How are we going to find him?" I panted.

Carrig stopped short ahead of us. Sinead and I halted just behind him. Shock screamed through me at the sight, wrenching my insides, keeping me frozen. All I could do was stare.

Ricardo hung from a tree trunk, held in place by a silver stake pinned straight through his heart and into the bark. It was more like a petrified image of him. Blood streaked his shirt and the tree trunk below him.

Sinead threw her hands over her mouth. Carrig pulled her into his arms, and she sobbed against his shoulder.

A pendant dangled from a silver chain around his neck. My legs were shaky as I shook off my stupor and stumbled over to the tree. The stone features of Ricardo's face looked peaceful. The pendant had twisted around so the back showed. Etched in the silver base was the name Faith. I turned it around. It was a gothic-style pendant with a circle of thorny, silver-stemmed roses surrounding a blood-red crystal. *He did care about her.*

I undid the clasp of the necklace and removed it. With shaky hands, I refastened it around my neck. Faith would want something to remember him by. The thought of telling her about his death sickened me.

"I'm so sorry, Ricardo." My voice trembled. "How could they be so cruel?"

Carrig came to my side, swiping tears from his cheeks. "Crazy eejit, you should have left me here." He choked back a sob. "Rest in peace, my friend, for your soul be saved." He yanked the stake out of Ricardo's body and it crashed to the ground, breaking into several pieces. The pieces turned into ash and flew off in the breeze.

"Carrig!" Edgar's voice came from the direction of the castle. He raced down the hill, slipped to his knees, and scrambled back to his feet. "Hurry! Get to the exit. The guards are coming."

Sinead grabbed Carrig's arm with her slender hand. "We must get Gia to the shelter."

Carrig shot me a puzzled look. "Gia?"

Carrig's eyes, the same green as mine, stared at me. He mumbled something under his breath. Looking from

Sinead to me he said, "You be Gianna?"

I nodded. "Yes, I'm your real daughter.

Tears glossed his eyes, and he took a deep breath, pulling me into a tight hold. "When they took me, I worried you be found. I be out of my mind worrying that you were alone, facing this unknown world without me."

I swallowed hard, trying not to lose it right there. "I'm fine."

"I have dreamed of this meeting many times. Of course, it be in a better surrounding."

"Sweet reunion," Edgar said. "But it'll be short lived if we don't get out of here."

Carrig released me and looked at Sinead. "Diedre?"

"She's safe," she said, her tears different. It was like they had glitter in them.

"A'right, then." Carrig patted my back. "Keep running and don't stop or look back."

"Okay."

We ran, not stopping at the sounds of men and growls behind us.

My heart ached as I trekked back along the tunnel with Edgar, Carrig, and Sinead. In the little time I'd known Ricardo, he had been kind to me. Both Carrig and Merl considered him a friend. He must've been a better person than Faith had led me to believe.

"Why did you say Ricardo's soul was saved?" I asked Carrig, regaining my composure.

"Laniars lost their souls long ago," he said. "It be said one killed an angel. The entire race was damned to Hell, unless they be giving up their life to save another. When they do, their soul comes back to them. I've known Ricardo a long time. He saved me life once—and now, twice. He'll be greatly missed."

"I'm sorry," I said.

Carrig nodded with a grateful smile. He was quiet all the way through the tunnel and to the library.

Sinead sniffed back tears as she searched the gateway book for a library.

We had to jump in and out of three libraries to avoid Conemar's forces. When we made it to the Senate Library in France, the sprites had a Sentinel from Couve waiting for us. He led us to the shelter through a small, two-hundred-year-old library in a French countryside village.

The black of night had turned purple with the morning rising. The neoclassical manor of the shelter stood stoic in a pasture. To the south of the manor, a clear lake glistened like ice beneath an enormous moon.

A river ran beside the manor and dumped into the lake. We crossed a bridge arching over the river and walked on a cobbled pathway that cut through a row of tiny cottages. Most of the early risers greeted us in French. Sinead spoke to them in their own language.

Warm light engulfed us as we entered the foyer of the manor. Familiar voices echoed down a hallway. We followed the voices into a large room. Arik, Bastien, and the other Sentinels sat around a game table in deep conversation. Pop sat with Afton, Nick, and Deidre by a large hearth with lit logs. There was a collective intake of breath when we moved into the room.

Pop got up, charged over, and pulled me into a death hug. "Thank God you're safe. When they said you should've been here, and you weren't, it worried me sick."

"Easy." I wrapped my arms around him. "You're going to crush me."

He released me, his eyes assessing me for damage and mine looking for Arik.

It was like a family reunion with everyone embracing each other around the lodge-style room. I finally found Arik across the room. Edgar was telling him something—probably informing him about what went down in Esteril. Arik was definitely confident. A real leader. He shoved his hands into his pockets, tilting his head as he listened. Just the sight of him ignited tingles in my stomach. I wanted to hold him and tell him how glad I was that he was okay. That I missed having him with me in Esteril. I was more confident as a warrior and conjurer with his leadership guiding me.

"We were so worried about you," Afton said.

Bastien approached. "You certainly know how to make an entrance. And she's right. *We all* were concerned. So glad you all made it out safely." Again, the way he looked at me with such tenderness stirred something deep. Arik was a leader, all right, but Bastien was also—his ability to rise above his grief to show compassion for others inspired me, too.

"I'm sorry—" But we all hadn't made it out. Ricardo was dead. For some reason, I couldn't say that. Saying it would make it real.

"What's this?" Nick motioned to my coat as he ambled over. "I thought you were against wearing fur?"

"Well, it was cold, and there wasn't anything else. You know what?" I said, exasperated. "It's not like I killed the poor thing myself." I angrily removed my scabbard, wiggled out of the coat, and draped it over my arm.

"Whoa, no worries. I'm just teasing you." Nick sniggered.

I ignored him. "Besides, it smells ancient. The animal would probably be dead by—" The way the light hit Nick's face stopped me.

His brows were crinkled, the right one higher than the other. "Gia, I said I was teasing."

Conemar's eyebrow had done the same thing when he attacked my globe. Nick's eyes were the same deep brown and shape as Conemar's eyes. Same thick eyelids. Same dimple on their left cheeks. If Nick were thicker and had graying hair, he would be the exact copy of Conemar. My breath hitched. All noise in the room vanished behind the blood rushing in my ears. I had to get out of here. I couldn't let him see my fear. *Arik.* I had to find Arik.

Bastien captured my elbow. "What's the matter?"

I cleared my throat. "Um. Nothing. I'll be right back."

"After what you've been through, I want you to rest," he said.

"*You* want me to rest?" Again with the arrogance. Someone else telling me what to do. I slipped from his grasp. "I'm not one of your subjects or whatever you call them." I had more important things to worry about. Like what I'd just noticed about Nick.

I kept my breath even and slowed my anxious steps as I crossed the room. *It can't be. I've just been through too much. I'm seeing things.*

Carrig was sitting beside Arik, recapping our escape. "Her instincts are amazing," Carrig said. "She just broke the hinges on the cell without thinking."

"Excuse me," I interrupted. "Arik, can I have a word with you—*alone*, please?"

As I turned to go, I was barely aware of Arik's hand brushing mine lightly. He gave me a curious look as he walked with me out into the hall.

Arik turned to face me. "What's the matter?"

I rubbed over my scar. "I'm not sure. It's kind of crazy, but I think I just discovered something. It has to do with Jacalyn Roux."

It startled me when his hands came down on my shoulders.

"Easy there. You're nervous. Take a breath and tell—"

Carrig came into the hall. "Is there some'ting wrong?"

"I believe this is a private meeting," Arik said.

"No, it's okay. He can stay."

I inhaled and released the breath. "We found letters in Jacalyn's room. She had a baby. My mom helped her hide out in Boston until the baby was born."

"I did na know she had a baby," Carrig said.

"Well, she did. Her baby—" I couldn't bring myself to say it. If I did, what would happen to him?

"It's all right," Arik said. "Go on."

My heart was hammering so hard it surprised me that neither of them could hear it. On the one hand, I couldn't believe it could possibly be true, but on the other, it made so much sense. So much horrible sense. I gulped, then said in a rush, "When Conemar had a grip on my throat, something familiar struck me about his face, his mannerisms. Just now, in that room"—I pointed to the den for effect—"I saw his face again. The eyes, the nose, the hair, and the jawline are all the same."

"Who is it?" Arik said.

I had to force out the words. "I think Nick is Jacalyn's son, and Conemar is his father."

"He has parents. I've seen them," Arik protested.

"Nick's mother is always telling a story about how she couldn't get pregnant for several years," I said, my mind racing to put it all together. "They had tried everything, but nothing worked until they had Nick. One day, Nick's mother said it a little differently than her normal way. She *said*, until Nick was *given* to them. I remember it clearly because she corrected herself right away, making sure I understood that she had indeed *had* him.

"Before my mother died, she and Nick's mother were

best friends. I think Jacalyn wanted to hide Conemar's son from him, and my mother helped her. Don't you see? It all fits. We were raised together, sort of what my mom said in the letter. We had classes together. Even took Italian lessons together. Who does that?"

"The only way to know for certain is for you to perform a truth globe on him," Arik said.

Although that's what I should do, the idea churned my stomach. "I can't. What if I'm wrong? And if I'm right—well, it will devastate him."

"Why don't you ask *him*?" Nick leaned against the door-frame.

CHAPTER TWENTY-SIX

"I'm pissed, Gia. We've been best friends since diapers, and you couldn't come to me about this before them." Nick unhitched himself from the doorframe and stalked over to me. "Don't you know me by now? I've always wondered why I was taller than my parents were. Why my *nose, face,* and *eyes* didn't match anyone's in my family."

"I'm so sorry, Nick," I said, shaking. "It just clicked now. I'm not even sure I'm right."

He pulled out a photograph from his pocket. "I stole this from my mother's dresser. It's been in my wallet for years. I wanted to ask my parents about this, but I let them keep their secret. As long as they're happy, I don't care if I was adopted, but now the hint of it makes me wonder who I really am."

"Okay, now *I'm* pissed." I crossed my arms. "Why didn't you come to me with *that*?"

"I assumed you got it. You're always teasing me how I don't look anything like my family, and I must be my ma's yoga instructor's son."

I looked at the floor. I had been so mean to him. "I'm

such a shit. You're right. That had to be awful."

He handed me the photo. A crease from where he'd folded it in half ran vertical across my mother's face. Jacalyn and Nick's mother sat on an old orange couch with my mother wedged between them. My mother held up a pink baby dress as she balanced the remains of a present on her lap. Jacalyn's belly was a round basketball, and Nick's mother was as slender as ever. My mother and Nick's mother both wore wide smiles, while Jacalyn's face was pinched and sad.

I turned the photograph over and read the neat script on the back. "Baby Gia's homecoming—5 May." My gaze met Nick's. "I don't get it."

"Since you and I are only a few months apart, my mom should be pregnant in this photograph, but she isn't, and this woman"—he placed his index finger on Jacalyn's face—"is about seven months, wouldn't you say? I want you to perform that globe thing on me. I need to know the truth."

My heartbeat sped up again. I shook my head. "We don't have to. You're right. You have parents. They love you, and you love them. What does it matter?" I didn't want him to face the fears that I had. Once he knew for sure, he could never go back to normal. His entire world would change.

Nick placed his hand on my cheek. "I'm not afraid, Gia. Besides, we have each other, and you worry enough for the both of us."

"All right, you two," Carrig said. "This be pointless. You won't know if he be Conemar's son unless you perform that globe. So get at it, already."

"He's right," Arik added. "Let's see the truth."

Nick held out his hand. Arik poked Nick's skin with the tip of his dagger and a ruby drop splashed into my cupped hand.

...

Within the shimmering skin of the globe, Jacalyn lay in a hospital bed, cuddling a baby swaddled so tightly I was surprised his face wasn't as blue as the blanket.

"Not to worry, my beautiful boy," Jacalyn said softly. "Katy has put a charm on you." Her fingertips ran over a cross-like brand on the side of the baby's head. "It's different from baby Gia's brand, for this one protects your soul. I pray you never learn about your father. Conemar will never know you exist.

"I wonder what they will name you, dear one. If it were up to me, I would name you Tiege. It means the rule of the people, and you are destined to rule, my son. Within your blood flows the energy of two powerful wizards—one good and one evil. May you take after your great-grandfather, Gian, and not your father."

She paused when Mr. and Mrs. D'Marco came into the room holding hands and looking nervous. The D'Marcos looked a lot younger.

Jacalyn's eyes didn't leave her baby when they came in. Instead, she gazed lovingly at the bundle in her arms. I felt just as awkward as the D'Marcos seemed as they waited for Jacalyn to acknowledge their presence.

When Jacalyn finally tore her gaze away from the baby, her wet cheeks glistened in the fluorescent light. "Your mummy and daddy are here, little one. I have chosen a lovely family for you." Jacalyn kissed the baby's head. "Good-bye, little one." She handed the baby to Nick's mother. "What will you name him?"

"Nicklaus," answered Mrs. D'Marco. "Nick for short."

...

The image cut out and the globe hardened to an icy shell that exploded on my palm, cutting my skin. I screamed. "What happened?"

A pixie-like woman dressed in dark green was half-hidden behind a statue of a wizard, cackling her amusement. Arik darted across the corridor and caught the woman before she noticed him.

"Who—" Carrig began. "Blimey, I know you. You drugged me, you banshee."

I winced at the pain stabbing my palm. "*Who is she?*"

Nick pulled off his T-shirt and wrapped it around my bleeding hand.

Arik dragged the woman into the light.

"Aunt Eileen?"

She looked completely different. Gone were the loose black clothes and the teased crimson mushroom. Instead, her green shirt and black pants hugged her curves, and her red hair fell softly around her face. The black cat-eye glasses and heavy makeup were also missing, replaced with light makeup and pink lip gloss.

Sinead blew into the hall, followed by Bastien and Demos. "What's all the commotion?" She spotted Arik holding Aunt Eileen and yelled, "Let her go! She's an ally."

"No, she's hurt Gia," Arik said.

Bastien stormed over to me and bent down. "You're injured?"

"I'm okay," I said, leaning over to see around him.

Aunt Eileen struggled in Arik's hold. "She's probably aiding Conemar," he said.

"Lorelle, is it true?" Sinead asked Aunt Eileen.

Lorelle? Why is she calling Aunt Eileen that?

"Oh please," Aunt Eileen said. "You had your chance to serve Conemar, but you wanted to shack up with an overgrown elf."

Carrig pulled his knife out of his belt. "Watch your tongue, banshee, or I'll slice it off."

Sinead eased Carrig's arm down with a gentle hand. "Don't let her antics upset you. It happened a long time ago, and I chose you, not him."

Wow. Conemar's a player. He's been with Jacalyn, Sinead, and Aunt Eileen. Gag.

Sinead slanted a look at Aunt Eileen. "How did you get into the shelter?"

"Our queen gave me *carte blanche* to get in."

"Why would she do that?"

"I told her you were in danger, *sister*." There was so much hate in Aunt Eileen's voice.

"Okay," I cut in. "Who is Lorelle, and what happened to my aunt?"

"I'm Lorelle, you stupid girl," she said, a snarl in her voice. "I killed your aunt years ago. Oh, and it was too easy. We became instant friends at a witches' convention in Salem."

Lorelle shook her head, and a flurry of glittery dust blew into Arik's face, blinding him. She slammed her heel on his toe and threw a sharp elbow into his groin. He stumbled back, losing his hold on her, and she quickly backed away from him. From her belt, she pulled out a dagger and held it up, daring anyone to make a move.

"I sliced your aunt's throat from here"—she ran her index finger across her throat—"to there. I dumped her bleeding body off a pier and waited for the sharks to circle, and before long...sharks' bait."

Fury rose in me as Sinead inched toward Lorelle. "How did you know how to find Gia?"

"You told me Carrig believed Marietta had fled to America."

The look Sinead gave her was a cross between pity and hate. "What happened to you? Why are you doing this?"

"Love. I would die for Conemar." Lorelle smiled. She clearly enjoyed talking about her conquests. "Conemar is brilliant. He knew Marietta must have had a Pure Witch shield her and the baby, so he sent his followers to stake out the most talented ones, and we waited for a sign. My assignment was Katy Kearns because of my close resemblance to her husband's child. It made it easier for me when Eileen told me that she and Katy hadn't seen each other for over eight years due to a dispute. I glamoured myself to look like that hideous woman. Katy immediately forgave me, or rather, she forgave Eileen, after I groveled about how sorry I was and turned on the waterworks. What a pathetic woman."

"You're the one who's pathetic," I hissed through gritted teeth.

"Whatever. And you're a brat. It was always Gia this and Gia that. And you were right under my nose the entire time. I never met Marty, or maybe I would have put it all together. She had a different last name, and she was already dead when I arrived. There wasn't a clear picture of her anywhere. The ones I did find looked nothing like Marietta. She'd gained weight and cut her hair short. And you never showed any signs of magic."

She took a few steps backward.

Arik took a few steps forward.

"Then Carrig showed up," she continued. "We all know what happened next."

"Wow, you're stupid," I said. "My name didn't clue you in?" I wasn't going to mention I hadn't put Gian and my name together, either.

"Shut up, bitch." Lorelle backed down the hall, her eyes shifting from face to face until she stopped at mine again. "I never heard of Gian. I'm fey. I skipped Wizard History in school. It was such a boring subject."

I bit my lip, trying to stay calm, but inside I was dying. "You're a liar. You said you loved me."

She sent me the ugliest hate-eyes I'd ever seen. "I wanted to barf each time I said it. I'd never love a human child. When I get the chance, I will kill you. And I want my cat back."

"Cleo?"

"I'm going to skin her for turning traitor on me. She was supposed to spy on you and report back."

"If you harm her, I'll scratch your eyes out!" I started toward her, rising to my knees, but Nick grabbed my arm and stopped me. "What did you do to my globe?"

"I eliminated it," Lorelle said. "You'll never be able to use it again."

I pulled off Nick's T-shirt and opened my palm. Nick's dried blood from my earlier reading was a rusty smudge against the bright red blood oozing from the tiny cuts in my skin.

"*Mostrami la verità*," I spoke the charm to ignite my truth globe. A flicker of light zapped and vanished. I tried again, and nothing, not even a flicker. "It can't be. How—" A sob cut off my words. Nick wrapped his arms around me, and I leaned into his embrace.

"What did you do to her?" Carrig said, the vein in his forehead throbbing.

"Conemar is obsessed with her and her powers. He wants

her." Lorelle's face brightened. "I used an ancient charm straight from a book I found in Katy Kearns's house. It destroys globes. Were any of you aware Katy had such a book? There are some powerful charms in it. Conemar won't want you now."

"Good! You can have him," I yelled.

"Where be this book now?" Carrig demanded.

"Like I'd tell you," Lorelle said. "Oh, poor little Gia has lost her globe. Go ahead, someone tell her. Tell her she can't be a Sentinel unless she has a battle globe."

"Too bad for you, *biatch*," I mocked, a pink globe balancing in my hand. "Oops. I have another globe. How did that happen?"

I lobbed it at Lorelle, not sure what would happen when it hit her. A wave of energy knocked her on her butt and the dagger flew from her hand.

"You forget," Carrig said, crossing the room. "She be the daughter of two Sentinels. Therefore, she has two battle globes."

Lorelle clambered to her feet. "Not so fast," Lei said from behind Lorelle, pressing the tip of her sword to Lorelle's back. I hadn't seen Lei come up behind Lorelle. She was quick like that.

Carrig strolled the rest of the way to Lorelle and glared down at her. "Now, tell me where this book of charms be, and I won't send you to the scryers. Do you remember your fey lessons? You know the part, where scrying an unwilling party can cause the brain to become soggy. I'm certain you do."

Lorelle lifted her head. "You wouldn't."

"Ah, it'll be a fight, won't it? Take her to the scryers. I've no time for her games."

Arik and Demos each snatched one of Lorelle's arms.

"When Conemar finds out he has a son, he'll kill the lot

of you to get to him," Lorelle threatened as Arik and Demos dragged her away. "You all will die."

"Conemar has a son?" Sinead stared at Carrig with disbelief. "Who is it?"

Bastien aided me to my feet with a firm hold on my arm and a gentle hand against my back. "Are you all right?"

I glanced at my hands. "Yeah. They're just small cuts."

Nick stood and gave me a forced smile. "I guess I'm not the yoga instructor's kid, huh? I'm the Antichrist's son."

I buried my head farther into the down pillow, refusing to yield to the sunlight tickling my eyelids. Every muscle and nerve ending in my body ached. Some moron decided to knock on the bedroom door at the ungodly hour—I checked the antique table clock—of nine thirty. "Come in," I called angrily.

The door eased open, and Arik came into the room.

I quickly ran my hands over my hair, smoothing it down. I yanked the comforter up to my chin to hide my ratty old Hello Kitty tank top. "Hey, what's up?"

"I need to talk to you." He sat on the bed and rested his elbows on his knees. "That was a gloomy funeral yesterday, eh?"

"Yeah, most are. I feel bad for Bastien's mother with Odil missing and all. Who will replace Bastien's father?"

"The French Council has chosen Augustin Orfevre as Couve's High Wizard."

"Why didn't they choose Bastien?"

"Bastien is still a novice wizard," he said. "He'll reach senior wizard soon, but only a master wizard can be considered for High Wizard. Augustin is approaching three hundred, so he shan't last many more years. I think that's why they chose him. All Couve wants Bastien to rule. He will be a master wizard by the time he's twenty-five. When Augustin dies, Bastien will be ready to take over."

"Crazy. Is Bastien going to live to be *that* old?"

"If not more, and if you marry him, you'd be the first of many wives."

I shuddered at the thought until— "Wait. We're part wizard, aren't we? How long do we live?"

"Unfortunately, we haven't enough of it. We live a normal human lifetime."

I scowled. "Well, good thing I don't want to marry him."

He gave me a mischievous grin.

I sat up, keeping the comforter at my chin. "Pop will kill you if he finds you on my bed."

He raised an eyebrow at me. "Déjà vu?"

I smiled, recalling the morning in my apartment before we left for Asile when he sneaked into my bedroom.

His mischievous grin returned. Black eyelashes framed his intensely focused eyes, and they studied me. I wanted to run my fingers through the dark waves of hair falling over his forehead. If it weren't for the laws and the severe punishment, I would've kissed him right then.

"I haven't been fully honest with you." He stared at his hands. "Rather, I must seem dodgy to you. I fancied you the first time I spotted you in the library. And then I pushed you away. The laws say we can't be together. I'm promised to another, and yet, you are always on my mind. You make me question my beliefs. With the threats lately, none of it matters any longer."

I was tired of his jabbering, and besides, he had me at fancied. I grabbed his arms and pulled him to me as I fell back onto the pillows.

He wrapped me in his strong arms and kissed me. Our legs intertwined and his hands pulled through my hair, cradling my head with gentle fingers. I slipped my arms around his neck and closed my eyes, wanting to savor his touch.

The kiss deepened and incredible sparks ignited through my entire body. I pulled him closer to me. His tongue parted my lips. He tasted of maple syrup, like he'd just eaten breakfast.

His hand slid up my side, and I shivered. His mouth explored mine with such vigor my lips tingled. He drew his head back and watched me, his dark eyes pools of liquid chocolate. He leaned forward and kissed my neck, sending a blaze of heat across my skin.

"You're beautiful." The softness in his voice tickled my ear. "I love how you're so stubborn." He kissed my earlobe.

My lip trembled.

"I love this little twitch you get when you're nervous." He kissed the corner of my mouth. "I really fancy you, Gianna."

I shot up onto my knees and stared down at him. "Okay. Replay. What did you say?"

"You heard me. I don't *replay*." He smirked and sprang from the bed. "We're late. Get into your gear. We have drills. We only have a few weeks before we go to Asile."

I assessed my rumpled pajamas. "Wait a minute. Are you kidding me?"

"I don't kid." He walked over to the door. "We have practice."

"I'm not talking about that." I blew the bangs out of my face. "I was referring to the replay statement."

He opened the door, amusement in his eyes. "In the future,

when someone says he fancies you, it's a serious moment." The door clicked behind him.

"You're a tease!" I yelled at the closed door.

He laughed, his boots thudding down the hall.

"Guys," I huffed, plopping my butt onto the mattress. My lips stretched into a smile. "He likes me," I whispered to the room. I wasn't sure what I thought about that, but it felt pretty damn good.

CHAPTER TWENTY-SEVEN

Over the next several weeks, the master wizards from Couve sent probes to Asile. Probes were stronger than the tracers Sinead used to find people or spy within the libraries. The probes detected wards and gathered information. Each one sent had come back with the same results. Merl's wards still held, which was good news. The probes also brought back news of Conemar's army blocking the entry into Asile. Esterilians, Bane Witches, Writhes, some Laniars, shifters, and various others had joined him. There were also creatures the probes couldn't read.

The Italian, Irish, Spanish, and Greek havens had sent two Sentinels, a few wizards, and several guards to aid us. It was all they could spare, since they needed to protect their own havens. Pure Witches, ferals, fey, Laniars, werehounds, shifters, and a variety of creatures trickled into the shelter to join our side. Artisans worked endlessly to erect temporary housing. Within days, the shelter had become a refugee camp.

As the Sentinels waited for the elders to come up with a battle plan, we spent our days sparring and our evenings soaking in the lake's hot springs. Along with the French

Sentinels, the Sentinels from the other havens joined in on
our practice drills.

I waded in the water. Along the bank of the lake, several
pairs of eyes gleamed under the moon's glow. The eyes
belonged to werehounds. It was as if I had my own pack of
watchdogs. They followed me everywhere I went, whether
they were in hound or human form. A preteen werehound
girl named Katarina told me they protected me because of
Gian, like Ricardo said. He'd been dead since the 1930s, and
they still revered him. My heart lifted to be his namesake
and it made me work even harder to do him proud.

I hadn't spent much time with Pop, Afton, or Nick
except at meals. Pop helped the Curers—women with
healing powers—set up a medical center for when we went
to battle. Afton assisted him by organizing the supplies,
sterilizing the rooms, and doing whatever was asked of her.
A Pure Witch had charmed Afton's parents into thinking she
was on some sort of travel thing for school. Pop simply told
Nick's parents the truth. Nick's mother already knew about
the Mystik world because of my mother. Of course, she
freaked and made Pop promise to watch over him.

Sinead and Deidre became Nick's security guards, never
letting him out of their sights. Bastien, along with the higher
wizards, taught him charms and spells. Their efforts were
futile; Nick's power seemed suppressed by the cross branded
on his scalp. An elder wizard determined the only way to
remove the brand was through surgery. Pop assisted one of
the Curers as the older woman lanced off the brand. Nick
was still recuperating in his room.

I leaned back in the water and floated on the surface.

The ripples against my cheek grew larger as Arik swooshed
over and cradled me in his arms. "You're deep in thought."

I wrapped my arms around his neck and bobbed with

him. "I hate all this waiting. Why don't we just go rescue Asile now?"

"We have to be ready. If we go unprepared, we'll lose."

"Hey, Gia!" Afton called from the edge of the lake.

Arik released me and I waded over to Afton. She watched the Sentinels jumping from the rocks into the lake. "Nick's asking for you." She bent over, picked up a towel from the grass, and tossed it to me as I came out of the water.

As I dashed, I busted Arik checking me out in my bikini. I flung the towel around myself. "I'll see you later. Nick's awake," I said to Arik, and followed Afton up the hill. The dog pack plodded after us.

When we were far enough away from the others, I said, "Are you okay?"

"I'm fine," she said. "It's strange how they all act like they're not about to go into battle. That they could die. That you..."

"That I might die?"

She stared ahead. "Yes."

Back home we never fell into awkward silences, but now we did frequently. I figured it confused her having two Gias around.

"You and Deidre have been hanging out a lot lately," I said, and then wished I hadn't. "Not that that's a bad thing. I was just wondering how she was doing, is all." *Yeah, you didn't just sound like a jealous friend.*

"Well, she never leaves Nick's side." She sucked in a breath and let it out slowly. "They really do love each other. As for me, I always pick the bad boys. It's my own fault. You'd think I'd learn by now."

"Quit being hard on yourself. You just haven't found the right one yet."

"Thank you," she said with a grateful smile. "I sure do miss chilling with you."

"I miss you, too." I gave her a hug. I glanced back at the lake, where the rest of the Sentinels were still splashing around. "Have you seen Bastien lately?" The last time I'd seen the wizard was at his father's funeral. He'd looked so devastated, and I'd had to swallow the compulsion several times to comfort him.

"I see him a lot. He works with Nick every day. His father's death must really be messing with him. He hardly speaks to anyone." She gave me a questioning look. "Why? Are you into him?"

"No, of course not. Just worried about him." I did have an unhealthy urge to see him, but I reminded myself I needed to stay away. The last thing I wanted to think about was that betrothal hanging over us. I decided to change the subject. "So, what have you been up to?"

The chatterbox was back. Once Afton began talking, I couldn't get a word in. She rattled on about her forced friendship with Deidre and her homesickness. She told me working with Pop made her want to go into the medical field. Before long, we stood together at the side of Nick's bed. His closed eyelids flickered and their long mink lashes fluttered as if he were dreaming.

With Conemar for a birth father, what suppressed powers did Nick have? And what if that power changed him? The uncertainty scared me. How stupid and hypocritical was I? I hadn't changed. Had I? This was Nick. We grew up together. I knew him. He'd never hurt anyone.

I placed a shaky hand on his arm. His eyes fluttered and opened.

"Hey, cuz," I said. "Do you think you'll need a toupee, or will you go with the comb-over thingy?"

"Ha-ha," he said weakly. "Very funny. Did someone dunk you underwater or is this your new look?"

"Touché." I was relieved he still had his sense of humor, and it must've shown on my face.

He frowned. "I didn't have a lobotomy. They just lanced the surface of my skin. They've assured me the hair will grow back."

"I know." I patted his arm. "You're going to be fine. I won't let anything happen to you."

He tried to get up, and Afton eased him back onto his pillows. "You have to stay in bed," she said. "Watch him. I'm going to get your pop. He'll give Nick something to help him sleep."

"I have to go see my parents." He lifted his head. "It's still me. I won't be evil like him."

Does he mean Conemar?

Afton returned with Pop, and he gave Nick a shot.

"I'm not evil," Nick whispered.

I held his hand, tears stinging my eyes. "No one thinks that."

"You do."

"I'd never think—"

His eyes closed just then and he fell asleep, so Afton, Pop, and I crept out.

All the way to my room, Nick's words replayed in my head. I wanted to take away his fears. I knew dread well. I'd lived with it the last several months. Conemar had to be defeated. It was the only way to keep Nick safe. To get us back to our old lives.

...

The elder wizards had finally devised a plan. The shelter was buzzing with preparations for the impending battle. I worked alongside Arik, sharpening and cleaning my sword. The other Sentinels busied themselves with readying their gear for the fight scheduled for the morning.

The screaming of my blade under the sharpening stone drowned out Carrig's approach. "Gia," he snapped.

I jumped, practically falling off the boulder I was sitting on. "Omigod!" After righting myself, I glanced up at him, squinting against the sun. "Maybe give a warning next time, like clear your throat or something, before startling a girl messing with a sharp object, huh?"

"Me apologies, didn't mean to frighten you. I would like a word in private." He abruptly turned and walked off. When I didn't follow him, he called over his shoulder, "Are you coming, or do you need a proper invite?"

I plodded down the hill after him. He led me through trees until we stopped at a clearing by the river.

"This should be private enough." He sat on the grass. "Come join me."

I hesitated.

"Come on, trust me." He patted the grass.

I dropped down beside him. It was cool and refreshing under the shade of the trees after being in the sun all day. "What are we doing here?"

He fished a powder-white stone from his pocket. "Don't let losing your truth globe upset you. It served its purpose by revealing whom you could trust at a time when you were vulnerable. There be other ways of knowing the truth. One way be scrying. Only High Wizards are allowed to perform a scrying; it be illegal for the rest of us, because of the dangers."

"You mean like what the wizards did to Lorelle?"

"Yes. Except for Lorelle's be forced, which is extremely

painful. This be a scrying stone." With the stone still in his hand, he grabbed my hand, nesting the stone between our palms. "I want to show you something. Close your eyes, and don't fight it. Just let the stone work its magic."

The stone heated. Sparks danced against my closed lids. Visions flashed across my mind. It showed Carrig finding out I was Gia and not Deidre, and I could feel his excitement at the news. Then Carrig huddled in a corner of the dungeon, cold and thirsty. Lorelle, disguised as Aunt Eileen, drugged him with spiked tea.

"Is this playing backward?"

"Tis," he said.

A little girl resembling me at about age five or six ran into his arms.

"Is that Deidre?" I asked.

"She be nearly six then."

I closed my eyes. Sinead stroked his hair as he cried and trembled on her shoulder. He watched me—I had to be four—having a picnic with Pop on the Common. A dark depression overwhelmed me as he realized my mother was dead. He was across the street as a white delivery van hit my mother. My heart broke watching him discover Marietta had run away from Asile. Love warmed me as Carrig danced with a pregnant Marietta.

Tears slid down my temples. "You were there when she died. How come you didn't take me with you?"

"You were safe where you were. It *broke* me heart to leave you. Now, focus."

I returned my attention to the rewinding visions of Carrig's life. When Carrig saw Marietta for the first time, he said the word "beautiful" under his breath as she approached him.

"The first time you met her, you thought that?"

"Pay attention."

Fearlessly, he fought in battles within the most stunning libraries of the world. He was a little younger than I was as he trained on rolling green hills cut with white-stone walls. Night approached as he and his coach trained. I sensed Carrig's loneliness as a little boy weeping in a dark corner and his sadness cut through me.

"Stop. Why are you showing me this?"

"I never wanted you to feel that lonely. I saw you with your da, how much he loved you, and I couldn't take you from him."

He stood and reached his hand to me. I took it and he pulled me to my feet. Instead of releasing my hand, he towed me into an embrace. "No one could replace you in me heart. I've loved you ever since Marietta told me she was with child."

I buried my face in his chest, wanting to hold on to that moment. I'd always dreamed of my birth father loving me, and now I knew he always had. Seeing my mother in his memories was a true gift. They were memories of a woman we both missed and loved.

A cloud of sadness hovered over us. Carrig cleared his throat and let me go. My pocket crinkled and I stuck my hand in, retrieving the photo of him and my mother, along with her note to him. "I think these are yours." I handed them over.

He took them, and when he realized what they were, a sob escaped his mouth. "I thought they were lost forever."

I wrapped my arms back around him. "I'm so sorry. I've been so standoffish." I gulped the tears down. "It's just—I feel like I'm betraying Pop."

"Oh, Gia, you can love many people. Love isn't jealous." He squeezed me tight.

I was proud to be Carrig's daughter. He could never be Pop. Maybe he didn't even want that.

We sat back down on the grass and Carrig told me stories about my mother. I smiled at her insistence on teaching him how to dance. I laughed when he said they'd spar against each other, and my mother would beat him just as many times as he would beat her, if not more.

His face went serious after he finished telling me how my mother would burn everything she cooked.

I laughed. "I can't cook, either. I set off the smoke alarm burning butter in a pan once."

He took my hand, and a slight smile pulled on his lips. "It's because the both of you had more important things to be grand at."

That thought warmed me.

"You be a victor, Gia," he said somberly. "You were born for it. Killing will come as naturally to you as winning all them trophies your da brags about."

"I didn't have to kill anyone to get them. I mean, I don't want to kill anyone—or thing."

"Not even those who would destroy all you love?" He glanced sideways at me. "Because make no mistake—if the Mystik world falls, the human world will follow."

I studied our hands—his large, mine small. "I-I could die."

"So you could," he said. He paused before saying, "We each have an appointment with death. I'd rather die for a cause than die of old age never having done something important."

"I'm still scared."

"No matter how many battles I've fought, I always go in afraid. It keeps me on me toes."

This was a conversation I so didn't want to have. I refused to dwell on tomorrow's fight or who might die.

Nausea filled me when I thought about all that we had at stake. "We should get back," I said. "I have a lot of work to do before dinner."

"I need you to do something first." By the look on his face, it wasn't something he wanted to ask me but obviously had to.

"What?"

"The wizards recovered the whereabouts of your nana's ancient charm book from Lorelle's mind. I want to send you alone to retrieve the book."

"Did you say alone?"

"You're shielded. No one can detect you in the libraries. A spell be on the charm book and can't be removed from Katy's home. You can release the spell with your globe and bring it back."

I took a step back. "Are you crazy? I can't go by myself."

"I wouldn't send you if there be another way." He gave me a reassuring smile. "I'll be watching through the gateway book. It's a charm. I'll teach it to you. Once you're in the library, you're home."

"Can I have a minute to process this?"

He lifted his arm and checked his wristwatch. "Okay, one minute."

I rolled my eyes. "I didn't mean literally one minute. If you're going to time it, then give me five."

"Certainly, but remember no one can detect you in the libraries."

"Ugh." I kicked at a rock. "I have to do this, don't I?"

He shrugged. "You got a bit more time to agonize on it, if you want."

...

Getting to the library went smoother than expected. Carrig came with me to the library to show me how to charm the photos in the *Libraries of the World* book into moving pictures, or rather windows, to see if anyone was in the Boston Athenæum's reading room before I transported. It was morning in France, which meant it was about three in the afternoon in Boston.

Carrig had had the artisans sew me normal clothes. The women made me black pants, a shirt, and a jacket that all totally hugged what little curves I had, which brought back all the insecurities ever to haunt my mind. The low boots were ugly but comfortable. The curers created energy wafers for me to counter the side effects from using my globe. Though the side effects of the truth globe had stopped before Lorelle destroyed it, the pink globe's aftereffects were sporadic. I shoved the wafers into a pocket in the jacket.

When the coast was clear, I jumped into the book and hid in the farthest staircase in one of the protruding bookcases. A man departed the elevator and sat at one of the large tables. After grabbing a book from a nearby shelf, I crossed the room to the elevators. It was taking the elevator too long to reach the fifth floor, so I took the stairs, ditching the book on a step.

Okay, this is easy.

The reception desk was busy as I hurried down the white marble steps and out the red saloon doors. It was a clear, hot day in Boston. I flagged down a taxi, opened the door, and slid in. The driver let me off about a block from Nana's house. My heart squeezed at the thought of her. Merl had said he'd keep her safe, but we hadn't heard word since. I prayed she was still fine.

I knelt behind a lilac bush across the street, making sure the coast was clear, then darted across the street and peered in the front window. A shadow moved across the half-closed sheers. A twentysomething guy, a chubbier version of Bastien, stumbled over to the window, and I ducked down.

"It's an oven in 'ere," Veronique said from somewhere in the house. "Odil, open more windows."

Crap. This is not going to be easy.

The window squealed as Odil opened it. His heavy feet thudded back into the living room. "Where do you want to start searching?"

"Oh please, do I 'ave to babysit you? It's a *book*. Search in ze bookcase."

I eased up and peered over the windowsill. Veronique shuffled through a stack of books on the coffee table. Baron came out of the bushes and meowed. I slipped back down as he thumped up onto the sill and went inside.

Veronique gasped. "Oh kitty, you frightened me." She picked him up. "Poor kitty, I bet you're 'ungry."

Wow, the bitch had a heart, even if it was the size of a cherry pit.

The can opener squealed in the kitchen, and then a can clanked onto the floor. "I bet you 'ave been eating ze scrapes out of ze garbage. Go on, eat."

Duh, it's scraps…French girl.

I peeked through the window again. Odil was tossing books onto the floor.

"Good little kitty." Veronique's heels clicked across the tiles, and she returned to the sitting room.

Odil was waiting for her. He wrapped his arms around her and brought his mouth to her ear. "You know we're alone in a house with bedrooms."

"Quit it," she ordered. "That's all you think about. We must find ze book."

"I've looked at every book in the bookcase and it's not

there." He kissed her ear. "Shall we check the bedrooms for it?"

Veronique let out a deep sigh. "All right. But afterward we make a clean sweep of ze place."

"Whatever you wish," Odil said, leading her down the hall.

A door slammed somewhere in the back of the house, and I listened to make sure they were preoccupied before I crawled through the window.

Gross. I so don't want to know what they're doing back there.

Lorelle's scrying lobotomy revealed that the ancient book of charms was hidden behind the jacket cover for *Don't Knit the Small Stuff*, a book on how to knit big throw blankets. I shuffled through the knitting books on the end table by Nana's favorite chair and ottoman. The book was close to the bottom of the stack.

I peeled back the jacket. Underneath was a leather-bound book. The title was in a language I didn't know. After re-covering the book with the jacket, I formed a pink globe and dropped it onto the book, releasing Nana's charm.

A creak came from the hallway, and I dropped to my knees, hiding behind the loveseat.

"Do you want water?" Veronique called down the hall. She buttoned up her shirt as she walked past me. "*Magnifique*," she said. "Ze zings I 'ave to do for that man."

That was fast.

I was thankful she didn't see me as she passed. A glass clinked, and then the water faucet turned on in the kitchen. Veronique headed back to the bedroom, carrying two glasses.

When she was gone, I grabbed the book and stood.

"What are you doing here?" a startled Odil blurted from the hallway.

CHAPTER TWENTY-EIGHT

Veronique came running up behind him.

I skidded across the floor, twisted the doorknob, and pulled. Locked. A fire globe hit the wall just above my head.

I shifted the book to one arm and raised my palm to form my globe. Another ball of fire whizzed by my head and I ducked. *Shit.* I formed my globe and tossed it, hitting Odil in the chest. He rolled to the floor and crawled behind the couch.

Veronique readied another fireball as I fumbled to unbolt the door. The lock slid back, and I jerked open the door. Nick stood there with electric currents dancing on his fingertips, and just behind him was Afton.

"Move," Nick ordered.

I flung myself against the wall.

Blue currents shot through the open door and hit Veronique before she threw her next fire globe. The globe landed on the floor, and the carpet ignited into flames. Odil crawled to Veronique's side and dragged her away from the fire.

"Run!" Afton yelled.

Nick grabbed my hand and hauled me down the steps after Afton. We ran down the street, around corners, and through alleys before we stopped and rested behind a large tree.

"Why are you guys here?" I asked between pants. "You got a death wish or something?"

"Are you complaining? I just saved your life," Nick protested. "If it weren't for me, you'd have been fried. You should thank me."

"I know, thanks," I said. "But seriously, you surprised me. I was supposed to do this alone. Who told you I was coming here?"

Afton held her side. "I overheard you and Carrig in the hall. How could he send you alone? What was he thinking? Anyway, I told Jaran and he told the Sentinels. We decided Nick and I should help you search for the book because we'd go undetected through the gateway with our shields. Plus we know Boston."

"How did you get by Carrig?"

"That was tough," Afton said. "Arik distracted him."

"And you went through the gateway book alone?"

"Yep. I'm a wizard. Remember? The surgery released my suppressed powers the charm on my head blocked. It all came rushing back to me. It was like a bad LSD trip or something."

"Thanks to our tattoos, we were the only ones who could pass undetected. He practically killed me jumping through that book." Afton held up her hands. "Look, I have rug burns on my palms."

I turned to Nick. "Why did you bring Afton? She doesn't have any powers to protect herself."

"Right. I'd like to see you try and stop her once she's made up her mind to go."

I hugged the book. "How did you know where I was going?"

"When you took off in the direction of Mission Hill, I knew you were going to Nana's place," Nick answered.

"We grabbed a taxi and followed you," Afton said.

"Okay, then let's get one back to the library." I headed toward a busy street and flagged the first approaching taxi. It pulled up beside us and Nick opened the door. Afton slid across the seat.

Before entering the cab, I hugged Nick tight.

"What's that for?"

"Thank you for coming after me."

"It's you and me, right?" he said.

"Always." I pulled away from him and slipped in beside Afton.

Nick ducked into the cab. "We have to call Arik when we get to the library. He's going to escort us back to Paris."

Nick's unkempt hair was brushed to the side to cover the bald spot from the surgery, and he wore rumpled clothes. Old Nick never did rumple.

Under his skin. Watching Nick made me remember the scene from my globe where Jacalyn held Nick as a baby. She had said the charm on his head was to prevent him from turning evil or from evil finding him. She mentioned he was from the line of two great wizards. Whatever the charm did, removing it released his suppressed powers. I just hoped it hadn't released something else—something terrifying.

I grabbed his hand, and he smiled at me. There was no way Nick would be like Conemar. I'd known him all my life. We were more like brother and sister than just friends. We had each other's backs.

The taxi pulled up to the curb and we scrambled out. Nick pulled a window rod out of his pocket and contacted

Arik, then hid in the shadows and waited for him to arrive. A few moments later Arik opened the door and we hurried into the library.

"Are you trying to kill me, Gia?" Arik closed the door.

"I was following Carrig's orders—" I tried to explain, but he grabbed my arms and kissed me.

He pulled back and gazed into my eyes. "Don't ever listen to him again without consulting me first. You understand?"

"Don't tell—"

"Okay, Romeo and Juliet," Nick said, interrupting my protest. "Let's go."

"We must hurry," Arik said. "Someone may have picked up my jump."

"Then why did you come?" I adjusted the bulky, ancient book in my arms as we rushed to the stairs.

"Carrig is a great fighter but a terrible time manager. How did he think you were going to get back into the library after it closed?"

When we reached the fifth floor reading room, Bastien soared out of the gateway book and slid across the top of the table. Demos followed. Lei shot out of the book with Kale and Jaran right after her, and two werehounds were behind them.

Bastien hopped off the table. "There's another gateway book in this library."

Blue threads of electricity filled the room, hitting everyone near the table. The threads wrapped around Arik and the others. They dropped, immobile, to the floor.

Nick shoved Afton and me behind him. He aimed his outstretched hands in the direction where the strike had come from, and light crackled from his fingertips.

Conemar glided into the room with several of those

muscled Sentinels from Russia trailing him. "What a lovely surprise, Gia. We didn't sense your presence here. I come to kill Arik and I get such wonderful added prizes."

I formed a globe in my palm and tossed it on top of Arik and the others. The threads snapped and vanished. The Sentinels jumped up, pulled their shields from their backs and their swords from their scabbards, and charged after Conemar's Sentinels. The werehounds growled before attacking. Metal clanged against metal like many church bells going off at once.

Arik helped Bastien to his feet.

"Bastien, glad to see you weren't stunned to death," Conemar said. I could barely hear him over the battle sounds happening around us.

"You murdered my father!" Bastien made for Conemar. "I'll kill you!"

"That should be fun." Conemar stretched his fingers.

Arik held Bastien back. "Keep your head straight."

A Sentinel made for them, and Arik swung his sword, their blades meeting with a loud *clank*. They shuffled around each other, throwing blow after blow, their dance moving them off from us. My eyes darted from Arik to Conemar, not knowing what to do.

Conemar glanced at the book in my arms. "I see someone found my book. I sense shielding charms. Three. Did Katy cloak you with a brand, Gia? Furthermore, why did she cloak your friends? *Puzzles. Puzzles.* I do so love to figure them out."

One of the werehounds sprang from a table and landed in front of me, baring her teeth at Conemar.

Nick pointed his hands at Conemar. "Stand back or I'll zap you."

Conemar threw his head back and laughed. "Boy, I

can smell you from here. You're a fledgling wizard. I could destroy you with my pinky." He wiggled his finger at Nick.

The werehound readied to make a jump for the wizard, but Conemar was quicker and hit her with his magic. She yelped and crashed to the floor.

"No!" I made for the werehound, but Afton grabbed my arm to stop me.

"She's breathing." Fear sounded in her voice. "Help Nick. He's going to get himself killed."

Nick shot a wave of blue light at Conemar, and the wizard blocked the current with his hand and sent it back. Nick pushed me out of the way and shoved Afton to the side. Afton landed on the floor and slid until she collided with a bookcase. Nick tried to catch the current but he fumbled and it hit the floor, knocking him back.

"Nick!" I screamed, grabbing his arm and trying to keep him from falling to the floor.

He righted himself and gave me a quick look. "I'm fine."

Bastien hurried over, magic sparking in his hands, blocking us from Conemar.

"Nick? Nice strong name for a wizard," Conemar yelled over the fight noises. "Bravo. That was an impressive attempt, boy. Too bad it wasn't good enough. It's dark in here. I'd like to see your face when I kill you. Let's put some light on the situation, shall we?" He lifted his palms and the room illuminated.

Bastien stepped in front of Nick.

Conemar gave him a curious look. "Now this is interesting." He took a heavy step forward. "The next High Wizard of Couve risking his life for a fledgling."

Demos propelled a green globe at Conemar. The globe spun with great force, and Conemar threw up his hand to block it, not even flinching. The globe busted against an invisible shield, sending a gust of air at a nearby bookcase and knocking the books from the shelves. Loose papers floated in the aftermath.

A female Sentinel tackled Demos and they wrestled on the floor until Lei kicked her off him. The Sentinel whisked to her feet, stopping Lei's katana with her sword. They scuffled, moving into the fray.

I began to form another globe in my right hand as I held tight to the charm book in my other. The globe rose up to the ceiling, and I scrambled in front of Bastien and Nick, shielding them with it and blocking Conemar's view of Nick.

"What's special about this fledgling? Why are you and Bastien worried about protecting him?" He took a few steps to the right and looked at Nick. "It can't be." A confused look shadowed Conemar's face before it lit in awareness. "Well, well, Jacalyn, you minx, you gave me a son." He grinned at Nick. "You're the spitting image of me at your age."

"You murdered Jacalyn, you bastard," I said. "You stay away from him."

My accusation actually surprised him. "Jacalyn and I were in love, until she met Phillip Attwood. I do admit I killed her. I couldn't help myself. After all, she was mine, not his. How can you blame me?"

Born evil. Sinead's words replayed in my mind. He believed he was the one who had been wronged and had every right to take her life.

Demos jumped off a table and landed in front of Conemar with his sword extended in front of him. "Come on, fight like a man."

"Silly boy, I'm not a man. I'm a wizard." A spark snapped out of Conemar's hand and hit Demos in the chest, and he flew back onto the table. The table crashed to the floor, sending the gateway book sailing across the room to land at Conemar's feet.

Arik exchanged blows with an Esteril Sentinel who flanked Conemar on his right. Lei came out of nowhere and swung her foot at Conemar. Her boot connected with his chin and he stumbled back.

Kale shot his stun globe at Conemar, but he threw up a shield to block it. The globe backfired and hit Kale, and he fell motionless to the floor. Jaran tossed his water globe, and the mini tsunami knocked Conemar to the floor.

"Give me the book," Bastien said.

I handed it to him and he flipped through the pages.

"What are you trying to find?" My arm burned under the strain of holding the globe.

"A spell to contain him," he answered. "Keep him busy."

"Trust me. He's busy," I said, watching Conemar slip and fall before he got back on his feet. He wiped the water from his face and regained his stance.

Nick put his hand on my shoulder. "Remove the globe and we can hit him back with power."

"No."

"You have to release Kale from the stun before he stops breathing," Bastien said.

Kale's motionless body lay on the floor. I didn't want to mess up with him again. I almost killed him the last time. This time, I could save him.

I let the globe recede until it was a small sphere in my hand and pitched it at him. The globe spread across him and he took in several deep breaths. Kale staggered to his feet and dived behind a table that was teetering on its side.

Swaying on my weak legs, I yanked out a wafer and shoved it into my mouth. It tasted like earth, but the result was like drinking three energy drinks. I instantly felt better.

Both Nick and Bastien shot a stream of energy at Conemar.

An electric ball swirled between Conemar's hands. Bright blue and red light reflected in his evil obsidian eyes. I threw up another shield around Nick, Bastien, and myself at the same time Conemar shot the electric ball. The charge bounced off my globe and blew up a nearby bookcase. Splinters and books showered the pink sphere.

Conemar spotted Afton struggling to get to her feet, and in an instant, he was beside her, pulling her up by her arm. Afton screamed. He wrapped his arms around her, removed a dagger from his belt, and placed the point to her throat. *No!*

She froze in his grasp, her eyes wide.

"Here now, see what I've caught," Conemar said, eyeing me. "Tell your Sentinels to back away."

Nick pushed against my globe.

"Get me out of this thing." Nick shoved the globe harder. "Let her go!"

Conemar looked at the book of libraries on the table.

"Get him!" I screamed. "He's going to jump with her!"

I dropped the globe and Nick sprinted toward Conemar and Afton.

Arik tackled Conemar just as he was saying the key to jump through the book with Afton. The three of them fell into the book and disappeared into the open pages. The book flew up, landed on the floor, and slammed shut.

"Afton!" I yelled, sloshing through water to the book. I flipped through the dampened pages. "Help me! We have to find them."

Bastien, who was clinging to the ancient charm book, slid to my side. We searched each picture in the gateway book. We didn't find Afton, Arik, or Conemar within the photographs. With each flip of the page, my heart sank. Finally, at the back of the book, we spotted Conemar dragging Afton across the great hall of the library in Mafra, Portugal. *But where is Arik?*

Without thinking, I spoke the key and jumped into the photo. Bastien grabbed my leg and was towed in with me. We flew fast through the dark hole until it deposited us onto a marble floor. He landed on top of me and we tumbled across the floor together. We lay in a heap—legs and arms tangled. The book of charms Bastien held dug into my back.

We had landed in a rotunda that joined two great halls on either side of us. An elaborate cupola stretched overhead. About a dozen windows lined each of the long halls, the moon casting light on the white and gold arches. Each hall was the length of a football field but half the width, and their ceilings were extraordinarily high. There was no movement in either hall.

Bastien rolled off me and onto his knees. "Can you get up?" he asked.

"I think so." I lifted my head. He took hold of my elbow and helped me to my feet.

"This was planned," he said.

"What do you mean?"

"The book is here in the middle of a hall. It should be by a bookcase. Someone put it here for a reason."

I spotted someone lying in front of one of the arched windows between the bookcases. "Who's that?" I rushed to the body with Bastien on my heels.

Arik was facedown on the marbled floor. My chest tightened. I pulled him over onto his back. He bled from a large gash in his head.

I looked up at Bastien. "Do you see *Afton*?" My voice cracked with so much emotion it scared me.

He squinted as he searched the room. "No."

Arik's eyes fluttered open. "The compelled man was right. I failed again. I failed her. Just…like…Oren."

"No, you didn't fail anyone," I said, hugging him. "You were so brave. You didn't even hesitate. You just jumped."

He coughed. "Leave me. Save Afton."

I gripped his arm. "You're going to be fine. Hold on. You *have* to hold on for me."

"You're such a bother sometimes," Arik teased, and then closed his eyes.

Bastien squeezed my shoulder. "He's still breathing. Get up. We can't let Conemar harm Afton. I found a ritual to send him away, but I need your help to distract him."

I leaned over and kissed Arik gently on the lips. "Don't you give up. I'll be back," I whispered in his ear and kissed it, too. I pulled his sword from his scabbard, picked up his shield, and got to my feet. "Ready. What do you want me to do?"

"We have to draw Conemar out of hiding." He gave me a weary smile. "I know you'll think of something."

I slid my arm through the straps of Arik's shield and centered my body. As I inched down the hall, I readied his sword.

"Come out, come out, wherever you are, Conemar!" I shouted. "Are you afraid of me? 'Cause you should be. I'm the one Agnost foretold. I'm the *end*, all right—for you. Let Afton go. She's just a human."

The hall remained silent.

"So you *are* afraid of me," I baited him. "You're just a loser! You intimidated Jacalyn, and you betrayed her." I hoped that pissed him off enough to come out of hiding. Just in case, I added, "Coward!"

Conemar stepped out from behind a bookcase with

Afton struggling in his arms. "As I said, I did not *betray* her," he said through clenched teeth. "We were betrothed, and she had an affair with that weasel professor."

Here we go.

I took a deep breath. "Release her, you big dumb bully! Do you always hide behind girls?" *Really, Gia? You couldn't think of anything better? You sound like a second grader.*

"I don't need her. She's served her purpose—she's separated you from the others and brought you here to me. Run, you vermin," he ordered, pushing Afton away.

Afton ran toward me. Conemar raised his hand, and a mix of blue and red lights danced across his fingertips. I had no idea what Bastien was doing behind me, but I worried his plan wouldn't work.

I switched the sword to my other hand and made a pink globe on my empty palm.

Before Conemar could throw an electric charge at Afton, my globe engulfed her, and his strike ricocheted off it, hitting an iron candelabra overhead. The candelabra collapsed to the floor, sending an explosion of sound reverberating down the great halls. I stuffed two wafers in my mouth.

"Quick reflexes. You get that from your father. Your beauty and brains are from your mother." He walked down the hall with measured steps.

When Afton reached me, she fell into my arms, trembling violently. "Listen to me," I murmured. "Run into the other hall and hide. Do you understand?"

She stood planted to the spot. "I can't leave you."

I kept alert, watching over her shoulder. Conemar was almost a third of the way down the hall and would reach us soon. I lobbed another globe, and it landed just in front of him. It was like a big splash of Pepto-Bismol. The pink membrane flew up and out, reaching the walls and ceiling, blocking Conemar's path. He shot electric currents into the pink mass. Ripples ran down it, melting its surface with each blast.

"If you stay, you'll distract me. *Go*," I said sharply.

Afton sprinted to the other hall. I turned to watch her. Bastien was writing something on the ground with blood. Maybe Arik's?

"What are you doing?" I yelled, horrified.

"The charm requires Sentinel blood. Don't pay attention to me—do *your* job."

"That is so wrong!"

"Watch *him*," he yelled back at me.

Conemar had stopped blasting the globe and was studying it. He gave me a treacherous smile. Then he blew across his palm, and a frosty burst of air hit the pink wall. The surface turned to a frozen shell. He punched it, and pink shards shattered to the ground.

"You're trying my patience, Gia. How about I introduce you to a few of my new friends? They're newly hatched, so I'm not certain what they'll do or if I'll have any control over them. Shall we see? Come out, my pets!" he shouted.

A dozen dark figures sprang out from behind the bookcases and hopped down from the balconies above. Their stench, like rotting flesh, hit me where I stood nearly half a football field away. Black tongues darted in and out of sharp yellow canines. The deformed figures slithered and slinked across the floor, growling and hissing, ending their contorting dance behind Conemar.

CHAPTER TWENTY-NINE

"Do you like my creations?" Conemar asked. "I couldn't have made them without your help. Thank you for delivering Ricardo to me. I needed Laniar DNA to complete the transformation. They can crush a man's skull with their hands. Just think of what an army I'll have when I've changed all the Writhes."

"You're *crazy*!" I chanced a glance in Bastien's direction. "*Hurry*, Bastien. Do you see them?"

He looked up from the book and his eyes widened. "Can you block them? I'm almost done!"

"I'll try." I turned back to face my impending doom. Nausea curdled in my stomach; the stink of his creatures made me feel faint, but I couldn't fail now. I willed steel into my muscles.

Conemar was looking pointedly at Bastien. *Strange.* He didn't seem to care that Bastien was working on a spell. He had to know it was something that would stop him.

He refocused on me, and I tossed three globes in a row, blocking the hall with a thicker shield.

"I'd hate to kill you. Think of how powerful we'd be if

you and Nick joined me." His voice sounded muffled behind
the wall of pink. Conemar attacked the new shield with
frosty air. I watched hopelessly as it shattered to the floor.

"Let me tell you Agnost's true prophecy. Only I know
the full version. I killed him just after he scribed it. I wasn't
aware of his false start on the crumpled paper in the trash
bin, or I would have taken it, too. For, when the wizards
found it, they knew a child of two Sentinels would bring the
coming of the end.

"For an untalented wizard, Ian Sagehill was clever, I'll
give him that. He convinced the Wizard Council to forbid
Sentinels from conceiving together to prevent the prophecy.
Then he started arranging marriages for the Sentinels. Ian
pointed suspicion at me, but they couldn't prove I killed
Agnost. Still, Couve exiled me to Esteril because of that
suspicion. It was good for me, since I found Mykyl's recipe
to create my pets." Conemar snarled at one of the Writhes
that broke the line. "Get back, you!

"Sorry for the interruption," he said with his eyes on
Bastien, who knelt beside Arik with his back to Conemar.
"Let the boy die, Bastien. You can't save him."

Thank God. He hadn't noticed what Bastien was doing.

Conemar returned to me. "I no longer need you,
Gianna, but I want you. There's a difference between need
and want. One you can do away with and still survive. I'm
certain if you knew the full prophecy, you'd understand why
I'd prefer keeping you."

Why is he telling me this? He's stalling. But why?

He pulled a thick aged sheet of parchment from his coat
pocket and unfolded it. "Listen carefully. I won't repeat it.

"From the union of two Sentinels the beginning of the
end shall come, more powerful than any that has come before,
to lead and guard the one. The dyads from the Seventh move

secretly through the gateway door, the knowledge to finding the trinkets filling their minds."

That must be me, but—

"A High Wizard poisoned by greed seeks to release the four powers of old."

That's Conemar searching for the Tetrad.

"An ancient rhyme from a long-ago time will send the evil to a prison where power upon him is bestowed, a price to pay for reciting the charm to avoid harm."

Ugh. That makes no sense.

"A time will come when the evil one will break free, and the battle begins for the four. Whosoever rules the four rules the worlds."

Is that now? Or sometime in the future. I struggled to put the pieces together.

"You see, I'm destined to be the ruler. I'm the greediest of all wizards. I just need one of the dyads—an heir of the Seventh wizard—to help me recover the Tetrad."

Dyad? Ah! It means two. Nick and me. We both *can read the chart and find the Chiavi.*

Something behind me distracted Conemar.

Bastien stood in the middle of a circle with pie slices drawn in blood, and within each slice, he had sketched a character. The only character I could make out at my distance was a bird. Bastien chanted over his creation.

"I'll die before I join you!" I shouted at Conemar, hoping to distract him away from Bastien. This time I sent a globe directly at Conemar. He blocked it. For being old, he certainly was quick. But Conemar watched Bastien with amusement, not anger.

"*An ancient rhyme from a long-ago time,*" I mumbled to myself, repeating Conemar's words. "*A price to pay for chanting the charm to avoid harm.*"

Conemar's grin widened.

"Bastien, stop!" I yelled. He didn't break from his trance.

Conemar glared at me, his fingertips sparking. "I'm disappointed. I had hoped I wouldn't have to kill you. Thank you for returning my son, Gianna. From Jacalyn, he is an heir of the Seventh wizard, as are you, but I only need one to lead me to the Tetrad." He motioned to one of the things beside him.

The creature slithered quickly to me and tackled me to the ground. The sword knocked loose from my grasp and clanked onto the floor. I kept my shield between us. The creature's foul breath made my stomach heave. It chomped at me, spraying phlegm into my face as it gnashed at my neck. Its toenails scraped against the marble floor. A scream escaped my throat as its claw sliced my shoulder. Pain ran up my neck and warm liquid soaked my shirt and jacket.

I brought my knees up and braced my feet against the shield. Its nails slashed my side. I took in a painful breath and kicked out, flipping the Writhe onto its back.

Grabbing the sword, I leapt to my feet, but the Writhe was faster and it backhanded me, sending me sliding across the floor. I clutched tight to the sword, trying desperately not to lose it. I crashed into the wall, rolled to my knees, and scrambled back to my feet.

The Writhe charged at me. In spite of the pain in my shoulder and side, I lunged at it with my sword extended. The sword sliced through its throat, spraying rancid blood across my face. The Writhe wiggled and released a sound like a siren before it fell still beneath me.

I whirled to face the other Writhes.

Another creature stormed at me. I spun around and faked a blow to the right. The creature went left. I swung left and low, the blade driving deep and across its stomach.

Another siren scream sounded, and the creature crumpled to the floor.

"I'm having such fun," Conemar said. "Let's see how you handle this." He signaled two Writhes and they dashed down the hall.

"Shit." I rushed to the shield and snatched it up, smashing the first creature that reached me in the head with it. I squatted and did a roundhouse kick against its legs, and it toppled down.

The other Writhe knocked me to the ground. The creature kicked me in the gut, punching the air from my lungs. I groaned and tried to catch my breath. It kicked me again, this time connecting with my hurt shoulder. Pain lanced through me, and I let out a horrific scream, locking my hands together behind my neck and moving into a fetal position.

I wanted to give up. Be home. In a reality where none of this existed. But if I failed, Bastien and Arik would be next.

A growl sounded above me, and I rolled away from it. The creature's claw barely missed me, pounding the floor instead. I stumbled to my feet.

The Writhe's nails scratched the floor as it got up, and I swung my sword at it. Its severed head thumped to the floor. The remaining Writhe sped toward me. I gripped the hilt tight, cocked my arm back, and thrust the blade up, piercing the creature through the heart. I yanked the sword from its chest. It flopped to the ground and wiggled around on the floor as its earsplitting wail faded.

"Impressive," Conemar said. "They've trained you well." He raised his hand to send more demon Writhes at me.

I collapsed to my knees. This was it. I was done. My vision blurred and pain screamed across my body.

Behind me, Bastien spoke his charm louder. Before

Conemar could signal the Writhes, a glowing ball soared over my head. Then a bright light filled the room like a massive camera flash.

When my eyes came into focus, the hall before me was empty. *They're gone. Thank God, they're gone.* A shaky hand dropped onto my shoulder. I winced in pain.

"You all right?" Bastien said.

"Yeah," I said, voice shaky. I wanted to cry, but I was too tired. I stumbled to my feet.

Afton rocketed up the hall and into Bastien's arms. "Oh my God! You did it," she said with a voice so high and squeaky it hurt my ears.

I dropped the sword and shield. "*He* did it? He had the easy job."

Afton's nose wrinkled. "Eww. Gross. What's on your face?"

I ran a hand across my chin, collecting dark liquid on my fingertips. "It's that demon Writhe's blood. I think I swallowed some."

"But it's *black*." She covered her mouth with her hand.

"Yeah, it's pretty rotten tasting." Bile rose to my mouth. "Oh man, I feel—" I bent over and hurled the contents of my stomach onto the floor.

Bastien removed his shirt and handed it to me. "Here, use this."

"Thanks." I took his shirt and wiped my mouth.

"Gia, you're hurt. Let me see." Afton examined the cut through the tear in my jacket. Blood oozed from my shoulder. "You might need stitches."

"I'll be okay. Don't worry about me." I shrugged her hand away. "Can you check on Arik, though?"

Afton rushed to Arik, dropped to her knees, and wrested off her sweater, her shirt underneath pulling up slightly.

She tugged it down. "He's breathing," she called to us. "The wound doesn't look all that bad. I think he has a concussion. He must've hit his head hard when we landed out of the book."

Arik was alive. I squeezed my eyes tight. He'd be okay. He had to be okay.

The Writhes' bodies sprawled across the floor looked like black oozing mounds. Just beyond them, I spotted the yellowed parchment with the prophecy written on it. The paper contrasted against the white marble floor. I limped over to it and picked it up.

"What is it?" Bastien asked.

"You didn't hear me." I shook my head as I handed him his shirt. "I tried to stop you from sending Conemar to wherever you were sending him."

He examined the gunky black blood on his shirt, shrugged, and dropped it on the floor. "Why did you want to stop me?"

"'An ancient rhyme from a long-ago time will send the evil to a prison where power upon him is bestowed, a price to pay for reciting the charm to avoid harm.'" I read the prophecy on the parchment to him. "Don't you see? Conemar is in a place where his powers will grow stronger. He'll return someday."

"Conemar might've been lying to you."

"No. I'm sure it's the prophecy. I can't explain it, I just feel it is."

"Well, we can have the penmanship tested to determine if Agnost wrote it. While Conemar's gone, we'll just have to find the Chiavi and destroy the Tetrad before he returns." He winked and hurried over to Afton's side, where she was struggling to rip her sweater to use as a bandage for Arik.

"Yeah right, like that's going to be easy."

"Stay positive," he threw over his shoulder, pulling a pocketknife out of his pants pocket and opening it. He stabbed Afton's sweater with the blade and ripped it into strips. He handed the longest piece to Afton and she worked at wrapping Arik's head wound.

Bastien strode over to me with two chunks of the fabric in his hand. "Remove your jacket and top."

"Bite me."

"Later, perhaps, but right now, I think I need to stop your cuts from bleeding."

I sighed, shrugged off my jacket, and eased my shirt down to my waist, flinching when the pain shot down my arm. I glanced at my white sports bra, wishing I'd worn a lacy one. Who was I kidding? I didn't even own anything that could pass as lingerie.

He eyed me. "Nice."

"You're enjoying this, aren't you?"

His smile widened.

Blood stained my bra and my stomach. He wrapped the long strip around my waist to cover the nasty gash in my side. I sucked in a painful breath when he tied the ends together. After he finished mending my shoulder, he helped me get my top back on, his fingers lightly stroking my arm as he did. My skin prickled under his touch.

I stepped away from him. "What are we doing? We have to get help for Arik."

"We will, once Afton has him stable enough to move."

"We need the book." I searched the hall for the gateway book, slowly lifted it, and then leafed through the pages. Conemar had torn out most of the pages. The library in Paris was missing, so we decided to go back to the Boston Athenæum and to the others.

Bastien lifted Arik on to his shoulders. "Holy mother of

God, he's a load."

He jumped through the gateway with Arik, and I went with Afton, who held on to the ancient charm book. We landed in a different room in the Athenæum than the one where we had departed. It was a small sitting area with three leather chairs and sage walls. It must've been where Conemar had entered to ambush us earlier. Bastien eased Arik to the floor.

With great effort, I squatted to my heels beside Arik, my cuts protesting angrily, and brushed a dark strand of hair away from his forehead. He sighed and tried to roll over.

"Arik?"

When he didn't respond, I bit my lip. We had to get him to Pop, and quick.

Afton placed her hand lightly on my shoulder. "He's going to make it."

Bastien picked up the gateway book we had jumped through and flipped the pages. "The library in Paris is gone from this book as well," he said. "Conemar didn't want us returning home."

"Or he didn't want anyone coming to aid us," I said.

"Let's find the others." Bastien shut the book and handed it to Afton. She hugged it to her chest with the charm book. He hoisted Arik back on to his shoulder.

We went to the large reading room and slogged across the flooded floor. Nick held a soggy book in his hands while the Sentinels surrounded him. Bastien cleared his throat as we got nearer to the group.

Nick's head popped up. "What happened?"

Kale and Demos got to us first and relieved Bastien of Arik. Demos wrapped his arms around Arik's chest while Kale supported his legs.

"Is he *dead*?" Lei asked, worry coating her voice.

Bastien wiped his brows with the back of his hand, his bare chest glistening with sweat. "No, but we must get him to the shelter. He needs a Curer."

My stomach rolled at the sight of Arik's blood staining Bastien's hands.

"How did you guys get back?" Nick asked, holding up the soggy gateway book. "This book doesn't work. We couldn't get to you. Someone threw too many water globes."

"I was trying to—" Jaran grumbled, raising his hands in frustration.

"No worries," Afton said. "We have another one."

"I can't figure out how Conemar managed to bring another gateway book into this library without alarming the Monitors," Bastien said. "There hasn't been an alert about any missing gateway books."

The talk around me sounded like it was coming from a tunnel. It was hard to concentrate on what they were saying. Arik was out cold, his beautiful face scrunched in pain. No telling what was happening with his brain. It might be swelling.

"He got the book from Esteril," Jaran said. "There used to be two libraries in Russia. One library burned down and the book was reported destroyed. My guess is the Esterilians lied and removed the tracking charm from the book so the Monitors couldn't detect it."

"I bet you're correct," Bastien said.

"By the way, what happened to Conemar?" Kale asked.

Shut up. Shut up!

"Shut up!" I finally snapped. "Talk about this later. Arik needs help." My chest hurt. My head pounded. It was like I was inside a bubble watching their shocked expressions. "Which way are we going?" But my outburst got them going.

"We'll go through Spain and on to Paris." Bastien

barked orders. "You two, grab Arik. Nick, help Afton."

Demos and Kale jumped through the gateway with Arik in their arms. I went after them, falling into the darkness, my mind racing. Agnost's prophecy scared me. If it were real, Conemar would be back one day, and he'd be stronger. I strangled the parchment with the prophecy scribed on it. Just as the fear of that thought squeezed the breath out of me, I broke into the light of the library.

CHAPTER THIRTY

Carrig was waiting for us when we returned to the library in Paris. The guards rushed Arik ahead, ordering me to stay back when I attempted to go along. As we followed, we all debriefed Carrig on what had happened. He told us Asile was recovered and Nana and Faith were safe. I desperately wanted to see them, but I needed to make sure Arik was okay. Plus, Carrig said I had to get my wounds attended to and rest before going.

A crowd greeted us as we stepped out of the outbuilding and into the shelter. Sinead and Deidre bolted to Carrig and Nick, giving them bear hugs.

I stepped around the side of the building to calm down before facing everyone.

Bastien cornered me. Thankfully, someone had given him a shirt. "I know you feel our connection."

I did, and that unnerved me. But it was just because we both understood what it felt like to lose a parent. That's all.

"You amaze me, Gianna. How you stand up against a powerful wizard like Conemar, your compassion for others, your intelligence and quick reflexes. Everyone admires you and your strength. As do I. You are meant to be a queen," he said. "With time, I'll prove to you we belong together. Go ahead and have your fun with Arik, but it's my arms you'll end up in one day." He kissed my cheek and headed over to the gathering crowd.

I slammed my gaping mouth shut.

Sure, he was beautiful, with a nice ass, and moved with such confidence. I could watch him all day. But he was arrogant, and I was so not going to get involved with any *betrothed*. He wasn't really interested in me anyway; he just wanted to prove he could steal me from Arik. Fat chance. My heart was already on another path. I sighed and headed for the Curers' station to see Arik.

"You did well," Lei muttered as she walked past me.

I smiled, knowing it was her way of saying she forgave me for almost getting her boyfriend fried.

A squat, gray-haired woman at the medical center stitched and bandaged my cuts properly. She shot down my request to visit Arik, saying he couldn't have visitors yet. Reluctantly, I went to my room and gave myself a sponge bath, avoiding my clean bandages. The hot sponge lathered with floral soap soothed my aching muscles as I dragged it across my skin.

I was alive. Was it over? I washed my face and dropped the sponge in the sink.

After slipping on a pair of pajamas, I fell onto the bed, stretched out across it, and stared at the ceiling. Conemar haunted me and worrying about Arik weighed on my mind. I pushed aside all those uncomfortable thoughts about Bastien's promise. Somehow, despite the laws, Arik and I would find a way to be together.

A knock at the door startled me. I staggered over and pulled the door open. "Pop!" I cried and stepped aside so he could enter.

He balanced a tray with two steaming cups and a plate of chocolate biscuits. After he placed the tray on the tiny table by the window, he wrapped his arms around me. I tried to lift my arms and squeeze back, but the pain in my shoulder and side prevented me.

He kissed the top of my head. "Are you okay?"

"I'm fine. How's Arik?"

"He's going to pull through." He released me and sank onto my bed. "We contacted Asile. The wards are down. The Sentinels are taking Arik there for further treatment as we speak."

I dropped onto the bed beside Pop and rested my head on his shoulder. I told him everything that had happened. I didn't hide anything from him. He stared off to some place across the room as he listened. When I was done, he drew me into his arms again, and I sobbed against his chest.

"I promise you, kid, it'll all work out." He rubbed soothing circles on my back. "You're safe now."

"I'm not too sure."

I longed for the days when I believed no one could harm me with Pop around. But I had seen evil, tasted it on my tongue, even. No one was invincible. Not even Pop. After we finished our tea, I got under the covers. Just as he had when I was little, he tucked me into the bed and hummed Irish songs until I fell asleep.

T he smells of coffee, eggs, and bacon filled my nose, and I rolled onto my back under the comforter. Afton hovered over my bed, holding a breakfast tray. The items on the tray rattled as it moved. An oversize tote dangled from the crook of her arm.

"Bad dream?" she asked.

"Yeah."

"Are you hungry, or was Writhe blood enough for you?"

"Very funny." I scooted up against the pillows into a sitting position.

She placed the tray on my lap. "Can you believe we made it through *that*?"

I picked up a piece of bacon and bit down on it. "It's unbelievable. Have you heard anything about Arik?"

"Yes, that he's recovering fast." Her face was a question mark and her hands wrung a napkin nervously.

"Okay, what gives?"

"I know I shouldn't feel this way—well, don't think I'm going all Jerry Springer and shit, but—" Her face pinched as she gathered the nerve to finish.

"But what?"

Her face flushed. "I'm in love with…"

"Nick?"

"What am I going to do? He's with the other you."

"The right thing to do is to wait it out. They probably won't last."

"I know. It sucks."

I snorted. "It'll work out." I sounded like Pop.

Her face softened and she placed the crumpled napkin on the tray. "After you eat, get dressed. We're leaving for Asile."

"Great! I can't wait to see Nana."

"Oh, I almost forgot. Carrig took me home to get a few things and I picked this up for you." She opened her tote, pulled out my mother's faded red umbrella, and placed it beside me.

"Thank you. I thought it was gone forever." I picked it up, thinking of my mother, picturing her holding it over her head, the loose handle rocking back and forth and rain waterfalling over the sides.

"Someone at the Athenæum called your dad and said it was left behind. Your dad called and asked me to get it for you the next time I was there. I know how special it is to you, so I got it right away."

"Thanks so much. You know, it makes a great weapon." I swung it over my head. The top came off and its body went flying, barely missing Afton.

"Watch it!" she yelled. "You could poke an eye out." Her eyes narrowed on the handle, which was still in my hand. "What's that?" She pointed at a shiny chain hanging from it.

I tugged the gold chain free from the handle's cavity, and a bedazzled cross slipped out.

I clamped my hand over my mouth and gasped. "I think it's the missing Chiave. My mother had it all this time. Gian must've hidden it in the handle before he died. This was probably *his* umbrella."

"You eat and I'll get Carrig." Afton hurried to the door.

I laced the chain between my fingers. A pain hit my chest and my brand started bleeding. I rubbed the blood onto my palm and spoke the charm. Nothing happened. The truth globe was definitely gone forever. I needed a globe, and I knew where to find one. After getting out of bed, I slipped on my robe as I headed for the door.

I found the Monitor for the shelter perched on a globe in the map room.

"*Arrrk!* What is it?" the colorful parrot asked when I entered. He had vacant eyes, like Pip.

"I found a Chiave." I held it up to him. "I'd like to use

my blood and your globe to see what the spirit seer wants. Do you mind?"

"*Arrrk!* Be my guest."

I smeared my blood across the glass. The Monitor stepped to the other side of the perch. A tiny silver twig sprouted from the blood and grew into a branch until it was a miniature tree. From the hollow of the tree, a small silver squirrel emerged. It stood on its hind legs and continued changing until an extremely buff silvery man stood on the sphere before me. To my relief, he wore a loincloth.

"That's a little much," I mumbled to myself.

"Greetings, Gianna, me name is Declan. I do like to make a show of meself. I be the Keeper of the Chiave you hold." Declan had an Irish accent. "Not only is it one of the keys to release the Tetrad, but it also be having an individual power. The wearer can see things that have come before within the location he or she be in. May you survive the trials that be ahead. The trinkets you find will protect the chosen one while venturing to the monster's prison." He bowed, and both he and the tree shrank back into the blood that had dried on the globe.

"*Arrrk!*" the bird screeched, moving his head from side to side.

"Thank you." I slipped the cross into the pocket of my robe.

When we returned to Asile, a crowd greeted us in the corridor. Nana held me so tight I thought she'd break my back. Merl complimented me on a job well done. When I saw Faith, I let her know about Ricardo and gave her his pendant. It was actually hers. She'd lost it many years ago. He may have been a womanizer, but he kept Faith close to his heart. She kissed the pendant and put it over her head, a slight smile passing over her tear-drenched face.

As for Professor Attwood, he choked up when I told him about Nick being Jacalyn's son. Nick came over, I introduced the two, and they shook hands. Professor Attwood promised to show Nick photographs of Jacalyn and letters she had written. An easy friendship settled between them.

Before Professor Attwood walked off, I hugged him. It was a stiff and awkward one. I stepped back and gazed up at him. "You know, I've always wanted an uncle. Do you think I can start calling you Uncle Philip?"

A surprised expression crossed his face, then warmed as he smiled down at me. "I would love that, Gia." And this time, he hugged me, one that was tight and full of warmth.

We released each other. "I should go."

"I'm proud of you, Gia."

His words swelled my heart. "So, I'll catch you later, then?"

He nodded and headed down the corridor in the direction of his office.

High Wizards from every haven descended upon Asile for a summit. The wizards decided neither Nick nor I was safe in the havens, so they were sending us into hiding. More meetings ensued as the details of our secret refuge were worked out.

I passed Arik's unconscious days by reading to him or by playing games with Jaran's iPad as I sat by his bedside. There was a hint of antiseptic and something that smelled suspiciously like mothballs clinging to the air.

"How long have I been out?" Arik's hoarse voice startled me.

"You're awake!" I set down the iPad, then rushed to the

water pitcher on the nightstand and poured a glass. "You've been out for a few days. Can you sit up?"

"I think so."

After pushing the button to raise the bed, I put the glass to his mouth and he took a long sip.

With some effort, he swallowed. "Thank you. What happened to Conemar?"

For what seemed like the gazillionth time, I told the story of what had happened in the National Palace Library in Mafra, Portugal, leaving out the fact I was almost lunch for those scary Writhes. I let him know I had found a Chiave in the handle of Gian's umbrella. Then I filled him in about the High Wizards' meetings that had taken place all week. When I finished, he reached his hand out to me, and I took it.

He stared at the bandage peeking out of the collar of my shirt. "You were hurt?"

"It's just a scratch."

"You could have been killed," he croaked.

"You could've, too"—I gave him a reassuring smile— "but we weren't."

"The garden has changed the girl." He gave me a weak smile.

Emotions clogged my throat, and I couldn't think of anything to say to that. His secret world had changed me. And I didn't feel like I belonged to his world or to mine. I was in a sort of limbo. I gave him a quick kiss on the lips. And then I thought of Nick. "I did discover Nick's my cousin."

"How is he faring with his changes?" he asked, still groggy.

"I'm not sure. He's struggling."

"Well, it will take time. And what did the council decide at their meeting?"

"Nick and I have to go into hiding," I said. "We can't

go back to Boston. Pop, Nana, and Carrig have gone to get Nick's family. They won't be happy. They'll have to give up the restaurant."

"I want you to stay here with me."

"You're going into hiding with us, too. Several Sentinels are. The council is splitting the rest of the Sentinels among the havens. They're also bringing the retired ones back into service. A delegate of wizards and guards went to Esteril to gain peace there."

"That gives us two Chiavi." He coughed. "And five left to find."

I brought the glass up to his lips again and he leaned forward, taking several sips before his head landed back on the pillows.

"So where are we hiding?"

"I'm not sure. The council will purchase two houses and one building somewhere. Nick and his family will live in one house. Pop, Deidre, and I will live in another—"

"Deidre's going to live with you?" he interrupted.

"Well, if Deidre lives with Carrig and Sinead, people will wonder why we're identical. We don't want to raise suspicions. We're going to pose as Pop's twin daughters. Carrig and Sinead will open a boarding school for troubled teens nearby."

Arik gave me a sour face. "And the Sentinels are going to be the *troubled teens*."

"You got it."

"As long as I'm with you, I won't mind the stigma." He raised my hand to his lips and kissed my fingertips softly. "I'd go anywhere with you."

My heart belonged to Arik.

"I was so worried about you." I leaned over and pressed my lips to his. "If you're lucky, when I come back later, I'll give you a sponge bath," I said against his lips, then laid my head against his chest, the rhythm of his heartbeat soothing me.

His arm wrapped around my back. "You're such a tease." He lifted a weak smile, then paused before adding, "I apologize for not being able to help you in that fight."

I sat up. "Like I said before, I can take care of myself."

"Yes, you can." He gave me a naughty grin. "Come back here."

I bent over and kissed his forehead. "You should rest. I'll be back later." I stood and walked to the door.

He turned his head to watch me. "You do realize this is only the beginning, right?"

I stopped in the doorway. "Yeah, I know," I said.

It was the beginning, all right: the beginning of my new life as a Sentinel and the beginning of the end of my life before I got sucked into that damn book. The door slowly shut and I caught a final glimpse of Arik's gorgeous face.

And I wouldn't have it any other way.

Find out where Gia's story goes next in

GUARDIAN OF SECRETS

Available in stores and online February 7, 2017

GUARDIAN OF SECRETS

CHAPTER ONE

I f you could drown in boredom, I was about to gulp my last bit of air. Seriously.

I leaned against the tree I sat under and pulled my knees up to my chest, watching the frail-looking neighbor girl clamor up the porch of our newly purchased home on Pine Orchard Road. She handed a plate of something to Pop. They exchanged pleasantries before she pirouetted around and scrambled back down the steps. She looked like Snow White with her dark hair and pale skin. The widow's peak on her forehead and her sharp chin made her face look like a pasty heart.

You'd think I'd be happy for quieter times after accidently jumping into a gateway book in Boston and transporting through a portal to a library in Paris. Not to mention having my normal life change so drastically. Being a Sentinel and able to fight unfathomable beasts would be cool if it was just a video game and not real life. In real life, people died.

Permanently.

The image of Ricardo staked to a tree had haunted my dreams. I wondered if Conemar and his band of rogue Mystiks would ever stop searching for us. Uncle Philip had said I shouldn't worry and that there wasn't a threat anymore, but I seriously doubted it.

Unfortunately, even after defeating Conemar, I *still* had to go into hiding with my family and friends just in case his followers wanted to seek revenge. Having a price on your head would be bad enough in the human world, but having one in the Mystik realm was more than terrifying.

I glanced at the fancy new phone Pop had bought me so I could video chat with everyone I missed back home. Which was mostly my best friend Afton, since Nana's cell phone was from the Stone Age and didn't have the feature. I found Afton's name in the recent calls section, tapped the call button, and waited for her to answer.

Stuck in Branford, Connecticut, alone without my boyfriend, Arik, and the Sentinels for two weeks was driving me insane. My other best friend and newly discovered cousin, Nick, moved into a home down the street with his parents four days ago, but I hadn't spent much time with him, not with my "pretend twin" Deidre taking up all his free time. Living with my Changeling was like having a walking mirror around constantly.

Then there was Faith. Though she was assigned to protect me, she was more of a friend than a guard, and we hung out a lot. Or at least we did when one of us wasn't sleeping. It sucked that Laniars slept during the day. It only gave us a few hours together at night before I went to bed. With her odd appearance—greyhound-like body, sharp canines, and pale skin—she had to hide from our new neighbors. Which meant we spent most of our time in the attic converted into a living space for her.

Afton's face popped onto my phone. Her large brown eyes looked kind of buggy over the screen. "You know I love you, girl, but this is the third time in less than an hour." Another call beeped through and I ignored it. I really needed my best friend. "I'm at work," she was saying. "I can't chat right now. I promise I'll call you as soon as I'm off."

"Okay, I'm sorry… It's just…well, I miss you."

I waved at Pop zipping by in his Volvo. With his focus fixed on the road, he didn't see me.

"I miss you, too." Afton leaned back, glanced over both shoulders, and brought her face close to the screen. "Why don't you hang out with Nick?"

"'Cause Deidre's with him again. Those two never separate. It's sickening—" I stopped when I noticed the disappointment cross her face. "Shit. I didn't mean…"

"No worries. I'm fine," she said over a slurping espresso machine somewhere off screen. I knew every one of her expressions. The forced smile and sad eyes told me she was lying. "I had my chance. He's moved on. Anyway, why don't you go to a movie or something?"

"I just got back from one. This has to be the longest Saturday *ever*."

"Hey, I've got to go. Customers. Talk to you later." She hung up, and my face flashed onto the screen. I pushed the end button.

Though I was lonely, I kept to myself out of fear of saying something I wasn't supposed to. I needed to talk to someone who knew about the Mystik world. Someone to listen to my worries and assure me I wasn't certifiably insane. I needed my friends, but Nick and Afton were too busy.

The neighbor girl came down the pavement from my house. Why didn't this neighborhood have sidewalks? Any driver could swerve and hit a pedestrian on the side of the road. She hadn't noticed me earlier when she passed on her way to my house, so I hoped she wouldn't on her way back to hers, which was a lot bigger than ours. Still, we had more than three thousand square feet in our gray Victorian home with the pointy turret, sitting at the end of a quiet road with a crooked street sign.

When the girl neared, she spotted me in the shadows of the tree and practically skidded to a stop.

Please don't come over. Please don't come over. Shit. She's coming over.

She stepped cautiously across the grass as if she'd kill it with her scrawny frame. Before long, she hovered over me.

"Hi, Deidre," she trilled. "Did you get my text?"

I stood, the fall leaves crunching under my feet. "Um, Deidre's my sister. I'm Gia."

"Oh, right, she did say she had a twin. You're identical."

This one's observant.

"We are."

She smiled. "I'm Emily…Emily Procter. I live next door."

"I know. I saw you with your dad yesterday."

Her smile slipped, and she looked down at her hands. "He's my uncle. My parents are gone. The house used to be my grandparents' home."

"I'm sorry," I said lamely.

When she looked up, the sun hit her cotton-blue eyes and glistened against the tears gathering on her bottom eyelashes. "Thanks. It's been a few years now, so, you know…"

No matter how long ago or how young you were at the

time, when a parent passes away it leaves a wound. One that is always gaping, making you vulnerable to attacks of emotions at the most awkward moments. Like now. "Yeah, I do," I said softly. "My mother died when I was four."

She smiled again. "Now I'm sorry. That sounds stupid, right? I never know what to say in these kind of situations."

Note to self: Don't go with first impressions. She seemed nice enough.

"How do you know Deidre?" I asked, hoping to change the conversation to something less depressing.

"She's in my biology class."

"Oh, right—" A loud motor cut off my words. And as if on cue, Nick's junkyard special pulled up, dark exhaust smoke coughing out of the pipes in the back. I plugged my nose at the burned-oil smell.

Nick got the motorcycle even though his parents protested. Nothing said, *We're sorry for lying to you* all *your life about being adopted and about being the son of the Antichrist aka Conemar* than turning a blind eye to his new rebel attitude.

Deidre swung her leg over the seat and hopped off the bike. She removed her purple and black helmet, and I wasn't sure if it was me or Emily or both of us who gasped. Her long brown hair was gone. The new style was bleached and short with lavender bangs that hid one eye.

"Oh my *gosh*," Emily squealed. "I love your new hairstyle. You look so…um…couture."

Nick unsaddled from the bike. "She looks biker chic to me."

I lowered my head and rolled my eyes. The girl was a good liar, and Nick was a moron. It was obvious what Deidre was going for—the complete opposite of me. Who could blame her? After all, she was born to be me, and finding that out had to have messed with her head.

"You look amazing." I feigned excitement in my voice.

Nick cocked a brow and gave me a look that spoke more than words. That he knew I was faking it.

I gave him a wide grin. "What's up?"

"Not much," he said, "just dropping off Deidre."

Deidre stared into the bike's mirror, fixing her helmet hair. "You and Nick have some sort of meeting with Pop."

"Really? Pop just left. Why didn't he take me with him?"

"He said he couldn't find you." She frowned at her reflection. "He had to overnight a package before the post office closed. You can go with Nick and I'll hang out with Emily." She looked over at her. "If you're not busy, anyway. I'd love to do some shopping today, and I like your style."

Emily beamed. "I'd love to."

"I'm not riding that thing." I nodded toward the rusted metal.

Nick patted the cracked seat. "It looks like shit, but it runs."

"But is it safe?" I gave the bike a curious eye. "I'd rather walk."

Deidre threw down a gauntlet. "What are you scared? I rode it."

I wasn't one to pass up a challenge. I snatched the helmet from her and put it on. "If you wreck, I'll kill you," I said to Nick as I straddled the bike.

"See you later, babe," Nick said and planted a firm kiss on Deidre's lips. "Later, Emily."

"Bye," Emily said. "It was nice chatting with you, Gia."

I paused at seeing the frown on her face. *Did she see me roll my eyes at Deidre's hair? Or see Nick and I exchange looks?*

"Yeah, it was great," I finally answered.

Nick revved the bike, and I quickly wrapped my arms

around his waist before he sped off.

"Where are we going?" I yelled over the loud motor.

He turned his head to the side and yelled, "The library. The new librarian arrived Friday. She's a plant..." He adjusted on the seat. "From the Wizard Council. She's here to monitor the gateway book."

He took a corner fast, the tires squealing, and I gripped him tighter.

"Hey, easy there! You'll crack a rib."

"Stop complaining," I said. "You're such a baby!"

Nick sped the bike around another corner, revved the engine, and released the throttle, obviously to freak me out, which worked. I squeezed him tighter, and he winced.

After another horrifying turn, we ended up at The James Blackstone Memorial Library adjacent to the town square. Made out of white marble and with four pillars holding up an overhang draping the porch, the place resembled a state building. It looked like some Greek architecture Afton had shown me in one of her books. Nick slowed the bike into an open parking spot.

I yanked off the helmet and shoved it at him. "You are certifiably insane, you know that? You could have killed us."

"I had it all under control." He lifted the seat and packed in the helmets.

"You're an ass."

He snickered and slammed down the seat. "Yeah, but you love me anyway."

A big, stupid grin spread across my lips. He was right, but I'd never admit it. "I'm glad we finally have some alone time."

"Me, too," he said.

Pop pulled his Volvo into a space down the row from Nick's bike. He swung open the door and crossed the parking lot, meeting us at the steps. Beyond the opened bronze doors was a rotunda. The walls were pink marble with varnished wood doors and frames. I gazed up at the dome above our heads, my mouth dropping in awe. Eight large paintings with scenes illustrating some sort of history timeline adorned the inside, and medallion-shaped portraits of important-looking people created a circle between arches exposing the balcony just below it.

"Isn't it beautiful?" A young woman, wearing black-rimmed glasses that matched her thick, straight hair, stood next to me. "The paintings depict the history of book making. The portraits are of famous authors. Harriet Beecher Stowe"—she pointed each out—"Nathaniel Hawthorne, Ralph Waldo Emerson—"

"Are you Kayla Bagley?" Pop interrupted her.

"Oh…n-no, sorry, I'm Maira. I volunteer here. Miss Bagley is new. She's filling in for a librarian who's on a leave of absence. Maybe I should get someone with more experience to help you?" She looked nervous about what she had said and quickly corrected herself. "I mean, Miss Bagley is still acquainting herself with how things run around here."

"They understand what you meant, Maira," an overly sweet voice came from behind us. "You may continue with whatever you were doing. I'll take care of our guests."

"Yes, Miss Bagley," Maira muttered.

Miss Bagley was a ginger, in her midthirties. Smaller than what I was expecting. Her apricot-colored hair was pulled back in a bun. Her plain white shirt, loose gray pants, and sensible chunky shoes said she wasn't obsessive about her appearance, which apparently Pop didn't mind. He was giving Miss Bagley that awkward smile he gets when he likes someone.

"It was nice meeting you," Maira said, and shuffled away.

"Mr. Kearns, I assume," Miss Bagley said through nude-colored lips. "And you must be Gianna?"

"It's just Gia."

"Oh, that's right. Sorry. Professor Attwood did a wonderful job describing both of you." She pulled out a tube of lip balm from her pocket and applied it. "Sorry, my lips get so dry and I hate wearing lipstick."

A woman after my own heart. I preferred my Root Beer Lipsmacker, too.

Pop turned on a bright smile for her. "Please, call me Brian."

She smiled back, and it was like the sun came out to blind us. "And you may call me Kayla." They were totally flirting in front of us.

"I'm Nick," he said, elbowing me and nodding at Pop and Miss Bagley. He had noticed the flirting, too.

"Well, if I knew I would be working with such handsome men, I would have dressed better."

She winked at Pop. She actually winked at him.

"How old are you?" I blurted out.

"Gia…" Pop gave me that glare again.

"No, it's fine. I just turned thirty-six," she said.

That could work, so I decided to offer, "Pop's forty-two. He'll be forty-three in a month."

"You don't say? You look so much younger."

Miss Bagley turned, and Pop gave me the warning eye again.

She headed for a freshly polished door. A lemon scent hung in the air. "Shall we get your library cards?" she asked. "Then I'll give you a tour. We just received a new reference book this morning. It contains photographs of the world's most beautiful libraries. You simply must see it."

"That will be fantastic," Pop said, and then mouthed to me behind Miss Bagley's back, *Behave.*

"Dude, you're in trouble," Nick whispered to me.

"Shut up," I hiss-whispered back. "Why were you smirking, anyway?"

"Did you see them? Your pop likes librarians."

I wrinkled my nose at him. I didn't want to think about my pop and his possible fantasies. "Please stop. Besides, she's not a real librarian. You do know that, right?"

He laughed. "Well, your pop forgot."

I elbowed him. "I will cut you."

"You could try."

Pop scowled at us over his shoulder.

At her desk, Kayla issued us library cards, then took us on a tour of the library.

She guided us to a room off the rotunda with book stacks and a staircase leading to a balcony. "This is the reference room where I put the gateway book." She pulled a familiar-looking leather-bound book from a bookcase behind the stairs. "I'll keep track of it, so it will be here whenever you need it." She slipped the book back into place. "There's a quiet study area in the mezzanine. Follow me."

She went up a staircase with Pop right behind her. I wanted to vomit witnessing Pop check her out. I glanced at Nick, and he was holding back a snicker.

Nick mouthed, *Nice butt.*

"Really?" I hissed at him, holding onto the wood railing as I climbed.

"Hey, what can I say," he whispered through a smirk. "I'm a proponent of well-formed structures."

"Is that right?" Kayla said from above us. "I'm always impressed when kids appreciate historical landmarks and architecture."

"Oh, I appreciate it," he said.

I rolled my eyes at him and stepped onto the landing. Directly off the stairs was a long desk. It was a circular space with tables against the curved wall, facing the many windows looking outside.

"You could make your jumps here if you want," she said.

"This is a great spot," I said.

"You'll have to make sure it's vacant before starting." She went to the stairs. "Shall we continue?"

"Lead the way," Pop said in that swoony tone that was sure to make the movie popcorn I consumed earlier come up and be the feature presentation on the library floor.

"We'll stop by my office on the way out," she said, stepping off the last stair. "I'll give you a brochure with the times of operation. Also, I'll write down my cell number. I'll be on call. Anytime you need to make a jump, just text me, and I'll meet you here."

Pop stalked after her like a lost puppy as I stood there, on the last step, dumbfounded. Pop hadn't dated much. I think he worried about disrupting my life or something heroic like that. Maybe Miss Bagley was a good thing for him. I wasn't going to be around forever, especially if I make it into New York University. It was time for Pop to find someone special.

"You okay?" Nick asked.

I gave him a sideway look. "You weren't helping."

"Come on," he said. "It was cute. Your pop. Miss Bagley. I can see it now. A big wedding in a library."

"Why do you have to be so irritating?"

Two girls about our age walked by. They could have been younger, but with all the makeup, revealing clothes, and expensive-looking accessories, it was hard to tell.

"We should catch up to Pop and Miss Bagley," Nick said,

trailing the girls.

"You're hopeless," I said.

"I prefer the athletic type to pompous peacocks like them." Arik's voice came from the other side of a bookcase.

I gasped and reeled around. Every noise in the library quieted, and all I could hear was my pulse, quick and loud in my ears. The bookcase between us blocked my view of him, except for his lopsided smile and his almost-perfect teeth.

Am I dreaming?

I took a step forward and placed a nervous hand on the top of the books lining the shelf.

He grasped it.

"It is you."

ACKNOWLEDGMENTS

There is one name on the cover of this book, but there are many names of people who supported and guided it (and me) to publication. The journey was long, painful at times, but worth every trial to realize this dream. And thank you doesn't seem strong enough to express my gratitude, but I offer it to the following amazing friends, peers, and family members with my entire heart.

To my agent, Peter Knapp, for all the support while getting this book out in the world. At times it was tough, but knowing you were on my team, helped me through the darkest moments. I'm so happy to celebrate this success with you. Thank you for taking this jump with me.

My publisher and editor, Liz Pelletier, thank you for believing in me and loving this story as much as I do. This book wouldn't be the story it is today without your guidance. Thanks for being tough on me and pushing me to do better. I won the editor lottery when you took me on.

A grateful thanks to Stacy Abrams, Editorial Director of Entangled Teen, for all your support and helping with copyedits. You have to be the sweetest person I know.

Thank you to Meredith Johnson, Robin Haseltine, Julia Knapman, Lydia Sharp, Fowler Martens, and Beth Hicks for edits and ensuring each page sparkled. A big thank you to Heather Ricco for keeping everything organized. To the publicity team, Melissa, Debbie, Katie, Jessica, Rhianna, & Anita, along with the entire Entangled family, I'm amazed by the support the authors and employees of this house extend to each other every day. I'm proud to be included in this talented group. Your kindness and generosity is greatly appreciated.

A warm thank you to my publicist Jen Halligan for your support and marketing prowess.

Thank you to Louise Fury for your wonderful guidance and being a great friend. You have such a big heart and I love you bunches!

A huge thank you to my critique partners without whom this story would never have been good enough to get a publisher in the first place. Erica Chapman for the endless phone calls hashing out plots, unloading concerns, and laughing until it hurt. And most of all, for telling me, "Get rid of the cats." Your advice is always spot on. Shannon Duffy for helping me get my characters in shape and warming my heart with your generosity. To Jami Nord for your quick and accurate notes and for just being tough on me. Shelley Watters for helping me get that icky love thing right and for talking me off the ledge more times, than I'd like to admit. Trisha Wolfe and Cassandra Marshall who contributed to this book in its infant stages. And to Veronica Bartles, Paula Ashmore, and Julie Diercks who helped me tidy a few things up during drafts. My first readers, Kayla Ashmore, Heather Anderson, Emily Bartles, and Lucia Gregorakis who made me smile often.

A special thank you to Mandy Schoen, Hallie Tibbetts,

and Sue Zaynard for your wonderful edits in the earlier stages of this book's publishing journey. I appreciate the hard work and kindness you each gave me.

A shout out to my blog and contest assistant, Nikki Roberti. Without you, I would have gone insane ages ago.

A huge thank you to my best friend since middle school, Joannine Kramarsic, for reading every single version I sent her and being enthusiastic each time, and always cheering me on. Gratitude to Connie Kallman for all our long, brainstorming walks. I miss them and you greatly.

I would never have ventured out of my writing cave or learned my weaknesses without the help of the talented ladies who run the *Adventures in YA and Children's Publishing* blog, Martina Boone and Lisa Gail Green. Thank you for your wonderful contests and workshops. And to Jessica Soulders who helped me get my query and logline in shape during one of them.

Thanks to all the writers, critique partners, and friends who support me always: K.T. Hanna, Donna Munoz, Rebecca Coffindaffer, Marieke Nijkamp, Maggie E. Hall, Dee Romito, Mónica Bustamante Wagner, Krista Van Dolzer, Sharon Johnston, Summer Heacock, Jami Montgomery, and all the other writers who contribute to my contests or participate in them. Your advice and friendship made this journey even sweeter. Also, a thank you to my friends on Twitter and in the blogosphere, you entertain me each day during breaks, cheer my successes, and pick me up when I'm down.

Thank you to the young girls who inspired the character Gia, Tarah Ashmore her athleticism and ponytail, Kayla Ashmore her love for books and libraries, and Eugenia Woods her spunk.

A shout out to my family living in Massachusetts, the LaPointes and Yacovones, and all the branches thereof. You all are the reason my heart remains in Massachusetts and my stories often find their homes there.

I'd like to thank my mom, Jean LaPointe, for always reading and giving me the love for books, and my father, Walter "Skip" LaPointe, for passing on his stubbornness, which my parents probably thought wasn't good when I was a teen, but turned out to be a blessing on my quest to get published.

To my sister, my soul mate, Paula Ashmore. Thank you for always being there from day one. I'm so happy to have shared a room, and now, a deep friendship with you. My brother, Mark LaPointe, thank you for making me tough and for protecting me. I needed a tough skin during this journey.

My boys, Eric and Jacob, thank you for letting me steal your personalities for Arik and Nick, and for dragging me to fantasy movies when you were younger. You are my world. Thank you for your love and support. My girls, Cara, Annika, Fallon, and baby Stevie thank you for all the love and happiness you give me each day. I am truly blessed.

For my husband, Rich, who is the most understanding man on the planet, my best friend, desk mate, and love of my life. Thank you for asking me on that fateful day just after our wedding, and because you were feeling a little smothered, if I had a hobby. Because of you, I found my voice, and my life is so much more enriched with you in it.

Thanks to my family and friends for understanding when I couldn't go out or answer the phone for weeks during intense edits. And a heartfelt thank you to my readers, fantastic book bloggers, and librarians for taking a chance and reading this book.

Grab the Entangled Teen releases readers are talking about!

REMEMBER YESTERDAY
By Pintip Dunn

Sixteen-year-old Jessa Stone is the most valuable citizen in Eden City. Her psychic abilities could lead to significant scientific discoveries, if only she'd let TechRA study her. But ten years ago, the scientists kidnapped and experimented on her, leading to severe ramifications for her sister, Callie. She'd much rather break in to their labs and sabotage their research—starting with Tanner Callahan, budding scientist and the boy she loathes most at school.

The past isn't what she assumed, though—and neither is Tanner. He's not the arrogant jerk she thought he was. And his research opens the door to the possibility that Jessa can rectify a fatal mistake made ten years earlier. She'll do anything to change the past and save her sister—even if it means teaming up with the enemy she swore to defeat.

LOST GIRLS
by Merrie Destefano

Yesterday, Rachel went to sleep curled up in her grammy's quilt, worrying about geometry. Today, she woke up in a ditch, bloodied, bruised, and missing a year of her life. She's not the only girl to go missing within the last year...but she's the only girl to come back. And as much as her dark, dangerous new life scares her, it calls to her. Seductively. But wherever she's been—whomever she's been with—isn't done with her yet...

INFINITY
by Jus Accardo

Jump dimensions. Save the world. Don't fall in love.

Nobody said being the daughter of an army general was easy. But her dad sending a teenage subordinate to babysit her while he's away? That's taking it a step too far.

Cade, as beautiful as he is deadly, watches Kori with more than just interest in his eyes. He looks at her like he knows her very *soul*. And when he saves her from a seemingly random attack, everything changes.

Turns out, Kori's dad isn't just an army general—he's the head of a secret government project responsible for jumping between parallel dimensions. Which means there are infinite Koris, infinite Cades...and apparently, on every other Earth, they're madly in love.

Falling in love is the last thing on Kori's mind. Especially when she finds herself in a deadly crossfire, and someone from another Earth is hell-bent on revenge...

ISLAND OF EXILES
by Erica Cameron

On the isolated desert island of Shiara, every breath is a battle.

The clan comes before self, and protecting her home means Khya is a warrior above all else. But when obeying the clan leaders could cost her brother his life, Khya's home becomes a deadly trap. The council she hoped to join has betrayed her, and their secrets, hundreds of years deep, reach around a world she's never seen.

To save her brother's life and her island home, her only choice is to turn against her clan and go on the run—a betrayal and a death sentence.

SHADOWS
by Jennifer L. Armentrout

The last thing Dawson Black expected was Bethany Williams. As a Luxen, an alien life-form on Earth, human girls are…well, fun. But since the Luxen have to keep their true identities a secret, falling for one would be insane. Dangerous. Tempting. Undeniable.

Bethany can't deny the immediate connection between her and Dawson. And even though boys aren't a complication she wants, she can't stay away from him. Still, whenever they lock eyes, she's drawn in. Captivated. Lured. Loved.

Dawson is keeping a secret that will change her existence…and put her life in jeopardy. But even he can't stop risking everything for one human girl. Or from a fate that is as unavoidable as love itself.